The Cape Light Titles

CAPE LIGHT

HOME SONG

A GATHERING PLACE

A NEW LEAF

A CHRISTMAS PROMISE

THE CHRISTMAS ANGEL

A CHRISTMAS TO REMEMBER

A CHRISTMAS VISITOR

A CHRISTMAS STAR

A WISH FOR CHRISTMAS

ON CHRISTMAS EVE

CHRISTMAS TREASURES

A SEASON OF ANGELS

SONGS OF CHRISTMAS

ALL IS BRIGHT

TOGETHER FOR CHRISTMAS

BECAUSE IT'S CHRISTMAS

CHRISTMAS BLESSINGS

The Angel Island Titles

THE INN AT ANGEL ISLAND

THE WEDDING PROMISE

A WANDERING HEART

THE WAY HOME

HARBOR OF THE HEART

Thomas Kinkade's Cape Light

Christmas
Blessings

KATHERINE SPENCER

BERKLEY
NEW YORK

BERKLEY
An imprint of Penguin Random House LLC
375 Hudson Street, New York, New York 10014

Library of Congress Cataloging-in-Publication Data

Names: Spencer, Katherine, 1955- author.
Title: Thomas Kinkade's Cape Light Christmas blessings / Katherine Spencer.
Other titles: Cape Light Christmas blessings
Description: First edition. I New York : Berkley, 2017. I Series: A cape light novel ; 18
Identifiers: LCCN 2017030564 (print) I LCCN 2017036119 (ebook) I
ISBN 9780451489180 (eBook) I ISBN 9780451489173 (hardback)
Subjects: LCSH: Cape Light (Imaginary place)—Fiction. I City and town
life—New England—Fiction. I Christmas stories. I BISAC: FICTION /
Religious. I FICTION / Christian / Romance. I GSAFD: Christian fiction. I Love stories.
Classification: LCC PS3553.A489115 (ebook) I LCC PS3553.A489115 T48 2017
(print) I DDC 813/.54—dc23
LC record available at https://lccn.loc.gov/2017030564

First Edition: October 2017

Printed in the United States of America
1   3   5   7   9   10   8   6   4   2

Cover design by Annette DeFex

To Jane Stine, Joan Waricha, Theresa Labreglio,
Arleen West and Ellen Steiber at Parachute Press, and
Cindy Hwang at Berkley Publishing—because "it takes a village"
to make a village. With deepest gratitude for making
Cape Light come alive again this year.

CHAPTER ONE

THAT MEAL WAS DELICIOUS. Now I KNOW HOW A STUFFED turkey feels." Jessica's stepfather, Ezra, patted his stomach while the rest of Jessica and Sam Morgan's guests smiled and laughed.

There were only ten around the table this year, but enough food for twenty, Jessica decided, surveying the leftovers. Family holidays were often at her house, and there were often many more guests. But their Thanksgiving dinner had been quiet and relaxed this year with just her mother and stepfather; her sister, Emily, and her husband, Dan, and their younger daughter, Jane. Emily's older daughter, Sara, who lived in Boston, was spending Thanksgiving with her husband's family this year. Sara and Luke would come to Cape Light for Christmas. Of course, there was also Jessica's husband, Sam, and their three children—Darrell, Tyler, and Lily.

"No room in that turkey for dessert?" Emily's tone was teasing. She emerged from the kitchen with an apple pie in one hand and a pumpkin pie in the other. Her daughter, Jane, followed with a bowl of rice pudding and a carrot-nut loaf.

Ezra smiled, taking in the bounty of sweets. "I might need a taste of each. And a small scoop of vanilla ice cream on the side?"

Jessica laughed at his hopeful look. She cut a generous slice of each pie and served him first. "Don't worry, I didn't forget the ice cream."

"I'll get it." Lily, Jessica's youngest, headed back to the kitchen, eager to help.

"I hope you didn't forget the stomach antacids either." Jessica's mother, Lillian, turned to her husband. "Will I be kept awake all night by your moans and groans?"

Ezra smiled in his good-natured way. "If the need arises, I shall take my moans and groans into the guest room. While I concede your point, I must ask, what would Thanksgiving be without a little over-indulgence? I've heard the first Thanksgiving revelers carried on for days."

"Three days." Lily returned from the kitchen and placed a carton of vanilla ice cream and a chrome scoop on the table next to Ezra. "Mrs. Gibson read us a book about it."

"Thank you, Mrs. Gibson." Ezra ladled a generous lump of ice cream on his apple pie and picked up his spoon. "Let us honor our brave Pilgrim forefathers."

Just as Lillian seemed poised to for another volley, Sam lifted his glass. "And let us honor the cook. We may not keep everyone here for three days, but I bet we've had the best Thanksgiving feast in town."

"Hear, hear. To the cook," Dan echoed.

Jessica blushed. "Correction—the *many* cooks. Thanks to Emily and Jane, for their side dishes and the pudding. And Tyler," she added, smiling at her middle child. "He made the sweet potatoes and the pumpkin pie entirely on his own."

Tyler glowed with pride. It was becoming apparent that he had both interest and talent in the kitchen, and was even considering a career in that direction.

"Nice job, Ty." Darrell, Jessica's eldest, home from college for the long weekend, reached over and ruffled Tyler's hair. "We should call you Iron Chef."

Lillian raised her glass then leaned toward her husband. "What does that mean? Iron Chef?"

"A cooking show, dear. On TV," Ezra explained.

"I thought so. All these people cooking on television. I don't get the point," Lillian murmured. "In my day, you ate what was set in front of you. No fuss or fanfare."

"Thankfully, that day has passed," Sam said. "Before I forget, there's another part to my toast. Only about Jessica."

Jessica knew what was coming. She stared at her plate and took a breath. She and Sam had debated all morning whether or not to share her news today. Sam had been eager to tell the rest of the family, but she had felt unsure. He had promised he would leave it to her. It was her news to tell. Or not tell, if she chose.

She also knew Sam could never keep a secret. It was one of the things she loved about him—he was always so forthright and honest. But it was not an endearing trait at this particular moment. "Jessica has some news," Sam announced. "Right, honey?"

Finally, he looked at her.

Jessica tried to telegraph her displeasure to the far end of the table where he sat. But all eyes were on her. There was no avoiding it.

"Don't tell me. You're pregnant." Her mother practically groaned the words.

Jessica almost laughed. "Three is enough for me, Mother. And I'm a bit past that stage."

"Who knows these days? Movie stars seem to be having babies well into their senior years," Lillian observed.

"That might be true. But not me."

Emily had poured herself more coffee but didn't touch the cup. "What is it, Jess? Please tell us. I can hardly stand the suspense."

Jessica smiled and took a deep breath. But before she could speak, Lily interrupted. "Mommy started an animal shelter. We're going to take care of animals that are homeless."

"What a nice idea. You have plenty of property here, and you've always loved animals. Especially the strays." Emily smiled softly. "Remember that stray cat you found when we moved to the house on Providence Street?"

Jessica did remember. But she was surprised that Emily did.

"Don't remind me," Lillian said. "The minute your sister showed that mangy creature attention, it set up shop under the porch and had a boatload of kittens." Leave it to her mother to blame a poor stray cat for seeking shelter for her offspring. "It took us all summer to give those kittens away. Are you really eager to go through all that again . . . and again? That's quite a time-consuming hobby."

Jessica twisted her hands in her lap under the table, a nervous habit, perfected during endless and often stressful meetings at the bank. Sam gave her look. If she didn't tell all of her news, he would.

"It's not going to be a hobby, Mother. I mean, not any longer. I'm leaving the bank. I'm going to rescue animals full-time."

Jessica paused, her gaze sweeping over the surprised expressions around the table. Her relatives looked something just short of stunned.

Her niece Jane recovered the fastest. "I think that's great, Aunt Jess. You have so many pets already. I don't think it will be much different around here at all."

Jessica smiled, grateful for the vote of confidence. "I don't think so either, Janie. Though we do have plans to build some stalls in the barn and fence off different sections of the property."

"You'd be surprised. A lot of animals don't get along. Goats and sheep, for instance," Sam offered.

Her mother stared at him, her lips a tight line. "Is that all you have to say?" She turned to Jessica, her gaze withering. "You quit your job at the bank, manager of the loan department. In a few more years, bank manager, to be sure. You tossed all that in the . . . dung heap, let us say, to fuss over a pack of stray animals?"

"I don't expect you to understand, Mother. Please don't try to change my mind," Jessica said. "It's all settled. I've turned in my notice and started taking in more animals."

Lillian pressed her hand to her chest and took a deep breath. Ezra leaned toward his wife, looking concerned.

"Now, Lily . . . don't get yourself into a state. Jessica's old enough to know her own mind."

"Sounds like she's lost her mind to me," Lillian retorted. "And what do *you* think of this?" she asked Sam. "You don't care if your wife ruins a perfectly good career for some midlife, wildlife crisis?"

Jessica watched Sam rub the back of his neck, a gesture he used to buy time and gather his patience. "I'm totally in favor of the career change, Lillian," he said. "Jessica has wanted to take this step for a long time. She's certainly paid her dues at that bank. She's just not happy working there anymore. At this stage of her life, I think she should work at a career that's fulfilling and makes her happy."

"Fine words," Lillian replied. "What about her paycheck? I assume it takes two salaries to run this house and take care of your children. Jessica certainly won't make the same income running an animal shelter—if she makes anything at all from the endeavor."

"Mother, really. That's none of your business," Emily cut in.

"I'm just curious. Since I happen to be the person most likely to be asked for a loan, if the need should arise," Lillian added.

Jessica thought Sam's temper was going to flare at the dig. But to Jessica's great relief, he sat back and shrugged.

"It's nice to know you're ready to lend a helping hand, Lillian," Sam said, intentionally misinterpreting his mother-in-law's words. "But there won't be any need. My business is doing well, thank goodness. And we have plenty of savings. We know it will take time for the shelter to turn a profit. We've already planned for that."

"Not worried about making ends meet?" Lillian sounded as if she didn't believe him. "Well, time will tell. That's all I have to say."

"Yes, it will," Sam agreed.

Jessica smiled at her husband, meeting his dark eyes with a look of thanks. And love. All her annoyance about the way he had given up her secret faded. She was immensely grateful for Sam's understanding and the way he had encouraged her to follow through on this "someday" plan—to open and run her own shelter. Not just dabble with the work on the weekends.

Emily cut a slice of pumpkin pie and passed it to her husband. "Life is short. We must follow our bliss, whether it leads to Thanksgiving pie . . . or caring for God's creatures, great and small. Congratulations, Jessica. I think we should toast to your new career and great success."

"Yes, Aunt Jessica. That's very exciting news," Jane said.

Everyone raised their glasses again. Everyone but her mother, Jessica noticed. "Go ahead. Clink away. I won't toast to this harebrained idea. No pun intended," Lillian added.

"Oh, Lily, don't be a spoilsport," Ezra muttered.

Her mother ignored him. "I'll give it a month. Maybe two. By the new year, you'll regret this impetuous decision, Jessica. But by then it will be too late."

Was her mother right? Jessica hoped not. She shook off the doubts her mother had just planted and reminded herself that she couldn't let her mother's dire predictions get under her skin.

"Think what you like, Mother," Jessica replied calmly. "By the new year, I'm sure I'll be thanking my lucky stars I had the courage to take this leap . . . and thanking my husband for encouraging me every step of the way."

"Aww, Jess. That's so sweet." Sam smiled at her from the far end of the table.

"Hear, hear . . . to supportive husbands, everywhere," Dan said, toasting again. Just as Jessica clinked glasses with her brother-in-law, she heard her mother shriek and saw her tilt back in her chair, her arms raised in alarm.

"Good gravy—what's going on?" Ezra turned to his wife.

"Something is crawling up the tablecloth." Her mother stared down at her lap and Jessica saw a soft, gray head emerge. One of the kittens she was keeping had escaped the enclosure in the family room.

While everyone laughed, it scampered in confusion and fright, straight through her mother's dessert dish, leaving pumpkin-colored footprints on the tablecloth.

"For heaven's sake. Don't just sit there. Someone catch it," Lillian snapped.

Several swipes were made but the kitten eluded capture. Finally, it settled on the table, cowering in a small ball. Lily gently lifted the cat, cooing softly as she removed it from the table, then cradled it to her chest.

"She must have wiggled through the enclosure. Lily will put her back," Jessica explained, wondering if there were any other escapees on the loose.

Jessica expected her mother to reply with some tart comment, but Lillian just pushed her dessert plate aside. "I'd like another slice of pie, please. On a fresh dish. This one has cat footprints."

"Coming right up," Jessica replied, barely able to keep a straight face.

She knew it wasn't going to be easy, this new path she had chosen. A path "less traveled by," as the poet Robert Frost had written. But she was so eager to set off and put her whole heart into it. Nothing could dim her high hopes.

"EVERYTHING'S READY. FINALLY. I DIDN'T EXPECT THE TURKEY TO take so long," Jean Whitman admitted to her mother. "It's only a turkey breast. I thought that would be enough for just the two of us."

"More than enough. It seems a waste to do all this cooking for just two people. Though I will miss the dark meat."

Jean had forgotten her mother's preference. Should have bought some drumsticks. Oh well, next time.

Cynthia had refused any help walking from her bedroom to the dining room, though Jean felt anxious, watching every step as her mother maneuvered her walker. When her mother reached the table, Jean pulled out a chair and waited to help her mother sit.

"My place is on the other side, don't you remember?"

"Yes, of course. I'll move your place setting."

Jean had remembered, but the other side of the table was so much harder to reach with the walker. But she patiently took the dish and silverware to the spot her mother preferred, then waited as her mother made her way around.

Jean had set the table with good china and silver flatware. The dishes, rescued from the china closet, had been full of dust, and the silver had needed polish. She had also bought a centerpiece of autumn-colored flowers and found candles for the silver holders.

She thought her mother would appreciate the special touches. Cynthia was an artist—or had been. Jean also thought the extra fuss might lift her spirits a bit. But her mother didn't seem to notice anything special about the table. She opened her napkin and took a sip of water from a crystal glass with no change of expression. She could have been eating off a tray in her bedroom, Jean thought.

Jean returned to the kitchen and carried out the many dishes she had prepared. It did seem like a lot for two, but they would definitely use the leftovers. Jean's mother had not been a very good cook. She was more interested in her painting and would toss together a hasty supper after hours in her studio—often sandwiches and soup from a can or pasta with bottled sauce.

But Jean loved to cook. She was always taking classes and gleaning tips from TV shows and the Internet. She had already found some interesting recipes for Thanksgiving leftovers and would try a few this week. She wasn't just visiting Cape Light for the holiday but had moved down from Portland, Maine, to take care of her mother indefinitely, taking over the cooking and housekeeping from the aides who stopped in daily.

She placed a bowl of string beans on the table. She would have preferred to have made Brussels sprouts, oven roasted with a touch of balsamic vinegar, but she didn't want her mother to find the food too challenging. Her mother had always made string beans. Not fresh, with slivered almonds, the way Jean prepared them, but they would be familiar nonetheless.

Her mother peered at the dish then sat back in her chair. "No potatoes?"

"Coming right up." Jean ran back to the kitchen and retrieved a dish of sweet potatoes, baked with cinnamon, butter, and a pinch of brown sugar.

"Oh . . . I meant plain potatoes. I always made mashed, remember?"

Jean remembered. Granulated bits from a box. Just add water. Her mother's specialty. Jean would never cook anything like that. Her mother probably still had a family-sized box of the wretched stuff stashed in a cupboard.

"I thought I'd try something different. Sweet potatoes are traditional, Mom. I'll make you mashed potatoes another night."

"All right." Cynthia sighed and took a small piece of sweet potato. The she poured an ample amount of gravy all over her dish. Though her mother was supposed to watch her diet, Jean didn't say a thing.

At least I left out the salt, Jean consoled herself. She knew it was dangerous to her mother's condition—congestive heart failure. *Failure* being the operative word these days, according to Cynthia's doctors. No surgery could repair her mother's heart, and all the drugs in the world couldn't stop the muscle from weakening and eventually failing altogether.

But Jean forced herself to focus on the moment. She was here now with her mother, and they could enjoy a nice meal together.

"Shall we say grace?" Jean asked. Her parents had taken Jean and her brother to church most every Sunday, and her father had always started Sunday dinner by saying grace. Jean hadn't gone to church much since leaving home, but she knew her mother still belonged to the church on the village green, even though she had not been to Sunday service in a long time.

Cynthia shrugged. "Why don't you say it? I don't feel very grateful lately."

Her mother's admission made Jean sad. Cynthia claimed she didn't mind living alone—in fact, preferred it. But being confined to the house with only aides and a visiting nurse for company would take its toll on anyone. Sometimes friends came by, her mother reported. Or her minister, Reverend Ben, who visited at least once a week, sometimes more. That was something.

Jean would never say her mother had a sunny personality, even when she was younger. But her mother had always displayed a lively intellect and could carry on an interesting conversation, up-to-date about the news and the latest books and movies. Little by little, her intellectual interests had faded. Cynthia seemed to have shrunken back, into a shell. That was the only way Jean could describe it.

Jean could see a decline, even since her last visit in late October. Her mother's doctor had told Jean that Cynthia should not be living alone any longer. The obvious choice was a nursing home, where she would get more attention and social contact. And medical assistance would be quickly available.

But Jean knew her mother's most dreaded nightmare was having to leave her cozy house and end her days in such a place. That was the main reason Jean had decided to move back home and take over her mother's care. She had only arrived Tuesday night but could already see this plan was going to be more challenging than she'd expected.

"All right, I'll say grace." Jean bowed her head and folded her hands, trying to remember what her father would say before the meal. "It's been a while. Let's see . . . Thank you, Lord, for this delicious food we're about to enjoy, for this comfortable house and all of our blessings. We're grateful for your gifts all year round, and especially today, on Thanksgiving." She looked up at her mother and smiled. "I guess that covers it."

"More than covers it, I'd say." Cynthia had already picked up her fork and was picking around her dish, as if the offerings were exotic. What could possibly be so mysterious about turkey, stuffing, sweet potatoes, and string beans?

"Is everything all right, Mom?" Jean took a bite of turkey and stuffing.

"It's fine. You've gone to a lot of trouble. I don't think I can eat half my dish. Is there any salt?"

"Here you go." Jean handed her the salt substitute.

Jean's mother stared at the shaker. "Oh . . . this stuff. Did you cook with that? No wonder the stuffing doesn't taste right."

Jean took a moment to gather her patience. "Salt is very bad for you right now, Mom. You know that. It holds water in your body, and that's the last thing you need."

"Yes, yes. Believe me, I know all about it."

Jean continued eating. She had thought she would miss the salt in the food but hardly noticed it. Perhaps her mother expected to get a day off from doctor's orders since it was a holiday.

Cynthia wasn't eating much, just picking at her dish. Jean didn't comment, though she knew her mother needed to eat better if she wanted to stay out of a nursing home. She would address that later, maybe talk to the visiting nurse about it. One thing at a time. There were many fronts to cover.

"So, are you really going to live here with me? Is that really your plan?"

Her mother's question surprised her. They had discussed this move several times over the past few weeks while Jean was still in Portland. Was her mother growing senile as well?

Jean helped herself to more cranberry sauce. "Yes, that's the plan. We talked about it. Remember?"

"Oh, I do. But now that you're actually here, I wonder if you're having second thoughts. You're moving in because you were fired from your job, is that it?"

"There was a merger, Mom. The advertising company I worked for was bought by a larger firm, and I was laid off. With a lot of other staff in the same boat. Not fired."

Her mother shrugged. "You lost your job. It's more or less the same boat, isn't it?"

"Not exactly. But yes, I lost my job. I could have found another one, in time. But I decided to come down here and help you. Dr. Nevins says he doesn't think it's safe for you to live alone anymore."

And you should be in a nursing home at this point. That was what he had really said. But her mother knew that.

"I'm not alone. The aides are in and out every day. I should install a revolving door. That Nurse Crosby. She's here a few times a week. Too many people coming and going, if you ask me."

"That's just it. They're coming and going, visiting an hour or so. You're alone the rest of the time and alone every night."

Her mother sighed. "All I do is lie in bed. What's the difference if anyone is here or not?"

"There's a lot of difference." Jean decided not to argue further. Her mother knew there was a difference between having someone in the house full-time and not. She was just being obstinate.

"The doctor said you need more attention, and I'd like to take care of you. I'll take care of the house, too. We can get rid of the aides coming and going. You'll have more privacy, Mom," she added, knowing that point would appeal. "Once I get things in order, I'll find some freelance work."

Jean also planned to work on the special project she had started—a children's picture book. The idea had just come to her one day. She had started with some rough sketches and soon had a cast of quirky animal characters, a story, and a few watercolor and ink drawings in the works.

"What about the shop? Will you run that, too?" The question broke into Jean's thoughts.

There was a little shop on her mother's property, which sat at the end of Main Street, on the edge of the village. Her mother had run the shop for extra income, serving coffee and tea and desserts. Cold drinks and ice cream in the summertime. The shop also displayed an array of knickknacks and semi-antique bits of bric-a-brac that her mother had collected here and there, sometimes culled from their own attic. But the main line of merchandise consisted of her mother's watercolor paintings, which were prominently displayed, covering every wall. Scenes of the local beach, marshes, and other natural sights. Cynthia had been a fairly good artist and had even won some local competitions, though she never seemed truly satisfied with her work, Jean reflected. The shop was, in fact, a private gallery, and Jean guessed her mother would be very happy to see it reopen.

"Yes, I can run the shop if you want me to. How long has it been closed?"

Her mother looked down at her dish, reluctant to meet Jean's gaze. "Oh, I don't know. A month or two." Jean knew it had been much longer but didn't contradict her. "What does it matter? All you have to do is unlock the door and turn on the coffeepot."

It would take more than that to get the place up and running; Jean was sure of that. Chase out some squirrels, maybe, or other nesting creatures? But she didn't want to get her mother upset by raising that possibility.

"I'll take a look in there tomorrow and figure out what needs to be done."

"You might as well. If you'll be living here." Her mother shrugged.

"If it helps you get back on your feet, Jean, I suppose I'm willing to see if it works out."

"Well . . . good. Let's see how it goes." Jean took a huge bite of turkey to keep from laughing. Leave it to her mother to turn things around and make it seem as if she was the one helping Jean out of a rough patch.

Jean knew she could have easily found a new job at another advertising agency or publishing house. A lot of companies hired graphic artists, and her references were excellent. But after talking to her mother's doctors over the past few weeks, she understood that Cynthia was certainly facing her last days—and Jean didn't want her to face them alone.

Jean cleared the table and brought in dessert. She had made an apple pie and bought a pumpkin pie at a bakery in town.

"Oh, dear. Two pies? One for each of us?" Her mother sat back, eyeing the pies as if they were about to explode.

"I'd claim the apple all for myself, but I know it's your favorite," Jean replied, unfazed by her mother's reaction. "You can have some later if you're too full now."

"I'm sitting here now, might as well get it over with. I'll try some of the apple, please."

Jean cut her a slice and then a taste of each for her own plate.

Her mother was silent, too busy eating her dessert to talk for a moment or two. "Not bad. Willoughby's does a good job," she said finally.

"I got the pumpkin pie there, but I made the apple myself."

"Really? The crust, too?"

"Yes, the crust as well." Jean didn't think it was her best piecrust ever, but her mother seemed impressed.

"Where did you learn to cook like that? Not from me, that's for sure," Cynthia added with unusual candor.

"I like to cook. And bake. I've taken quite a few classes."

"Cooking never interested me. But I guess you have the time, being single. Seems a waste though, with no one to cook for."

The words stung, though they were true. There was no one special in her life to cook for and share meals with. Certainly no husband or children. Jean had been married for a short time, but it hadn't worked out. There hadn't been anyone really special since. *But that could change,* Jean reminded herself. Even if her mother doubted it.

"Not a waste at all, Mom. Now I'll cook for you," Jean said brightly.

Before Cynthia could answer, the phone rang. Her mother sat up in her chair. "What time is it? That must be Kevin."

Jean's older brother, Kevin, had gone to law school in California and had been living there ever since. He called their mother once a week, without fail, though he rarely visited.

"Could be. I'll go see." Jean rose and answered the phone in the kitchen. She greeted Kevin and wished him a happy Thanksgiving.

"Hello, Jean. Happy Thanksgiving to you, too. How's it going? Did you really move in with Mom this week?"

Jean had told her brother her plans and had explained on the phone and in e-mails about their mother's failing condition. Though she didn't feel Kevin truly understood the gravity of the situation.

Perhaps he, too, thought she had given up her apartment and independence because she was down on her luck.

"Yes, I came on Tuesday night. I'm not quite unpacked, but I didn't bring that much. I left a lot in storage." As she talked to Kevin, she walked back to the dining room. She could see how eager her mother was to get the receiver, practically squirming in her chair.

"I'll catch up with you later, Kevin. Here's Mom."

Jean handed the phone down to her mother, who lit up like a

firefly at the sound of Kevin's voice. Jean could only hear half the conversation as she started to clear the table, but that was enough.

"Oh, I'm fine," Cynthia insisted. "Don't you worry about me. You have a big job to focus on and lots of other concerns. These doctors love to exaggerate every little tick and twitch. I'll outlast them all," she boasted, her voice sounding heartier and livelier than Jean had heard it in the last two days.

Kevin was speaking and Cynthia listened attentively. Her gaze followed Jean as she came back into the dining room again to take away more plates and cups. "Yes, she's here. Cooked a huge turkey dinner. We could barely make a dent. I'll be seeing more of that turkey as the week goes on, I'm sure." Cynthia chuckled.

Jean felt annoyed at the joke. As if she had done something wrong by making a special dinner. Sometimes it seemed, from her mother's perspective, she could never do anything right.

On the other hand, Kevin could never do anything wrong. He had always been her mother's favorite. They shared a special bond, as if they both belonged to an exclusive club, and Jean was not a member. And never would be. She didn't know why it should still bother her after all these years, but it did.

"Oh, isn't that nice. You deserve a vacation. You work so hard," Jean heard her mother say. "You take care, too, dear. Thanks so much for the call. It gives me such a lift to hear your voice, honestly. You have a good week. Take care of yourself."

Jean waited until her mother had hung up before returning to the dining room. "How's Kevin doing? Did he have a good Thanksgiving?"

"He went to a neighbor's house for dinner. Said it was very nice. But there were a lot of children there and he came home with a headache." Her mother laughed. "It's a good thing your brother never had kids. I don't think he would have the patience for them."

Jean didn't agree. Kevin had always loved children. He had even done some babysitting as a teenager. There was a reason that Kevin's marriage had broken up, and perhaps it had been fortunate that no children were involved. But Jean always thought her brother would have wanted children. With the right woman, that is.

"He's working hard, of course. I do worry about him. So much pressure at those big firms. He sounded tired, as usual."

Jean didn't comment. Tired or just bored? Kevin's conversations with their mother were usually short and sweet. But she knew for a fact that Kevin's work was very routine. He had taken a job at an insurance company right out of college and had never left. He had once described his job as a big snore that paid very well. It was hardly the high-powered legal firm her mother imagined.

"He's going on vacation. Skiing in Utah. Doesn't that sound nice?"

"Lovely," Jean agreed. Kevin was often on vacation—skiing or scuba diving or traveling through Europe. A single man in his early forties, with no children to support, he had plenty of time and extra money.

"When is he going to Utah?" Jean sat at the dining table again.

"Over the Christmas break." If her mother had hoped Kevin would visit Cape Light for the holiday, she didn't show it. "I think it's nice for him to get away with friends. I hate to think of him all alone at Christmas."

If he came home and spent Christmas with us, he wouldn't be alone, Jean thought. This could be their mother's last Christmas. Didn't Kevin get it?

Cynthia yawned. "I feel tired. I should go back to bed. All this eating and talking has worn me out."

"Here, let me help you." Her mother was trying to push herself up from her chair but was having trouble. Jean came around and helped her maneuver onto the walker. She knew her mother must be tired when she didn't protest.

Jean helped her wash up and get into bed. Then she watched as Cynthia took several pills from a box on the nightstand and swallowed them with water, every movement slow and deliberate. She sank back on a pile of pillows with a deep sigh. Her color wasn't good, Jean thought.

Jean felt relieved when her mother asked for the oxygen. "I think that's a good idea." The small tank, in a metal holder with wheels, was set up near the bed, and Jean helped her mother fit the breathing apparatus to her nose.

"I can do it. Please don't fuss over me," Cynthia said.

Jean didn't think she was fussing, exactly. But she stepped back from the bed. "Should I turn out the light?"

"Not yet. I'd like to read awhile. That book with the red cover. And my reading glasses, please." Her mother pointed to a book on the night table.

Jean handed it over. "Good night, Mom. Call me if you need anything."

"I'll be fine." Her mother spoke without looking up from her book. "And thank you for the dinner. I know you made an effort," she added, her gaze still fixed on the page.

"You're very welcome. Sleep well."

Jean left the door ajar so she could hear her mother call. She would come back and check on her later.

A mountain of pots and pans in the sink greeted her as she returned to the kitchen. The rest of the mess wasn't too bad. She put away the leftovers and wiped down the countertops and kitchen table. She turned on the dishwasher and took out her cell phone, then dialed Kevin's number.

He picked up quickly. "Jean? Is everything all right?"

"Everything's fine. Well, not really. But Mom is in bed, probably asleep by now. I wanted to talk to you privately."

"Sure. What's up? Having second thoughts already?" Kevin sounded amused. Doubts had popped up since she arrived Tuesday night. She did wonder if she had made a huge mistake. But then she would remember the alternative.

"It wasn't my first choice. I'm sure you know that. But I'm not sure you realize how bad Mom is. She's really lost ground. Dr. Nevins wanted us to move her into a nursing home, one with quick access to medical care."

Kevin didn't answer for a moment. Then he said, "It would be hard to talk her into leaving that house. But maybe it would be for the best, Jean. In the long run."

"That's just it. There is no long run. Both of her specialists agree. She's in the end stages. Her doctors won't give a time frame, of course. They hate to do that. But it doesn't sound good, Kevin. Two months more? Maybe three, if she's lucky. That's if she doesn't catch pneumonia. Or even a cold."

She heard her voice rise on an emotional note and tried to calm herself. She hadn't meant for this to be a melodramatic conversation. For one thing, she knew her brother didn't respond well to that sort of appeal. She had told him all this in her e-mails, hadn't she? It sounded as if he didn't read her updates very closely. Or was in denial about the situation.

"I didn't realize it was that bad."

"It is, Kevin. You can call the doctors if you want to speak to them personally. I think they'd like to hear from you."

"All right. I will. I'll call this week," he promised.

Jean felt relieved to hear that. Proximity was all-important when an older parent was sick. But there were going to be some hard choices to make in a little while. She did wish Kevin would get more involved, even at a distance.

"I know you have plans for the holidays. Mom told me about your trip to Utah. But I was hoping you'd come home for Christmas and visit with Mom. It would mean so much to her."

And will most likely be her last, she wanted to add. But she didn't want to play the guilt card too hard. Surely he understood what was at stake?

"I want to visit her . . . before. Well, soon. You know what I mean." He was usually so well-spoken, but now his words faltered. "I'm just not sure I can come for Christmas. I'll think it over, okay?"

Jean decided not press any further. Kevin could be self-involved at times, and he, too, had issues with their mother, despite her doting on him. Still, Kevin wasn't heartless or without a conscience. He usually did the right thing, Jean reminded herself. Eventually.

"Good luck, Jean," he said sincerely. "You're a braver man than I."

"Thanks. I'll keep you posted."

"Yes, let me know what's going on." They said good-bye, and Jean ended the call.

She returned to the kitchen where the pile of pots beckoned. She was tired but she knew she would feel better facing a clean kitchen in the morning when her mother would need her attention. She filled the sink with sudsy water and searched for the scouring pad.

Her brother hadn't said it outright but seemed to think she had made a mistake coming back to Cape Light. Not a mistake, exactly, but a miscalculation, choosing a path that might prove too challenging.

Had she made a mistake? Each corner of this house held memories, and most were not happy ones. Her relationship with her mother had always been strained, though Jean wished it could be otherwise. While some seniors would have been thrilled to have an adult child care for them at this stage of life, Jean knew her mother would offer little thanks or recognition. That's just the way it was and had always been.

But coming back to care for her mother was still the right thing to do. What her father would have wanted her to do. Her mother's attention had been spare, but her father's love and affection had given Jean comfort, encouragement, and strength. Though he had died when she was ten, she still sometimes felt his presence, especially when she was lonely or confused. She felt it at that moment and pictured him looking down from heaven, heartily approving of her decision. The notion made all the difference to her.

CHAPTER TWO

*H*OW YOU DOING UP THERE, SAM?" BART BEGOSSIAN, ONE
of Sam's workers, held the bottom of the ladder steady as
Sam slowly climbed to the top.

"I'm good, Bart. I'm just going to take a peek at the chimney seal.
I'll be right down."

"You're not going on the roof, right?"

A wintery mix of snow and sleet had started falling an hour ago
and was now coming down heavier. Sam had sent the rest of his crew
to lunch early. When they came back, he would assign indoor work.
The house they were working on was a gut job, needing a complete
renovation, indoors and out. The outside was just about completed
except for a few finishing touches. A new roof and chimney had been
rebuilt last week. Sam wanted to make one last check of the tar seal
around the base of the chimney. Bart had stayed with him, insisting

on holding the ladder steady while Sam climbed, though Sam didn't think the precaution was necessary.

"Not in this weather. I'm not totally crazy."

"No comment, boss," Bart shouted back.

An unexpected gust of wind blew through the trees, and Sam felt the ladder sway. He gripped the edges with his gloved hands and held perfectly still for a moment. Maybe it was a good idea to have Bart holding the ladder today.

He had been lucky with the weather this winter, managing to get all his outside work done before the snow fell. Even though this weather couldn't be called snow, it did make things messy.

He reached the top of the ladder and peered over the gutter and roof edge, his gaze searching out the chimney. The seal looked smooth and solid, though he couldn't see the opposite side. But the roof was much too slick for him to scramble up and check at close range. Despite what Bart thought, he was not crazy enough to attempt that.

"How's it looking?" Bart asked.

"Pretty good from here. I'll get a look at the far side some other day," he added.

"Good idea. Some *sunny* day. Better yet, send Mike up. He'll be happy to crawl all over that roof for you."

Mike was the youngest on the crew and by far the nimblest.

Sam didn't think he was too old for such work, but he knew Bart had a point. There were some parts of this job that didn't come that easily to him these days. Not that he was likely to admit it.

"I can still crawl around on a roof with the best of them." Sam started down the ladder. "I'll show you sometime."

"Of course you can, Sam." Bart sounded sorry for having hinted otherwise. "I wasn't saying that. Exactly."

Before Bart could say anything more, another gust of wind pushed at the ladder, catching Sam by surprise, midstep. He felt one boot slip on the slick metal rung and gripped the side of the ladder with both hands, fighting for balance. But the metal was wet and his hands slipped as both feet flew out from under him.

"Sam, hang on, man!" Bart shouted.

But Sam could only cling to his perch for a second. He felt the ladder slip away from him and he began to fall. Nothing between his body and the ground but thin air. As his own shocked scream and Bart's shouting rang in his ears, he had no time to think or brace himself. His body landed in a heavy, painful heap on the icy ground.

"Sam!" Bart ran over and touched his shoulder. The man's panicked face loomed over him. "Can you hear me?"

Sam nodded weakly, feeling searing pain flash through his body, like electrical currents. Bart had already pulled out his cell phone. "I'm calling 911. Don't move. They'll be here in a minute."

Sam couldn't answer or even move his head. He tasted blood on his lips. Bart had grabbed a tarp and tried to shield him from the icy rain. "I'm sorry I can't get you inside, but it's probably best I don't move you. They say to never move a person after an accident."

Sam's tongue felt thick and strange as he mumbled a reply. "Thass right," he managed.

He stared up at the muddy tarp then closed his eyes. Bart was talking, but Sam could barely make out the words. His shoulder hurt so much, like a hot knife stabbing him. And his left leg felt the same, unbearably painful. He glanced down and saw blood and a piece of bone protruding through his jeans. He felt like he might be sick.

Call Jessica. Call my wife, he wanted to tell Bart, but it hurt too much to talk.

He heard a siren in the distance and focused on the sound as it grew closer.

"The ambulance is here. Thank God." Bart's face swam into his field of vision again. Sam couldn't answer. His entire body throbbed with pain, especially his legs.

He heard footsteps rushing toward him through the muddy yard. He closed his eyes again and sank into a white haze of pain.

SAM OPENED HIS EYES SLOWLY AND BLINKED. THE ROOM WAS DIM and the pale blue walls blank, except for an empty bulletin board and a flat TV hung high in one corner. His head pounded and he closed his eyes again, then felt someone squeeze his hand.

"Sam? Can you hear me?" He turned his head on the pillow and saw Jessica leaning toward him, her pretty face lined with worry. She sat beside the bed. Behind her, tubes, wires, and plastic bags of fluid dangled from a metal pole.

Sam nodded and tried to sit up but he felt weak as water. He couldn't move the right side of his body at all. His legs felt hot and encased in cement. He looked down at the sheet that covered his body and could see the odd shape underneath: both of his legs in plaster casts. The sight startled him and he tried to sit up again. "I can raise the bed. Just a minute, let me find the button," Jessica said. He heard a whirring sound and felt the back of the bed lift. He was soon at an angle, almost but not quite sitting up.

"How's that? Any better?"

He nodded. He tried to speak but his mouth felt so dry. "Some water?" he croaked.

"Sure, you can have water." Jessica quickly handed him a paper cup with a lid and a straw. He drank quickly, trying to remember when water had ever tasted so good.

"You had an accident at work. Do you remember?"

He met his wife's searching gaze and nodded. "Most of it. I was on a ladder at the Marino property and I slipped off."

"That's right. You fell nearly two stories to the ground."

"Wow . . . don't remember that part. Or landing," he added honestly.

"Maybe that's a good thing," Jessica said quietly. "You have a mild concussion."

"Yeah, I figured. I have a rip-roaring headache."

"I'll ask the nurse if she can give you something for that. You're already on a lot of painkillers." She glanced at the metal pole. "Intravenously."

"Is that why the rest of me feels numb?" He looked back down at his body. "Did I break both my legs?"

Jessica nodded. "The right leg was fractured. They had to put a plate in. On the left leg, the ankle and foot are broken. And you broke your right shoulder," she added. "Luckily, they didn't need to operate."

Sam glanced at his right shoulder and arm, completely immobilized.

"Are you in any pain right now?"

He shook his head. "I'm all right. My shoulder hurts a little. I guess the medication is strong."

"They said the shoulder might bother you."

"I should have fallen on my left arm. Why did it have to be my right? I can't write, I can't drive. I can't do anything—" Sam stopped. He hated to hear people complain, and hated the sound of his own voice complaining even worse. He glanced at Jessica. "Sorry, I didn't mean to start whining like that. You must be exhausted."

"I'm all right." She reached over and smoothed the hair off his forehead with a featherlight touch. "You can complain if you want. It might help you feel better to vent. You've been through a lot today,

Sam. You don't need to be all manly and stoic, you know." She stuck out her jaw, making a mock-grave face.

"I'm not," he replied, laughing at her. "It has been a long day. A long, blurred, lost day," he added. He glanced at the half-closed curtain. It was dark outside. He hadn't noticed. "What time is it?"

Jessica checked her phone. "Half past seven."

"That late? What about the kids? Don't you need to get home for them?"

"They're with Emily. She picked them up after school and is giving them dinner. They can do their homework at her house. She waited here until the doctor came out to speak to me and told us you were being moved to a room. She said to give you a big hug. She and Dan will be by tomorrow to see you."

Sam was glad to hear Jessica's sister had kept her company while the doctors were taking care of him. "That's sweet. But I really don't want any visitors, Jess. Maybe once I get home. They won't keep me here long, will they?"

"I'm not sure, honey. The doctor didn't say yet. I hope not. I called Darrell. I didn't want to keep anything from him."

"Of course not. You had to tell him," Sam replied. "Was he upset?"

"Well, he says he's coming home."

"Coming home? He just got back to school last night. There's no reason for him to come home. I look like a mummy in this plaster outfit, but there's nothing he can do."

"That's what I told him. But he's worried about you. You know how he gets."

Sam didn't answer. Sam and his adopted son had always shared a special bond, one that had only grown stronger with each passing year. Sam had met Darrell when he was nine years old. The boy was living at New Horizons, a Cape Light center for inner-city children who were at risk. Darrell had never known his real father, and his birth mother struggled with drug addiction. He had been left in his grandmother's care, but she had grown too old and sick to keep up with him. The boy had begun hanging around with the wrong kids and had gotten into minor trouble shoplifting and skipping school. He had been placed at New Horizons to help get onto a better track.

Sam met Darrell while working as a volunteer at the center. He and Jessica had been married a short time and were trying to start a family, though Jessica had suffered two miscarriages and they were not sure that dream would ever come true. When it came time for Darrell to be placed in foster care, Sam couldn't give him up. He knew that the boy was meant to be his child—his and Jessica's—a gift from heaven above he could not turn down.

A lot of Sam's friends reported tension and conflict when their sons reached adolescence. Growing pains that were par for the course, Sam had heard. But he and Darrell had never hit a rough patch in their relationship. Now twenty-two, Darrell was about to graduate from Boston University, and Sam was very proud of his son and proud of their close relationship.

"Give me the phone. I'll call him. He'll calm down if he hears me tell him I'll all right."

Jessica dialed Darrell's number and handed Sam her phone. It felt odd holding the phone in his left hand, but he managed, listening while it rang and rang. "These kids, they never pick up the phone. If you don't text, they won't talk to you."

Suddenly his son picked up. "Hello?"

"Darrell, it's Dad. I know Mom told you I had a little accident. But I'm all right. Well . . . not perfect. But nothing that won't heal. There's no reason for you to rush back home and miss classes this week," Sam said. "Maybe you could come home on the weekend and—"

Darrell laughed. "Too late, Dad. I'm already at the hospital. I'm on my way up to your room. See you in a sec."

"He's here," Sam said.

"Yes, I heard." She took her phone back and shrugged. "We didn't want him to go far from home for college, so . . ."

Sam couldn't deny that. He had felt comfortable knowing Darrell was in Boston, about a two-hour drive away, where they could visit him easily or he could come home quickly if he wanted to. Though he had been very independent the past four years and rarely came back to Cape Light unless it was for a holiday or a vacation.

Or a family emergency, which, thank goodness, happened rarely.

Jessica stood up and refilled Sam's cup with water. "He just wants to see for himself that you're all right. He doesn't need to stay long."

"Right. I'll tell him that and you do the same," he added, just to make sure they were on the same page. "Help me sit up a little more, will you?"

He wasn't quite as comfortable sitting up as he had been lying down, but he thought it would make him look as if he felt better, and give Darrell a better impression.

As Jessica hit the bed control again, Darrell appeared in the door-way. Sam smiled and waved, the bed still moving under him so that he felt as if he were on a parade float. "Hey, buddy. What are you do-ing here? You didn't need to make that drive again today."

"Of course I did. I wanted to see you." Darrell walked over to the bed, leaned down, and kissed Sam's cheek. Then he took in the casts on Sam's shoulder and legs. "Man, you look bad. Mom told me what happened. Next time, you'd better wear a parachute."

"And a crash helmet," Sam added. "It was a long way down. I have to admit it—and admit that I'm a real idiot for climbing up there in that weather in the first place."

"It was an accident, Dad. It could have happened to anybody." Darrell moved a second chair close to Sam's bed.

"Anybody who's thickheaded and a know-it-all, you mean. Bart told me not to climb up there. I'm lucky he stayed back to hold the ladder. I hate to think what would have happened if I was alone."

"Let's not even go there," Jessica said quickly. "All the doctors said you were very lucky."

"That's funny, because I don't feel very lucky," Sam replied honestly. "I feel very stupid."

"Darrell's right. You can't blame yourself, honey. Your injuries could have been permanent. Or worse."

By "worse" she meant he could have broken his neck or ended his life with that fall in some other way. Maybe he should count himself lucky to get off like this, coated with enough plaster to cover a ballroom ceiling.

"How long will it be before they take all this plaster off?" he asked with a surge of impatience. "Did the doctor tell you yet?"

"Not yet. But the nurse indicated . . . probably at least . . . six weeks. Maybe eight," she added quietly. So quietly he could hardly hear her. Which had been her intention, he was sure.

"Eight weeks? For the shoulder, too?"

Jessica nodded. "I think so. The doctor should be by later. Let's see what he tells us."

"Calm down, Dad. It won't do any good to get yourself worked up," Darrell said. "Six weeks isn't such a long time in the bigger scheme of things. Get the big picture. Isn't that what you're always telling me?"

Sam glanced at his son, annoyed to have his own classic advice tossed back at him. Whenever Darrell got impatient about waiting for some big life event—to find out if he passed a test, to hear if he was picked for a team, to get his license, to get accepted to colleges—Sam had always told him to get the big picture. Time has to pass, through the joyous events and the sorrowful, the most onerous and annoying.

"I took a walk down this hall while you were sleeping, Sam," Jessica added. "It looked to me like most of your fellow patients would give a lot to hear that they'll be back up and running in six or even eight weeks."

Sam knew that was true, too. He was just too angry to acknowledge her point. Angry at himself, mostly.

"I know but . . . I want to hear what the doctor says. Let him tell me eight weeks." He noticed his wife and son share a glance and knew that he sounded belligerent, as if he planned to talk the doctor out of such a long recovery time.

"Looks like you've got your wish." Jessica turned to the doorway. "I think I hear Dr. Bradley's voice in the hall. He must be doing his rounds."

Sam smoothed the sheet across his lap with his good hand and once again forced himself to sit up straighter, trying to look as if he had already started to recover. Though it was hard to pull off such an act, attached to all the tubes and wires and wearing the flimsy hospital gown.

The doctor walked up to Sam's bed. "Hello, Mr. Morgan. I'm Dr. Bradley. I was on call when you came into the ER today. I'm the one who slapped all that plaster on your legs. You weren't in great shape. You may not remember that clearly."

"I don't really remember. Not all of it," Sam admitted. "But I have been wondering who to blame."

"We were just wondering about Sam's recovery," Jessica said. "How long it will take?"

"I can't say exactly. A lot depends on how fast your bones heal, Mr. Morgan."

"Call me, Sam, please. And I'm very fast healer, believe me."

Dr. Bradley smiled at Sam's testimonial. "Best scenario, six weeks for the legs. Perhaps a little longer for the shoulder. Though at some point, you'll get soft casts. But no driving and no putting weight on that foot for a while. You'll need physical therapy, too."

"That's the best you can do, six weeks?" Sam asked. Even in his hazy state, he knew he had a long list of jobs that had to be completed.

Dr. Bradley nodded. "Any sooner and there would be a risk of a new injury. That would be even harder to mend, Sam. You don't want to be left with a permanent limp or chronic pain."

"Of course he doesn't," Jessica answered before Sam could reply.

"I'm sorry . . . I don't mean to sound unreasonable." Sam looked down at his legs again. "But I have a business to run. I have projects going. I can't be immobile for that long."

"We'll work it out, honey," Jessica cut in. "Dr. Bradley can't do anything to solve that problem."

The doctor stood at the foot of the bed. He did look sympathetic. "I'm sorry, Sam. I wish I could help you solve that issue. Patients are often shocked when they hear the recovery period. But they always seem to find a way to take care of their obligations. It might take a while, but I think you'll sort things out."

Sam wasn't so sure about that. *What if you had to take a six-week leave from setting bones, Doctor? How would you like that?* he wanted to say. But he held a tight rein on his temper, feeling his jaw set in what Jessica called his manly, stoic mode. He tried to cross his arms over his chest, in a further pose of defiance, but could only succeed in folding his left arm over, which felt awkward and silly.

The doctor spoke to them for a few more minutes about practical matters—the medication Sam was taking, how the nurses would soon get him up and sitting in a chair, the sort of foods he was allowed to eat. Sam didn't hear half of it, simmering over the six-to-eight-week sentence that had been handed down.

"Any other questions?" Dr. Bradley met Sam's gaze again.

"Just one more. How soon do you think I can get out of here?" Sam knew he sounded curt but couldn't help it.

Dr. Bradley smiled mildly. "Very soon, Sam. There's not too much more we can do for you here. I'd say Thursday, barring anything unforeseen. I hope that's enough time to prepare the house," he added, turning to Jessica. "You'll need to rent a wheelchair and maybe a hospital bed. No climbing stairs, of course. Not even at night."

"We'll have everything he needs, Doctor," Darrell said. He quickly turned to his father. "Don't worry, Dad. We'll get you out of here pronto."

"Thanks, pal." Sam offered Darrell a small smile, though the truth of the matter was he wanted Darrell to go back to school the next morning.

Sam waited until the doctor left the room then leaned back and closed his eyes.

"Are you all right, Dad? Are you in pain?"

Sam looked over at Darrell, his son's handsome face full of concern. "I'm all right. Just a bad headache."

"Oh, I was going to call the nurse and get you something." Jessica stood up. But Darrell was faster.

"I'll go ask. You stay here with Dad," he said, and was soon out the door.

Jessica cast a wistful glance at the empty doorway. "I know you didn't want him to come, but it's good to have him here."

"Yes, it is," Sam agreed. "Maybe you want Darrell to stay until I come home—to help you set up the house and all that?"

Despite his own wish to have Darrell return to school, he didn't want to deprive Jessica of Darrell's help. His son was tall and strong, definitely able to move furniture and hospital beds, and do whatever heavy work was needed.

"Only if he's not going to miss anything important at school, but we can figure that out later." She sat down next to him again and took his hand. "What do you think of Dr. Bradley? I hear he's a very good orthopedist. I liked his bedside manner. Those specialists usually seem so rushed. But he spent a long time with you, answering our questions."

"He's all right. I just wish he'd had some better answers." Sam sighed. "I can't just drop off the face of the earth for six weeks, Jess. I have three projects going and more lined up to start soon. My clients will be furious. I'll get bad-mouthed all over town . . . I don't even want to think about the lack of income."

"Calm down, Sam. Everyone understands when there's an illness or an accident. This is not going to ruin your reputation. As for an income, I'll go back to work. It's probably not too late to get my old job back, despite what I told my mother. But even if that position is filled, I think the bank can find something else for me to do. If not in Cape Light, then at another branch. Or I can find a job at a different bank," she added. "Or some other sort of work."

Sam was not surprised by Jessica's solution. That's just the way she was, at any moment ready to put aside her own desires and priorities for their family's sake. But her selfless offer didn't make him happy or ease his anxiety. "I don't want you to do that. You just left office life. It's not fair to you at all. Just because I'm a dumb idiot who climbed a ladder in a snowstorm—"

"It wasn't a snowstorm. And you're not an idiot," Jessica overrode him. "And it doesn't have to be permanent. It doesn't even have to be at a bank. I can find something to cover the bills until you're ready to go back to work. And you can file for some benefits, too. Workers' comp?"

Sam had already thought of that, but he doubted the workers' compensation check would make a dent in their monthly budget. Maybe it would cover the pet food? But he didn't want to worry Jessica any more than necessary now.

"Finding a decent-paying job takes time. I don't want you taking some minimum-wage job as Christmas help in the mall, so put that out of your mind right now. I could be recovered by the time you find a job that makes sense. We have savings," he reminded her. "That's what it's there for. A rainy day. We'll be okay." Jessica didn't answer. She looked doubtful, Sam thought. "Honestly, Jess. We'll be fine."

"Yes, I know we will." Jessica nodded. He couldn't tell if she really believed that or was just trying to make him feel better. But he believed it. He was trying hard to, anyway.

"I wish Joe Kelley was still around," Sam said as Darrell walked back into the room.

Joe Kelley, one of Sam's longtime workers, had managed projects whenever Sam found himself overbooked or in a bind. But Joe had recently moved away, leaving Sam without that sort of backup. Sam knew it was his own fault. He preferred to be the one in charge, to oversee his jobs down to the smallest detail. He believed it kept the quality of his work high, resulting in a sterling reputation. But at times like this, he could definitely see a downside to his perfectionist tendencies.

"Joe could have taken over in a heartbeat. But there's no one on the crew to replace him," Sam said to Jessica. "Bart is a hard worker, but he doesn't like being in charge."

Darrell stepped closer and stood at the foot of Sam's bed. "I can be your foreman, Dad. I can watch the jobs and let you know what's going on."

Sam was touched by his son's offer. "Thanks, Darrell. I appreciate you stepping up, son. But I can't see how that could work out. For one thing, you need to get back to school and finish the semester." Darrell's expression fell and Sam felt bad at refusing his offer. "Maybe when you come home for Christmas break you can help me. If there's any business left to manage," he added in a quieter voice.

"The semester is practically over, Dad," Darrell told him. "There's only one more week of classes, then the study period before finals. I can tell my professors it's a family emergency. I only have one final. The rest of what I've got due is all papers and projects."

"It's still schoolwork, important work. You need to keep your grades up if you want to get into a good grad school," Sam reminded him.

Darrell was studying engineering and architecture, and wanted to be an architect, which required a graduate degree in order to become fully certified. Sam was more than willing to see him continue his schooling, though Darrell hadn't yet applied to any graduate programs. He had told his parents he wanted to work for a year in between, at an engineering or an architecture firm. Sam wasn't so keen on the idea. He worried that one year might stretch to two or more, and Darrell would never get his graduate degree.

But that was a debate for another day. Right now he needed to make his son see that finishing his fall semester of senior year on a strong note was what mattered. Sam had started college but had quit after two years. Though he loved his work, he had often regretted his lack of a college degree. He wanted better for his children. He didn't want anything to hold them back from achieving their full potential. Darrell was so smart and talented, the sky was really the limit for him, and Sam wanted to see him get there. Even if he had to nag at times or play the heavy.

"I'll get good grades, Dad. No worries," Darrell assured him. "The next week is all review. Most of my projects and papers are practically done, too. I can easily finish them at home."

"Maybe Darrell should call his professors and see what they think," Jessica said before Sam could answer. "He's worked for you every summer since he was in middle school, Sam. He does know the business and most of the men working for you, too."

Sam met Jessica's gaze. She did have a point. But he was annoyed that she was taking Darrell's side.

"I'm sure I could be just as good a foreman for you as Joe Kelley," Darrell chimed in. "Maybe even better."

Sam sighed, suddenly noticing a throbbing in his shoulder and his head. "I know you can do it," he said, though he wasn't convinced. "And I know you want to help. But let's not figure it out right now. I'm tired. It's hard to think. Is that nurse coming any day soon?"

"She said she'd be right here. I'll see what's taking her." Darrell nodded and left the room again.

Sam looked up at Jessica. "I want him to go back to school. I didn't even want him to miss school today."

"I know. But he wants to help you. He wants to help our family," she added. "That's the way we raised him. It's a good thing, nothing to complain about."

"I know he wants to help, but—"

"And he's persistent once he gets an idea in his head. Just like you," she added.

He couldn't argue with that either. Sam sighed and closed his eyes. "He is. But I still want him to go back to school. I'll figure out some way to keep the jobs going. Just not right now."

CHAPTER THREE

~~~

"THAT NURSE CROSBY. IS SHE HERE AGAIN?" JEAN'S MOTHER looked up from her book when the doorbell rang. "She just came on Sunday."

"And she comes every other day, and today is Tuesday," Jean reminded her mother as she headed to the front door.

"Oh, bother. I could do without seeing her for a week or two," Cynthia grumbled.

"Actually, you couldn't," Jean muttered. She had gotten her mother washed and dressed and settled in the living room, but none of that required medical expertise.

During the short time she had been home, Jean had quickly learned her mother disliked the visiting nurse. Jean had just as quickly decided the woman was a breath of fresh air. Especially on a drizzly winter day, like today. Jean also knew that the nurse's visits were essential to Cynthia's survival.

Despite that fact, her mother's attitude toward "that Nurse Crosby!"—which was what she always called her—was a mixture of fear and disdain. While her mother considered Barbara Crosby far too irreverent, Jean found her upbeat and witty. Barbara was caring and competent, but she didn't handle Cynthia with kid gloves or seem the least bit fazed by Cynthia's crankiness and complaints.

Jean opened the door, and Barbara greeted her as she came in. "How's it going? You look a little tired. Her ladyship wearing you out already?"

"Not yet," Jean replied. "We seem to be falling into a routine. She's in the living room, in her recliner, reading."

Jean did feel a little tired. But not due to caring for her mother. Not entirely, anyway. After her mother had gone to sleep the night before, Jean had been working on sketches and paintings that were part of the children's picture book she had started a few months ago. As usual, once she took the work out, she had lost track of the time and had gone to bed much too late.

"Good morning, Cynthia," Barbara said. "What are you reading today? Anything interesting?"

"It is to me. But I doubt it would catch your fancy. A biography of Pablo Picasso?" Her mother prodded the nurse with her question, as if Barbara would not be familiar with the world-renowned artist. Her mother could be an intellectual snob at times. Most of the time, Jean decided.

"I bet he led an interesting life. But you're right. I'm not big on biographies. I like an easy, fast read with plenty of romance and a happy ending. Mysteries can be fun, too." Barbara set her bag down. "May I examine you in here, or would you prefer the bedroom?"

"This room is fine with me."

"Let's start with your blood pressure." Barbara took a blood-pressure cuff from her bag and unrolled it. She wrapped the cuff around Cynthia's outstretched arm and began pumping it up. "How about you, Jean? What do you like to read?"

"Oh, all types of books. It depends on what I'm in the mood for. I enjoy serious novels at times. Then a light book with romance or a mystery next. Sometimes I even read cookbooks."

Barbara laughed. "My husband would probably say I should read a cookbook, too. But I'd rather wait for the movie."

"How is my pressure? Can you tell me that?" Cynthia interrupted.

Barbara gave her the numbers as she jotted them down on a pad. "Not bad. Jean tells me she's been cooking salt free. I think it's already helped."

"It may have brought my blood pressure down, but it hasn't helped my appetite. The food tastes so bland." Cynthia stuck out her tongue.

She looked like a child, acting out in a doctor's office. Jean shared a glance with Barbara and nearly laughed out loud.

"Really? I've heard you're eating well. Much more nutritious meals since your daughter came than you had on your own. Your weight and color already look better," Barbara noted as she took out her stethoscope.

Cynthia shrugged. "I really haven't noticed. I eat whatever she puts in front of me."

Jean was sure that her mother had noticed but didn't want to agree, thereby admitting that she had not been eating very well on her own. Jean had been preparing healthy, whole foods, with lots of fresh vegetables, fruit, and lean protein. If the refrigerator and cupboards were any indication, her mother's diet had been sorely lacking all of that. Aides had been making breakfast and lunch, though there was no telling if Cynthia ate much of it. Jean knew Cynthia's bad habits and guessed that she had probably been surviving on cheese and crackers, with some tea, cookies, and chocolate added in.

Barbara's face took on a serious expression as she listened to Cynthia's heart. Then she moved the stethoscope to her back and listened again. "In and out please, Cynthia, deep breaths." Cynthia did her best, though it tore at Jean's heart a bit to see and hear her mother labor for a good, deep breath.

Barbara put the stethoscope aside and took Cynthia's wrist to check her pulse. Jean noticed the nurse did not comment on Cynthia's breathing; she just moved on to the next task.

"Your pulse seems good," she said after a moment or two.

Cynthia pushed her sweater sleeve down again and sat back in her chair. "If you can still find a pulse, it's a good report. That's the stage I'm at now."

"You're not at that stage yet, Cynthia. Not by a long shot," Barbara assured her. She was writing in the notebook again, her reading glasses balanced at the tip of her nose. "Let's take your temperature. Then we're almost done."

Cynthia looked impatient with the thermometer—an electronic model—in her mouth. A few moments later a beep sounded.

"Ninety-six point seven. We'll take it." Barbara turned to Jean. "Did you collect a sample for the blood-sugar test?"

"We did," Jean said. "It's in my mother's bathroom."

"Good. I'll just pop in there and check her sugar." She patted Cynthia's shoulder as she went by. "We'll see if you've been eating too much Thanksgiving pie."

Cynthia let out a long, noisy sigh as Barbara left the room. "I wish she'd leave. All this chatter. So annoying."

Barbara soon returned and began to pack her equipment. "Your sugar is a tad high. Nothing serious. You know what to cut back on. I won't give you a lecture."

Cynthia rolled her eyes. "Thank heavens for that small mercy."

Barbara laughed. "Why don't you do something fun today? With your daughter," she added. "Start a project together—an afghan? Or a scrapbook? I bet you have plenty of old photographs around here."

Did they ever. Crammed into drawers, tucked away in shoeboxes, and even hidden in the pages of old books. No telling where photos might pop up, considering the state of the house—an unholy mess, in Jean's opinion.

"The fun boat has sailed for me, Nurse Crosby. I doubt I'll live long enough to finish anything like that. Why even start it?" The unvarnished admission made Jean sad. She would have been happy to start some handicraft project with her mother, but it was probably true she would end up finishing it alone. "I'm content with my book," Cynthia continued. "That's about all the fun my old ticker can take."

"You know what Henry Ford said? 'Whether you think you can, or you think you can't—you're right,'" Barbara returned. "Every day is a gift, Cynthia. That's why they call it the present."

Her mother groaned. "Please, spare me the greeting-card inscriptions."

"I knew you'd love that one. I couldn't help myself," Barbara admitted with a grin. "See you Thursday."

Cynthia nodded and returned to her book. Jean followed Barbara to the foyer. "How is she doing today? She seemed to have more energy this morning."

"As well as can be expected, Jean." Barbara zipped up her jacket and pulled on a wool hat. "I think she's benefited already from you being here. And doing some craft or something productive would do her good," she added. "But she's stubborn—and partly right. We can't expect any miracles. Keep a close eye on her. You can always call me with questions. But call the doctor or 911 if anything major happens."

"I will, thanks."

Back in the living room, Jean found her mother sitting back in the recliner with her feet up. "Would you like some lunch, Mom? Or a cup of tea?"

"Not right now."

"How about the oxygen? Do you need that?" Her mother's complexion looked a bit ashen.

"You can bring it in. I might take some later. That woman always tires me out. I need a nap."

"Good idea. I'll get you a throw for your legs." When Jean returned from the bedroom with the oxygen and a light throw, she found her mother sitting with her eyes closed. But she opened them again as Jean fixed the blanket around her. "I think you should open the shop today, Jean. We might as well try to make a little money from that space. You have nothing better to do."

Nothing better than keeping up with the wash, the shopping, and the cleaning. Not to mention tackling the piles of junk in every room—stacks of mail, newspapers, magazines, and assorted odds and ends that filled every corner of the house. Her mother had never been the type of woman who was devoted to house cleaning. But somehow the house had always been tidy and clean when Jean was growing up. At some point, Cynthia had let the place slide. The daily aides could only do so much, and it now looked like a scene from the TV show about hoarders.

But Jean guessed there had been enough changes in her mother's routine for one week. She would wait a bit before proposing a major cleanup.

"Sure, I can go out to the shop. When was the last time you were in there? I think you told me, but I forgot."

Her mother looked annoyed by the question. "Oh . . . I don't know. I can't remember precisely. Not too long ago."

"I'll bring some cleaning supplies out. To dust and clean the floor."

She stopped in the kitchen and put supplies together in a bucket. Then she brought a monitor in from her mother's bedroom and set it up near the sofa. "I'll take the receiver. Call if you need anything."

"I'm just going to sleep. I won't be dancing a jig."

"Maybe not. But if the mood strikes, just remember, I can hear you," Jean warned in a teasing tone.

Her mother was lying back again with her eyes closed and didn't reply.

"I'll be back to check on you in an hour," Jean called out.

She listened for a reply but could only hear deep breathing. Her mother was already fast asleep.

Carrying the bucket, broom, and mop, Jean tramped across the muddy ground toward an outbuilding, about fifty feet from the house, a small building protected by a stand of pine trees. The house itself was not quite Victorian, more of a small farmhouse, and the shop was originally built as a guest cottage. Jean's great-grandparents, who purchased the property—a good-sized parcel, at the far end of Main Street, about a mile and half from the harbor—lived in the house and found it overflowing with guests in the summertime, so they built some extra accommodations.

Eventually, after Jean was born, her mother inherited the property. This allowed Jean's parents to move to Cape Light from Northampton, easing financial pressures and making it possible for Cynthia to pursue her passion—painting—and to take care of her children. Usually in that order of priorities, too, Jean reflected.

Her mother had used the cottage as an art studio for a time. But after Jean's father died, Cynthia converted it to a coffee and tea shop to bring in extra income. These days one might call it a bookstore café, Jean thought, except that her mother had much more than old books for sale.

It was a sweet little cottage but looked neglected now. The familiar wooden sign that hung over the door looked faded—*Wayside Coffee & Tea Shop*, it said in hand-painted letters. And beneath that: *Ice Cream, Cakes, Antiques & Books.*

Jean gazed up at the sloping roof. It was covered with pine needles, and the sagging gutters overflowed with leaves. Shutters that framed the windows were loose, the paint peeling. The same for the door, Jean noticed, as she unlocked it and pushed it open.

A few dry leaves had blown in, and she pushed them aside with her foot. The room smelled musty and she propped the door open with a chair, despite the chilly weather outside. It was cloudy out and looked like it might rain again. Still, the place needed a good airing out—and a good cleaning from floor to ceiling.

Not to mention the dusting, a day's work right there. There were shelves and small tables covered with bric-a-brac, bits of china, costume jewelry, quasi-antiques, picture frames, vases, and books. None of it had been touched in months, or maybe years, she guessed. Just as Jean remembered, the walls were still covered with watercolor paintings, mostly scenes of local landscapes and all by the same artist—Cynthia Randolph Whitman.

Jean shrugged off her jacket, set up the receiver for the monitor, and got to work. Her mother's perception of the shop was definitely stuck in some distant day when the place did attract a fair number of customers each afternoon: villagers out walking; mothers pushing strollers, small children in tow; schoolchildren who weren't allowed to stray too far from home but found the Wayside Coffee & Tea Shop within their permitted range. Jean doubted many people would stop in these days when there were other, more attractive choices in the village—Willoughby's Fine Foods and Catering and the Beanery, to name just two. But if it made her mother feel better to know the shop was up and running, Jean didn't mind making the effort. Cleaning the place brought back memories, mostly unhappy ones. Jean worked in the Wayside almost every afternoon after school and on weekends, too. Kevin was supposed to share the job, but he was older and had more after-school activities, especially sports practice and games. It seemed as if he was on a team for every season. Jean didn't play any sports or belong to after-school clubs. So she was stuck with running the Wayside, doing her homework at the counter in between customers. Sometimes one of her friends would stop by and keep her company. Other times, the cool girls from school would come and tease her, making her run back and forth to wait on them.

Her mother rarely greeted Jean when she got home from school, asked about her day, or helped with homework. She was in her studio and did not like to be disturbed. "Pretend I'm working in an office or a store," she would tell Jean. "You couldn't run in and talk to me when you got off the bus, could you? I know your father doesn't think so, but my painting is real work, Jean." Then when her mother emerged, around dinnertime, she was often in a bad mood. "My work didn't go well," she might say. Or sometimes it was going well, and she was annoyed that she had to stop.

Jean sneezed at the dust. She'd better get started before she wound up with a full-on allergy attack. She began by washing down the countertop and tables. She soon had them clean, and the area behind the counter, too, dumping all the metal utensils in a sink of sudsy water. She started on the floor next, lifting the chairs to the tables to sweep and then mop. Luckily, the shop was small and it didn't take long to make progress.

As she waved the broom near the ceiling to pull down some cobwebs, a painting caught her eye. A small sailboat, heeling into the wind, heading around the bend of a rocky shoreline, a beach that looked familiar to her, though she couldn't recall the name.

Jean took down the small painting. The small craft, tossed by white-capped waves, was a sixteen-foot daysailer called *The Cuttlefish*. The man at the helm was her father, Thomas Whitman. Her mother rarely included people in her paintings, and when she did, the figures were always at a distance, too small and blurry to identify. But Jean could easily recognize her father, his wide shoulders and lanky form, the way he faced into the wind and spray, undaunted.

Jean returned the painting to its place. Never well-matched, her parents were unhappily married most of the time. When Jean got older, she realized it wasn't anyone's fault. But her mother had been discontented with nearly everything in her life.

When she was a young woman, Cynthia had a chance to study in New York at a famous art school where many of the cutting-edge artists of the day taught. But her parents didn't have the means to send their daughter there. Cynthia was going steady with Jean's father at the time, and her family pressured her to marry and settle down.

Jean had often heard the story, along with a warning about marrying too young. "People change so much in their twenties. Even in their thirties. You shouldn't marry young, Jean. Take your time. Get out in the world. Have a sense of yourself, what you really want in life," her mother would advise. *The way I should have done,* Jean would always hear her mother's silent refrain.

To this day, Jean was sure her mother still believed that she had missed her chance at a different sort of life. A life far from quiet Cape Light. A life that would have been more exciting and sophisticated, and filled with a higher level of accomplishment than a room full of watercolors and two small children.

As much as she had idolized her father, Jean understood that he had played a part in her mother's unhappiness. He would often come home late, well after dinner. Jean remembered eating quietly with her brother while her mother smoked cigarettes and brooded. On those nights, Jean would run to greet her father at the door, but her mother barely said a word.

Later, after Jean and her brother were in bed, she would hear her parents argue. The words "affairs" and "divorce" often floated through the walls in the darkness. Though Jean was always braced to hear the worst in the morning, life went on as usual.

She later realized that her parents stayed together for the sake of her and Kevin. Perhaps they would have divorced once she and her brother were out of the house, but her father died when she was ten, of a sudden heart attack. As an adult, she wondered if her mother grew difficult because of her father's roving eye, or if Cynthia had always been difficult and hard to please, and had driven her father away.

Jean wiped out the coffeemaker with vigor, as if trying to wipe away the past. She had put those childhood years and traumas behind her. She had grown and changed and even forgiven her parents for her less-than-perfect upbringing. Still, she could feel those old buttons being pushed, just by being back here.

She walked around the shop and took the chairs down, setting them under the tables. The place was clean and fresh-smelling. Ready for business, she realized, if she had anything to sell. She had listened at the monitor a few times and only heard the continued sound of her mother's steady, deep breaths as she slept. But it was time to check on her, Jean thought, and get some coffee and maybe some leftover Thanksgiving pie to sell.

She grabbed her jacket and headed for the house just as a rain began to fall. She doubted there would be any customers today, but she was ready for some coffee herself.

She entered the house quietly then peered into the living room. Her mother was fast asleep, the blanket pulled up to her chin. Jean walked closer. Cynthia was breathing well without the oxygen, and the snack Jean had left—half an apple, cheddar cheese, and crackers—had disappeared.

Jean took a container of coffee from the kitchen cupboard, along with milk and sugar. She also took what was left of the pumpkin pie. More than half, she noticed, enough to put on a cake stand.

She made one last stop in the laundry room, where she had left her black leather artist's portfolio containing the sketches and paintings from her picture book project. She had stashed the artwork there last night, seeking a place beyond her mother's range. No one had seen the work yet, and she sometimes wondered if anyone ever would. She doubted the paintings were good enough for a published book, but she enjoyed working on it. If this first attempt didn't get published, she would start another. Unlike the work she had done at advertising agencies, she never knew quite what was going to happen when she picked up her pen or paintbrushes. There were always surprises, the heart of truly creative endeavors.

She ran through the rain for the short distance back to the cottage, and hung her wet jacket near the door. Then she slipped on the white apron and fixed a pot of coffee. The rich smell filled the small shop quickly, even before she arranged the pumpkin pie on a stand.

She poured herself a mug of coffee then spread out her artwork on a table at the back of the shop. The coffee tasted good, made from freshly ground beans she had bought from the Beanery.

Raindrops pattering against the windows gave the shop a cozy feeling. *I could get a lot of work done out here,* Jean realized. She was close enough to help her mother if needed. But also far enough to have some physical and mental space. Which she definitely needed in order to concentrate.

Jean wasn't so sure of her writing but hoped that her paintings would carry the story. The main character, a city mouse named Stanley, finds himself trapped in a delivery truck and "delivered" to a small village out in the country. He's a bit of a know-it-all but finds he must gain trust and make unlikely friends if he's going to survive. She was happy with the way she had captured Stanley's jaunty personality in his furry, rounded body and whiskered face. Drawing some of the other animals was harder. She had studied photographs she'd found online and visited a farm to make sketches and take photos.

As Jean looked over her sketches, she was distracted by her mother's paintings—as if the paintings had eyes and were peering over her shoulder. Jean had always been intimidated by Cynthia's talent. Now she could see that the paintings were good. The bold brush strokes showed both talent and skill, marked by a distinctive, abstract style. But her mother's paintings were not works of genius.

Though Jean had always loved art while growing up, her mother never praised her projects. Only her father was encouraging and gave her confidence. Jean always felt she had to hide her light under a barrel, mostly to avoid her mother's critiques, couched in "helpful" suggestions. By the time her mother was done with a "helpful review," Jean felt two inches tall. Then Cynthia would get annoyed, saying, "How can you ever improve if you can't take advice?"

Perhaps that was what she felt now, with the watercolors taking the place of her mother. Jean considered turning the paintings over so that they faced the wall, then laughed at the notion.

The bell over the door rang and a customer came in. Jean was so startled, she felt sure there was some mistake. He wore a khaki green, army-issue field jacket, threadbare around the hem and collar, an oil-cloth vest with a lot of pockets underneath, and a denim shirt beneath that.

She couldn't see his face, just his unshaven jaw and chin, the rest hidden beneath the brim of a beat-up tan fedora that reminded her of Indiana Jones. She had to smile at that and smiled again when he stood just inside the door, shaking off the wet weather like a dog.

Finally, he pulled off his hat and looked up. He needed a haircut, along with a shave. But he was definitely attractive, in a scruffy way. She wondered if he had been out hunting or maybe even fishing, despite the cold. But something about him didn't seem the type for either of those pursuits.

Jean made a neat pile of her work and stepped behind the counter. He smiled and pulled up a stool, then studied the chalkboard menu that was propped on a shelf.

She had forgotten about that menu. She should have taken it down and wiped the board clean. The lettering was faded and most of the items listed were unavailable.

"Let's see . . . I'll have a cappuccino, please. With extra cinnamon?"

"I'm sorry, there's no cappuccino today."

He looked disappointed and scanned the list again. "How about an espresso? A double would be good."

"Sorry, no espresso either. The machine is broken." And had been for a few years, Jean recalled, though she didn't add that information.

His disappointed expression had turned to a gentle, amused smile. He had hazel eyes and dark brown hair tinged with gray. She guessed his age to be early forties, a few years older than she was.

"I think I smell some coffee. Is that for sale?"

Jean nearly laughed. "I just made a fresh pot. Sumatra roast."

"Sounds perfect. I'll have a large cup. And a slice of pumpkin pie, please."

Jean poured the coffee then looked around for the milk and sugar she had brought from the house.

"Just black is fine," he said, as if reading her mind.

She sliced the pie, wishing there was a can of whipped cream handy to garnish it, but he didn't seem to notice and dug in eagerly.

She would have to buy some supplies for this place the next time she went to the supermarket. She would check around later and make a list.

He finished the pie quickly then picked up his mug and wandered around the shop. He strolled slowly in front of the long wall of watercolors. "You sell a little bit of everything in here."

"That we do," Jean replied.

"Who's the artist, Cynthia Whitman?"

"That's my mother. It's her shop."

"And her gallery, too," he noted. "She's not bad. I like this one, of the marshes. It really captures the light in the reeds, the quiet, swaying sense of the place. Is it for sale? I'd like to buy it."

Jean stared at him a moment, shocked by the question. As far as she knew, no one had bought a painting in years.

"Yes. Definitely . . . There's a notebook with prices around here somewhere . . ." She rummaged around behind the counter, pulling out drawers and opening cupboards. She finally spotted the notebook in the back of a drawer that held dish towels, the book's cover stained and the pages yellowed from the passing years. "I'll see if that one is listed. Is there a number on the back?"

Her customer removed the painting from the wall and checked. "Yes, it's number fifty-three."

Jean leafed through the pages and found the painting and the price. A few hundred dollars. Not much for original art, but judging from this man's appearance, she doubted he would buy it.

She told him the price but he didn't seem put off. "I don't have that much cash with me. Can I come back tomorrow and pick it up?"

"Yes, certainly." Jean wondered if his reply was just a graceful way of saving face. Perhaps the painting was out of his price range after all, and he didn't want to admit it. "If the shop isn't open, just come next door and knock. We're usually home."

"You live next door. How convenient. Have you lived here very long?"

"I grew up here. But I was living in Portland, Maine, until recently. I came back last week to take care of my mother. She's not well."

His expression turned thoughtful. "That's good of you. Most people I know . . . well, they love their parents, but they wouldn't move back home to care for them."

Jean's feelings toward her mother were complicated. They always had been. She knew in her heart she had not returned out of pure filial love. Or even out of guilt, exactly.

"There was a merger at the company where I worked, and I was laid off. So it was a convenient time for me to come back," she admitted.

"What do you do for a living?"

"I'm a graphic artist."

"So you're an artist, like your mother." He'd been looking at the watercolors on the wall again but turned to Jean when he spoke.

"Not really. What I do isn't real art. It's advertising layouts and brochures. That sort of thing."

They were standing in the back of the shop. "What about these sketches, aren't they art?" Before she could stop him, he picked up a sketch from the pile she had been working on. "This is lovely. His face has so much character. Not overly sweet either."

She leaned over and quickly snatched it away. "Please don't touch my drawings. You should ask before you do something like that."

She slipped the drawing in the leather portfolio, along with a few others that had been left on the table.

"I'm sorry . . . You're right. That was very rude."

Jean let out a breath and shrugged. "Apology accepted. I didn't mean to snap at you. But I haven't shown that work to anyone yet. It's not ready."

"I understand. Totally. I would scream bloody murder if someone did that to me—just grabbed one of my photographs without asking."

"Are you a photographer?" Jean had guessed by the way he spoke about the painting that he was an artist. When he nodded, she said, "What sort of work do you do?"

"I work for myself," he said simply. "Right now, I'm doing a photo essay on the village and the open spaces around here. I came through a few months ago and promised myself I'd return and take pictures."

"It is beautiful. I'm not sure I appreciated how lovely this place is when I was growing up here," Jean said. "There's more to see than people realize. Most just think of the beaches. The marshes are very beautiful, and the farms and orchards. Not to mention the harbor, especially when the fishermen are there."

He met her gaze with a look of agreement. "Exactly. It's hard to capture all that. But I'm trying. My name's Grant, by the way . . . Well, my last name isn't 'by the way.' It's Keating. Grant Keating."

Jean smiled at his small joke. "Nice to meet you, Grant. I'm Jean Whitman. So, what will you do with the photos when you're done? Sell them to a magazine?"

"Maybe. I'm not sure. I might make a book out of them. Or send them to a gallery and see if I can have a show. I'm not sure when I'll be done."

Jean found his attitude a refreshing change from the profit-driven advertising world, though she wondered how he supported himself.

"I've been renting a room in town, a big old house. The landlady's name is Vera Plante. She's been very helpful."

Jean was sure of that. Vera knew everyone in town and most of their business, too. But she wasn't really a gossip. "I know Vera. She and my mother have been friends for years."

Jean had set her own coffee mug on a table and now heard a splashing sound. She turned to see a thick drop of water fall from the ceiling onto the table and into the cup, and a moment later, another.

"Oh dear. What a mess." Jean grabbed a roll of paper towels from behind the counter, along with the plastic bucket she had used for cleaning up.

"I didn't think that coffee cup could handle the leak. But I didn't want to say something and seem too nosey again."

Jean looked up at him, wondering if he was serious or not. He was looking up at the leak, which dropped steadily from a brown ring on the ceiling. When their gazes met, she could tell from the light in his eyes that he had been teasing her.

"That spot on the roof has been leaking forever. No one ever seems to fix it for good."

Grant took another look and turned to her again. "I can fix it. At least, I can try."

"Are you a handyman, too?"

"I do the odd job here and there to earn extra money. I've already done some work at Vera's house and a few places around town, if you want references."

"I'll talk to my mother about it. I'll let you know when you come back for the painting," she added. *If you come back.* With a possible job dangling like a carrot, maybe he would return, Jean thought.

The property had become very run-down over the last few years. Jean could easily make a long list of needed repairs. She wondered if her mother had even noticed, or cared. Perhaps she had reached a point in life where such matters didn't seem very important.

"Jean . . . are you there? I just woke up. I need some help."

Jean heard her mother's voice on the monitor and stepped behind the counter to answer her. "I'll be there in a minute, Mom. Let me just close up here. Don't get up. Wait for me to help you."

Grant had followed her and stood close by. He pulled on his jacket and fitted his hat on his head. Then he extended his hand. "Good to meet you, Jean. I'll be back for the painting tomorrow. Any special time?"

Jean was distracted by his touch. His grip on her hand was warm and firm. "I'll be around all day. Either in here or at the house."

"Then I'll find you." He tipped his hat and walked out the door.

Jean watched his departing figure, feeling as if she had imagined him and his promise. The same way she conjured up the characters in her book. She doubted she could trust half of what he said. But she couldn't help liking him anyway. Would he show up tomorrow? She certainly hoped so.

Jean crossed the muddy ground to the house, then shrugged out of her wet jacket. "What took you so long?" her mother called from the living room. "I've been waiting here for half an hour."

"It's only been a few minutes, Mom. I couldn't leave right away. A man came into the shop. He had some coffee and pie."

And we talked a lot, she nearly added.

"I'm sure there will be plenty of customers if you go out there in the afternoons." Jean did not share her mother's confidence, but didn't argue. "Help me up. Is there any mail?"

"I left it in the kitchen." Jean set up the walker and helped her mother stand. Then she watched as Cynthia took tentative steps, pausing at the window to pull back the curtain and look outside. "Not even five o'clock and dark out already." Her mother let the curtain drop. "Such a dull day."

"Maybe not," Jean countered. "The customer who came into the shop wants to buy one of your paintings. He's coming back tomorrow to pick it up."

Her mother turned quickly and stared at her. "Really? Which one?"

"A scene of the marshes. It was hanging above the bookcase."

"I know the one. Not a bad little landscape." Her mother didn't seem as happy as Jean expected, but her spirits seemed brighter. "How much did you ask for it?"

Jean named the figure. Her mother's expression soured. "That's all? It's worth much more than that."

"I looked up the price in your notebook. That's what was listed."

"Those prices are outdated by now. You should have asked me first."

"I should have," Jean agreed. "Do you want me to give a higher price when he comes to get it? He told me that he's staying at Vera's house. I can call him there and let him know."

"No, no . . ." Her mother waved her hand as if batting away an insect. "Don't do that. You've given him a price. That's that. Just make sure he pays in cash. No checks."

Jean smiled at the stipulation. "Very wise. But I believe he already plans to pay with cash. Why don't you come into the kitchen. You can look at the mail and we can talk while I make dinner."

Cynthia was soon settled at the kitchen table, carefully reading each piece of mail, though most of it was junk mail—requests for donations, flyers marketing insurance discounts or cable TV service.

Jean stood by the sink, peeling potatoes. Mashed tonight, her mother's favorite. But not from a box.

"The man who's buying the painting also does home repairs. You know that leak in the back of the shop? The rain started coming through the ceiling again today. He said he could fix it."

"Many have tried. And failed." Her mother had moved on to the catalogues. She pushed a medical supply catalogue aside and opened one called *Home & Hearth*.

"If we're going to reopen the shop, I think we should try again," Jean said. "Water has been coming in through that hole, Mother. It's worn a spot on the floor and gives the whole place a musty smell."

Cynthia turned a page without looking up. "I suppose we can hire someone. But we don't know this guy from Adam."

"He's done work for Vera and other people in town. He said he'd give some references."

"I'll ask Vera about him. She's a good judge of character. Then again, that leak has been there for ages. And it only leaks when it rains," her mother added.

The observation struck Jean as funny, though she didn't dare laugh out loud. "That's the way leaks are, I guess," she noted. "There are a lot of things around here that need repair. It's an old house and it needs some attention. It's starting to look a bit run-down."

Her mother turned another page of the catalogue. "Some fixing up so it will sell quickly when I die—is that what you mean? Or maybe you and your brother plan to put me in a nursing home."

Jean was cutting up the potatoes and nearly sliced into her finger, she felt so taken aback by the accusation. "I've come back home so that *won't* happen, Mom. I thought you knew that."

"That's what you say. For now anyway," her mother mumbled.

"No one plans on selling the house," Jean assured her. "But there are basic repairs that need to be done. Other leaks in the roof of the shop and the house. Loose floorboards. Anyone could fall. And a few windows in the sunroom are broken. Those can be fixed easily, and it will cut down on the heating bill," she added. "Besides, the cardboard that's covering them now makes the house look a shambles."

"You seem very concerned," her mother noted. "Though you know Kevin will get the house. I hope you didn't come back planning to change my mind about that, Jean."

Did she really suspect such a devious scheme? Jean turned to look at her mother but was unable to read her expression.

She scooped the potato pieces into a pot, added water, and set it on the stove to boil. "We both know your wishes, Mom. But you don't want to leave him a falling-down heap."

Jean noticed her mother's slight reaction, pursing her lips and knitting her brow. Though she did not concede the point aloud.

"I'd like to clear out the piles of newspapers and things that have collected around here. I know it must have been hard for you to keep on top of the housekeeping the last few months," she added. "But it has to be bad for your breathing, all the dust on that stuff." Not to mention that the assorted piles made Jean crazy, and she had barely been home a week.

Her mother finally closed the catalogue and looked up. "It is important to keep the property value up. I suppose this fellow can take a look at the repairs."

"Let's make a list after dinner. We can ask him for an estimate when he comes to pick up the painting."

"All right. If he charges too much, we'll find someone else."

Jean hoped that was not the case. For reasons she didn't want to examine too closely, she hoped Grant Keating's fees seemed reasonable. Even to her mother's penny-pinching pocketbook.

CHAPTER FOUR

*H*ERE YOU ARE, HONEY. HOME SWEET HOME. I BET YOU
feel better already." Jessica walked a few steps ahead of
the wheelchair while Darrell pushed from behind. The path from the
driveway to the side door was clear and flat, but Sam had no idea how
his wife and son would get the chair up the steps, even though there
were only three.

"Maybe we should call Dan to help get me in the house," Sam
suggested. "And Bart is probably around. He'll help. I don't think you
two can do it alone."

"No worries, Dad. We've got this covered," Darrell promised.

Darrell turned the chair around the side of the house, and Jessica
turned to smile at Sam. "Look . . . Darrell built a handicapped ramp
for you. He had it up before I even knew what he was doing."

Sam's eyes widened at the sight. A sturdy ramp, built at the perfect
angle for his chair to be rolled easily to the door.

"Nice job. You even matched the paint to the house trim?"

Darrell shrugged, but Sam could tell he was proud of the project. "Glad you approve, Dad. Now for the real test," he said, pushing the chair toward the house. "Tyler tried it on his skateboard, but we haven't driven a loaded wheelchair over it yet."

"Now you tell me?" Sam was not alarmed but didn't mind teasing Darrell a bit. The ramp was as solid as it looked. He didn't feel the planks budge, not even a slight buckle or dip.

They reached the door and Jessica held it open while Darrell pushed Sam inside. Tyler and Lily were at school, which was just as well, Sam thought. They would be home soon enough.

The rush of leaving the hospital had tired him out, along with the pain medication he still needed to take. But he was eager to get into his office and try to sort out his tangled business problems.

Once they were inside, Darrell helped him remove his hat and jacket and the one glove he was able to wear. Once again, Sam felt reduced to a childlike status, with his son playing caretaker. It was an odd feeling and one he didn't care for.

"Would you guys like some lunch?" Jessica asked. "How about some soup or a sandwich?"

"I'll take both, please," Darrell said.

"Just soup for me, Jess, thanks," Sam said. "Can you bring it into my office, please?"

"Sure. I'll bring a tray in, in a few minutes." Jessica turned and headed for the kitchen, stepping over the baby gate she used to corral any animals she was keeping indoors.

Darrell carefully steered the chair through the doorway of Sam's office. "We took the couch out and set up the hospital bed in here. The wheelchair won't fit behind the desk, but Mom thought this wood table would work for you."

Darrell parked the chair near a small table that was just the right height for Sam's use. Sam saw his laptop along with a pad of paper and a jar of pencils and pens from his desk, and his cell phone charging station. "Nice setup," he said. "And thanks for the ride." Though the chair was motorized, Sam hadn't yet learned how to use the controls. It was going to be a bit challenging with his left hand. "I'd better learn how to drive this thing. You'll be going back to school tomorrow, and I won't have anyone to push me around."

"You'll get the hang of it once you practice. If ninety-year-olds can drive one of these, you can, too . . . Do you need anything else from your desk?"

"I'm fine for now. This is great. Thanks." If only the rest of the problems his injuries had caused could be solved so easily. Sam picked up the pad and a pen, and began to make a list. He felt Darrell watching and looked up to meet his son's dark brown eyes.

Sam knew that Jessica had needed Darrell's help until he got home from the hospital. But Darrell had been in Cape Light since Monday, the day of Sam's fall. Now it was Thursday, and Sam was worried that Darrell was missing too much school.

"Thanks for springing me from the hospital, buddy. When are you heading back to Boston?"

"Oh, I don't know. In a while, I guess." Darrell stood in the doorway and crossed his arms over his chest.

"No sense driving back in the rush-hour traffic later. It will take you twice as long."

"Yeah, I know," Darrell said lightly.

Before Sam could prod his son further, Jessica called from the hall. "Sam? You have a visitor—"

Sam waited, expecting Emily and Dan or maybe Reverend Ben.

But it was Bart Begossian.

"Hope you don't mind me stopping in, Sam. I should have called first, right? The guys got together and bought you a little get-well present. It's DVDs—the complete series of that fishing show you like. I just wanted to drop it off, see how you're doing."

"I'm doing fine. It's good to be home. You don't need to rush off, Bart. Sit down a minute," Sam said eagerly.

Bart sat in an armchair and set the gift bag he was carrying on the table. He seemed uneasy, Sam thought. But maybe he felt self-conscious, stopping by without warning or an invitation.

"How do you feel? Are you in much pain?" Bart looked over Sam's leg casts and shoulder.

"Sometimes," Sam admitted. "Then I think of the alternative, and it doesn't seem so bad. If it wasn't for you, I wouldn't be here to tell the tale. I can never thank you enough for sticking around that day. Especially considering I was telling you not to."

Bart looked embarrassed by Sam's gratitude. "Good thing I didn't listen to you," he joked. "I didn't do much. Nearly had a heart attack when I saw you take a dive off that ladder."

"Good thing that didn't happen. So, any news from the crew?"

"Not much news to tell, Sam. You know that."

The work on Sam's three jobs had come to a grinding halt with his fall. Sam guessed that Bart—along with the rest of the men on the payroll—wanted to know if it would start up again anytime soon.

"I do, Bart. I'm sorry about that. I'm still trying to sort things out. It's going to take a day or two more." Or even longer, Sam knew. But he didn't want to alarm anyone.

"I know you're in a bind, Sam. I wouldn't wish this on anyone, especially you. But everyone wants to know if we're going to pick up the work again. Or should we look for other jobs? Christmas is coming. It's hard to do without a paycheck," he added.

"I know it is, believe me. Everyone will get paid for this week, their full hours," Sam promised.

He had called each man on his crew and assured them they would receive their pay at the end of the week. But he felt bad that he couldn't promise more than that right now. He knew most were restless, even after three days. He couldn't blame them if they looked for other work.

"I understand where you're coming from, Bart. I'd be asking the same thing. Could you please wait a day or two more? I'm trying to keep the work going. I really am. But I'm not sure yet how I can work it out."

"Sure. I know you are, Sam. I didn't mean to pressure, honest. You have enough on your shoulders right now. Your good shoulder," he added. Bart came to his feet and pulled his gloves from his pocket. "I'll tell the guys I saw you and try to slow them down. I'll wait to hear from you," he promised.

"Thanks, Bart. I appreciate it. Tell the guys I really appreciate the gift—gives me something to look forward to. And Bart, I'd hate to do without you on the job," Sam said sincerely. Lots of men tended to come and go in Sam's line of work, but Bart was a keeper. He sure hoped Bart didn't jump ship.

Bart seemed pleased by the compliment. He gently patted Sam's good shoulder. "You're looking better already. You'll be up and shouting orders at everyone before you know it."

Sam smiled. "I hope so."

Jessica came in carrying Sam's lunch tray. She set it on the table and chatted with Bart a moment.

"I'd better be going. I'm visiting my father in Rockport," Bart said, glancing at his watch. "You take care, Sam."

"I will. Thanks again for stopping by," Sam said.

Jessica showed Bart to the door then returned to Sam's office. His wife's homemade chicken noodle soup looked and smelled appetizing, but he only took a few spoonfuls before setting it aside. He was too eager to start making phone calls, and he searched his contacts for the numbers he needed.

Jessica had taken a seat at the other side of the table. "Something wrong with the soup? Is it too hot?"

"Tastes great, honey. But I'm trying to get some work done while I eat. No time to lose. Bart says the crew is losing their patience. They're looking for other work." He picked up a cracker and took a bite. "If I can't get the projects going again somehow, I won't have workers to do the jobs."

"That's too bad. It's only been three days." Jessica took a cracker off his plate. "Did you talk to Bart about being a foreman?"

Sam shook his head. "He's a great guy and a great carpenter. But managing other men is not his thing. I might be able to find someone if I call around. Or find other contractors who will take over the jobs . . . if the customers will agree to let them finish the work." Sam showed her the list he'd been working on. "I already called a few of these guys from the hospital. The good ones are super busy this time of year. And I don't want the unreliable fast-and-dirty guys ruining my reputation."

"Of course not. That wouldn't do you any good in the long run."

"You need to know—if I can find some good outfit to take over, I'll need to pay them the bulk of the fee. I won't end up with much profit, Jess. I might even lose money."

Jessica stood up and began smoothing the bedding, folding an extra quilt. Trying to hide her concern, he thought. "What about your customers? How do they feel about the delay? They were all very concerned when they heard about your accident. Some called the house.

Others sent get-well cards. They might not mind a break from construction right now, with the holidays and everything."

"That's one way to look it." Sam was trying not to squash her hopeful note. "Most of them wanted their new kitchens and dormers done in time for Christmas. I don't think they'll be happy decorating around some stalled-out construction."

"It's a complicated situation," Jessica agreed. "But there is a solution right under your nose."

"Darrell has to finish his semester. That solution is not under my nose; it's off the table, Jess. You know how I feel about that." He hadn't meant to snap at her, but she shouldn't have brought it up again. "Maybe I can find a reliable guy to oversee the work for me. I've been sifting through all my contacts and asking other outfits for recommendations. If I make a few more phone calls, I'm bound to find someone."

Sam didn't feel nearly as sure of that outcome as he was trying to sound. All the best foremen already had jobs. He also knew the way friends in this business tried to throw each other work, giving a good reference that wasn't always accurate. He was down to calling guys he hardly knew, and they were recommending men who were total strangers to him. It would be hard to trust someone he knew well with his customers and business reputation, much less a stranger.

Jessica walked over and stood behind his chair. She placed her hands on his shoulders. "You'll figure this out, Sam. I know you're between a rock and a hard place, but you always manage to find solutions. You will this time, too," she said quietly. "Is there anything I can do to help?"

He smiled, despite the way he felt, and reached back to cover her hand with his own. "Thanks, honey. You're already helping me."

His cell phone sounded, and he snatched it up, hoping it was one of the contractors he had called earlier. But he quickly saw that the caller was a customer—Suzanne Prentiss, who had hired him to remodel the second floor of her house.

"Suzanne, how are you?" Sam greeted her.

"I should be asking you that question, Sam. Are you still in the hospital?" she asked with concern.

"Out early, on good behavior. I just got home this morning."

"That's great news. I'm so happy for you. There's nothing like resting and recovering at home."

"Absolutely. My wife is already plying me with chicken soup." Sam was fine with friendly chatter with his customers, but he was sure Mrs. Prentiss had called for a reason beyond checking on his recovery. "What's up? Anything I can help you with? I'm so sorry the work on your house has been delayed. But I'm doing my best to get the job up and running again."

"I know you are, Sam. And I'm sorry to bother you. But I have a real problem here today. A big truck pulled up this morning, and now there are bales of insulation and all sorts of wood and heaven only knows what in our driveway. It's not only inconvenient, but I'd hate to see any of these materials ruined in this weather."

The delivery from Harbor Lumber . . . he had forgotten all about it. And she was right. A lot of those supplies would get ruined if it started raining again, or possibly snowing.

"No worries, Suzanne. I'll get that cleared out for you, ASAP. Are you home today?"

"Yes, I am. All day."

"I'll call you back and let you know when some men will be over to move it. Thanks for letting me know."

"No problem, Sam. Thank you for taking care of it. By the way, any idea when the work will start up here again? I'm sorry to pressure you, but we're having some family in from out of town over Christmas. If we can't use the second floor, we'll have to find them hotel rooms. I'd need to make those reservations right away. You know how it is."

"Yes, I know." Sam felt his heart sink at her tone. Despite her kind words, she was losing her patience. And Suzanne Prentiss knew everyone in town; he didn't need her giving his company bad reviews. He wondered if he should offer to pick up the hotel expenses but decided to wait on that. Her project could be finished by Christmas. *If there was some kind of miracle,* he thought.

"I'm making a million calls today, trying to get my ducks in a row. I'll let you know the status of the work very soon. Thanks for your patience, Suzanne."

"Not at all. You take care."

Sam sat back in his wheelchair, his shoulder and head throbbing. He suddenly felt hungry but now the soup was cold.

Jessica looked over at him. "A problem already?"

"I've got to get some guys over to the Prentiss house. But somebody's got to tell them what to do . . . and smooth things over with Mrs. Prentiss."

"Why don't you call Bart? Is he good with the clients?"

"He can be. If I coach him. But he told me he was headed to Rockport today. He's probably gone by now."

Sam was so lost in the quagmire of his problems, he didn't notice that Darrell had come into the room until his son stood right in front of him.

"I'll go for you, Dad. I know how to talk to your clients."

Sam knew that was true. Darrell had great social skills, especially for someone so young. When he worked for Sam in the summers, all the clients loved him. But Sam still wasn't persuaded.

"I thought you were heading back to school today. I thought you came in to say good-bye to me."

"It's too late to make any classes today. What's the difference if I go now or tonight or tomorrow?"

Sam stared at him, his eyes squinting. "That's what you said yesterday. And the day before."

"And I know Mrs. Prentiss. She was an art teacher at the high school. She always liked me," Darrell added with a wide, cheesy grin.

"That's right. She loved Darrell. She'll be happy to see him," Jessica said. "Besides, he can take care of the problem. I'm sure he can. He's practically a certified architect. He knows as much about building as Joe Kelley ever did. Or Bart Begossian, for that matter."

Their points were persuasive, and all his problems crashing down at once had worn down Sam's defenses. Still, he was reluctant to send his son out to fill his shoes.

"I can visit your other jobs while I'm out, too, Dad. Talk to the clients, see where the work is at. If you find another contractor or foreman to take over, you'll need to give them a project status report."

"So now you're flinging architect talk at me, is that it?" Sam countered.

"It's more the way engineers talk," Darrell replied. "You know what I mean."

Sam sighed. "Okay, you can go. I'll call the other clients and find out who you can see then text you the info. I'll also have a few guys meet you at the Prentiss house. Be superpolite and find out where we can store the materials. Maybe in her garage or basement. Make sure the men are moving everything carefully. If you can't leave the stuff there, you'll have to bring it back here and we'll put in the barn."

Jessica made a little sound and Sam glanced at her. "I hope there's room. I'm expecting a pony tomorrow. She's so sweet. Her name is

Sassy. She was dragged around for children's parties and abused by her owner for years. Someone heard that he was going to put her down just because he's retiring and moving away. So they called me. Just in time, too."

"That's one lucky pony. Good for you, Mom," Darrell said.

"I'm glad you could save her, Jess," Sam said evenly. He was actually dismayed that the pony was going to take up space he might need to store the supplies. Couldn't one thing go his way today? But what could he do? He had agreed that Jessica could start this animal rescue work in earnest, and abused ponies were part of the deal. He winced inwardly. There were definitely more needy animals to come.

DARRELL OFTEN DROVE HIS FATHER'S TRUCK, BUT THIS TIME FELT different. As he rode down the Beach Road toward the village, he was careful to ease up on the gas pedal. The truck had a lot of power, a lot more than his small, aging Subaru. He didn't need a speeding ticket today. Not after he had finally gotten his father to agree to let him help with the business.

Darrell felt sure he could get his dad's projects up and running again. He already knew enough about the field to design a skyscraper, let alone a finished basement. But writing papers and making models for his courses were a whole lot different than dealing with half-finished dormers and annoyed clients.

As he turned down Cherry Lane and pulled up at the Prentiss house, he felt a fit of nerves. He parked the truck and took a few deep breaths before he jumped out. Two men stood talking by a small blue truck. Darrell recognized them from working last summer for his dad. Darrell walked toward them and smiled. "Terry . . . Bobby . . . good to see you." Darrell held out his hand and greeted them warmly.

"Hey, Darrell. Too bad about your father. Sounds like he was hurt bad." Terry shook his hand then stuffed his big, chapped hands in the pockets of a down vest he wore over a hooded sweatshirt. Red block letters on the shirt said MORGAN CONSTRUCTION & HOME IMPROVEMENT.

"He's coming along. He got home from the hospital today," Darrell replied, trying to put a positive spin on his father's condition. "He's definitely getting up to speed."

"Bart told us he's trying to keep the jobs going," Bobby said. "I hope so. We all need the work. Especially with Christmas coming." Bobby was older than Terry, but still in good shape for his age. He also wore a down vest over a sweatshirt, but his said Boston Red Sox, matching his cap, which hid his thinning hair.

"My dad knows that. Believe me, he's trying every which way to get the work started again. I think he will, too." *He will if I have anything to say or do about it,* he wanted to add.

"So what do you want us to do?" Terry gestured to the mountain of insulation and supplies in the Prentiss driveway. "Load this stuff on your truck? I think we'll need to make a few trips."

"Just hang out here a minute. I'm going to talk to Mrs. Prentiss. Maybe we can store it on the property somewhere."

Bobby shrugged. "Sounds good. But try to speed it up. I need to get over to the high school for my son's basketball game. He's a starter this year."

Darrell wasn't sure what to say. He knew that his father was paying both men for a full day's work. He doubted that when his dad was in charge, Bob quit at two in the afternoon and ran off to games at the high school.

"Let's see how it goes. I'll be back in a minute."

Bobby looked like he might argue about leaving early. Darrell turned and headed for the house before he could. But as he started up the drive, he heard the men continue to talk.

"I'm leaving at two," Bobby said. "I don't have to take orders from Sam's kid."

"He's trying to help his father. And we're lucky to get paid the full week. Some guys wouldn't do that."

"Sure, I'm glad to get paid, too. But what happens after that?"

You'll be taking orders from Sam's kid, Darrell wanted to tell him. *That's what's going to happen.*

Mrs. Prentiss opened the door as Darrell came up the walkway. She ushered him inside. "Thank you for coming by so quickly, Darrell. It's good to see you. How's school? What year are you in now?"

"School's great, Mrs. Prentiss. I'm a senior. I'm going to graduate in the spring."

Mrs. Prentiss looked shocked. "Graduate? Already? You make me feel so old," she said with a laugh. "Your father told me that you're studying engineering and architecture. You certainly have the artistic talent for it. I'm sure you'll do well."

"Thanks. I hope so." Darrell looked around. "This is a lovely home. I love the housing stock in Cape Light. I didn't really appreciate it growing up."

Mrs. Prentiss looked flattered. Just as he'd hoped. "We try to keep it in good repair. That's the problem with old houses. It's always something. So can you move those supplies out of the driveway today? That would be a great help."

"That's what we came to do. Is there somewhere on your property we can store this stuff?"

"Store all that here? No, I don't think so. Doesn't your father have a yard or a storage area or something?"

"Not exactly. I can take it someplace else if that's what you want us to do," Darrell replied in a solicitous, calming tone. "But it would be more convenient to keep it here. That way we won't waste any time packing it up again and bringing it back and then unloading everything . . ." He dragged out his explanation, hoping his excuse was working. "When we start working again, I mean."

She had looked doubtful at his question, but her expression brightened at the hint that the renovation might start up again soon.

"When do you think that will be? I spoke to your father this morning about it, and he couldn't say."

Darrell hesitated. "I don't want to make any promises. But . . . things are moving in the right direction," he said finally. He thought that much was true.

Mrs. Prentiss considered his prediction, her expression stern, an expression he remembered from the times when the class acted out or didn't clean the art room properly.

"I guess it can go in the basement," she said at last. "I'll show you the spot. Your men can take it through the garage and downstairs. Just leave a path to the Christmas decorations."

"Thank you. We're happy to do whatever's convenient for you."

Mrs. Prentiss quickly showed him the way. The basement was clean and dry. Not completely finished but it had Sheetrock walls and a linoleum floor. The supplies would be fine down here temporarily, he decided.

Just to be on the safe side, he took a picture of the space and texted his Dad with the plan. Then he gave instructions to Terry and Bobby and worked alongside them. With the three of them working, it didn't take as long as Darrell had expected to empty the driveway. Though at the end of the task he felt more tired than he expected and had a few muscle aches, too.

Outside again, he said good-bye to the two men and thanked them for coming on such short notice. Bobby was already in his car and waved as he drove off. Two o'clock had come and gone but he had not asked to leave for the basketball game. Maybe he had been afraid that Darrell would complain about him to his father. Or maybe he realized he should work for a few hours, until the task was done, when he was getting paid for a full day.

Terry lingered on the sidewalk before getting in his truck. He slapped Darrell on the back. "Good to see you, kid. Tell your father I was asking about him. Maybe we'll see you around? Maybe you'll be stepping into the old man's work boots for a while?"

Darrell laughed. "I hope so," he said honestly.

Back in the truck, Darrell found a text from his father. There was no one at the Hendersons', so he couldn't check that job today.

Okay. Heading home, Darrell replied.

He drove around the block, intending to retrace the path he had followed into the neighborhood, but soon realized he had taken a wrong turn somewhere. He found himself driving on a deserted road with only a cottage or two to be seen behind marsh grass and overgrown shrubs.

A high, chain-link fence came into view, and behind that, a huge, old brick building. Most of the long, mitered windows were boarded up. The rest were broken, providing a convenient portal for the birds that flew in and out. Darrell parked the truck on the road's sandy shoulder. He got out and walked closer, stepping over beer cans and other litter. He saw more trash on the other side of the fence and figured that there must be a hole somewhere. He walked around the building, to the side that was not visible from the road, and soon found an opening in the fence, large enough to squeeze through.

He walked carefully; the concrete around the building was fractured, with weeds growing through. He saw a double door that must have been the main entrance. It was secured with a padlock, but he was able to peer through the window and look inside.

Late-day sun filtered through the holes in the roof, just enough for Darrell to discern that the building must have been a factory of some kind. Most of the walls had crumbled, but the iron beams that framed the structure still looked solid. Around another corner, he noticed the double rails of train or trolley tracks overgrown with weeds, but still leading to a loading dock.

From the construction—what he could see of it—he guessed the place was built around 1900, maybe even earlier. Despite its ruin, there were many fine decorative touches in the brickwork and stone trim. Darrell pulled out his phone and took pictures, wandering around the entire perimeter until he came to the hole in the fence again.

Something about this place excited him. He had a million questions about it. Mainly, why had it been left to rot like this? Practically every old warehouse on the Boston waterfront had been renovated and turned into living space. Pricey living space. Hadn't anyone spotted the potential here?

He jumped back in the truck and checked a map on his phone to figure out his location, now glad that he had lost his way.

Not all who wander are lost. He recalled hearing that phrase somewhere. He had not exactly been wandering, but veering off course had definitely resulted in the bright spot of his day. He glanced at the map on his phone again. He wanted to know more about this place, that was for sure.

He was just about to start off when a text came in from his mother. She wanted him to stop in town and pick up a prescription at the pharmacy. Don't forget to drop off that donation can at the bakery, she added.

I didn't forget, he replied, though the task had slipped his mind. His mother, aided by his brother and sister, had made containers out of coffee cans to collect donations for the Grateful Paws Rescue Center. Tyler had taken close-up photos of the cutest animals, and printed them out with a caption requesting donations. Their aunt Molly— their dad's sister—had happily agreed to keep one on the counter in her bakery, and Darrell had tossed it in the back of the truck cab that morning. He glanced back. It was still there, safe and sound. A close-up of Pinky, a tiny orphaned piglet, stared back at him.

Out on the Beach Road, he headed for the village. The pharmacy was on Main Street. He found a parking spot quickly and picked up the prescription. Then he headed to Willoughby's Fine Foods and Catering. He was definitely ready for a snack and was sure Aunt Molly would feed him well. Even if he didn't need to drop off the donation can, she would never forgive him if she caught him eating anywhere else. She did serve the best food in town. No question about that.

The bakery was just around the corner on a street that faced the harbor and a park. It was about half past two, and the park was filled with kids burning off energy after being cooped up in school all day. Darrell watched them play, remembering when he was one of them.

On the nearby village green he saw the old stone church, Reverend Ben's church, and the town's Christmas tree, decorated with lights. His family had come down for the annual tree lighting, as usual. It wasn't the same since his aunt Emily wasn't mayor anymore, but it was still fun to watch his little sister, Lily, who was almost eight. She claimed that she didn't believe in Santa anymore but still grew wide-eyed when the big, red-suited guy arrived on the back of a fire truck.

Darrell knew that he hadn't really appreciated the town, all the years growing up here. Now that he was studying housing and how neighborhoods evolved, he understood what made Cape Light such a special place. It didn't matter if you were rich or poor or somewhere in between. The village of Cape Light had much to offer all—with its schools and churches, and its many shops and restaurants that made a trip to the mall, or even larger towns, unnecessary. Decorated now for Christmas, it was even prettier than usual.

Willoughby's wasn't as crowded as usual. A girl behind the counter quickly asked for his order, but before he could answer, he heard his aunt's unmistakable greeting.

"Darrell, are you still around? I thought you went back to school." Aunt Molly had been checking a display case full of amazing-looking cakes but turned to give him a huge hug. "How's it going? I heard your dad was sprung from the hospital today. Driving all the nurses crazy, right?"

Darrell grinned. "No comment. He's doing well, all things considered."

"Poor guy. This is a tough break for him, no pun intended. It's been years since he's had to deal with anything more than a bad cold." His aunt's tone was sympathetic. "My heart goes out to your family, too. I know how your father gets when he's stuck in the house. Like a restless tiger in the zoo."

Darrell laughed at his aunt's accurate description. "It'll be fine. We'll just throw a little steak in his room a few times a day and slam the door shut. Which reminds me, speaking of wild animals, my mom said to give you this." He handed her the donation can.

Molly took the container and looked it over. "Grateful Paws? Great name, and the photo is adorable. Tell your mom I'm putting this front and center, and giving customers dirty looks if they don't drop some change in."

"I'll relay the message," Darrell said with a laugh.

His aunt's expression changed, suddenly all business. "What can

I get you? A sandwich? Some muffins or cake? All of the above? At your age, I bet you can eat six meals a day. Good metabolism is wasted on the young, that's for sure."

Darrell eyed the selection. Everything looked good. "A brownie?"

"Coming right up. How about two?" His aunt bustled behind the counter and set two brownies on a plate. "Some milk with that?"

"That would be excellent," Darrell said. He thought he should order something more adult, like espresso, or even regular coffee. But he really did like cold milk with a brownie.

"I could use a break, too. Let's sit down and chat." Molly carried his dessert and a cup of tea for herself to a table by the window. Darrell followed and took a seat across from her.

"When I saw your dad in the hospital, he was all hot and bothered about you getting back to school. Did you stay to help your mom get him home today?"

"We had to get the house ready. We rented a hospital bed and an electric wheelchair. I built a ramp at the side door so he could get in and out easily."

His aunt looked impressed. "You built that for him? I bet he was pleased. At least the restless tiger can get some fresh air once in a while."

"That was the basic idea." Darrell took a big bite of his first brownie, glad his aunt had given him a second. "Great brownie, Aunt Molly. Even better than I remember."

"Thanks, honey. Enjoy." She leaned closer and practically whispered. "I changed the recipe a few weeks ago. I'm adding some coffee to give the chocolate a little backbone."

"It's just right," he said, finishing off the first.

"When are you going back to school? I'm sure your mom can use more help with him than just today."

"Agreed. And Dad's in a panic about his business. His projects are at a standstill, and he's not sure how to get them up and running again. I finally talked him into letting me visit clients today and sort out a few emergencies."

"Good for you." His aunt poured an extra dollop of honey in her tea from a jar on the table. "Too bad you can't stick around and help until he gets better."

"That's the thing. I can. I talked to my professors, and they all said it was fine if I finish the semester online, as long as I hand in my papers and projects in a few weeks."

"That's great. Problem solved."

"I wish. I had to twist Dad's arm—his good arm—just to get him to agree to let me go out today. He's still looking for contractors to take over his work. Or maybe a temporary foreman."

Molly rolled her eyes. "Morgans are a hardheaded clan. Probably the reason why your dad's head is still in one piece after that fall. He's lucky you're willing and able to help him like this. Sooner or later, he'll figure that out."

"He needs to have that revelation in the next few hours. He expects me to leave tomorrow."

His aunt leaned over and patted his hand. "You never know, honey. Stranger things have happened."

Darrell had started the second brownie, which was going down a bit slower than the first, though he doubted he'd leave a crumb behind. His aunt had finished her tea and cleared away her empty cup. "Back to work for me. Can I get you anything else?"

Darrell shook his head emphatically. She smiled, looking pleased. Molly Willoughby was never happier than when she watched someone enjoy the food she cooked. "I'll make a care package for your father. It will cheer him up."

One of Aunt Molly's care packages could cheer anyone up, Darrell knew. "Thanks, that would be great."

He walked back to the counter and watched as she filled a big white box with a selection of cookies, pastries, and muffins. "I was out near your neighborhood today, Aunt Molly, and I noticed an old warehouse, just off the Beach Road. It's all boarded up with a fence around it. Do you know anything about that place?"

"I think it was a paper mill, or maybe a cannery? It's been shut down for ages." She placed the box on the counter and taped down the flaps. "The town has talked about knocking it down a few times. But nothing ever happens. I wish they would. It's a bit of an eyesore."

"It is a wreck right now. But it has lots of possibilities. I wonder who owns it."

His aunt put the box in a shopping bag then filled another bag with loaves of fresh bread—sunflower, cinnamon raisin, and his dad's favorite, pumpernickel. "Ask around at Village Hall. Someone should be able to tell you. Why do you want to know?"

"If Dad lets me stay to work for him, I need to do an extra project for one of my classes. Figuring out a way to reclaim and renovate an old building would be a great topic."

"Good idea. I bet professors love stuff like that."

"Yeah, they do." Darrell grinned then picked up the shopping bag. He thanked his aunt for the bounty of baked goods and headed back to the truck. He was eager to get home and look over the pictures he'd taken of the warehouse. Maybe even show them to his father.

CHAPTER FIVE

~~~

*C*YNTHIA HAD STARTED THE DAY WITH A SURPRISING AMOUNT of energy, supervising as Jean tackled the piles of junk that filled the sunroom. They began the project soon after breakfast, and while Jean was pleased to see her mother finally enlivened and interested in some activity, Jean knew the job would have gone twice as fast without her mother's oversight. Still, these were her mother's belongings, her memories. *In her place I might be just as fussy,* Jean reminded herself when she lost patience.

But the effort of merely directing wore her mother out, and after lunch she returned to her room. Jean was worried that her mother had overdone it and was glad when Barbara Crosby arrived around four p.m. "Sorry I'm here so late today," Barbara said as she unwound her wool scarf. "I had two new patients this morning, and it takes a lot of time to do an intake."

"It's perfect timing," Jean said. "Mom started off the day fine, but she's been resting since lunch and needed her oxygen. She wanted to help me clean out the sunroom. She was just telling me what to keep or throw out. But I'm afraid that was too much for her."

Barbara patted Jean's arm. "Let's see what's going on. I'm sure you couldn't have stopped her from taking part, even if you wanted to. So don't look so guilty."

Jean smiled. "I do feel guilty. Though, of course, she didn't lift a finger."

"I can see you did all the heavy lifting, no worries. If you want to jump in the shower while I'm here, that's fine," Barbara added.

Jean knew she looked a total wreck, wearing worn jeans and a baggy sweatshirt she had found in her old bedroom. Her long brown hair was pulled back in a ponytail that had mostly come undone, and dust smeared her hands and even her cheek. "I can wait. I still have to put out all the trash."

Barbara opened her bag, taking out the book she used for notes on her patients. "I know you want to help your mom as much as you can, and this place needs cleaning up, no question. But it took years for the house to get into this state. And taking care of her is a big job, too. You can't fix everything in a week. You'll just burn yourself out, honey."

Jean smiled. She was sure she looked like a madwoman today, which must be part of the reason Barbara felt obliged to offer advice. "I'm starting to see that. I'll try to slow down."

"Good. And you need some time of your own. Some distractions and entertainment," Barbara advised.

Jean knew that was true, too. But she wasn't sure how she would manage time away from the house . . . or where she would find any "distractions and entertainment."

Meeting Grant Keating the other day had been both. He had

promised to come back for the painting on Wednesday, but here it was, approaching five on Thursday, and he had not even called. She'd taken a little extra care with her appearance yesterday but didn't bother today. Her mother had not asked about him. Jean was glad of that. She was secretly disappointed he hadn't come back, or even called, but not entirely surprised.

Barbara went into Cynthia's room and Jean pulled on a down vest and gloves, then began lugging out the bags of trash. She had just dragged two to the curb when a beat-up truck pulled up. She saw Grant in the driver's seat and waited as he shut off the engine and jumped out.

"Hi, Jean. I've come for the painting. Sorry I couldn't make it here yesterday."

Of course you'd come today, when I look like a dog's breakfast, she wanted to reply.

"No one bought it out from under me, I hope."

Jean was sure he was teasing, though he looked perfectly serious. "No one has topped your offer yet." Her reply was sarcastic, she realized, even though it was true. She began walking back to the house and he followed.

Yesterday morning Cynthia had woken up with a renewed interest in the piece. She had asked Jean to bring it in from the shop then propped it up on the dresser in her bedroom. Jean wondered if she was willing to part with it, after all.

Barbara was in the foyer, putting on her jacket as they came in.

"Your mother is fine. All her vitals were good. She just needs to rest this afternoon."

"Thanks. I feel relieved," Jean admitted. Then realized it was rude not to introduce them. "Grant, this is Barbara, my mother's nurse. Grant is going to buy one of my mom's paintings."

"So I heard. Cynthia told me." Barbara slung the strap from her bag over her shoulder. "It's a good choice."

"I thought so," Grant replied with a smile.

"See you on Saturday," Barbara called, and slipped out the door.

"She seems nice. Very upbeat," Grant observed.

"She's a good nurse . . . and almost too upbeat, according to my mother," Jean replied, making them both laugh.

As if on cue, her mother called from the bedroom. "Jean? Who's there? Is that Reverend Ben?"

"It's Grant Keating. He's come to pick up the painting," Jean called back. She wondered if her mother would remember Grant's name.

"Oh . . . finally. I thought he was going to come yesterday."

Jean noticed Grant duck his head. At least he had the good grace to look a bit embarrassed. "Sorry about that. I should have called."

"No big deal," Jean said, though it had seemed a big deal to her at the time.

"Come and help me, Jean. I want to meet him," Cynthia called.

Jean looked at Grant. "Do you mind?"

"Of course not. I'd be happy to meet your mother."

He seemed sincere but Jean wondered if he was just being polite. He had probably expected to grab the painting and go. The issue of fixing the roof still dangled, she recalled. Perhaps that made it worth his while to stay a little longer.

Jean went back to Cynthia's bedroom to find her mother's hair combed, her sweater and skirt smoothed out, and a bit of lipstick applied. She was up on her walker, heading for the door. "Get the painting, please. Be careful with it."

Jean grabbed the painting off the dresser and followed. "Mrs. Whitman, it's an honor to meet you," Grant greeted her.

Cynthia was wheezing a bit but didn't ask for her oxygen. She landed the walker in front of her armchair and sat down. "An honor, huh? I don't know that I'd go that far. But you have good taste. That little painting is one of my favorites. I'd forgotten how much I like it."

Grant smiled. "Then I'm glad I was able to remind you. Still sure you want to sell it?"

Her mother considered his question a moment. "I was nearly going to tell you that it isn't for sale anymore. But then I decided that artwork is meant to be sent out into the world, for other people to enjoy. Not hoarded and hidden away."

"Very true. I tend to be a hider and hoarder myself," he admitted with a laugh. "I'll have to remember that."

"Jean told me you're a photographer and you're doing a photo study of this place."

"That's right. There's a lot to document. A lot of beauty. I'm afraid with all the development going on, a lot of these sights will soon be lost. That's one reason I wanted to do this."

"The area has changed a great deal over the years," Cynthia agreed. "Some of the scenes in my paintings no longer exist. But the marsh is one place that stays the same. It's always been too difficult and costly to build on. Someday, I fear, they'll solve that problem, too."

"I hope not," Grant replied. "I took a thousand shots of the beach grass and wasn't really happy with any of them. But you captured it perfectly."

He held the painting at arm's length, and they both gazed it a moment. "The light was perfect that day," her mother recalled.

"Most people are interested in the big attractions around here— the lighthouse or the cliffs at Angel Island. I painted my share of those sights, no denying it. But I always got more satisfaction painting a fresher, more uncommon subject. Like the marsh grass or even a bug settling on a leaf."

"It's hard to find that fresh perspective. I want to show you something. Tell me what you think . . ." Grant reached into one of the many pockets of his field jacket and pulled out two prints, then handed them to Cynthia.

She had already slipped on her glasses, which hung from a cord around her neck. "These are good. You bring something new to the party," she said quietly, looking from one print to the other. "Years ago, I started to paint that same view of the lighthouse. Maybe I'll use this photo to finish it . . . if I can borrow it awhile?"

"I'd be honored," Grant replied. He sounded as if he really meant it, too. Her mother certainly looked pleased as she placed the photos on a side table.

Jean guessed that her mother had not painted anything in years. At least that's the way it seemed from the look of her studio. But she would never raise that point and embarrass her. Cynthia was clearly enjoying herself, talking shop with Grant. It was the most alert and convivial she'd been since Jean had come home.

"I asked Vera Plante about you," Jean's mother said suddenly. "She gave a good report about your repair work."

Grant grinned, caught by surprise. "That's good to know."

"Jean said you'd be willing to take a crack at the leaky roof in the shop."

"Ready, willing, and able."

"Well, I'm willing to hire you. For a fair price," she added. "There are plenty of other leaks, creaks, and holes that need patching around here, too. Let's see how it goes with the roof, and maybe you can tackle the rest in due course."

"Fair enough," Grant agreed. "I can start on Monday."

"Monday will be fine," her mother replied.

Grant glanced at Jean, waiting for her reply. "Monday is fine with me," she said. She did wonder if he would actually show up. Or come on Wednesday with no call or apology. She wasn't sure how, but Grant had definitely wrapped her mother around his little finger, which was no small feat.

Grant took an envelope from his pocket and paid her mother for the painting. Her mother, who had been holding it in her lap, finally handed it to him. "Hang on to that one. It might go up in value when I'm gone."

Grant smiled kindly. "It might. But I hope that's a very long time from now."

Cynthia glanced at Jean. "Give him a bag or something. To protect it from the weather."

"Good idea. I'll get something from the kitchen."

She hadn't meant for Grant to follow her but he did, watching as she wrapped the small painting in paper towels then slipped it into a shopping bag.

"Thanks. You didn't have to go so much trouble."

"It wasn't any trouble," she said, handing him the bag.

He looked down a moment then back up at her. "I did intend to come back yesterday, like I promised. But I went out with some fishermen, to take shots of them at work, and it turned out they didn't plan on coming back until late last night. They kept finding more fish on their radar. Before I knew it, we were practically in Nova Scotia."

"Nova Scotia?" Jean asked, her voice skeptical.

He smiled and laughed at his exaggeration. "Well . . . practically. It's hard to tell in the middle of the ocean. We were far from Cape Light, that's all I know."

"Get any good photographs?"

"Plenty. I'll show you sometime."

Her mother called out, interrupting them. "Jean? Have you started dinner yet? I'm hungry. I hardly ate a bite of lunch."

"It will be ready soon, Mom," Jean called back.

"I'd better go." Grant sniffed the air, his expression appreciative. "Smells good. Roast chicken?"

Jean nodded. Was he angling for a dinner invitation? It sure looked that way. She nearly gave in, then decided not to be such an easy mark. "Sorry to rush you. My mother likes to eat early."

"I understand." He said good night to her mother, and Jean showed him to the door.

"He's an interesting man," her mother said, which was high praise for her. "More interesting than I expected from Vera's description."

"Yes, he is. I'm glad you liked talking to him. Dinner will be ready in a few minutes," she added, changing the subject.

"Very well. I'll watch some news." Her mother picked up the remote and turned on the TV. She also picked up the envelope Grant had left and checked the contents, looking pleased at the bills she found there.

Jean went into the kitchen to finish cooking. Yes, Grant Keating was an interesting and attractive man. Jean had been impressed by the way he engaged her mother in conversation, his kindness and respect for her mother's intellect. But Jean could already see he was not the type of man to get involved with. That road would surely lead to disappointment. Even as a "distraction" from her caregiver duties.

Other women might manage it, but Jean knew she gave her heart too easily. Grant was clearly the type who could make a woman incredibly happy one minute, only to disappear the next. Not her type at all.

SAM HAD BEEN NAPPING WHEN DARRELL GOT HOME. WHEN HE woke up, it was time for dinner—a chaotic one, even for their house, with several lop-eared rabbits hopping around the kitchen while Lily and Tyler did laps around the table, trying to catch them.

Darrell must have noticed that the rabbit wrangling was getting on Sam's nerves. "Ready to talk about the jobsites, Dad? I can bring my notes into your office."

"Good idea. I'm eager to hear what went on today." Feeling thankful for his motorized wheelchair, Sam finished off his last bite of beef stew, wiped his mouth, and spun the chair in the direction of his office.

Jessica stood up and began clearing off the table. "Your sister sent a ton of cake and cookies. I'll bring some back to the Sam Cave for you."

Jessica's nickname for his office had irked him at first, but he now found it amusing. He not only worked there, but slept, watched TV, and often ate meals there, too. The office really was his lair, and he had started to think of himself as a bear, in hibernation for the winter. The accident had shrunken his world considerably, and he wouldn't really emerge in one piece until it was almost spring. Sam tried not to think about that too much—or he was liable to get depressed.

"Thanks, honey. Just one or two. It's not like I can work off the calories at the gym tomorrow."

The thought of dieting had never crossed Sam's mind, not once in his entire life. He always ate as much as he wanted, of whatever he wanted, even into his forties. All the hard work he did and an enviable metabolism kept him in great shape. But he worried now about packing on the pounds while he recuperated. It was hard to resist Jessica's cooking and all the sweet treats in the house that the kids liked to eat. Meanwhile, his only exercise was pressing the buttons on his wheelchair. He couldn't even start physical therapy until he got his heavy cast off, and that would take weeks.

Sam steered the chair into his office, and Darrell soon appeared in the doorway, carrying a legal pad and his cell phone.

"Have a seat, pal," Sam said, positioning his chair closer to the wooden table. He smiled up at his son. Darrell looked so serious. Sam hoped the site visits had gone well. Darrell hadn't reported any problems in his text messages during the afternoon. But maybe he was waiting to deliver some bad news?

"Did everything go all right?" Sam tried his best, but a note of anxiety crept into his voice.

"I think it went well. But that's for you to say," Darrell replied. "Here are my notes on each of the projects."

Darrell showed him the long legal pad, filled with crisp handwriting. On the first page, Sam saw the name of a client, a project description, and a progress report, with any problem or impending complication summarized at the bottom.

He leafed through the top few sheets of the pad and saw the same type of report for each client. He skimmed the information quickly, knowing he would look back later with a closer eye. Darrell was leaning forward in his chair, waiting for Sam's response.

"Very thorough, Darrell. Very professional. You did a great job today," Sam said sincerely.

"I took photos, too. I have them on my phone." Darrell handed Sam his cell phone. The screen held a shot of the Prentiss garage, with bales of insulation packed to the ceiling. In the next shot, Sam saw a close-up of the inside of a wall, with framing all set for a new window insert.

"What's this about?" he asked, turning the photo toward Darrell.

"That's the Turners' bathroom renovation. Mrs. Turner decided that she wants an arched window over the new bathtub, instead of the one you ordered. I checked the plans and found one that will fit. But there's a load-bearing beam a little too close to the frame. All we need to do is fit a joist in there. That should fix it," Darrell explained. He took the pad and flipped to the next page. "I made a note about that in the remarks, at the bottom of the page."

Sam noticed how Darrell said "all we need to do" instead of "all you need to do," but he didn't comment. His son gave the pad back, and Sam read the section.

"Good catch. She keeps changing her mind as we go along, but we . . . I mean, I . . . need to keep the customer happy."

"She was happy to hear we could do the arched window. I think it will add a lot to the room design."

"Yeah, nice touch," Sam agreed. From the way Darrell was talking, Sam was fairly certain his son had charmed his clients. "Sounds like you got along with Mrs. Turner?"

"Sure. I think I got along with all the clients."

"Good. It's important to make them all feel special. A contractor goes from job to job, and the details of each can start to seem routine. But every client feels that their project is totally unique. The only arched window over a bathtub *ever*," he explained, making Darrell chuckle. "Seriously, the smallest detail is very important. And it should be. A builder leaves in a few weeks. It's on to the next house. But the home owner lives with that window and bathtub forever."

"Good point. I'll remember that."

"Happy to pass on my words of wisdom. I guess I am getting old," Sam added with a laugh. "And these notes will come in handy when I find a contractor or foreman."

Darrell's smile sagged. "You're still looking? Really? Wouldn't you have found someone by now if anyone was available?"

Darrell had a point. Sam had called all the top firms and possible foremen he knew and could trust, but they were all too busy to take the work. He was now calling firms and site managers that had been recommended. He didn't have a very good feeling about that, though he would never admit that to his son.

"I just showed you I can handle this. I can be your foreman, Dad. You just said I did a great job today."

"Of course you did. I knew you would," Sam replied, though in truth he hadn't been all that sure. But Darrell's report and their conversation had truly impressed him. "Listen, buddy, just give me a day or two more to beat the bushes. In the meantime, I guess you can keep the jobs up and running. But I'm still not happy about you missing school. This is an important semester for you."

"I know, I know." Darrell looked somewhat mollified by Sam's offer. "But I already told you, all my profs say I can finish the semester at home. I can take finals online and hand in my papers and projects by e-mail. Even if I need to make a model or two, I can easily drive back to BU one day and drop that off."

Sam didn't want to argue with his son. He would worry about that if he actually found a professional to take over the work. Which was looking more and more unlikely. "Let's see what happens in a few days and decide then."

Jessica came in with a dish of cookies and two mugs of tea. She set the cookies on the table, and Darrell grabbed one, scarfing down half of it in a single bite. Sam watched with a pang of envy.

"I'm going to the gym. Want anything from the outside world?"

"No, thanks. I'm good. Don't get back too late. You have work tomorrow," Sam teased him.

Darrell turned in the doorway and shot him a grin. "I know."

Jessica sat at the table, opposite Sam. She picked up a cookie and chewed with a thoughtful expression. "I know it's your decision, but I have to say, I'm very proud him. He feels a very deep responsibility to our family, Sam."

"Yes, he does. I'm proud of him, too."

"I think you should let him do it. It sounds like he's good at it, and he really wants to help you. I think he'll feel very bad if you refuse the gift he's offering. As if you don't respect or trust him enough."

"Of course I respect him. Darrell's highly intelligent, and he's got a real feel for building. He's going to make a fine architect. Once he gets his four-year degree and goes to grad school," he added.

Jessica sipped her tea. "No one is saying that plan is in jeopardy. But honestly, listening to you, it sounds like it is."

Sam wondered if that was true. "I'm thinking of what's best for Darrell. And that's going back to school and finishing his semester, so he can get good grades and get into a good grad school."

"I understand. But he already has excellent grades. I think he can finish the term from here just fine. Don't you?"

Sam sighed. "He's very responsible. I know he'll do his work. Even if he has more distractions here."

"So what's the problem?" she asked bluntly. "It's not as if you have a guy like Joe Kelley around to take over. You told me yourself: if you found someone, it would be a stranger. Don't you trust Darrell to do this job more than you would a stranger?"

Sam met his wife's dark blue eyes. Jessica had a knack for boiling things down and making a point in a way that was hard to refute.

"And if Darrell keeps the projects running, it would be much better for the family financially," she added. "I think you know that's true, too."

Sam picked up a large chocolate chip cookie. Finally giving in to temptation, he took a giant bite. "If the animal rescue business doesn't work out, I think you should become a lawyer," he said finally. "Have you rested your case?"

She smiled, looking pleased at the compliment. "I have, Your Honor."

"Good. I'll sleep on it," he promised, then finished off the rest of the cookie.

JEAN THOUGHT A TRIP TO CHURCH WAS TOO AMBITIOUS. FOR ONE thing, the temperature had dipped down into the low thirties and she didn't want her mother to catch a chill. For another, she had hoped to linger over coffee and read the Sunday paper this morning. She had been working hard all week, cleaning out the house. Wasn't Sunday supposed to be a day of rest?

She thought to ask her mother that question, but instead said, "Are you sure you're up to it, Mom? You didn't have much energy yesterday."

"I feel perfectly fine today. I don't even need to lug this old tank around." Cynthia slapped the oxygen tank that was attached to her wheelchair. "I haven't been out of this house in weeks except to visit the doctor. The least you can do is take me to church, Jean. If you really don't want to, I'll call a taxi. Just help me get dressed."

Her mother stared across the breakfast table with her chin raised at a defiant angle. It was true; she rarely left the house anymore, and the confinement would wear on anyone's nerves.

"Of course I'll come with you. I'll help you dress, and then I'll take a fast shower."

Jean had been helping her mother bathe and dress since she had arrived. Most of the time, her mother wasn't fussy about her clothes and didn't even seem to care if items matched. But now, she was acting like a five-year-old getting ready for the first day of school as Jean tried to pick out an outfit with her.

"Not that sweater. I said the blue one," her mother snapped. "Powder blue. Not navy."

Jean returned to the closet, sifted through the hangers again, and finally found the sweater her mother wanted.

"That's the one. There should be a matching a cardigan in there somewhere, too."

"'Somewhere' being the operative word?" Jean wrestled with the bunched-up hangers. The closet was packed with clothes, most of them decades out of fashion. She recognized dresses her mother had worn when Kevin was in high school. "A lot of these clothes can go to charity, Mom. I bet you don't wear half of them."

Cynthia took the cardigan from Jean's hand and smoothed it on her lap. "You can do that when I'm dead. You can give everything away at once. It will be a lot be easier."

Jean couldn't deny that was true, but her mother's blunt reply took her breath away. Did her mother really accept her mortality so easily? Or was the remark just bravado, meant to draw a reaction?

"I'm going to get dressed. I'll be down in five minutes," Jean said.

It was another ordeal to get her mother properly bundled up and out to the car in her wheelchair. Then get her mother into the car and the wheelchair stowed in the cargo area of Jean's Subaru.

Luckily, they lived very close to the church, which was in the village green, at the harbor, on the opposite end of Main Street. Still, Jean doubted they would get there on time.

"I hate to go into the service late. You know that, Jean," her mother said as Jean searched for a handicapped space in the parking lot.

"We'll slip in the back. No one will notice," Jean promised her.

"Reverend Ben will. He'll be looking right at me."

"Reverend Ben will be happy that you've come at all," Jean said. She knew that was true, too.

A few minutes later, with the help of one of the deacons, Jean pushed her mother's chair through a side door of the sanctuary and searched for an empty rear aisle where they could sit.

Reverend Ben stood in front of the altar and began the call to worship. Jean handed her mother a program and pointed to the prayer. "We didn't miss too much. Just the announcements."

"And the Advent candles," her mother replied. "I like that part. We won't miss it next week."

Next week? Was this going to be a regular Sunday morning activity? Jean sighed and sat back in the pew. *You came home to help your mother in her final days,* she reminded herself. *If she wants to go to church every week, that's what you have to do.*

Jean focused on the program again. It was time to sing a hymn. Jean couldn't find a hymnal, but the music was printed out in her mother's "large type" program. Her mother nudged Jean with her elbow and held out the page, indicating they should share it.

Jean leaned toward her and began singing, listening to her mother's raspy voice rise and fall with the notes. Her mother once had a lovely singing voice but could hardly hold a note now. Still, she sat up straight and sang as loud as she was able. As if she didn't notice her voice was gone. Or maybe, just didn't care.

When the song was over, she smiled and met Jean's gaze and nodded. For the first time in a long time, Jean saw joy in her mother's expression. Jean sat back, knowing she would take her mother to church every day if simply singing a hymn could make her this happy.

The service continued with more prayers and the Scripture readings. The Gospel reading was from the Book of Mark, and Jean followed along in the small Bible that she found next to her seat. The reading was about the Second Coming of Jesus Christ, describing the end of days.

"'But about that day or hour no one knows, neither the angels in heaven, nor the Son, but only the Father . . . '" Reverend Ben read. "'Beware, keep alert; for you do not know when the time will come.'"

Jean's thoughts turned to her mother, her days clearly numbered. Yet no one knew exactly how many more there would be, not the doctors or nurses or even the angels above.

Jean hoped that however difficult it might be, she would help her mother enjoy these last days as much as she possibly could. Not just oversee her mother's physical care, or even get the house in order, but try her best to bring some joy back into her mother's life, which anyone could see was a dark, lonely place.

Maybe they didn't have the close, warm relationship some mothers and daughters shared, but that didn't mean she couldn't give her mother this one last gift. Maybe it was all the more reason she should try.

After the sermon, it was time for the congregation to share their news and ask for prayers during Joys and Concerns.

Reverend Ben called on Vera Plante, who sat a few rows in front of them. "Yes, Vera. Do you have a joy to share with us today?"

Vera stood, then turned and smiled at Jean and her mother. "I'm very happy to see Cynthia Whitman and her daughter, Jean, in church today. It's wonderful to have you with us, Cynthia."

Someone started clapping and everyone else joined in, everyone turning in their seats to smile at her mother. Jean could practically feel the waves of warmth and affection.

Her mother looked surprised, then overwhelmed. She couldn't stand but waved her hand. "Thank you, Vera. Thank you, everyone. Very much." Jean thought her mother might start crying, her eyes looked so glassy. But she dabbed her nose on a tissue and smiled at Jean for a moment. "Silly Vera. I hate to have all that attention focused on me. She knows that."

"Very silly," Jean agreed.

After the service, many of Cynthia's friends came over to greet her. So many that Jean couldn't budge the wheelchair.

"The Christmas Fair Committee is meeting right after Fellowship Hour. They're serving lunch, too. Why don't you come, Cynthia?" Vera asked. "You always have so many good ideas. I can wheel you around. Jean doesn't have to stay."

Her mother considered the invitation. Jean was sure she would refuse. "I think I will," she said. She turned to Jean. "You can come back in a while and pick me up."

"I can take you home, Cynthia. That's no trouble," Vera said.

Jean had been sure her mother would want a nap after church and had planned to use that time to work on her children's book. She would have even more time now with her mother occupied and in Vera's watchful care.

"If you're sure you're not too tired, Mom," Jean said.

"Not the least bit," Cynthia assured her.

"All right, but make sure you call me if you want to leave early, and use the oxygen if you need it," she added. Despite her mother's vow at the breakfast table, Jean would not go out without attaching the trusty tank to the back of the wheelchair.

"I've been taking care of myself for a long time without your help, Jean. I think I know by now if I need my oxygen or not."

The rebuke stung, but Jean knew it was true. Her mother had been left on her own for far too long.

"I'll take good care of her, don't worry." Vera's breezy tone smoothed things over. Vera took the handles of her mother's chair and began steering her out of the sanctuary. "We'd better get over to Fellowship Hall," Jean heard Vera say. "Sophie Potter is hosting coffee hour, and you know how fast her cakes go."

Jean watched the two women for a moment as they disappeared down the hallway. She had come to the service thinking of her role as her mother's chaperone. Or even her chauffeur. Jean hadn't expected to feel involved in the service at all. But she had enjoyed it. She felt refreshed, her spirits lifted. Jean buttoned her coat and pulled on her gloves before heading outside. Maybe it wouldn't be such a chore to take her mother to church on Sundays, after all.

A cluster of people stood at the big wooden doors, slowly making their way out. Jean waited behind a mother with two children, a girl and a boy. The boy, who looked about four or five, was having trouble zipping up his jacket, and the woman turned and crouched down to help him. Jean stared down at her a moment then edged her way to the other side of the line.

Laurel Milner? Jean suddenly doubted her own eyes, then sneaked another look. It was definitely Laurel. Her features had matured and she had cut her hair. But there was no mistaking her. Laurel hadn't changed much. She was still very pretty in a natural, "girl next door" way.

What was she doing here? Jean had heard that Kevin's old flame had gotten married and moved somewhere down south. North Carolina? Maybe she was in Cape Light visiting family. Her parents or siblings could still be in town.

Jean wondered if she should tell Kevin. The relationship had not ended well. Even though years had passed and her brother had married—and divorced—and had probably dated many women since, Jean had a feeling talking about Laurel would still disturb him. There was really no point, she decided.

And no point telling her mother either, who never had a nice thing to say about Laurel and certainly would not now. Still, Jean had always liked Laurel. She wondered what her life was like now and what had brought her back to Cape Light. But for many reasons, Jean didn't stop to talk to her.

Jean stepped out into the crisp winter air and headed for her car, feeling more contented than she had since coming home. She was about to dive back into her children's book, and her mother was helping out with the Christmas Fair. Despite this being such a difficult time, the two of them were genuinely enjoying the day. Surely, Jean thought, that was a blessing.

CHAPTER SIX

ISPROVING HER DOUBTS, GRANT KEATING ARRIVED bright and early Monday morning. Jean had been taking care of her mother—serving her breakfast, washing and dressing her, the usual routine—but hadn't yet taken care of herself yet when he came to the door.

She and her mother both heard the doorbell. Cynthia looked at her while Jean looked down at the sweatshirt she wore over flannel pajama bottoms printed with polar bears, her fuzzy slippers peeking out at the bottom. Not the most alluring nighttime attire, that was for sure. The upstairs bedrooms were frigid this time of year, and Cynthia insisted that the thermostat be kept very low at night.

"That must be the handyman," her mother said. "Don't just stand there. He'll think we're not home and go away."

If only, Jean thought. She headed to the foyer, deciding she could hide behind the front door and all he would see was the sweatshirt.

The bell sounded again and she opened the door a crack, just her head poking out. Grant wore his usual utility jacket with a denim shirt underneath and a black T-shirt underneath that. His thick brown hair, tinged with gray, was still damp from a shower and combed back from his forehead. He looked very handsome, she thought. Too handsome for this early on a Monday.

"Good morning, Jean. Hope I didn't wake you up."

"Not at all. We're up. Wait here a moment, I'll get you to the key to the shop."

Jean intended to shut the door and have him wait on the porch, but her mother had quietly made her way into the room on her walker, and planted herself so close that Jean nearly knocked her over when she turned around.

"Let him in, for goodness' sake. Where are your manners?"

Before Jean could respond, her mother made her way to the door and opened it again. "No need to stand out in the cold. Please come in."

Grant looked pleased by the invitation. He smiled at her mother and rubbed his hands together. Bare hands, Jean noticed. Didn't he own a pair of gloves? It was cold out today, the sky a shade of crystalline blue that only seemed to appear in winter.

Jean thought she had left the shop key on a hook near the back door, but couldn't find it. She rummaged through a kitchen drawer, searching for a spare.

"Would you like some coffee, Grant?" she heard her mother ask. Jean stifled a groan as she waited for his reply.

"Thanks, but I don't want to trouble you," he said.

"No trouble at all. Jean? Is there any coffee left?" her mother called. "If not, put on a fresh pot. I'd like some more."

You're not supposed to have any coffee, Jean wanted to remind her, *much less extra cups in the morning.* But she didn't want to embarrass her mother, who always tried so hard to seem fit and "normal" in front those who didn't know her well.

Jean had noticed the ploy the other day on Grant's first visit to the house. And Sunday at church. Maybe being around strangers did make her feel better and it wasn't just a show? It was hard to say.

Jean found the key in the pocket of her rain slicker, right where she left it the other day. She walked out to the living room, ignoring her mother's offer of coffee. "Here's the key. The door sticks a little. Looks like the wood is rotten on the bottom."

"I'll take a look. Thanks." Grant slipped the key in a side pocket, then scanned her from head to toe. She could tell he was trying hard not to show his amusement. Especially when he got to the slippers.

"Is there any coffee left? You never answered me," her mother cut in.

"Yes, there's some left. Would you like some coffee, Grant?"

Jean didn't mean for her question to carry an irritated tone, but she knew it did.

"Sure . . . just black is fine. I'll take a mug and bring it back later?"

Great solution, Jean thought. She was sure that if he came any farther into the house, her mother would insist that he needed some bacon and eggs.

"Not a problem." Jean quickly returned to the kitchen, poured the coffee, and brought it back to him.

"Thanks. I'll get to work now." Grant opened the door with his free hand and smiled at her mother.

"When you're done with the roof, take a look at the door," her mother called after him. "See what needs to be done. We can talk it over later."

Jean had been hoping to avoid him. There was really no reason for him to be in the house, except to tell them he was there to work and let them know when he was done. But her mother seemed to have a different idea. Jean feared she would be setting an extra place for dinner before the day was over.

Jean helped her mother into her recliner and brought her the newspaper. Cynthia scanned the headlines and quickly put the paper aside. "No good news. What's the use? Will you help me up again? I'm going to get started on the handcrafts for the fair. They asked me to make ornaments. That was always my specialty."

"I remember. You made some very pretty ones when I was young." Jean helped her mother over to the dining room table and brought over the box her mother had taken home from the meeting.

"I'll need the glue gun and plenty of newspaper. Can you cover this table better? I don't want to get any marks on it."

"Good idea. I'll get the table-boards. That will be even better."

Cynthia frowned. "It would be even better if I could work in my studio. I'd love to get back in there, Jean. When will you clean it out for me?"

The studio wasn't a cleaning priority. Jean was focusing on the rooms they actually used. But remembering the promise she had made to herself in church yesterday, she could see that getting back in that space meant a great deal to her mother. Even if she was only gluing together bits of felt and Popsicle sticks.

"You can start in here and I'll start working on the studio today. Let's see how it goes."

Jean wasn't sure how long it would take to clear out the studio and didn't want to make any promises, but her mother seemed pleased enough with her reply.

Her mother paused, examining a long, felted pipe cleaner that was covered with sparkly fibers. "Thank you, Jean. I appreciate that."

Jean was already in the foyer closet, dragging out the covers for the dining table. Shocked by her mother's quiet words, she nearly fell into the coats.

The doorbell sounded. Was that Grant again? Jean hoped not, gritting her teeth as she pulled the door open. She was greatly relieved to find Barbara Crosby.

"Barbara, I didn't know you were coming so early today."

"Sorry. Didn't you see my text?" The nurse came in along with a gust of cold air. She stuffed her gloves in her pockets and shrugged free of her long down coat.

"I must have missed it. I've had a busy morning. Mom is dressed and doing crafts in the dining room."

Barbara's eyes widened. She looked pleased. "Are you making something together?"

"She's making ornaments that will be sold at the church Christmas Fair. We went to church yesterday. She hasn't been in months but she insisted. It was sort of an ordeal to get her there," Jean admitted, keeping her voice low. "I thought she would want to go straight home after the service. But she stayed for a meeting about the fair and reconnected with a lot of old friends. It was really a tonic for her."

"Great. I hope she's able to go back." The nurse took her notebook out of her bag.

"She'll definitely go back. She has to show off her ornaments," Jean replied, making Barbara laugh.

"Who's there, Jean? Is that Nurse Crosby here already? I wasn't expecting her until the afternoon."

"I had to come early today, Cynthia. I'm sorry to upset your schedule." Barbara's tone was utterly polite, as if Jean's mother was a busy executive, her day scheduled in fifteen-minute increments. Barbara shot Jean a secret smile.

Her mother turned as they entered the living room. "All right, let's get this over with." She pushed herself up with her hands on the table and managed to get to her walker all by herself.

"You look full of energy today, Cynthia. I'm glad to see that."

"Aren't I usually full of energy?" she demanded, despite the fact that it was not even close to the truth. "It's the health professionals who always want to find something wrong with you. Otherwise, you'd all be out of job."

Barbara gave her a doubtful look. "We're not pleased to see anyone feeling poorly, Cynthia. Our job is to help people get well. Since you're so feisty today, I'll race you to the bedroom," she added in a playful tone.

Cynthia waved a dismissive hand at Barbara and headed to her room on her walker at a steady but careful pace.

While the nurse was tending to her mother, Jean ran upstairs to shower and dress. She came down just as Barbara was preparing to go. "How is she doing?" Jean asked.

"Her pressure and pulse are fine. The edema seems under control as well." Jean knew the nurse meant her mother's tendency to hold water in her body, especially in her lungs and near her heart. "She may need oxygen today, especially if she plans to work with a glue gun or paints. Keep a close eye on her. I'm glad to see her in such good spirits, but her body is still seriously compromised."

"I understand."

Barbara headed for the door but turned just before letting herself out. "By the way, is that your friend Grant out near the shop? The guy who wanted to buy your mom's painting? I saw him setting up a ladder when I parked the car."

Jean sighed and crossed her arms over her chest. "He's doing some repairs. My mother hired him. He's not my friend . . . exactly."

"That's too bad. He seems friendly enough to me. You should work on that, Jean."

Jean gave Barbara a look. "See you Wednesday, Barbara."

Her mother emerged from her bedroom and headed back to the dining room table. Jean spent the rest of the day cleaning the studio, a small bedroom on the first floor with windows that faced north. She took only short breaks to check on her mother and make a quick lunch.

Cynthia was not satisfied with the art supplies the church group had chosen and had Jean hunting around the house for other materials she preferred. Most of the boxes and containers were in the studio, so the hunt helped Jean get the place in order.

By the time she served dinner, Jean was happy to report that she'd made good progress, though the room still wasn't done.

"When do you think it will be done?" her mother asked.

"Soon, Mom." Jean didn't want to say more than that. There was a row of cupboards she hadn't even opened and a few piles of paintings stacked on a work table. Not enough room in there yet to get the wheel chair through, even if her mother didn't mind the clutter. "I'm going to pick up some plastic boxes so you can store your supplies in a more organized way. But for now, I found some shoe boxes and labeled them."

"I'm usually able to find what I need when I need it. That's part of the process. Sifting through the materials gives me ideas."

"Did you make many ornaments today?"

"A few," Cynthia replied. "The committee chair, Emily Warwick, would have you slapping things together with no special touches at all. She may have been a good mayor, but she's definitely not the artistic type."

"I bet she's good at managing all the volunteers and keeping things on schedule," Jean said with a smile. "I don't believe artistic talent was ever one of Emily's calling cards."

"Well, my ornaments won't look like they came out of some cheap kit. Each one will be interesting and unique. I might not produce dozens, but I'm sure the church can sell each one for a much higher price."

"Good point, Mom. Can I see any yet?"

Her mother seemed suddenly flustered. "I can show you when I'm done. I'm still putting on finishing touches."

"Take your time. I'm sure they'll be very pretty."

"It's not about pretty, Jean. Not even with Christmas tree ornaments. Unique matters. Distinctive and memorable matter. Remember that, especially if you ever try to do any real artwork."

Her mother had never considered the graphic art Jean did for a living "real" art. Jean already knew that. She wondered what her mother would make of the paintings and sketches she had completed for her picture book. Jean was half tempted to show her mother, wondering if she would consider that work real enough. But memories of her mother's harsh critiques loomed in her mind, like a sea monster, ready to rise up with the merest encouragement. Jean decided it was not worth the risk. Maybe she would show her mother the work when she was further along. She couldn't risk being discouraged at this early point.

The phone rang and Jean located the receiver in the living room. She could see from the caller ID that it was her brother, Kevin. They exchanged greetings quickly.

"How's it going there with Mom? I must admit, I didn't think you'd last this long."

"It's barely been two weeks, Kev."

"That's long with Mom. You know what Einstein said about relativity. Five minutes talking to a pretty girl doesn't feel the same as five minutes with your hand on a hot stove? Something like that."

"It's not perfect," Jean said quietly. "But we're doing all right."

"Is that Kevin? He's called to talk to me, not you," her mother called from the kitchen.

"Mom wants to talk to you," Jean said as she brought the phone to her mother, who was already smiling widely.

"Hello, Kevin. Good to hear your voice. I thought you'd call yesterday. I would have been out anyway," her mother reported happily. "I went to church then stayed for a meeting. I'm helping with the annual fair."

Jean cleared the table and started washing up. She could only hear one side of the conversation but it was enough. Her mother loved to give Kevin the impression she was hale and hearty. No wonder he didn't seem to believe her own reports of Cynthia's failing heart. He was getting very mixed messages.

"—and I've decided to do some repairs on the property. The house and the shop both need attention," her mother reported. As if it was all her idea, Jean noticed. "I don't want to leave you with a falling-down heap."

Her mother paused, listening to Kevin's reply. "Yes, yes . . . a long time from now. To be sure. But I thought we should make a start. Before it got any worse. The handyman I found is an intellectual, a photographer who does odd jobs on the side. He bought one of my paintings," she reported proudly. "And he gave me some photographs. I may use one for a painting. Jean is cleaning out my studio. I'm going to get back in very soon. Maybe even tomorrow."

Tomorrow? Jean was sure she had never promised her mother that. She wasn't sure she could manage it. But every day counted for her mother now. Perhaps she should put the pedal to the metal and get it done.

"That's great, Mom. You're always happiest when you're working," Jean heard her brother say.

"That's just my way. I like to be productive. It keeps my mind active. I'm not one of these old people who likes to sit in a chair all day, staring at the TV."

That was true. Though Cynthia had neglected to admit that some days she didn't feel well enough to leave her bed. Or even to take a deep breath without the aid of her oxygen.

Her mother chatted with Kevin a few minutes more. Then she held out the phone receiver. "He wants to talk to you again."

Jean took the phone, and Kevin said, "I just wanted you to know I looked into canceling my trip to Utah. It's really difficult, Jean. I'm sorry. But my friends are counting on my share, and I'll lose my deposit. And my airfare."

Jean knew he was making a case for not coming East. She also thought he could come if he wanted to. Kevin was very well off with no family to support. "I'm sorry to hear that," she said honestly. "Maybe we can talk about this later." *Later, when Mom is asleep,* she meant. She felt sure he understood.

"Sure, call me back when you can. It's just the way things are working out. I wish I had known you wanted me there before I made plans." Jean doubted that would have made a difference in his decision. She suspected he would have found some other excuse not to come, but she didn't tell him that.

Kevin said good-bye, they hung up, and Jean picked up a dish towel and started drying a frying pan.

"What was that about?" her mother asked. "What are you sorry to hear? Is your brother all right?"

Jean was not very adept at lying and searched for some plausible reply. "Kevin had some bad news about a high school classmate of mine. She lives in California, and he runs into her from time to time. I'm going to send a note."

"Really? Are you sure?" She felt her mother's gaze following her around the kitchen. Cynthia might be ailing but she was still sharp. "You're not keeping anything from me, are you, Jean? You know I'd be very upset to find out later."

Jean turned from the cabinet and met her troubled gaze. "Kevin is fine. Perfectly fine. No worries, Mom. Honestly."

Her mother sighed, her expression relaxing again. "He works so hard. I worry about him, living alone with no one to take care of him. I wish he would find a nice girl and settle down . . . Do you know if Kevin is seeing anyone special?"

"I don't think so, Mom." Jean and her brother had been close once, but now he rarely spoke to her about personal matters. "He hasn't mentioned anyone in particular."

"I was just wondering. Perhaps there is someone special, and he doesn't want to say. I think he was very hurt when his marriage with Elaine broke up. I think he's still a little gun-shy."

"Maybe," Jean replied. It was true that Kevin's ex-wife had ended the marriage. But Jean did not recall her brother acting surprised or even hurt by the divorce. What she remembered was resignation and even indifference. Jean had never been totally sure that her brother really loved Elaine. Not the way he had loved Laurel Milner.

Using her walker, Cynthia went into the living room to watch the news. Jean stayed in the kitchen, tidying up and thinking about her brother. She wasn't at all surprised that Kevin's love life was a mystery to their mother. Perhaps Kevin was still afraid Cynthia would interfere in his relationships, the way she had interfered and eventually driven off Laurel.

Kevin was in his senior year of college when he announced that he and Laurel, his high school sweetheart, were going to get married when he graduated. Laurel had stayed in Cape Light, working in her family's plumbing business, which Cynthia thought was very low class. Laurel was taking a few classes at a community college but wasn't career minded, despite being quite intelligent.

Kevin had been crazy about Laurel from the day they met. Their mother predicted he would quickly find a new girlfriend at college and drop Laurel like a hot potato. But Kevin had barely looked at other girls during his college years, making frequent visits home on the weekends to be with Laurel. Cynthia didn't think Laurel was good enough for her son and did all she could to break up the romance. She promised Kevin he would meet a girl who was his "equal" in law school, and he would thank his mother later.

Kevin was brokenhearted when Laurel broke up with him. She loved Kevin but wouldn't marry him knowing his mother hated her. She feared that sooner or later Cynthia would turn Kevin against her, too. Kevin came home after graduation but barely spoke to their mother. He left for California—and law school—two weeks later.

He eventually married Elaine, another attorney who worked for the same firm. But they divorced after only a few years. Jean knew her brother had never gotten over his first love—or forgiven Cynthia for breaking up the romance.

Jean was sure the sad history was a big part of Kevin's reluctance to visit. But she also believed he would deeply regret it if he didn't spend Christmas with their mother this year.

She didn't think talking to him about this again would get them very far. She decided to send an e-mail instead. It would give him time to consider his decision carefully.

IT TOOK SO LONG TO DO THE SIMPLEST THINGS. THAT'S WHAT MADE Sam so frustrated. Despite the casts on both legs, his right arm out of commission, and even the pain, being slowed down to a snail's pace was getting to him. And he had been home barely six days.

He was trying to start Tuesday off with a good routine and had finally maneuvered into his office, only to realize he had left his reading glasses in the kitchen. It was no small feat to turn the wheelchair around and backtrack. By the time he got back to his lair, he was exhausted. Jessica was doing a great job watching over him, but she was already outside, checking on the animals. He hated to call or text for help unless he was desperate.

The project files and blueprints he needed were spread out on the wooden table and he began to work, making a list of tasks that needed to be completed next on each project and inspections that were due. Despite making a million calls in the past few days to contractors and potential foremen, Sam had come up empty. It looked like Darrell had the job. Though he hadn't told his son that yet.

Darrell had gotten the jobs up and running and was out again today, visiting the sites and watching over the crews. Sam had thought it would be a problem for the older men to take orders from Darrell, but his employees had been cooperative and respectful. Many of them knew Darrell, having worked with him during the summers since the boy was in middle school. Sam knew that was a big advantage and might not be the case if he hired a foreman from the outside who had never worked with the crew before. There were advantages to Darrell taking over for him. Sam was beginning to see that.

Sam dialed Village Hall and asked for the building department. The Turner project couldn't go forward without an inspection of the electrical work, and Sam was geared up to put the pressure on, but as he waited for the building inspector to come on the line, furious barking and a fierce, unholy yowl broke the silence in the house.

Then the sound of scampering paws and furniture being knocked over. Two sleek tabby cats raced by the office door followed by Daisy, the family's chocolate Lab, galloping with her head down and a determined look in her eye.

"Daisy! Stop that. Leave those cats alone." Sam hung up on the call and rolled to the doorway to see where the racing trio had gone. The dog paid him no mind. She didn't even slow down, skidding down the hall to the kitchen, barking her head off. Sam rolled back into his office and dialed Jessica. The line kept ringing as the frenzied cats flew down the hallway then careened into his office.

"Oh, no! Get out! Get out, cats!" Sam shouted. He waved file folders in the air, but they didn't seem to notice.

One cat darted around his chair, ran under his desk, scaled the bookcase, and finally perched on top. The other cowered on the carpet then scooted under his wheelchair, hunkering down under the seat.

The dog galloped in next and came to a screeching halt just seconds before crashing into Sam's chair. Daisy stepped back and barked even louder, her gaze fixed on the cat beneath him.

"Sam? Are you all right? What's going on over there?"

Sam heard Jessica's voice and picked up his phone. "You tell me. Daisy and these cats have me surrounded."

"I'll be right there. Don't move."

"As if I have a choice," Sam shouted back. Luckily, Jessica had already hung up.

Moments later, she stood in the doorway, surveying the standoff. Daisy had tired herself out and was now lying down, staring intently at her prey. If it wasn't for Sam, her master, sitting over the quaking feline, he was sure Daisy would have pounced long ago. Rolled in a tight ball, the cat gave off long, low meowing moans.

"I'm so sorry. They've been getting along so well," Jessica said. "If they hadn't, I wouldn't have left them loose in the house with you."

"Just get them out of here. There's another cat around here some-where, too. I'm not sure where he's hiding."

"I'll deal with Daisy first. She can go in her crate. The cats will leave once she's gone."

Jessica gently tugged the big dog by her collar. "Come on, Daisy. Come with me, honey. I'll give you a treat."

Daisy didn't want to go. She stared up Sam with mournful eyes, as if to say, "I need to protect you from those bad cats."

"Sorry, Daisy. I'll see you later," Sam said. "It doesn't seem fair that the dog has to be in her crate, Jess, while the cats roam free. Daisy was here before any of them."

Jessica had tugged the dog into the hallway, and Daisy was finally giving in. "I'll have Tyler or Lily take her for a long walk later. I don't know what else to do. At least the piglets didn't get out."

Piglets? "There are piglets in the house?" Sam had not meant to sound surprised, but he couldn't help it.

"They just came inside this morning. They're so cute. I put them in the sunroom."

"Why aren't they in the barn? I thought Darrell made some stalls for you and shelves for the crates and cages."

"He did. But it's really cold out there, and they're just babies. The space heaters aren't working well. I need to install a real heating sys-tem. I mean, when we can afford it."

Sam could see she was worried about the added expense. He felt bad about that. He didn't want Jessica to feel the least bit anxious or guilty about carrying out her plan. He certainly didn't want her to go back to an office job. She clearly loved this new career. He could rarely recall seeing her so happy.

"We'll figure it out. Maybe I can get a break on the price from one of the plumbing outfits I know. I'll ask around."

She rewarded the suggestion with a huge smile, still holding poor Daisy's collar. "Thanks, honey. That would be great. It's only going to get colder, and I don't know how many more animals we can fit in the house . . . without giving up our own beds."

Word had gotten around quickly about Jessica's shelter. She was getting calls and e-mails every day about animals that needed help, and she was taking in most of them. She kept a clipboard in the kitchen with a list of her adoptees and the care they needed. Tyler and Lily were being very good about helping her, and volunteers came and went all day, too.

"I draw the line at having piglets in my bed. Just sayin'," he teased her.

Jessica laughed. "Want some lunch?"

Was it that time already? Where did the day go? Sam wondered. But he was hungry. "Sure. That would be great."

Sam went back to his pile of papers and lists, and Jessica soon returned with a grilled cheese sandwich and a green salad.

"I doubt there will be any more animal uprisings today. But if you hear something starting up, call right away. Before it gets too crazy?"

Sam was just about to reply when a yellow canary flew into the room, swooped down to his dish, and stole a piece of salad.

He looked up at her. "I'm not going to say anything."

Jessica seemed about to laugh but managed to hold back. "Don't worry. I'll catch that bird before I go."

"Either you will, or the cats will be feasting on free-range canary for lunch."

"You're eating canaries for lunch?" Darrell walked into Sam's office, wearing a quizzical expression. "That looks like grilled cheese to me."

"Dad was talking about the cats," Jessica said. "If you want lunch, there's plenty in the fridge to make a sandwich. I need to get back to the barn."

Jessica left and Darrell sat down at the table across from Sam.

"How did it go this morning?" Sam asked.

"No big problems. A few of the windows ordered for the Prentiss house had to be returned. Wrong sizes. And we never got an inspection on the electrical work at the Turners'."

Sam took a bite of his sandwich and set it aside. "I called about that this morning, but I got interrupted."

"I went by Village Hall on my way home and spoke to someone in the building department. He said the inspector would take care of it this afternoon," Darrell said. "I'll check and make sure that he comes."

"Good work, Darrell. It's always better to nag in person instead of on the phone. Did they teach you all this stuff in architect school?"

Darrell laughed. "You taught me, Dad. I learned from hanging out and watching you."

Sam was surprised by the answer, and pleased. All the years of spending time with Darrell were yielding a harvest. "We hung out a lot together, but I didn't think you were listening that closely," he admitted. "I've been thinking. Maybe not finding anyone to take over my work is a good thing. I should be grateful for a son like you, willing to put his own life aside to help his dad out of a jam. To help his family. I'm going to stop looking for outside help, pal."

"Gee, Dad. Of course I want to help you. Wouldn't anyone?"

Sam thought about the question a moment. "No, Darrell, not every son would step up like you have. I'm grateful and blessed to have you here and willing to help me."

"I'm here as long as you need me. I love this work. It's what I want to do with my life—build things. You know that."

Sam nodded, knowing how much Darrell took after him, even though he was not Darrell's biological father. "Yes, I do. And you're darn good at it, too."

Darrell shrugged. "Working for you like this, it feels right."

He looked happy and confident, as if he were stepping into a role he was born for, Sam thought. Seeing his son so content made Sam feel good, too. He'd made the right decision, he told himself. At least for now.

CHAPTER SEVEN

⌒⊤⊼⊀

*D*O YOU THINK I CAN GET INTO THE STUDIO TODAY? YOU said Monday night that it would be ready soon," Jean's mother reminded her. "That was two days ago, Jean."

Jean couldn't argue with that. It was definitely Wednesday morning, and she hadn't finished her first cup of coffee. She was not fully awake, and not looking forward to another day of cleaning, sorting, and throwing out.

"I'll do my best but there's still more cleaning to do in there, Mom. I don't want you to have a coughing fit from all the dust."

Her mother was reading the newspaper at the breakfast table and shrugged as she turned a page. "I don't know why it would take so long. I always kept it well organized."

Jean's eyes rolled back in her head but her mother didn't see. "Except for the boxes of newspapers and magazines, and shopping bags full of all sorts of things." Including seashells, rocks, feathers, bits of fabric, dried flowers, and faded autumn leaves. Jean could not begin to catalogue the varied, dusty, crumbling contents.

Her mother finally looked up. "I need those materials for my work. They inspire me. Something catches my eye, I save it and refer to it later. You didn't throw it all out, did you?"

"No, not all of it," Jean said carefully. She had started to toss with fervor but could see now that she needed to be more selective. "Why don't I sift through and save the best items? Some of it's so old, Mom, it's already crumbled to dust."

"All right. Sort it out however you like. As long as I can get in there soon." Cynthia looked back at the newspaper and turned another page. "The way things stand, all those bits and pieces aren't much use to me now. Funny how you save things for *someday*, and then the time just runs out."

It made Jean sad to hear her mother talk that way. She had been on such a good track since their outing to church. Working in her studio might lift her spirits again, which was all the more reason to fix it up for her quickly. Jean rose and brought their breakfast dishes to the sink. "I'll try to finish this morning. Maybe you can work in there this afternoon."

Her mother was reading an article and didn't look up. "I hope so."

Good to her word, Jean started working in the studio first thing. It was barely nine o'clock. The weather had turned unseasonably mild, and as she opened the windows to air out the small room, she saw Grant's truck pull up. He parked in front of the shop and took painting supplies out of the truck's cargo space.

This was his third day of working for them. He had been arriving on time and leaving at around five o'clock but had not come into the house much. When he did, they barely exchanged a few words. He mostly spoke with her mother about his next repair assignments.

Jean had expected to have more contact with him but told herself it was better this way. Though part of her wasn't buying it.

It was tedious to sift through her mother's collection of scraps and inspiring tidbits, but Jean tried to be patient, carefully selecting a few pieces from each bag or box.

Just before noon, Barbara Crosby arrived. While the nurse examined her mother, Jean hauled black trash bags out the side door, then down to the sidewalk. As she carried the first load, she noticed that the doors of the shop were open. She could smell the wet paint and caught a glimpse of Grant through the window, paint roller in hand.

She was carrying out a second load when she heard him call her name. She turned as he walked up to meet her. "Jean, let me help you with that stuff."

"I can do it. You don't have to interrupt your work."

"Perfect timing. I'm letting the first coat dry." He grabbed two bags and Jean did the same, which left only one more. "Many hands make light work," he added.

"These trash bags aren't anyone's idea of light, but thanks all the same."

They reached the sidewalk and piled the bags with the others. "I've been cleaning up my mother's studio. She wants to work in there. Making those ornaments for the church fair got her in the mood to paint again."

"Good for her. How long has it been?" With his head tilted to one side, he looked sincerely interested. Jean had to like him for that.

"I'm not sure. She'd say it was only a few months, but it's probably been years. She's what you might call an unreliable narrator," Jean added with a smile.

Grant smiled, too. "Aren't we all, at times? I hope she enjoys it and doesn't feel frustrated."

"I didn't even think of that," Jean confessed. "I've pretty much promised her she can get in there this afternoon. It's almost ready. I just need to put the easel together, if I can figure out how. She took it apart for some reason."

"I can do that. No offense, but it will probably take me half the time."

"Or less," she admitted, grateful for the offer. She wasn't entirely clueless about fixing things. But she was sure Grant could do it better and faster. "That would be a big help. Thank you."

"No thanks necessary. I'll grab my toolbox and meet you at the house."

Jean went back inside and found Barbara ready to leave. "Another good report for your mother. Making tree ornaments seems to agree with her."

"Seems so. She wants to try painting again, too."

"Really? She's come a long way in a short time. Since you began living here, I mean." Barbara smiled as she zipped up her coat.

"Oh, I don't think my presence has anything to do with it," Jean said quickly.

"Of course it does. You give her such good care and so much attention. And everyone needs companionship, Jean. Even if they insist that they don't."

Is Barbara talking about my mother or about me? Jean wondered.

"See you on Friday." Barbara pulled open the door, and they saw Grant coming up the porch steps. Barbara glanced at Jean over her shoulder, a teasing light in her eyes. "Someone's here to see you. Enjoy the rest of your day."

While Grant was in the studio putting the easel back together, Jean served her mother lunch. He came into the kitchen just as they were finishing.

"That wasn't too bad. A few screws were missing. I had to make do with what I had on hand, but it's stable. That's the most important thing," he said. "I set it up near the window, so you can get the light. I'll move it if you want."

Her mother looked pleased and excited. She pushed herself up from the table and got to her walker without any help. "Let's go see. Jean, I'll need you to take out my paints and brushes."

Jean was already following them. When they reached the studio, her mother took one step through the doorway and looked around. She turned to Jean. "It looks different. I think you cleaned too much."

Before Jean could answer, Grant said, "Don't worry, you'll put your imprint on it again soon enough."

He shared a quick glance with Jean, and she silently thanked him for coming to her rescue.

Cynthia had maneuvered the walker to the easel, which stood near a window that faced north. Pale winter sunlight filtered in over her shoulder. "I suppose this will do. For now. Let me try it and see how it goes. You'll need to adjust the height for me."

Grant stood nearby. "I can't see how you'll manage standing in that walker. You'll get tired too quickly. You should sit in your chair, and I'll fix it for that height."

"I like to paint standing. I never sit," her mother insisted.

Grant tilted his head to one side, looking amused. "At this stage of the game, you might need to try things a little differently."

Her mother frowned. She picked up a brush from a jar that Jean had left on the windowsill and held it toward the easel, her other hand gripping the walker. Jean could see it was an effort for her to hold herself upright, much less maintain the balance and stability she needed to paint.

She turned back to her audience, holding the brush out like a conductor about to signal an orchestra. "All right. I'll try it in the chair. I suppose this old dog can learn a few new tricks. If absolutely necessary."

Jean found the wheelchair in the living room. The studio doorway was a tight fit, but with Grant's help they managed to bring the chair in and then get her mother comfortably seated. Grant began taking out painting supplies, and her mother was soon set up and ready to work, a stack of blank watercolor paper and a few jars of water within easy reach.

"Do you have everything you need, Mom?" Jean asked.

"I suppose so. I need to get my touch back. That's the most important thing. It's been a while. Can you find a painting I left in here, on top of that cabinet? A view of the beach and the lighthouse. It wasn't finished yet. I hope you didn't throw it out," she added with an accusatory stare.

"Of course not. I would never do that." Jean was sure she hadn't thrown out any of her mother's paintings, but she didn't recall seeing that particular scene.

Grant was already rifling through a stack of paintings stored in a special holder with wooden partitions. He carefully separated one painting from the pile and held it out to Cynthia. "Is this the one you mean?"

She nodded and held out her hand. "That's it. Clip it up on the easel for me, will you?"

Grant did as she asked, then stood back as Cynthia appraised her work. Jean thought it was a good start. Her mother's brush strokes had captured the powerful waves and moody, blue-gray clouds just before a storm.

"That's a good one. I can see why you want to finish it," Grant said.

"It has potential," Cynthia replied, still a harsh critic of her own work. "I started it so long ago. I haven't been to that place in years. I'm not sure I can remember it clearly enough to do it justice."

Jean heard the regret in her mother's voice. "We can take a ride out there and you can see it again."

"Oh, that won't help. I can't get down on that beach anymore. I could hardly see anything from a car parked way on top of the cliff."

Jean had forgotten that. There was a high cliff over that stretch of beach, she now recalled. A long flight of stairs led down to the shore. Another insurmountable obstacle for her mother these days.

"I'll go there and take photos for you," Grant offered. "Would that help?"

Cynthia eyed him skeptically. "Would you really do that?"

"Sure, I would. Anything to support the arts," he joked with her.

Cynthia ignored the joke. "When would you go?"

He shrugged. "How about . . . today? After I finish the second coat of paint in the shop. I was going to leave a little early anyway, to do some photography. There's not much more in the shop that I can work on until the paint is dry."

"That's all right by me," her mother said. "But I'm not going to pay you for your time out there taking pictures," she quickly added.

Grant laughed. "The thought never crossed my mind. It's a favor, Cynthia. Maybe Jean would like to come. She could use an afternoon off, too."

He glanced at Jean. Feeling self-conscious, she met his gaze a moment and looked away. "Thanks. But I'd better stay here. My mother might need some help."

Her mother glanced at Jean but didn't comment, though Jean could recall countless times Cynthia had insisted she was fine on her own, without Jean or anyone around.

"All right. I'll finish the painting in the shop and go." Grant met Jean's gaze a moment, then left the room.

Jean lingered in the studio. "Is there anything else I can get for you, Mom?"

"I'm fine for now. If I need anything else, I'll call you."

Her mother glanced at her, then dipped a brush into a jar of water and twirled it on her palette. Jean knew that dismissing look. Her mother wanted to be left alone. She also suspected that her mother felt guilty for not saying, "Go ahead, Jean. I'll be fine for an hour so."

It was just as well. For one thing, her mother might actually need her help. For another, spending time alone with Grant at the beach was not a good idea. In the three short days he had been working in the shop, she had grown to like him more and more. And today, the way he'd shown so much patience and concern for her mother, only made it worse.

While Cynthia worked in the studio, Jean decided to do something easy and rewarding—and started assembling the ingredients for a quick bread. She found dried cranberries and walnuts in one of her mother's cabinets, and the dry ingredients on another shelf.

She had just taken the loaf out of the oven when the doorbell rang. She wondered if Grant was back for some reason, and was surprised to find Reverend Ben on the doorstep. He greeted her with a smile, his blue eyes bright behind the gold frames of his glasses. "Hello, Jean," he said. "Hope I'm not interrupting? I was in the neighborhood and thought I'd see how your mother is doing."

"Please, come in, Reverend. My mother's in her studio, but I'm sure she'll be happy to see you. Walk back with me. Let's see what she's up to."

Jean took the minister's coat and hat, then led him through the house to the studio. Her mother faced the easel and seemed unaware of Jean and the minister standing in the doorway. Jean knocked lightly on the woodwork. "You have a visitor, Mom. Reverend Ben is here."

"I don't mean to interrupt your work, Cynthia. I just wanted to say hello," the reverend explained.

"Come in, Reverend. Tell me what you think of this painting."

Nothing like putting a friend on the spot, Jean thought with an inner smile, though she was curious to hear Reverend Ben's answer.

He stood behind her mother's chair and gazed down at the watercolor scene for a few moments. "I know that bend on the beach. I was out there this morning, with my rod and reel. You've captured it perfectly."

Her mother looked pleased by the compliment. "It's not finished yet." She looked up at him. "I thought it would be hard to paint again. Maybe that's why I put it off for so long. But it hasn't been that hard." She put her brush down and rubbed her hands. "My fingers are stiff. That's the problem. I think I'm ready for a cup of tea. Would you like some?"

"I would. Let me help you with your chair." Reverend Ben took the handles of the wheelchair and rolled it out of the room.

"Let's sit in the living room," Jean suggested. "I'll bring the tea in there."

As Jean prepared a tray with tea and slices of her cranberry-walnut bread, she could hear her mother and Reverend Ben chatting in the living room. As usual, her mother was putting on a show of health and high energy, and Reverend Ben seemed to be buying it, though Jean was almost certain he knew the truth about her mother's condition and her prospects for the future.

"Jean cleaned out my studio this week. I only got in there this morning, but I've been working on the ornaments for the Christmas Fair since Monday," her mother said. "I've been using my own materials—decoupage, acrylic paints. I don't mean to criticize. Goodness knows, I haven't volunteered to help with the fair in ages. But those kits we were given are fairly . . . well, pathetic."

"Pathetic?" He sounded surprised. "Why do you say that, Cynthia?"

"Just take a look inside one. Styrofoam balls. Pipe cleaners and little fuzzy bits. Glue-on glitter and stickers. Suitable for a kindergarten class, I'd say. But who's going to pay good money for something like that? I wouldn't," Cynthia said adamantly. "My ornaments are distinctive. Made from interesting materials. You'll get a good price for them, I'm sure. Perhaps the other ladies should take a page from my book."

"It sounds like they should," he agreed heartily. "Are they finished yet? May I see them?"

"Of course you can. I left them in the studio, boxed up. Jean will get them."

Jean was walking into the living room with the tea tray. "She did a wonderful job, Reverend. There's a nativity scene, an angel, Rudolph the Red—"

"Don't spoil it for him," her mother cut in. "You're ruining the surprise."

"Oh, that bread looks wonderful," Reverend Ben said. "And it smells as if you just took it out of the oven."

"Right before you showed up," Jean said with a smile. "I'll go get the ornaments. You'll see for yourself."

Just as she turned to head back to the studio, the doorbell rang again. She wondered who it could be. Vera Plante, maybe? They rarely had visitors, no less two in one day.

She opened the door, surprised to find Grant. "I got the second coat on the walls and I'm heading out for the beach."

She nodded. "Sure. Have a good afternoon."

Had he come by just to let them know he was leaving for the day? He had never done that before. Usually, he just finished his work and left. Her mother had already agreed that he could leave early.

"May I come in a moment? I just want to ask your mother something. About her painting."

"She's in the living room with a visitor, Reverend Ben."

"I'll just be a moment." He headed for the living room.

"Grant?" Her mother sounded equally surprised to see him. "I thought you were going to the beach to take those pictures for me. You didn't leave yet?"

"I was just heading out, Cynthia. I thought maybe since you had a visitor, Jean wouldn't mind coming with me, after all." He glanced at Jean. "I know you didn't want to leave your mother alone, but it looks like she's in good company. We won't be long," he added. "And it's such a beautiful day."

Jean felt ambushed. And embarrassed. Why hadn't he just asked her again at the door? She didn't need her mother's permission, for goodness' sake. But he knew she would find some new reason not to go with him. This was just a scheme to get around her excuses.

"It is a beautiful day," Jean said. "But I can't impose on Reverend Ben. He just stopped in to say hello. I'm sure he has a lot to do this afternoon."

"I don't mind at all," Reverend Ben cut in. "And I have no pressing plans this afternoon. Please, go out to the beach, Jean. It will be a nice break for you."

Jean was swayed. Grant's hopeful look was hard to resist. And so was his persistence. "Do you mind, Mom? We won't be long."

Her mother shrugged, then took a sip of her tea. "I've told you before, I'm used to being on my own. I can manage just fine."

"But you won't be on your own, Cynthia," Reverend Ben said

gently. "I'm happy to stay until Jean returns." He looked up at Jean and met her gaze. "Take a nice walk on the beach. Take your time."

"Thank you, Reverend Ben. My mom's oxygen tank is on the chair, if she needs it. Just call me if there's any problem. I'll come right back. We won't be far at all." Jean wrote her cell phone number on a pad for the reverend.

"We'll be fine," the reverend assured her.

Jean turned and headed to the front door. Grant stood in the foyer and politely held out her jacket while she put it on. She was a bit miffed at him for cornering her the way he had. But he looked so pleased to have gotten his way, and was being so solicitous as they left the house, that she decided not to complain.

As his truck pulled away from the curb, Jean looked back at the house through the passenger-side window.

Grant's quiet voice broke into her thoughts. "No need to feel guilty. I'm sure Reverend Ben will take good care of your mother."

"I know he will. And I don't feel guilty. Exactly. I leave her alone all the time, or with Barbara Crosby, to go shopping and do errands."

"But not to have fun or socialize," he guessed. He sounded amused and she felt self-conscious. He was making it sound as if she had sneaked out of the house for a date with him.

"Who said anything about fun? I thought it was a walk on the beach to take photos and get some fresh air."

"Yes, all very therapeutic. And with the blessings of a minister, too. Can't we have fun at the same time? You have a bit of a stubborn streak, Jean. I mean, for a sweet, easygoing person."

Jean had to laugh at herself. It was true. She could definitely be stubborn at times. So he thought she was sweet and easygoing? Was that good? She glanced at him. "All right. You win. I'll let you know later."

He looked confused. "Let me know what?"

"If I have fun with you." She pinned him with a bold stare, and he laughed again.

"You've raised the bar now. I'll have to make sure you do, or I really won't be able to pry you loose from that house again." He matched her teasing tone, and Jean felt her cheeks flush.

Was she really blushing? She was a grown woman, for goodness' sake. Wasn't there a statute of limitations for that silly reaction? She was glad to see his gaze was fixed on the road and he hadn't noticed. At least she hoped he hadn't.

"It's nice of you to take the photos my mother needs," she said. "But you must have taken plenty of the beach by now. I bet you had something else planned for today."

He shrugged. "I rarely plan, and this stretch of beach is as good a place as any. Better than most. I never get tired of shooting the ocean and shoreline. That's the amazing thing about photography. You can visit the same exact spot every day, and it will never look the same twice. That's the challenge, too. To capture the essence of a particular moment in time. The light, the tide. The mood of the place." He hesitated, then said, "May I ask you a personal question?"

Jean had been watching out the window. She turned and met his gaze. "Sure. Though I might not answer it."

"How are those drawings I saw coming along? The ones I wasn't supposed to see. For a picture book, I think you said?"

She let out a breath. She thought he was going to ask something a lot more personal than that. Not that her project wasn't personal. She hadn't shared it with anyone yet, had not even talked about it. But for some reason, she felt safe talking about it with him.

"The project is going well, I think." She smoothed the gloves that were folded together in her lap. "I've made steady progress since moving here. I usually work at night, after my mother's gone to bed."

He nodded. "It's good to have a set routine. Slow and steady does the trick for me, too." He glanced at her a moment then looked back at the road. "Has your mother seen it?"

Jean shook her head. "She doesn't even know about it. Why do you ask?"

He looked surprised. "Just curious."

"I haven't shown it to anyone yet. I'm not sure I ever will. It's really just practice."

"From the little I saw, I think that would be a shame, Jean. You're not the only artist I've met who's too hard on themselves. Being your own worst critic might feel like protection. But honestly, it's not. It doesn't help you at all in the long run."

Jean didn't know what to say. Was that true? She felt she just wasn't ready yet. Her work wasn't polished enough. But maybe he was right. Maybe it would never be. She did fear taking that risk and putting her work out there for all to see—and judge.

"I'm not far enough along yet to take in a lot of comments. I don't want to get confused. I'll know when I'm ready," she replied, sounding more sure of that than she felt.

"I hope so. And I hope when you are ready, you'll show it to me. I promise I won't confuse you."

He was already confusing her, in more ways than she could list. Not confusing her exactly, but making her thoughts and feelings a jumble and making her feel things she had not felt for a long time.

She didn't want to think about that too closely either. *Just try to enjoy this,* she told herself. *A walk along the beach on a fair day in December. It doesn't have to mean any more than that.*

They drove a short distance in silence. Jean saw the lighthouse come into view. Years ago, her mother had said that she thought of the lighthouse as being the very heart of the village.

"I think we're near the spot in your mother's painting," Grant said.

"Yes, this is it. The steps down to the beach are just up the road a little way." Jean had not been to this stretch of beach in years. The sight brought back a flood of memories.

"Oh right. I see them." Grant parked the truck on the shoulder of the road, near the stairway.

She got out of the truck and took out her cell phone. She didn't think there would be any messages from her mother, but she couldn't help checking. Grant was leaning into the back seat, pulling out cameras and a canvas knapsack. The sun was so bright. She felt the sunlight warm her cheeks and a light breeze tug at the loose strands that had escaped her hair tie. "A perfect day," she said. "I don't even need to zip my jacket."

"Not up here. Let's see what happens down on the beach." He waved his arm in a gallant gesture, indicating she should go first down the long flight of steps.

"My family came to this beach all the time when I was growing up. I always hated going down these stairs," she confessed. "I was afraid I was going to fall over the rail and land in the sand. Sometimes I'd just freeze in the middle and hold up everyone behind me."

"Are you afraid of heights?"

Jean shrugged. "Not really. I wasn't afraid anyplace else. Just these steps. My father would walk ahead of me and practically walk down backward, holding my hand to make sure I was all right."

"That's very sweet—a nice memory."

"It was sweet. That's just the way he was. It helped me get over it," she added. "Or maybe just getting older did."

It was breezier on the beach, as Grant had predicted, but still incredibly mild. Grant started off toward the lighthouse, and she quickened her step to catch up.

"Let's walk this way," he said. "The lighthouse is in the foreground of her painting. I want to find a spot with the right perspective."

He marched along through the sand, a serious expression on his handsome face. Jean walked beside him, her hands in her pockets. He was being very exacting about the photos, Jean noticed, taking her mother's request seriously. That was good of him. She hoped her mother would appreciate it.

Jean paused as they passed another familiar sight, one that brought back more memories—a long jetty where whitecaps crashed into a barrier of gray stones, where seaweed and tiny mollusks clung, somehow withstanding the pounding waves.

"It must be past the jetty. That's not in the picture," Jean said.

"Yes, you're right, it must be farther on. But that jetty is amazing. Maybe I'll get some shots there later."

Finally, he found a spot he thought looked right. "I think this is it. See the way the shoreline curves, an equal distance between us and the lighthouse?"

He stood behind her and rested one hand on her shoulder, pointing down the beach with the other. When he spoke, his warm breath fanned her cheek, a sharp contrast to the chilly spray coming off the sea. Jean was so distracted by his nearness, she couldn't answer for a moment.

"I think it's the spot, too. Or close enough," she said quietly.

He stepped back and checked the settings on one of the cameras that hung from a strap around his neck. Then he lifted the viewfinder to his eye. He seemed in a trance after that, the shutter clicking rapidly as he moved closer, then farther. He crouched, knelt down and stood up again, and even walked into the foamy edge of the rushing tide.

Jean watched him but didn't speak, afraid to break the spell. After a few moments, she walked back to the jetty and carefully walked out, selecting each stone to step on and then the next. The way she had as a child, calculating her moves as if playing a giant game of checkers.

Before she realized it, she had walked more than halfway out. The pile of stones began to narrow and waves slapped on either side. Sudden bursts of spray rose up like fountains. She knew her coat and even her hair were getting wet but she didn't care.

She tipped her head back to watch the sea birds that cackled and cawed above. Or floated in lazy loops then dove into the water and swooped up again, tidbits of fish dangling from their orange beaks.

Jean watched them, studying the graceful curve of their bodies and wings, filing the images away for some future time, a drawing or a painting perhaps. She heard Grant shout her name and turned suddenly, nearly losing her balance. She realized he must have been calling for a while. She had either been lost in her thoughts or the wind had carried his voice away.

He smiled and began to walk toward her. She began to walk toward him, too. With a short distance between them, he picked up his camera and began taking photos. Jean stopped in her tracks and waved her hand at him. "Please don't do that. I hate being photographed. I don't need any pictures taken of me. Honestly."

"Of course you do. It's a perfect shot. You look so free out here, just you and the sky and the water. It's beautiful."

She stopped in her tracks and crossed her arms over her chest. "I mean it. Will you please just stop? I look like a windblown mess."

At the words, her hair tie burst and her long hair, wavy from the mist, whipped across her face. She pushed it back with her hand to find Grant very close, still taking photos. Then, suddenly, he tucked the camera in his jacket, reached out, and brushed her hair off her face, his palm lingering there, cupping her cheek.

"Windblown, yes. But definitely not a mess. Just the opposite, I'd say." His tone was quiet but decisive, his face very close. Jean wanted to speak but the words got stuck in her throat.

With one hand resting on her waist, his dark head dipped down and he kissed her. Softly at first, then deepening as she responded to his touch. His lips tasted salty, like the sea, but felt warm and soft.

She wasn't sure how long they stood there. A big wave crashed on the rocks where they stood. Grant pulled her close and turned his back to the water, shielding her from the worst. As quickly as the wave had risen up, it washed away.

Jean pulled back from his embrace. "Your cameras. I hope they didn't get wet."

"No worries, I tucked them into my jacket. They'll be fine. But I think the tide is coming in. We'd better get back to dry land before we're washed away." He took her hand and they headed down the jetty to the beach.

Jean's mind was spinning on the ride back. She didn't know what to think. Was this the start of something? Was he really attracted to her—or just taking advantage of a romantic moment? Which it most certainly had been. One she would replay in her mind later, when she was alone.

Grant was as talkative as he had been on the ride out, acting as if nothing at all had changed between them. "I got some good shots of the shoreline. I think your mother will be pleased. I won't fuss over the prints. I'll make her some eight-by-tens when I get back to Vera's and bring them with me tomorrow."

"That sounds great. My mother couldn't ask for faster service than that."

"She *might* ask," he said, a teasing light in his eye. "But she wouldn't find it."

Jean laughed. He already knew her mother well, didn't he?

When they returned, Jean thought Grant would drop her off and be on his way. But he parked and walked back into the house with her.

"I want to tell your mom that I think I found the spot and will bring the prints tomorrow," he explained.

Jean didn't mind him coming in at all and considered inviting him for dinner. Then decided that would be too much. After all, it was only a kiss. She didn't want to seem too eager and overwhelmed by his attention.

As they hung up their jackets, Reverend Ben walked into the hallway from the direction of her mother's room. He smiled at them, looking pleased for some mysterious reason. "Did you have a nice walk?"

"Very nice," Jean replied. "Grant took a lot of photos that will help Mom finish her painting. How is she doing?"

"She's fine. We went back to the studio and looked over her ornaments. They're wonderfully creative. I'm sure they'll be the hit of the fair," he said. "Then she felt a little tired. She's in the bedroom, taking a nap."

Before Jean could reply, she heard her mother call out. "I'm awake now. I'd like some help getting out of bed, please."

Reverend Ben turned to go back to the bedroom, but Jean touched his arm. "I think you've stayed long enough, Reverend. I appreciate you keeping her company."

He smiled and patted her hand. "Anytime, Jean, anytime. You just call me. I always enjoy chatting with your mother."

He slipped on his jacket and headed out as Cynthia called, "I'm still waiting."

"Coming, Mom. Just a second . . ."

"I'll wait here. Maybe she'd like some privacy," Grant said. "Call if you need help."

Jean thought that was wise. She could tell from her mother's tone that she had woken up in a bad mood.

"There you are. Finally." Cynthia was sitting up in bed, her oxygen tubes dangling around her neck. She had obviously pulled them out of her nose, though Jean suspected she could use the help breathing.

Jean sat on the edge of her bed. "Are you all right? Reverend Ben said you got tired."

Her mother shrugged. "He's a good man, but small talk wears me out after a while. I wish you hadn't left me alone like that. You said you'd be right back. You were gone for hours."

Jean had already checked the time on the way back and knew for certain she had only been out a little over an hour. "Grant took some very good photos for you. He's going to make prints tonight and bring them tomorrow."

Her mother's sour expression didn't alter. "Is he still here? I think he should go. It's almost dinnertime. I don't want any more company today. I've had enough of that."

"Yes, of course. He wanted to speak to you, but I'll tell him you're tired. You can talk to him tomorrow."

"Please do. Can you fix the pillows behind my back? I'd like to read a little while you're making dinner. I don't think I want to get up, after all."

Jean leaned over and fixed the pillows the way her mother liked. "I can bring your dinner in here if you're too tired to eat at the table."

Her mother had already opened a book and found her place. She glanced at Jean over the edge of her reading glasses. "Maybe . . . I don't know how I'll feel from one minute to the next."

Jean didn't know how to reply. If her mother was trying to make her feel guilty for going out, she was doing a good job.

"I'll make your dinner. I'll cook something fast," she added. She left her mother and found Grant in the living room, sitting in an armchair.

"How is she? Did she survive being babysat by the reverend?"

"Just barely. Or maybe she's just acting that way."

"If she's mad at you, it's my fault. I wrangled you away and then stayed out too long. I'll talk to her tomorrow."

Jean was touched by his gallant intentions. "It's not your fault. She would have complained if we were gone fifteen minutes. Sometimes there's really no pleasing her," she added honestly.

His warm brown eyes met hers, his gaze thoughtful. "Maybe not, but you're a very good daughter to try so hard. I'm sorry she's out of sorts. I hope it was worth it?"

Jean felt herself blush and didn't know how to answer.

"So, what's the verdict? Did you have fun?"

She tried not to smile but couldn't help it. "Yes, I did. I must admit, I did have fun with you, Grant Keating."

He looked very pleased by her reply, and as his gaze locked with hers for a long moment, she had the feeling he was going to kiss her again.

Her mother's voice rang out from the bedroom. "Jean? Is Grant still here? I thought you were going to start dinner."

"He's just leaving, Mom. Dinner will be ready soon."

Grant headed for the front door. "She still has excellent hearing, all things considered," he whispered.

"Yes, she does. Remember that," Jean whispered back, a hint of laughter in her tone.

She walked him to the door and watched as he ran down to his truck, jumped behind the wheel, and drove away.

Jean turned and headed for the kitchen. It was a little early to start dinner, even in their house. Jean wasn't hungry yet and decided to fix something quick for her mother and have a bite by herself later. Her mother obviously wanted to eat and go to sleep. She had tired herself out today, maybe by starting to paint again. Or her visit with Reverend Ben. Or fussing over Jean's outing with Grant, despite her claims of being perfectly able to stay on her own.

Jean heated some leftover chicken in the oven and worked on a salad. Her thoughts turned to Grant. Did he really care for her, or did he just enjoy charming any woman—or two—he might encounter in his travels? An inner voice cautioned to keep her guard up. To be wary of a man who was obviously a rambler, rootless and resistant to commitments.

While another voice, a voice in her heart, encouraged her to let go and follow her feelings. She had been married once, in her twenties, and had been in a few serious relationships since. But Jean could barely recall feeling this drawn to anyone. The more time she spent with Grant, the stronger the urge to follow this attraction wherever it might lead.

CHAPTER EIGHT

⌐⊤✕

*D*ARRELL WAS ON HIS WAY HOME LATE WEDNESDAY AFTER-
noon when he realized that he had forgotten to stop at
Village Hall to prod the building inspector again about visiting the
Turner house. And he had promised his father that he would. He had
just finished working at the Prentiss renovation and had made the
rounds of the other jobs, too, to check the day's progress. It was already five o'clock, and he doubted that he would catch Inspector Hepburn in his office. The village employees were notorious for leaving at
five on the dot. But he turned the truck down Main Street anyway. At
least he could tell his father that he tried.

Village Hall was quiet and looked deserted. But back in the building department, Darrell found an assistant still at his desk. Just as
Darrell had expected, the inspector had left for the day.

"Would you like to leave Inspector Hepburn a message?" the assistant asked.

"I'm with Morgan Construction. We're waiting for an inspection of the electrical system at a jobsite—38 Tea Pot Lane. The resident's name is Turner."

The assistant jotted down the information. "He can probably visit by the end of the week—or maybe early next."

"I hope so. Please tell him our work is held up until we get that certificate. This is costing us money, and the client is getting impatient, too."

Darrell tried his best to sound firm and assertive. The assistant, who looked about his own age, maybe a year or two older, didn't look impressed. Darrell suspected all the contractors delivered the same complaints.

"I understand. I'll see what I can do to fit it in the schedule."

"Thanks. See you around." Darrell was about to leave when he had a sudden thought. "Do you know anything about a property near the Willow Tree Estates? A big old warehouse, just off the Beach Road?"

The young man looked puzzled by the question. "A warehouse? Oh, right. I know what you mean. That property was taken over for back taxes a long time ago. I think the bank owns it. Or maybe even the village."

"The village? That's interesting." Darrell was encouraged by that tidbit of information.

"That's all I know about it. You can ask Inspector Hepburn when you see him. I'm sure he can give you more information."

"I will. Thanks." Darrell turned and left the office and soon found himself face-to-face with Cape Light's mayor, Charlie Bates. Charlie, who owned the Clam Box Diner, had long sought the mayor's office and had finally won it about two years ago in a very close election against Darrell's aunt Emily.

Charlie was not his family's favorite person, for that reason and a few others. Darrell's parents didn't think he was a very good mayor, not as good as Aunt Emily. But Charlie had come a long way from his rocky start, and the Morgans had always taught their children to give a person the benefit of the doubt and try not to judge others harshly. At the very least, to be polite and respectful of their elders.

Charlie greeted him warmly, though he looked surprised to see Darrell in the Village Hall offices. "Hello there, Darrell. I heard about your dad's fall. Gee, that's tough. How's he doing?"

"He's coming along. He hates to be cooped up in the house. That's the main problem now."

"I bet. I'm the same way. My wife says I have two speeds, fast and stop." Charlie laughed at his own joke. "What brings you by today? Helping your father with his business?"

Darrell nodded. "I'm overseeing the projects. I came by to see Inspector Hepburn. We need a certificate for some electrical work."

Charlie looked impressed. "I hear you're studying to be an architect. What year are you in now?"

"I'm a senior at BU. I graduate in the spring."

"Wow, time sure flies. I remember the first time Sam brought you into the Clam Box. You were maybe . . . this high?" Charlie held his hand at hip level. "Staying at New Horizons."

"That's right." Darrell smiled but hoped Charlie wouldn't take too long a walk down memory lane.

But what Charlie had said was true. Darrell had come to Cape Light because of the New Horizons program, which was part boarding school, part country camp for city kids who were getting into trouble at school and were at risk of getting into even more serious problems, like drugs and crime.

Darrell had never known his father, and his mother drifted in and out of his life. He had been raised mainly by his grandmother. But when she became ill and couldn't handle him, he had started hanging with some bad kids and heading in the wrong direction.

A stay at New Horizons—and the love and attention he found there from Sam, who had been a volunteer at the time—had turned his life around. Saved his life, truthfully.

Darrell wasn't ashamed of his history, but he didn't feel comfortable hearing Charlie Bates rehash it. Darrell decided to change the subject and maybe get some information in the process.

"You know, Charlie, I was just asking in the building department about an old warehouse off the Beach Road. Near the Willow Tree Estates," he added, mentioning his aunt Molly's neighborhood. "The assistant in the building office told me that the town might own it?"

"Oh, that old place. It used to be a cannery. Tillerman's Clams. And before that"—Charlie's expression changed as he remembered the history—"it was owned by your grandfather, Oliver Warwick. But it was taken over by the bank and sold at auction when he had that financial setback that ruined him. You must have heard about that?"

Darrell nodded. He didn't know all the details of this dark page of family history. But he had heard how his grandfather, his grandmother Lillian's first husband, was the only heir to an impressive fortune but lost practically all of it due to his own poor judgment and gambling debts.

"That's interesting," Darrell said.

"Yup, your grandfather Oliver once owned it." Darrell could almost hear him add, "How the mighty have fallen." An attitude many people in town held toward the Warwick family. Darrell's relatives on his mother's side, the Warwicks, were once the wealthiest family in town. They lived on a big estate called Lilac Hall: Jessica and Emily had both grown up there. But Lillian sold Lilac Hall to the village after everything fell apart, and it now housed the Cape Light Historical Society. Although it had been decades since his grandmother lived in such splendor, she still acted as if the family were local royalty. Then again, Lillian's own parents had been Boston Brahmins. She had been "upper crust" from the day she was born.

"What got you so interested in that place?" Charlie asked.

"Oh, I don't know. I was just driving around the other day, and the building caught my eye. I thought it would be a good subject for my school project—mock plans to renovate and rescue a property. Who owns it now? Do you know?"

"The town owns it. We took it over years ago from Tillerman for back taxes."

"Do you have any plans for it?"

Charlie laughed. "I thought we could take the boards off the windows and make it a bird sanctuary, but nobody on the town council agreed with me."

Darrell smiled. He knew Charlie was joking, but he really wanted a definitive answer. "Has the council talked about it lately?"

"It's come up a few times—every time the neighbors complain it's an eyesore or kids get caught hanging out there. But that old heap isn't exactly a priority. Some on the town council think we should put it up for sale. A developer might buy it. But this village gets into such an uproar about new construction. Developers don't like that. They don't like to work here. Sooner or later, someone will see the potential. But we have a lot of other issues to worry about right now, more important than that pile of bricks."

"I'm sure you do," Darrell said, feeling excited to hear the town owned the building and had no plans for it. "Do you think I could take a look inside sometime?"

Charlie shrugged. "I don't see why not. If it's safe to walk around there," he added. "I'll speak to Inspector Hepburn for you. He'd have the final say about that."

"That would be great. I'd really appreciate it, Charlie . . . I mean, Mayor Bates."

Darrell thought Charlie could tell he was just being flattered, but he seemed to eat it up anyway. "That's okay, Darrell." Charlie patted Darrell's shoulder. "I'll see what I can do. Say hello to your dad for me. Maybe I'll stop by and see him sometime. I'll surprise him with a nice clam roll. I bet he'd like that."

Darrell knew for sure his father would not. His father vehemently disliked the Clam Box specialty and would not enjoy a visit from Charlie either. But Darrell smiled politely. "I'm sure he'd be surprised by that."

Darrell said good-bye to Charlie and left Village Hall feeling buoyant and encouraged. If the town owned the property, maybe he really could get something going with the warehouse. More than just a school project. Much more.

Darrell had a real vision for the place that was growing in clarity and detail with each passing hour. He could hardly wait to get home and begin working on his plans.

DARRELL DID HIS SHARE OF AFTER-DINNER CLEANUP, THEN HEADED to his room. He was eager to start working on the plans he had for the warehouse. Eager enough to miss dessert, though he did grab a brownie and an apple on his way out of the kitchen.

"Hey, buddy—the Celtics are on tonight," his dad called out. "Don't you want to watch the game?"

Darrell turned in the doorway. "I have some work to do for my classes, but call me at halftime."

"I'll watch with you, Dad," his younger brother, Tyler, said. His father reached out and ruffled Tyler's hair. "That goes without saying. Go get our hats and meet me in my cave."

Glad to see that his father would have some company to cheer with him and yell at the TV screen, Darrell headed upstairs with his laptop and a sketch pad on which he had outlined a few ideas.

Darrell had already sent pictures of the building from his phone to his computer and worked with the different aspects of the property on his sketch pad. Until he got inside the structure, many questions remained. But there was still a lot he could do with the information he had on hand.

He wasn't sure how much time had passed when he heard his brother calling from the bottom of the stairs. "Dad said to tell you it's halftime. Celtics are up by six, but Isaiah turned his ankle."

Isaiah turned his ankle? That wasn't good. "Okay, Ty. I'll be right down."

Darrell saved his work, snapped the laptop closed, and brought it downstairs. He found his father, Tyler, and their chocolate Lab, Daisy, on the leather couch in his father's office, in front of the TV. His dad and Ty were wearing Celtics hats, and Daisy wore a green bandana.

"Hi, guys. I forgot my hat." Darrell took a seat in an armchair next to the couch.

"It's right here." Tyler walked over to their father's desk and handed Darrell his hat. "I'm going to make popcorn. Call me if the game starts."

"Good idea, Ty. Bring me a glass of water? I need to take some pills," his father said. He turned to Darrell. "I'm glad you're keeping up with your schoolwork. Did you finish what you needed to do?"

"It wasn't homework exactly, Dad. But it's something I think I can use for my senior project. I found this old warehouse near Aunt

Molly's neighborhood. I took some photos and had a ton of ideas about how it can be renovated. Like those big warehouses on the waterfront in Boston?"

"Sure, I know what you mean. It's amazing what they've done to that waterfront. It was nothing special when I was young," his father agreed without looking at him. Sam was half listening to the sportscaster rehash the first two periods of the game and half listening to Darryl.

Undeterred, Darrell brought up the photos of the warehouse on his computer and one of the sketches he'd done of a possible renovation into an apartment complex. He held out the computer for his father to see. "Here's what it looks like now. And here's one of my ideas for renovation."

His father glanced at the screen. Then back at the TV. "Nice. That's very interesting. Where is this place?"

"Just off the Beach Road. Not far from Willow Tree Estates. I heard that it used to be a cannery." Darrell knew the full history of the place was interesting but didn't think his father was paying enough attention to appreciate it. "The building inspector might let me go inside and look around."

A commercial came on, and his father looked back at him again. "You be careful walking around an old place like that. Make sure he says it's safe, okay?"

Darrell nodded, disappointed that his father was missing the entire point. The possibilities of this property were mind-boggling. At least to him they were. He thought his father, of all people, would appreciate that. But it seemed like a bad time to show him and explain his ideas.

Just as Darrell snapped his laptop closed, a tiny pink piglet raced into the room. It ran in a circle around the coffee table and darted under his father's desk, giving out small but earsplitting squeals every few seconds. Daisy sat up and barked. Sam rested his hand on her head and held her back from jumping off the couch.

"Easy, Daisy. I know you love ham, but it's not good for you," he joked.

Darrell's little sister, Lily, was in hot pursuit. "Hold Daisy back, Dad. Pinky broke through her barrier. I guess she got over her cold."

"Great news. Maybe we should make her some more chicken soup. Oops . . . don't tell the chickens. And Pinky might feel bad eating soup made out of a roommate."

"Dad! That's not nice!" Lily was under the desk, trying to grab the baby pig, who darted from side to side, nimbly remaining out of reach.

Darrell's mother stood in the doorway, her arms crossed over her chest. "Very funny, Sam."

"Just answer one question. Why isn't that pig out in the barn with her little pig friends?"

"The space heaters aren't working very well. I told you yesterday, remember?" His father nodded, but Darrell could tell he didn't really remember. "It didn't matter much during the day, it was so mild out. But the temperature really dropped tonight. It's too cold in there for her. She's still on antibiotics."

Before his father could answer with another wisecrack, Lily emerged from under the desk, cradling the baby pig. "Here she is, Mom. I caught the little rascal."

Lily handed the pig to Jessica, who cradled her gently. "You bad girl. Back in your barrier."

"See you later, Pinky." Sam grinned and waved good-bye.

Tyler came in with a bowl of popcorn and a glass of ice water for their dad. He set both on the coffee table and took his seat on the sofa, on the other side of Daisy. "Did the game start yet?"

"No, but you missed a good halftime show," Sam joked.

"What?" Tyler looked confused. Sam just laughed and yanked the bill of Ty's cap down below his eyes, making him laugh, too. The rest of the game was exciting. Darrell was glad he had come down for the second half. It was fun to watch sports with his father and brother. He definitely missed that when he was away at school. Even though he watched plenty of games with his friends, it wasn't the same.

The game was a nail-biter right down to the wire. With two minutes left, the Celtics were trailing by three points. Their three-point shooter had gone cold but could tie it up with one shot. And win it all if he went to the line for a foul shot.

Sam sat on the edge of his wheelchair, his cap turned backward for a late-game rally. "Come on, you guys. Pass the ball! Bradley is wide open. Pass the ball, for crying out loud!"

Finally, the ball was passed, and the star player tossed the ball in a long arc. It headed for the basket, perfectly aligned for a three-point, game-tying shot.

Suddenly the screen went black. There was no picture or sound.

Darrell, his father, and Tyler sat stunned, then looked at each other. "What in the world?" Sam shouted. "What's going on now?"

"Looks like the cable went out, Dad." Darrell walked over to the TV and clicked the remote. "It's got power, but it's lost reception." He turned to his father. "Maybe a line went down or something. Maybe there's a problem in our area."

His father sat back in his chair, looking glum and exasperated. "Just at the biggest moment of the game. What luck."

Daisy sat up and barked. Darrell's father looked over at the dog. "Even Daisy is annoyed."

Suddenly Daisy jumped off the couch and ran to the TV cabinet.

She sniffed under the edge of the cabinet, then ran around the side and sniffed at the back.

Darrell saw a large brown-and-white lop-eared rabbit squeeze its way out the other side of the cabinet. Then it hopped in a flash across the carpeting and out the door.

Tyler jumped off the couch and followed it. "Buster! He's been hiding behind the TV cabinet the whole time. Lily couldn't find him, but she didn't want to tell Mom."

Tyler disappeared in pursuit of the rabbit. Darrell held on to Daisy's collar so she wouldn't follow, too. He leaned over and looked behind the cabinet. Just as he suspected, the cable wire had been gnawed through.

"Don't tell me." His father covered his eyes with his hand. "The rabbit chewed the cable wire."

Darrell winced. "Looks like it."

His mother walked into the room. "I heard you found the rabbit. The kids thought he wandered out of the house, but they didn't want to tell me."

"I wish he *had* wandered out. He chewed right through the cable, and we missed the end of the game. A very exciting game," his father added, his voice growing louder. Darrell could tell he was annoyed now. His patience and humor about the animals had worn thin. Sam could put up with a lot, but it was never wise to come between him and one of his favorite teams, like the Celtics, Red Sox, or Patriots. The critters had crossed the line tonight.

"We're lucky he didn't get hurt, chewing on that wire," Jessica said.

"Depends on how you look at it. I hear roasted rabbit can be very tasty," his father replied. "Any other animals on the lam I should know about? No cats about to spring out of a closet? No goats in the bathroom?"

"Maybe I can cut the cable wire down and splice it together again," Darrell offered. "I'm sure they'll show the ending on the post-game show."

Sam let out a long sigh. "Sure, Darrell. It's worth a try." He looked at Jessica again but didn't say anything.

"If that doesn't work, I'll call the cable company and get a repairman here tomorrow. I'm sorry the rabbit ruined the game for you, Sam," his mother said. "But I really couldn't help it. I didn't even know he was missing."

"I understand." His father's tone was overly patient, Darrell thought. "I think I'll just go live in a zoo. At least I'll know what to expect."

Jessica shrugged and turned to leave the room again. "Suit yourself. But I doubt you'll find any cable TV there either."

His father looked at him and rolled his eyes. A man-to-man look that made Darrell laugh. "I'll go get the wire splicer and see if I can fix this mess."

"Thanks, Darrell. Just promise me one thing. If your wife ever asks if she can start an animal rescue center, think it over carefully before you answer."

Darrell laughed. "I'll definitely remember that."

"I hope you do, son. I sure hope you do."

DARRELL HAD JUST PULLED UP IN FRONT OF THE TURNERS' HOUSE ON Thursday morning when his cell phone rang. He checked the screen and saw it was a call from his father. The first of many for the day, he knew by now. "What's up, Dad?" Darrell greeted him.

"Inspector Hepburn called. He said he can go to the Turners' this morning for the inspection."

"Fast service. His assistant told me sometime this week."

"Maybe your chat with Charlie Bates yesterday helped. Just make sure you stick around until he comes. Don't leave for lunch or anything. We need that certificate, and he might have some questions."

"I got it covered, Dad. No worries." It wasn't that his father didn't trust him. Not exactly. He was just a bit of a control freak, especially after his accident. Darrell tried not to let it bother him. Most of the time, it didn't.

"I know, I know. No worries," Sam parroted him. "That's what you always say."

"But it's true," Darrell replied.

"Sounds good. Keep me posted," his father said, ending the call.

True to his word, Inspector Hepburn arrived at the property at half-past eleven. The inspector reviewed the wiring, circuit box, and other details of the new electrical system. He also checked the carbon monoxide and fire alarms, which were hardwired into the construction. He had a few questions, which Darrell fielded easily. Finally, he took out the certificate, made a few notations, then signed and stamped it. "Here you go," he said, handing Darrell the paper.

"Thanks. And thanks for coming this morning. Your assistant said you might not make until the end of the week. Or maybe early next."

"My schedule opened up a bit. And Charlie put in a good word for you," he admitted. "I was sorry to hear about your father's accident. I hope he's recovering quickly."

"He's doing very well, thanks."

"That's good to hear. Charlie said you asked him about the Tillerman property. Is your father's company interested in doing something with it?"

Darrell quickly shook his head. "No, sir. It just caught my eye. I'm studying architecture. I thought it might make a good subject for my senior project. I could do a mock renovation of the building, a conversion to apartments, or something like that."

"I see. A developer approached the town a few years ago with an idea like that. But he got cold feet. Nobody's been interested since. The place is still a solid structure, last I looked," he added. "I think it could stand up to a renovation. Some of these old places aren't worth the bother."

Darrell felt his heartbeat quicken. "Do you think I could look around inside? I would be very careful, and I wouldn't take very long."

"Sure, why not? I'd be interested to see how it's holding up myself. Can you meet me out there this afternoon? Say, around two o'clock? I have an inspection to do in that direction. I'll be done by then."

"That would be perfect. I'll be there," Darrell promised.

"Very good. See you then, Darrell," the inspector said.

"Right. See you," Darrell replied. He was so excited, he couldn't say another word.

DARRELL ARRIVED AT THE TILLERMAN CANNERY A FEW MINUTES BE-fore two p.m. The forecast was calling for snow. It was due to start around dinnertime, but the air already felt frosty and the sky was heavy with dense, gray clouds. The mercury was definitely at the freezing point. Or lower. Darrell was eager to get a look inside the cannery before the snow started. He wanted to walk around the outside of the building again, too, but decided to wait until the inspector arrived.

He checked his phone and found a text from his father, warning about the snow and reminding him to turn the heat higher in the empty Marino house, the jobsite where his father's accident had happened.

Darrell quickly tapped back his usual reply. No worries. Got it covered, Dad. He looked up from the phone to see a black SUV pull up. Inspector Hepburn sat behind the wheel, wearing a yellow hard hat.

Darrell had his own hard hat and picked it up off the passenger seat before hopping out of the truck to meet the inspector.

"Ready for the grand tour?" the inspector greeted him.

"Absolutely. I have my hard hat, floodlight, and camera."

"Take one of these. The air might be bad in there." Inspector Hepburn handed him a face mask and put one on, as well. "Okay, follow me."

Instead of squeezing through an opening in the fence, as Darrell had done a few days ago, the inspector led Darrell to a gate in the fence. He took out a key ring and opened the padlock that was slipped through the fencing on a long chain.

Hepburn pulled open the gate and let Darrell walk through first. Then he led the way to a metal door on the side of the building, secured by another big padlock. He had a key for that lock, too, though the door was stuck and it took the two of them pushing with all their weight to ease it open.

They both turned on their floodlights. Darrell waited outside while Inspector Hepburn took a few steps inside. He coughed a few times, then signaled for Darrell to follow. "Musty in here. Make sure that door stays open."

Darrell turned back to the door and propped it open with a broken wooden chair he found near the doorway. Then he followed the inspector and stepped into a dark, cavernous space.

The inspector flashed his light around. Darrell saw large pipes running along a high ceiling, cables and wires hanging, and long steel tables that looked like parts of an assembly line.

On class trips, Darrell had toured buildings that had been converted from factory and warehouse space. But he had never seen an empty, abandoned building like this one, before it had been gutted and cleaned up.

Inspector Hepburn flashed his light along the floor and the brick walls, from the bottom up. "I don't see any cracks in the walls or the floor. Though I do see a few puddles—from holes in the roof, of course. But the cement floor looks solid."

He flashed the light higher, skimming the iron girders that ran across the length and width of the high ceiling. "Those beams are solid steel. And so are these supports," he added, flashing the light to steel girders than ran from floor to roof.

Darrell flashed his light straight up, to look over the roof. He heard the sound of wings flapping and a few birds swooped around above. One darted through a hole in the wood that covered a window.

"Well, the roof has a lot of holes," Darrell said. "But after all this time, that's to be expected."

The inspector checked the roof with his light, too. "Amazing anything is there at all." He turned to Darrell. "I think it's safe to walk around a little. Want to see more?"

"Absolutely." Darrell pointed his light at the floor to see where he was going. There was a lot of debris lying around, broken wooden crates, long pieces of pipe, and fallen chunks of insulation. Darrell could see spaces where machinery had been pulled out, the pipe fittings, wires, and other connections left hanging. When a big factory like this closed down, it was customary to sell off anything of value. There must have been valuable machinery in here at one time, Darrell realized. He imagined the space fully equipped and humming with activity, bustling employees in the midst of their workday.

"It's a great big mess, isn't it?" the inspector said as they walked toward the big metal doors that Darrell guessed once opened to a loading dock.

"A beautiful mess to me," Darrell replied. He had taken out his phone and continued taking pictures of different areas and angles. The flash helped, though he knew the photos would not really have enough light.

"Seen enough for your project?" the inspector asked.

"I think so. For now." Darrell slipped the phone in his jacket pocket. "It would be nice to see it with the boards off the windows. I wish I had a laser distance measure to measure the dimensions."

"We have one of those back in the office. I should have brought it for you," Inspector Hepburn replied. "But, better than that, I found a set of the plans in an old file. You can have a copy if you'd like."

"Wow, that would be great." Darrell felt so lucky hearing that news. He felt as if it was a sign that his vision for renovating the space was meant to be.

"I'll have someone make a copy later and leave it at the front desk in Village Hall." Inspector Hepburn took another quick look around, flashing his light up, down, and into the corners. Then he began to walk back toward the door they had left open.

Outside, they took off their masks, and the inspector secured the padlock. "This place has the potential to be useful again, in some way. I just can't say how."

Darrell thought he could but wasn't ready yet to fill in the blank. "I agree," he said, as they walked to the gate. "I think it has loads of potential. Thanks for letting me see it, sir."

"Not a problem." They walked through the gate and Inspector Hepburn locked it again. "I wanted to be an architect myself, once upon a time. But I stopped with a civil engineering degree and ended up in this job nearly twenty years ago. I don't mind it," he added. "I know I'm doing important work, making sure buildings are safe. But I still wonder about the road not traveled. About the houses and buildings I would have designed. You're lucky to be able to follow that path if it's what you really want to do with your life."

Darrell felt touched by his confession. "It is what I want to do. What I've always wanted. And I know that I'm very lucky I can pursue it."

Inspector Hepburn smiled and touched Darrell's shoulder. "Good for you. I'll leave those plans at the front desk. If I can help you more with the project, just let me know."

Darrell thanked him again and they parted. As Darrell drove down the Beach Road, his head was filled with ideas for the cannery. He had already done a little research on the Internet about the steps needed to make a real renovation happen. The first place he needed to go was the county seat. There were piles of applications to fill out, and he had read about some grants that were available for community improvements. More paperwork there, for sure. But if he could win a grant for this project, he would be home free. He knew the odds might not be in his favor, but it was crazy not to try.

He had completed the tasks he needed to cover on his father's jobsites and he could be at the county offices in half an hour, sometime around three p.m. He could do some research and easily make it back to the village by five. There was no reason not to go, Darrell decided as he took the turn off the Beach Road that led to the highway.

Darrell reached the county offices quickly but lost time finding out where he could pick up the applications he wanted. The county offices were ten times bigger and more bureaucratic than Cape Light Village Hall, and several people he spoke to contradicted each other. His cell phone had used up its charge—all those photos in the warehouse—so the reminder to head home never rang. But he kept his eye on the time, and at precisely four thirty he ended his hunt, knowing he could return another day.

Outside, the air was frigid. The temperature had dropped and icy bits of snow had begun to fall. He found a scraper in the glove compartment and cleaned off the windshield, with the defroster turned on high. Even with the bad weather, he would have made it home a few minutes after five, but he hadn't calculated for rush-hour traffic on the highway. It was slow going with the bad weather in the bargain.

By the time he pulled into the driveway and walked inside, it was nearly half past six. He could smell dinner in the kitchen. His family was probably waiting for him before sitting down to eat.

He paused in the foyer to hang up his jacket and slip off his wet boots. His father, who was sitting in the living room, spun his wheelchair to face him. "Darrell, where have you been? I must have called and sent a hundred text messages."

"Sorry, Dad. My phone died. By the time it got enough charge to see your messages, I was on the road. I sent a quick reply. Didn't you see it?"

"Yeah, I saw it. But 'Got delayed. Be home soon' doesn't explain much. I know you weren't at any of the jobs. I called around to the crew, and no one had seen you since lunchtime."

Darrell didn't realize his father had been looking for him so intensely. And had spies willing to report.

"I went to the county office. I had to look up some stuff for a school project."

"You could have told me that earlier."

"Yeah . . . I guess so. But it was sort of a spur-of-the-moment deci-sion. I finished all my work at the sites," he added.

"Really? There was one thing you forgot to do." His father looked angry, and Darrell felt alarmed. What had he forgotten? He couldn't remember. Before he could reply, his father said, "The thermostat and the faucets at the Marino house. I asked you to turn up the heat there so the pipes don't freeze tonight."

"Oh, man . . . I'm so sorry, Dad. It totally slipped my mind. I'll run over there right now." Darrell headed back to the foyer and grabbed his wet jacket off the coat tree. "I'll be right back. But don't wait for me to have dinner—"

"I took care of the situation. When you didn't answer my mes-sages, I sent Bart."

Darrell had already pulled the zipper of his jacket halfway up. "Oh. Want me to go over later and see how the house is doing?"

"No need. It will be fine. I'd rather you weren't out driving around in the snow. Wash up and see if your mother needs any help in the kitchen. Dinner is ready."

Darrell didn't answer. He took off his jacket again and went into the kitchen, where Lily was setting the table.

Jessica glanced at him as he walked in. He could tell by her sym-pathetic look that she had overheard his father's reprimands.

"Hungry?" she asked quietly.

He nodded. "Smells good. What are we having?"

"Pork chops." Lily looked unhappy as she placed a fork beside each plate. "I wish we were vegetarians, Mom. It's so mean to eat animals. They're, like, our best friends now. Would I cook Amy Cutler with potatoes and vegetables, and eat her for dinner?" she added, mention-ing her best friend at school.

His mother turned from the stove where she was stirring a pot of noodles. Darrell could tell she was trying not to laugh. Lily sounded so serious.

"That's a good point, Lily. I think we should discuss it, as a family, and see what everyone else thinks."

Darrell thought he wouldn't mind being a vegetarian. He would at least try it. But he knew what his father's answer would be. Sam could barely last a week without a steak or a big juicy hamburger, and he didn't care how friendly the steer who had supplied it was.

His mother gave him another concerned look. "How was your day?"

"It was good," Darrell said, his mind returning to visions of the warehouse. "Today was really good."

CHAPTER NINE

IT'S PILING UP OUT THERE. THOSE WEATHER FORECASTERS didn't expect this much snow." Jean's mother gave the front yard one last assessing glance then snapped the living room curtain closed. "Now they say it will snow all day tomorrow. Maybe even through tomorrow night."

It was Thursday night. They had just finished dinner, and Jean was drying the pots and pans. "That's a real blizzard, Mom. I didn't hear it would be that bad."

"Turn on the TV. See for yourself. The highway is full of fender benders."

"That's too bad. I hope no one was seriously hurt." Jean fit the last of the pot covers into a cupboard next to the stove and began to wipe down the counter.

Jean could not recall her mother paying much attention to weather reports when she was younger. Cynthia had barely seemed aware of what was going on outdoors, emerging from her studio to be surprised by a spring storm, the heat of a July day, or the piles of snow that had fallen during a long February night. Now she was an avid fan of the Weather Channel, relishing the daily barometric dramas. Jean knew it was a cliché, but old people did love to fret about the weather, and her mother had slowly but surely joined their ranks.

"I guess we'll be stuck in the house awhile," Cynthia said. "Good thing you went to the supermarket today. I hope you got some ice melt. I'd better call Grant Keating and tell him not to come until Monday."

Jean had only been half listening to her mother's chatter, but she turned from the sink at the sound of Grant's name. "Monday? That's three days from now. I doubt it will snow that long, Mom. No matter what the Weather Channel says."

Her mother sighed. "Don't be such a wise apple. What if he drives over in the storm and has an accident? I'd be responsible."

"Not really." Jean turned back to the pots to hide her true reaction to her mother's decision. She didn't like the idea of not seeing Grant for three days. It seemed like a long time. "I agree he can't come tomorrow. Sounds like everyone should stay off the roads. But what about Saturday? You've given him a long list of projects. I bet he doesn't want to fall behind."

Her mother shrugged. "A day or two won't make any difference. He's capable, but I doubt he has many clients clamoring for his time."

The phone was on the table and her mother picked it up. She had pinned a scrap of paper with Grant's number on it to the bulletin board near the cellar door. Jean watched her squint at the board to make out the numbers.

Jean wiped off more counters and turned on the dishwasher while her mother talked to Grant.

"Monday. Yes, that's right." A pause while her mother listened. "Oh, don't worry about that. Jean is very handy with a shovel. Don't trouble yourself. We'll be fine."

Grant had offered to come over and shovel them out. That was considerate of him, Jean thought. She wouldn't mind the chance to see him, even if it was just to shovel snow together.

Too bad her mother had fended off the idea.

"Thank you. You stay safe, too." Cynthia said good-bye and put the phone aside. "He wanted to come and shovel snow. He's missing a day's work. He must need the money."

Jean felt her temper rise. "Maybe he offered to be helpful. To do us a favor. Did he ask to be paid?"

"No, he didn't ask. But I bet he expected to be." The local newspaper, the *Cape Light Messenger*, was on the table. Her mother opened it and scanned the pages. "Honestly, Jean, you're so naive sometimes. It's hard to believe, for a woman of your age."

"I try to think the best of people. If that seems naive to you . . . well, I can't help it." She folded a dish towel and hung it over a rack to dry. "Grant went out of his way to take those photographs for you. He did it as a favor and didn't expect a penny in return. I noticed you barely thanked him."

Grant had brought prints of the beach photos over in the morning, just as he promised. He looked very excited to deliver them, too. Her mother took the envelope, thanked him briefly, and set the package aside. She didn't even open it to look at his work.

"I was perfectly polite. I just didn't fawn all over him and feed his ego. Like some people around here might do."

"And what is that supposed to mean?" Jean didn't intend to raise her voice but couldn't help it.

"Whatever you think it means. I've seen the way you look at him.

And I've noticed the way you defend him. Don't deny it," she added, before Jean could reply. "I've known a lot of men like Grant Keating. Artistic types. They're clever and charming and thrive on attention and compliments. But the starry-eyed looks of one woman are just as good as the next. They get bored easily. Very easily. Believe me."

She nodded, looking satisfied at having had her say and undermining any hopes Jean might have about Grant.

Jean waited a long moment before she answered. "He is clever and charming. And talented. And he's been very respectful and patient with you, though perhaps you never noticed."

Her mother looked down at the newspaper. Jean thought she felt a twinge of conscience but, of course, would never admit it.

"I don't mind defending him," Jean continued. "I think he's a good person, and I enjoy his company. But I'm not nearly as naive you think. Or starry-eyed. If he leaves here tomorrow, I won't be surprised."

It wasn't a lie or even tough talk. Jean knew she would be unhappy if Grant left Cape Light. But deep inside, she half expected it. Cynthia's mouth was pursed in a frown. "All right, if you say so. But I'll bet dollars to donuts he will up and leave without a minute's warning to anyone. Don't say I didn't warn you."

Her mother let out a long breath. Jean suddenly worried that their argument had been a strain and felt instantly sorry for giving in to the goading. "Do you need your oxygen, Mom?"

"I'm fine. Why do you keep asking me that?" Cynthia pushed the newspaper aside and pulled her walker next to her chair. "I'm going to bed. I'll see you in the morning. God willing."

Jean took a few steps toward her. "Let me help you."

Her mother shook her head but would not meet her eye. Jean could tell she was short on breath and trying not to show it. "You stay put." Cynthia struggled out of the chair but managed to grab the walker and turn herself in the right direction. "I can take care of my-self. I've been doing it a long time."

Jean's instinct was to help. But she forced herself to remain still. "Good night, Mom. Call if you need anything."

Her mother ambled slowly from the kitchen, her back turned to Jean. She didn't reply.

Left alone in the kitchen, Jean stared out at the backyard, covered with snow, thick clumps coating the bushes and trees. The blank white space reminded her of the three long days that stretched between the quiet night and the next time she would see Grant.

TYLER AND LILY HAD CHEERED THURSDAY NIGHT WHEN THEY SAW the school-closing notice on TV. Sam was secretly happy, too. He felt lonely at times, on his own all day with little to do.

Friday morning, he woke up and checked the snow piled outside and still falling, as predicted. He cleaned up and rolled himself into the kitchen, following the scent of fresh coffee and looking forward to a hearty family breakfast.

He did find the coffeepot full and poured himself a mug, but Jessica was not at the stove, fixing eggs or pancakes, as she usually did on such a day. The house was eerily quiet.

Daisy padded over to his chair and he patted her head. "Where is everyone, pal?" he asked the dog.

Then he heard voices out in the yard. He wheeled his chair to the sliding door in the dining room, coffee mug in hand. The doors to the small barn were open and he spotted Lily, red-cheeked, striped scarf flying, chasing a goat around a corralled space. She was knee-deep in snow, and the goat sometimes disappeared into a drift and popped up again, like a crazy game at a fun fair.

Darrell emerged from the barn and strode over to help his sister. He secured the goat with the tether around its slim neck and led it back to the barn. At the same time, Jessica and Tyler emerged, carrying big wire cages. Sam spotted Buster, the cable-eating bunny. "Oh no, not that guy. He is not coming inside again. I just got the TV up and running," he murmured to Daisy.

But Jessica and her crew of helpers were soon coming in the side door, carrying the crates of rabbits, baby ducks, and an assorted menagerie of other small animals.

"Let's leave them in the mud room for now. I think they'll be warm enough here for a while. We can put the babies in the kitchen later," she told the kids. "I hope you don't mind, Sam," she called out. "We have to bring some animals inside today."

"I don't mind," he said, though he did. A little. "What about installing heat in the barn? When is that going to happen?"

"I'm working on it," Jessica promised.

Before Sam could comment, Lily said, "Don't you think Sassy should be inside, too, Mom?" He remembered that Sassy was the party pony Jessica had rescued about a week ago.

"I think she'll be fine, honey," he heard Jessica reply. "A pony can't come in the house."

"Your mom is right. I draw the line at ponies," Sam called out.

"But she's having a baby. You said so yourself," Lily replied.

Sam sat up straight in his chair. "Sassy is pregnant?" he called out. "Nobody told me that."

Jessica had shed her jacket and boots but still wore a scarf wrapped around her neck. A bright blue scarf that matched her eyes. With her cheeks red from the cold and her curly reddish-brown hair framing her face, Sam was suddenly distracted, noticing how pretty his wife was, after all these years together. As pretty as the day they had met.

"We just found out the other day, when the vet came to look her over," Jessica replied. "I'm sorry I forgot to mention it."

"That's okay, I guess," Sam murmured. "Are we having breakfast now, or did you guys eat without me?"

"Of course we didn't have breakfast without you." Jessica picked up an apron and tied it around her slim waist, then pulled a big bowl from a cupboard. "How about pancakes? Is that all right?"

"Sounds perfect. With some scrambled eggs on the side?"

"Will do."

"And some bacon?" he added.

"Dad . . . *really*?" He turned to see Lily standing by his chair, looking crushed. "Eggs are bad enough. We absolutely can't eat bacon anymore."

"No bacon? I don't remember agreeing to that rule."

"Let's talk about it later." Jessica turned and gave him a look. "I actually forgot to buy bacon, so it doesn't even matter."

Forgot conveniently, Sam thought. He was about to make a joke about Pinky supplying the missing side dish, but he sensed that touch of humor would not go over well. Especially with Lily. His wife and children were so serious about the animals. He suddenly felt like the only one who was not in sync.

Maybe it was because he was worried about the business side of taking in all these furred and feathered friends. It had only been two weeks or so since Jessica had jumped in full-time, and he knew she would get the financials under control soon. She was so organized and knowledgeable, so good with budgeting. She had been a bank manager, for goodness' sake. But every time he heard about the cost of care and feeding these orphans, he felt a wave of anxiety. The vet bill for a pregnant pony, for example. How much was that going to cost?

After breakfast, Jessica headed back out to the barn, but Tyler and

Lily stayed inside and kept Sam company. They played video games on the TV, and when that got boring, took out some old-fashioned board games—Monopoly, Battleship, and Clue—which Sam liked even better. Jessica always said he was the biggest kid in the family, and Sam knew it was true. Even at his age, he still loved to play games and liked to win at them, too. Tyler and Lily started calling him the one-armed bandit, since his right arm was still bandaged and out of action.

After Tyler and Lily headed upstairs to their rooms, Darrell wandered into Sam's office. "How's it going? Can I get you anything?"

"Thanks, I'm fine. Hey, want to play chess?" Sam asked, suddenly inspired.

Darrell laughed. "Don't you want a break from board games?"

"Chess isn't a board game. It's more of an intellectual pursuit," Sam countered.

"Okay, I'll get the set. And I have something to show you. A project I've been working on."

Sam sat back in his chair. "I'd love to see it. Let's take a look."

Darrell left the room and soon returned, carrying the wooden box that held the chess set and his laptop tucked under one arm. He set up the computer on the table in front of Sam then opened a file that showed pictures of an old building with a chain-link fence around it. Sam thought it looked familiar. He knew it was in town somewhere but couldn't recall the exact location.

"I was driving around near Aunt Molly's neighborhood, and I saw this old building, just off the Beach Road. It used to be a cannery, owned by a company called Tillerman. And before that, it was owned by Oliver Warwick, Grandma Lillian's first husband."

Sam looked over the photos of the old cannery, wondering where all this was going to lead. "I know who Oliver Warwick was, believe me."

"I thought that was an interesting coincidence. All things considered."

"Considering . . . what, exactly?" Sam asked.

"How the building can be rescued and renovated." Darrell changed the image on the screen, and Sam saw renderings of an attractive building that looked like it might be apartments. He quickly realized it was the cannery, magically transformed.

Darrell changed the image and Sam saw plans, confirming his guess and showing the building sectioned off into at least ten units of living space.

"Wow, Darrell, that's amazing. How did you figure all this out? I bet you get an A plus on this project."

"Inspector Hepburn has been helping me. He showed me around the inside of the place yesterday, and he's going to give me a set of the original blueprints. I also did some research in the county offices." Darrell turned the laptop around and searched for another file.

Sam glanced at the screen and saw what looked like a spreadsheet or budget. Which made sense. Students like Darrell should know how to figure out the costs of the plans they created. They needed to know the practical side of things, as well as the aesthetic.

"Is that the budget for your renovation?" he asked.

"A preliminary one. Charlie Bates told me that the town owns the property now and has no plans for it. I think the space would be ideal for apartment units, affordable housing for families in the village who can't afford to buy their own home. It even costs a lot to rent a place in Cape Light now, Dad. Some families have to cut back on essentials, like food and clothing, just to keep a roof over their heads."

"Yeah, it's tough out there," Sam agreed. "We're very fortunate. Very blessed. I like the way you're thinking, Darrell."

"Thanks, Dad. But it's just the way you and Mom taught us to think. I'd like to work for the common good, not sit in a plush office, designing mini-mansions."

Sam felt gratified to hear him say that. He and Jessica had always tried to instill solid values in their children. It was good to see that Darrell had embraced them and wanted to help those in need.

Darrell had known what it was to live in a house where there wasn't enough food to eat and the landlord was threatening eviction. It had taken the boy a long time to feel safe and secure. Though he had put those fears behind him, Sam knew that his son had never forgotten the early years of his life.

"Well, maybe your mom and I had something to do with it," Sam said with grin. "Still, I'm very proud of you for thinking that way. For holding on to those values."

Darrell looked pleased at Sam's praise. "Thanks, Dad. That means a lot to me."

"So, what's the plan? Are you going to pass all this information on to Charlie? He might do something with it."

Or might not, Sam realized. Charlie wanted to bring in developers who would build high-priced housing and condos. He had even tried to change the zoning last year but had been slapped down. The opposition was led by none other than Sam's sister-in-law, Emily. Years would pass before Charlie could try that again.

"I'll need to get Charlie involved, in order to take over the title to the property. But I'd like to find the funding and supervise it myself."

Sam nearly laughed out loud. Young men could be so brash. He was like that once himself, wasn't he?

"You're not an architect yet, Darrell. You haven't even finished your four-year degree."

"I can find an architect and an engineer to sign off on the plans and oversee things. I think Inspector Hepburn might help me. He's always wanted to do something more ambitious than sign inspection slips all day. He told me so himself. And he's a civil engineer. I bet he knows of an architect who would help."

"Okay, I guess that's possible. But what about the financing? How do you expect to pay for it?"

"Yesterday, when you got mad at me because I forgot to turn up the heat at the Marino house? I was in the county office and did some research about grants. I can probably get enough money from the county or even the state for a project like that. And Morgan Construction can build it."

Having ambitious goals at Darrell's age was one thing. But this was just pie-in-the-sky talk now.

"Darrell . . . I've never taken on such a big project in my life. Do I look as if I'm up to that challenge right now?" Sam waved his good hand at his casts.

"You can still supervise it, Dad. Sending a million text messages every day? I know you can do that," Darrell said in a sly tone. "And we can find a foreman experienced in big construction projects. It won't be that hard, Dad. I know we can do it."

His son's use of the term "we" touched Sam's heart. But it still sounded like a lot of crazy talk.

Sam didn't answer for a moment. He didn't want to say the wrong thing and crush Darrell's hopes or his "can do" spirit. That was not the right way to handle this, he knew.

"It's great to see you so inspired," he said carefully. "I can see that you truly love this work and are going to be great at it."

Darryl gave a modest shrug. "Thanks. I do feel fired up by this idea. I'm going to start applying for these grants and funding opportunities. I heard that some of the committees give out awards very quickly, as soon as they review and approve a project."

"Really? That's unusual." Sam didn't know what else to say. He wasn't sure how to steer Darrell back to reality.

What about finishing the semester and graduating? he wanted to ask. *What about graduate school, which you need to complete in order to be a real architect?*

But what was the point of arguing with him? Darrell would hit the reality wall soon enough. What grant committee was going to award several million dollars to a college kid? It just couldn't happen. Sam felt sure that this wonderful-but-outlandish idea would not amount to much beyond a good grade and a great presentation to add to grad school applications.

"Sure, keep working on it. It's good experience for you. But I think you're going to see that it's very difficult to finance a project of this size, and get all the permits and such, and get everyone to sign off who needs to. Sometimes it takes years to find the money and untangle all the complications on a plan like this."

"I know that," Darrell replied in an overly patient tone. "But I can at least try."

Sam nodded. "Yes, you can try. Try your best. As long as you don't neglect any of my projects. And I know what you're going to say now, so don't bother . . . 'No worries, Dad. Got it covered.'"

Darrell laughed. "That's right. That's just what I was going to say. Still want to play chess?"

"I do," Sam replied, relieved that their sticky conversation was over. "Set up the pieces. The one-armed bandit is back."

CHAPTER TEN

*S*NOW FELL ON AND OFF ALL DAY FRIDAY, JUST AS THE WEATHER forecasters—and her mother—predicted. Main Street had been eerily empty, with only the snowplow passing from time to time. Barbara Crosby had called, promising that she would come, despite the weather, but Jean's mother insisted that the visit wasn't necessary. Jean would have welcomed Barbara's cheerful company, but agreed with her mother and thought it best for the nurse to stay off the road. Jean was not looking forward to shoveling Saturday morning, but found some heavy boots, leg warmers, and mittens on Friday night and set them near the door, knowing it had to be done.

On Saturday morning, she woke to a sputtering, motorized sound. She looked out the window and saw a man pushing a snowblower, clearing a path from the front door to the sidewalk. It took her only seconds to recognize Grant steering the machine, though he wore a wool cap pulled low on his forehead and large sunglasses.

He was almost done with the path, an arc of snow flying out the side of the machine as he smoothly walked along behind it. Work that would have taken her several hours was now finished, even better than she could do it, in a matter of minutes.

Grant pushed the machine up the clean path and started on the driveway. Jean pulled a bathrobe on over her pajamas and ran downstairs.

The noise had woken up her mother, and she called from her bedroom, "Jean, what's that racket outside? It sounds like the house is coming down."

Jean walked into Cynthia's room, bringing the walker with her. "Grant is digging us out with a snowblower," she said.

"A snowblower?" Her mother sat at the edge of the bed and levered herself up. "After I told him not come?"

"I guess so." Jean tried not to smile but couldn't help it.

She helped her mother into the bathroom then quickly put on a pot of coffee. Grant had finished the driveway and was clearing the paths around the house. When he came near the back door, she opened it a crack and held the neck of her robe closed against the frigid air. "Grant, would you like some coffee?"

He smiled and shut the machine off. "No, thanks. I have to get this blower back to Vera's house. She wants to loan it to a neighbor."

"Oh, sure. Well . . . thanks for doing all our snow. I would have been out there for hours."

His smile grew wider. "That's why I did it. You can tell your mother that I wasn't disrespecting her wishes entirely. She told me not to shovel. But she never mentioned a snowblower."

Jean laughed. "I'll give her the message."

He waved, tugged his hat down, and started the machine again.

He steered it down the side path, toward his truck that was parked on the street.

Back in the kitchen, Jean poured two mugs of coffee. Cynthia sat and sipped her coffee. "Well, is he coming in? I heard you invite him."

"He has to get back to Vera's. By the way, he wants you to know that he didn't mean to disrespect your wishes. But you never mentioned a snowblower."

"Very funny," Cynthia replied, sounding more annoyed than amused.

Jean hid her grin behind her coffee mug. "Yes, I thought it was, too."

DESPITE THE HEAVY SNOWFALL, JEAN WASN'T CONCERNED ABOUT taking her mother to church Sunday morning. The roads were clear and the temperature much warmer than it had been on Friday or even Saturday.

Her mother was eager to deliver the Christmas ornaments she had made, which were carefully wrapped in tissue paper and filled two large cardboard boxes. Her mother was looking forward to attending the committee meeting after the service and getting full credit in person.

"Leave those boxes in the car, Jean. You can come out later and get them," her mother said when they arrived. Jean thought that was a good suggestion. It was enough just to maneuver her mother into church in her wheelchair.

They were early, for once. Reverend Ben stood at the big wooden doors, greeting congregation members. He bid them good morning with a warm smile and looked especially pleased to see her mother. He took her hand as he welcomed her. "Good to see you out and about,

Cynthia. I hope coming to church in this weather wasn't too much for you?"

"Not at all. I haven't felt this well in years. It's just a little snow, Reverend. We have to expect it this time of year, living up here."

"Yes, we do. Very true," Reverend Ben agreed.

Jean had to smile at her mother's offhand attitude, when just the other night the snowfall seemed a major calamity.

Tucker Tulley, one of the deacons, found them seats at the end of the aisle that accommodated the wheelchair. The service started a few minutes later. Jean's mother was pleased that they hadn't missed the lighting of the Advent candles this time, though she didn't know the family who stood at the altar and led the liturgy.

"I used to know everyone at this church," she whispered. "But I've been away a long time. People come and go."

"Well, you're back now. That's what matters," Jean replied.

"Yes, I am. For a little while, anyway," her mother murmured in a wistful tone.

The service seemed to go by quickly. Jean enjoyed the music, which inspired a Christmas spirit. The sanctuary was completely decorated now, with big wreaths decked with red bows, garlands of fresh pine, and a Christmas tree set up to the right of the pulpit.

Jean wondered if there were any Christmas decorations stored in her mother's house that she could use to decorate. There had to be some left in the attic or basement, though she hadn't come across them yet during her cleaning adventures. If she couldn't find any, she would buy a few. Her mother would probably say it was an extravagance, but Jean thought she would like to see the house decorated nicely, nonetheless. Jean thought it was important to deck the house out properly this year, to do what she could to give her mother a nice Christmas.

When the service was over, Vera met them in the narthex. "Are you staying for the meeting, Cynthia?"

"Wouldn't miss it," her mother replied. "I brought my ornaments. I made quite a few."

"Very good. I'll help you get in there. Jean can come back later and pick you up."

"You go with Vera, Mom. I'll leave the ornaments in the meeting room for you."

"All right. Be careful with them," her mother said. "I'll see you later."   \

Jean went out to the car to retrieve the boxes. As she opened the hatch of her SUV, she noticed two children, a girl and a boy, run over to the car next hers.

"Don't run in a parking lot," their mother called out to them. "You know it's not safe. Wait in the car for me."

Jean heard the car beep and the doors unlock. The children pulled the doors open and climbed in the back seat.

Jean had turned at the sound of the woman's voice and saw that it was Laurel Milner. She looked straight at Jean, and Jean saw a flash of recognition. There was no hiding today from Kevin's old girlfriend.

"Laurel, how nice to see you," Jean said with a smile.

"Good to see you, too, Jean. I saw you in church this morning with your mother, but I was too far away to say hello. Are you in town visiting her?"

"I moved back here just before Thanksgiving. She's not well. I came back to take care of her," Jean explained. "But at least she can still get out and see old friends. That seems to have given her spirits a boost. How about you? I thought you lived in North Carolina."

"I did. But I just got divorced and moved back to be near my family. We've been living with my parents, but I'm starting a new job at

Southport Hospital this week. We'll find our own place around here soon."

"Congratulations. What will you do there?"

"I'm an RN. I specialize in maternity care."

"That must be fun, working with new mothers and newborn babies."

Laurel smiled. "It is. Most of the time."

So Laurel had not only gone to college but turned out to be an accomplished health-care professional. Her mother had been wrong with that prediction.

"I see you have children of your own. They're very cute. How old are they?"

"Avery is seven and Timmy is five. They can be a handful, but it's good to have my parents around. They've been a big help so far."

"Sounds like you made a good choice moving back here," Jean said.

"I think I did. How's your brother doing? Last I heard he was living in California."

Jean knew she wouldn't escape this meeting without some mention of Kevin, but it felt awkward nonetheless, even after all this time.

"Yes, he's still in California. He works at the same insurance company he joined right after law school. He was married for a few years, but he's divorced now."

"Oh . . . well, sometimes that can be for the best," Laurel said. "Please tell him I said hello and wish him well."

"I will. It was nice to catch up with you, Laurel. I hope to see you around town again soon."

"Same here, Jean. Say hello to your mom for me, too."

Jean thought that was good of her, considering the role her mother had played in Laurel and Kevin's breakup. Jean watched as Laurel got into her car and drove away.

Laurel Milner . . . After all these years, she seemed the same, still soft-spoken and kind. Still very pretty, too. Jean could understand why her brother had loved Laurel. And why he might love her still.

Jean brought the tree ornaments into the church and set them on the table at the back of Fellowship Hall. The meeting had started and Emily Warwick was up front, speaking to the group, but she caught her mother's eye. Her mother looked pleased to see the delivery and nodded, then turned back to listen to Emily.

Jean was happy to see her mother so involved, even though she couldn't work at the fair. Taking part meant a lot to her. Jean left the quiet church and started walking across the village green. Her mother's meeting would take about two hours, and she decided to have lunch at the Clam Box. Then maybe stroll Main Street and browse for Christmas gifts, though she didn't have many to buy this year.

The long slope of the green was filled with children on sleds and toboggans. Jean could remember sledding there herself, as a girl with her father and brother. She stopped to watch for a moment, excited children launching themselves from the top of the hill and parents at the bottom, waiting as sleds in all shapes and colors came flying by.

She felt a tap on her shoulder and turned to find Grant smiling down at her. "Enjoying the show?"

"I am," she admitted. "How about you? Have you been taking photos of the kids?"

That seemed obvious from the camera that hung around his neck. "I got some good shots. I've been experimenting with different angles. I found this old sled at Vera's. I'd really like a shot going down alongside them."

Jean laughed. "I guess that explains the clumps of snow in your hair?"

He laughed and touched his hair. There was a bit of snow, and her hand ached to reach out and brush it away, but she resisted the urge.

"The experiment has not been entirely successful. Yet."

"Too hard to steer the sled and take the photo at the same time?"

"Exactly. I can't quite work it out . . . but maybe you could help me?"

"Go down on the sled with you?" She thought he must be teasing.

"Why not? It's big enough and very sturdy. It can definitely hold us."

Jean eyed the old wooden sled. It was a big sled with metal runners and long enough for both of them to fit. But she still didn't want to. "I couldn't. Really."

"Of course you can. You're not afraid, are you? Look at those little kids. If they can do it, we can."

"Are you going to take photos on the way down?"

"This first run is just for fun." He was using a small camera today that she had never seen. He slipped it into his parka pocket and grabbed her hand, the other hand tugging along the heavy old sled.

"Come on, Jean. Let's show those little squirts how it's done."

His competitive spirit with the elementary school set made her laugh. And she liked the feeling of her hand in his as they marched to the top of the hill.

Grant parked the sled at the edge of the hill, away from the high traffic. He sat on the front of the sled and grabbed the rope attached to the steering piece. "Come on. Sit down. There's plenty of room."

Jean could not believe she had been talked into this stunt, but she sat down behind him, balancing her feet on the edge of the sled.

"Ready?" he shouted. She could feel him slip the sled around so it was pointing straight down.

"No, not yet!" she shouted back. "There's no place to hold on."

She tried to grip the edges of the sled, but her gloved hands kept sliding off.

"Hold on to me, silly. Or you'll fall right off."

"All right." She'd thought of that . . . and had felt too shy. But if he insisted. She rested her hands at his sides, lightly holding on to his jacket.

"Ready, set . . . go!" Grant pushed off with his booted feet, and they were suddenly flying down the slick hill.

Jean pressed herself to Grant's back and circled his waist with both arms, holding on for dear life.

She heard someone screaming—and realized it was her.

The world flew by in a white blur, and as quickly as it had started, it was over. The sled slowed, hitting a few bumps at the bottom of the hill, then glided to a stop.

Jean felt breathless and shocked. "Wow! That was really something."

"Glad you enjoyed it." He grinned at her. "Even though my ears will be ringing for a week. You have a loud voice when you put your mind to it." He jumped up and extended his hand. Jean took hold and jumped up, too. "I never would have guessed you could scream so loud."

"Sorry about that. You should hear me on a roller coaster."

Grant laughed. "Remind me to sit in a different seat when the time comes." He kept hold of her hand, and she walked beside him as they headed uphill again with the sled. "Now you're going to steer, and I'll sit in back and take some photos."

"Go down again? With me steering?" Jean wanted to help him, but she didn't really like that idea.

"That's the plan. If I get any good photos out of this stunt, I'll give you half credit. How does that sound?"

"Generous . . . though I may not live to share the glory."

He turned and met her gaze. His smile warmed her down to her toes. "Trust me, Jean. This is going to be even more fun."

The funny thing was she did trust him. Despite every good reason she had not to.

They climbed on the sled again. Jean felt very vulnerable in front, with nothing between her and the icy slope but thin air. Grant showed her how to hold the rope and steer, and how to point the sled forward when it was time to launch. Then he climbed on the back and took out his camera. "Ready?"

"I guess so." Her voice came out in a squeak.

He pushed off with his feet again and gravity took over. Jean heard herself screaming even louder this time. She felt one of Grant's strong arms wrapped around her waist and heard the clicking of the camera shutter. "Great . . . this is great, Jean."

Jean couldn't answer. The bottom of the hill was coming up fast. She pulled to the right, steering the sled toward an empty landing spot. But she yanked on the rope too hard and realized her mistake too late. Seconds later, the sled flipped up on one side. She and Grant slipped off the other, landing in a tangle under a big pine tree.

Grant was laughing at the crash, but she also heard him sputtering out a mouthful of snow. She had landed on her side and sunk into a drift. She felt stuck a moment and finally turned over, finding herself face-to-face with him.

"Sorry. I must have pulled the rope too hard."

He smiled into her eyes and brushed snow off her face with his hand. "No need to apologize. This is part of the fun, Jean. I think so, anyway."

Then he kissed her, his warm mouth a sudden contrast to the icy snow. Jean lifted her hand and touched his hair. Her head was swimming—from the ride and Grant's touch. She wasn't sure if she was freezing or melting, and didn't really care.

He pulled his head away and whispered. "We'd better get up. Before we get run over."

Jean laughed. "Good point."

They were actually far from the crowd and the busy lanes of sleigh riders, but it was still a possibility. Grant took her hand and pulled her up from the snow again. They left the sled near his truck and headed to the Clam Box to warm up.

The diner was very busy, but they were soon shown to a table near the window. Jean looked over the menu. It hadn't changed in all the years she had lived in the town—or since she had been away.

"What's good here?" Grant asked.

"Not too much, as I recall. Charlie Bates is still the cook," Jean replied with a smile. "The chowder isn't bad. We know it will be hot."

Grant closed his menu. "I'm sold."

After a waitress came by and took their order, Jean excused herself to check her cell phone. "My mother is in a meeting at church. I just want to see if she needs me to pick her up early."

She didn't find a message from her mother, but she did find one from Kevin, a reply to the e-mail she had sent after their last phone call. He had taken a long time to answer. For a moment, she thought maybe that was a good sign and meant he might be changing his mind. Her heart sank when she read his message. He knew she was disappointed, but he couldn't shake free of his commitments and come home for Christmas. He had tried again to work it out, but he couldn't change his plans. Her eyes skimmed his last paragraph.

I appreciate that you're taking such good care of Mom. Heaven
knows, she doesn't really deserve that sort of attention from you.
I understand that she's failing and I promise, I will come East
soon. Take care of yourself and don't overdo it.

Jean nearly laughed at the sign-off. "Don't overdo it?" she muttered. "What's that supposed to mean?"

Across the table, Grant gave her a curious look. "Bad news?"

Jean sighed and put the phone away. "Not exactly. And not a surprise either. I was trying to persuade my brother to come home for
Christmas. He lives in California and rarely makes it back here for a
visit, though my mother dotes on him. She's sure the sun rises and sets
on her son, Kevin." Jean couldn't help it. She rolled her eyes as she
explained the family dynamic.

Grant nodded and popped an oyster cracker in his chowder. "I get
it. Meanwhile, you're right under her nose, working day and night to
keep her comfortable, and she hardly has a kind word."

His observations were accurate but his delivery a bit blunt, Jean
thought. "I know what it looks like. But there's more to it. This is a
choice I've made," she explained. "The truth is that until now, I kept
my distance, too, in my own way—though I was living in Maine, not
quite so far as Kevin. But this is my mother's last Christmas. There's
really no doubt of that. Her doctor is surprised she's lasted this long."

"I'm sorry to hear that," Grant said. "I know she's got her health
challenges, but she always seems so feisty. I never realized that the
situation is so dire."

"She puts on a good act for visitors. And I will say, when I first
arrived, she seemed in very low spirits. But she's definitely livened up
the last two weeks, going back to church and helping with the fair.
Taking up her painting again."

"You've helped her a lot, Jean. Maybe the doctors are wrong. Maybe she'll live longer, since you're taking care of her."

"I wish that were true," Jean said honestly. "But there are indisputable signs that her heart is getting weaker. The congestion is increasing and her organs are shutting down."

"I'm sorry . . . Isn't there anything they can do?"

Jean shook her head. "Nothing short of a heart transplant would help, and her body is so worn and fragile, she would never survive the surgery."

"No wonder you want your brother to visit. Doesn't he get it?"

She shrugged. "I've tried to explain it to him. I don't know what else to do."

Grant reached over and took her hand. "It sounds to me like you've done all you can. The ball is in his court. You can't feel guilty if he doesn't face up to his responsibility."

Jean met his gaze. She appreciated the way he listened to her, hearing her out and not interrupting with a lot of advice. It felt good to have someone in her corner who understood.

But she still felt bad about Kevin's decision. She felt there must be something more she could do. She just wasn't sure what it was.

AFTER LUNCH, GRANT WALKED HER BACK ACROSS THE GREEN TO THE church. "It's a beautiful old building," he said, taking in the church from a distance. "I love those gray stones. I should take some pictures of it. I'd like to take a look around inside sometime, too."

"You've already met Reverend Ben. I'm sure he'd give you a tour sometime—or wouldn't mind if you wanted to explore on your own. There are some stunning stained glass windows in the sanctuary. And a huge, old pipe organ. I bet it's very photogenic."

"I bet it is. I'll have to check it out sometime soon."

Why soon? Jean wondered. Did that meant he was leaving town soon? Despite the wonderful afternoon they had spent together, her mother's harsh words rang in her head. *He'll up and leave without a word to anyone,* she had predicted. Jean didn't want to believe that. She pushed the thought away and focused on Grant's conversation again.

"My family didn't belong to a church when I was growing up," he said. "But my wife attended regularly. I didn't go with her either."

He had been married? That was news. "You've never mentioned that you were married," she said.

"I was. Happily, too. My wife passed away. Almost ten years ago now."

Jean felt sorry for asking. She could see it was still hard for him to talk about. "I'm sorry for your loss. That's very sad."

"Yes, it was. She was young. Too young."

Jean felt uncomfortable asking more questions. "You must miss her," she said.

"It was very hard at first. I was very angry. That's when my entire life changed. For the better, I'd say, now. But it was a difficult, confusing time for me. I'll always miss her, but I've accepted it." He glanced at Jean and then back at the church. "I still like to sit in an empty church from time to time, to gather my thoughts. To try to feel what she felt there," he confessed.

Jean didn't answer for a moment. She wasn't sure what to say. He was a very sensitive person. Another quality she felt drawn to.

"I was brought up in this church, but I haven't attended regularly since I left for college. I've been taking my mother to the service the last few weeks. I thought I'd be bored. But I don't mind coming at all. Reverend Ben always has something interesting and wise to say."

"Maybe I'll try it sometime," Grant said. They had reached the church. Jean thanked him for lunch and the sledding. "My pleasure, Jean. Even our crash landing was fun."

She had to agree with that. She thought he might kiss her good-bye. He seemed to be thinking of it but just touched her cheek a moment. Then his hand dropped away.

"I'll see you tomorrow," he said.

She nodded. "See you then."

She felt lucky to have met up with Grant today and to have spent a few hours together. She entered the church with a light, happy heart. Happier still to know it wouldn't be long before she would see him again.

CHAPTER ELEVEN

$\curlywedge$

*A*FTER ALL THE FAMILY TOGETHERNESS ON FRIDAY AND Saturday, Sam didn't mind being alone in the house Sunday morning. Jessica had taken Tyler and Lily to church and was probably still at the Christmas Fair meeting, he figured. Darrell had offered to keep him company, but Sam sent him off to the gym around noon. He knew that's what Darrell really wanted to do, not babysit his father.

Sam was content to work in his office, catching up on some invoices and billing. He had not been one hundred percent sure that Darrell would be able to supervise the business, but he couldn't deny the kid was doing a good job so far. Except for that one blip on Thursday afternoon. The fact was that Sam was able to keep billing his customers and have a bottom line, which was more than he had expected.

While an invoice for the extra cost of Mrs. Turner's arched window printed out, he considered what he might make himself for lunch. A sandwich, probably, if bread was in reach. Or maybe just some salad with anything he could grab from the fridge.

His plans were interrupted by a crashing sound coming from the kitchen. Were Jessica and the kids home? He wouldn't mind having someone make him a sandwich. "Jess, are you back?"

He turned his wheelchair to face the doorway. Three white cockatiels swooped overhead, crossing in mid-air, like fighter jets in an air show. Sam ducked and covered his head with his good hand while the birds gained altitude and circled near the ceiling.

Even more alarming was the parade of animals hopping, ambling, and tumbling down the hallway, many of them turning into his office—puppies chasing kittens, mother dogs chasing puppies, several guinea pigs running for their lives. He recognized Pinky, the piglet, and Buster, the cable-chewing rabbit.

He rolled toward the doorway to get a better a look. It was slow going, since he didn't want to run anyone over. He could barely make it close enough to the door to get a look down the hallway.

It was animal mayhem. All the crates and corrals Jessica had set up in the house must have fallen down, or opened somehow. The animals were taking over the house. Sam could hear them barking, hissing, and quacking at each other, and in between that, objects around the living room and dining room being knocked down. Including the sound of breaking glass.

He grabbed his cell phone and called Jessica. When he heard her pick up, he shouted into the phone. "Jess? Where are you?"

"On the way to Carlisle. I just got a call about some lambs at a fiber farm. Are you all right?"

"No, I'm not. Not at all. I mean, I'm not hurt or anything. But the animals are all over the place. I can't even get out of my office. You have to come home and put them back in their cages. Better yet, put them back outside, where they belong."

"Calm down, Sam. And stop shouting at me. Which animals got loose? The birds? I put some extra wire on their cage but it must have come loose."

"The birds are the least of my worries. You don't understand. They're *all* loose. I heard a big crash in the kitchen. The cages must have fallen down or something."

"Oh, dear . . . I'm sorry . . . But we just reached the farm. I'll grab the lambs and come right home. The kids will be so disappointed if we don't save them, Sam."

What about me? I need saving, too! he wanted to say. But he doubted even that would persuade her.

"Sit tight. I'll be home in less than an hour," Jessica said.

He doubted that. But he had no choice. He peered over the edge of his chair and saw a duckling waddle by. "I could not be sitting any tighter, believe me."

JESSICA FOUND HIM ASLEEP IN HIS WHEELCHAIR. HE HAD MANAGED to back it into his lair and had turned on the TV, then fell asleep watching a news talk show. He heard her come into the office and opened his eyes.

"Sam? We're back. Sorry for the mess. I think those pesky cats unlatched a few crates and it caused a chain reaction. I can't leave the cats loose. They're too smart for their own good."

He yawned and stretched his good arm. "Pesky cats, huh?"

"The kids are putting all the animals back in their crates and cages," she said calmly. "I'll clean up later. Were you able to get any lunch?"

The last question made him even more annoyed. His stomach was growling so loud, he was sure she could hear it. "How could I get anything to eat? You don't understand. I've been trapped in this room for hours. I was afraid to roll my chair and run something over. Then I'd really be the bad guy." He tried to hold on to his temper, but he couldn't help venting.

Jessica put a hand on her hip. "Was it really that bad?"

"Yes, it was. I'm not sure this animal rescue thing is working out, Jess. It's like chaos around here."

Her expression fell. "But you said it was the right thing to do. That you fully supported me and I should follow my bliss," she replied, an edge to her tone. "Didn't you say that?"

"I did," he agreed. "But I never thought it would be like this. There's no peace in our house anymore. I like animals. You know I do. But I don't want to live in a zoo."

She looked like she might cry, and he immediately felt a surge of regret. Still, he had to speak his mind. He and Jess were open and honest with each other.

Jessica took a calming breath. "I know I'm not managing things perfectly, Sam. But there's a learning curve here. The reason we've got so many animals in the house is because I thought the heat in the barn would be finished by now. I can't let the poor little things freeze. What kind of rescue center is that?"

"The heat isn't finished because it's not even started," he pointed out. "I thought you were taking care of that."

"The estimate I got from that plumber you told me to call was too high. I'm sure I can get the work done for less."

"No rush. It will be spring soon. Then we won't need to worry about it at all."

"Very funny." He could tell she was mad at him now. "I can't help it if these animals need attention. I thought you understood that. Many of them have been abused or are ailing and need extra care."

"What about me? I need attention. I need extra care. Pinky the piglet gets more attention than I do."

"You know that isn't true, Sam. You get more than your share around here."

Sam couldn't deny it. He was running out of arguments.

"I'll go back to a job in a bank. Is that what you want?" she asked.

"No . . . that's not it, Jess." He meant it, too. "I don't want you to go back to a bank job. To any office job."

"Then what do you want?"

She sounded exasperated and he felt the same. He shook his head and grabbed the controls of his chair. "I just want to be able to roll my chair into the kitchen and make myself a sandwich."

She frowned at him. "Stay there. I'll make it for you."

"No, thank you. I can do it." He heard his voice get loud again. He took a calming breath. "I need to get out of this room a little today. As long as the coast is clear."

"The coast is clear," she promised. She gave him one last look, then turned and left the room.

Sam turned his chair on and followed very slowly, scanning his path for stray critters who might still be on the loose. He hated to argue with Jessica. Especially when it didn't accomplish anything but leave them both with hurt feelings.

SAM WOULD HAVE BEEN HAPPY TO FORGET ABOUT HIS OUTBURST, BUT it seemed Jessica could not let go of it that quickly. Even after he apologized. Or at least tried to.

On Tuesday, the atmosphere between them was still tense. Never mind the poor creatures in the barn, Sam was feeling a distinct chill in his own house.

He had just finished talking to a client when he heard the doorbell ring. He rolled his chair into the hall just as Jessica opened the door. Reverend Ben was on the doorstep. Sam was happy to see him.

"Good morning, Reverend," Jessica greeted him.

"I just stopped by to look in on Sam. If he's busy, I can come back another day," their minister said.

"I'm the least busy guy in town, Reverend," Sam called from the hallway. "Come on back to my man cave and see for yourself."

Reverend Ben laughed and handed Jessica his hat and jacket. "We all need a room of our own."

"Some of us more than others," Sam heard Jessica reply quietly.

Sam rolled into his office and turned his chair. Reverend Ben soon appeared in the doorway. "How are you doing, Sam? Looks like you're very mobile in that chair."

"I can get around the house well enough, but it's hard to go out anywhere. I'll be glad to get rid of these wheels. The doctor said I should be ready for a smaller cast on my legs and crutches by next week."

"That's good progress. You must be healing well."

"I guess so. Yesterday was two weeks since my fall. It seems much longer," Sam admitted. "I'm going stir-crazy cooped up in the house. Especially with the snow. On Sunday, I was actually trapped in this room for hours."

"Trapped? How so?" Reverend Ben took a seat on the sofa, next to Sam's wheelchair.

Sam explained how everyone had gone out and he was fine being alone, at first. Until all the animals got loose and Jessica was too far away to come back and rescue him.

"I know it sounds funny, but it wasn't amusing to be trapped in here while Jessica's menagerie took over the house. And when she got home," he added, in a quieter voice, "we had a big argument. I tried to apologize, but she's still mad at me."

Reverend Ben's expression was thoughtful and concerned. "You argued about the animals getting loose or about her rescue work?"

"One thing led to another," Sam admitted. "It's not that I want her to go back to an office job. I really don't," he insisted. "But this is not what I expected. She's working even longer hours with the animals than she ever did at the bank. Running off at all hours to rescue sheep or ducks or a pony that turns out to be pregnant. I know that I told her it was fine with me to quit her job and try this, but I'm not sure anymore. It feels like a lot right now, on top of my accident and being stressed about our finances."

"I understand. You certainly have a lot on your plate, Sam," the reverend said. "How is Darrell working out? Has he been able to supervise for you?"

"I had my doubts, I'll admit it. But he's doing a great job, managing the crews and keeping the jobs on schedule. And he's a real natural at handling the clients when problems pop up."

"So the business is running smoothly?" Reverend Ben replied. "And you have an income from the work, the same that was expected when you were well?"

Sam suddenly realized what Reverend Ben was getting at. "Yes, we do. And I did tell Jessica that we'd be fine, and we didn't need the rescue center to turn a profit for a while."

"I'm sure she appreciated you saying that. She seems to have a real calling for caring for these creatures who would otherwise be abandoned or left sick to die. Or even slaughtered. She is truly doing God's work, watching over His creation. We have to give her credit for that."

"She sure is. And with amazing patience and compassion. It's rubbing off on the kids, too. Lily wants to be a veterinarian and says we have to stop eating meat."

Reverend Ben laughed. "How's that campaign going?"

"I might be the only holdout left." Sam smiled then sighed. "Maybe I just lost it Sunday because I feel so cooped up and unproductive. It's hard for me to be stuck in the house all day while everyone is out having a life."

Reverend Ben reached over and patted his shoulder. "But you do have a life, Sam. A good life and a family who loves you. You need to be more patient with yourself. You said it yourself. It's only been two weeks. Healing is a process. Perhaps this time of inactivity will be good for you."

"Good for me? How?" Sam couldn't see that.

Reverend Ben shrugged. "I don't know exactly. You'll have to wait and see. But it's all part of God's plan. You'll find the gifts, the things you can be grateful for in this challenge, if you look for them."

Sam considered his words. "A long time ago, you told me Darrell was a godsend, a wild card I didn't expect. I guess that's been a gift in all this mess. To see how mature and capable my son is."

Reverend Ben nodded. "God has a way of dealing a wild card when we need it most."

Sam thought a moment. "Maybe this experience is supposed to teach me to have more patience. Jessica needs to manage things a little better, but I was out of line on Sunday, blowing my top the way I did."

Reverend Ben looked pleased to hear Sam's admission. "You said that you apologized and it didn't help?"

Sam sighed. "I sort of apologized . . . I think I did, anyway. I'll try again. I'll be more sincere this time," he added.

"Good plan. If she doesn't make up with you, give her time. Try again after that, if you have to," Reverend Ben advised.

"I don't think it will come to that. Jess and I can usually talk things out. In a month or two, I'll be up and out of the house again. It won't matter if she has elephants roaming around the living room. I won't be here to see it."

Reverend Ben agreed with a grin. "It's important to focus on the big picture . . . and hide the peanuts."

Sam laughed. "Good point. I'll try to remember when the time comes."

Sam waited for a chance to talk to Jessica, but she was busy all morning in the barn and then had to speak with a vet who was nice enough to make a house call to examine the pregnant pony.

While the vet was visiting, Sam worked in the kitchen. He managed to set the table for two, heat up some soup, and even make two turkey sandwiches. He saw the vet's truck drive off and noticed a text on his phone from Jessica. Vet just left. I'll be right in to make your lunch.

Sounds good, Sam texted back. I'm waiting in the kitchen.

A few minutes later, Jessica came in the side door. He heard her hang up her jacket and kick off her boots. He could tell by her body language that she was still annoyed with him. But he greeted her with a smile.

She looked at the table and the food he had made and then looked back at him. "You did all this? By yourself?"

"Slowly, but surely," he replied. "It's just soup and sandwiches. I couldn't reach the chips or the pickles."

"I'll get the rest." Jessica washed her hands and was soon sitting at the table across from him. She took a bite of the sandwich. "What's up, Sam? The last time you cooked for me, you wanted to buy a new truck."

Sam laughed and felt color rise in his cheeks. "Did I actually do that?"

"Yes, you did."

"This is not about a new truck," he assured her. "It's a peace offering. I'm sorry I blew up at you on Sunday. I said a lot of things I didn't really mean. Since the accident, I've been feeling really cooped up. With the snowstorm and then getting stuck in the office . . . I just hit a wall. I know you love this work and you're great at it. The last thing I want to do is spoil it for you."

Jessica put her sandwich down. "I appreciate you saying that, Sam. I know you feel cooped up and frustrated. But I've been thinking that maybe this isn't the right time for me to try the rescue work. The well-being of our family and your well-being and peace of mind are more important, don't you think? I can go back to an office job for now and try the rescue work full-time someday in the future."

Sam shook his head. "I don't want you to, Jess. I'm sorry if I made you feel that's what I think you should do. I'm not worried about keeping our income going while I recover, honestly. Darrell really is keeping the business on track."

"Yes, I can see that he is," she agreed. She met his gaze and Sam felt a little better. It looked as if her anger at him was melting.

"I know things have started off a little rockier than we expected," she went on. "I should have realized that the barn needed heat, for one thing. And I can't take in every homeless animal on the planet," she added, making him grin.

"Thank goodness you realized that," he replied. "You'll get it under control soon, I'm sure. In the meantime, I can be more patient. A lot more patient."

Jessica looked pleased to hear that. "And you'll stop making jokes about eating them? I know you think it's funny, but Lily takes you seriously."

Sam smiled. "Agreed. No more eating-animal jokes. Especially no cracks about Pinky and craving pigs in a blanket. It would be okay to eat some, though, don't you think? If we call them tiny hot dogs wrapped in biscuit dough?"

Jessica laughed and took his hand across the table. "I think that would be all right."

"Good. Everything's settled. We're back on track."

Jessica smiled and nodded. "We're back on track, Sam. But since you're actually so able in the kitchen, despite that chair, I wouldn't mind if you started dinner?"

"Rats. I knew this fixing-lunch scheme was going to backfire." Sam laughed and Jessica did, too.

Sam doubted that Jessica was serious. But it sure felt good to laugh with his wife again.

LATE WEDNESDAY AFTERNOON, GRANT AND CYNTHIA SAT AT THE kitchen table, going over the list of repairs he had completed and a few more that were needed. Jean had made everyone mugs of hot tea and stood at the counter, sipping from her own and making a shopping list. It suddenly struck her, as she listened in on the conversation, that Grant would soon be finished working on her mother's house. What would happen then? Jean had grown accustomed to seeing him every day, though they didn't get to talk much, and when they did, her mother was usually in the room.

She would never admit it to anyone, but just the sight of Grant around the property and the possibility of spending some part of the day with him cheered her. It would feel lonely when he was gone, with just-every-other-day-visits-from-Barbara and her mother for company. Very lonely.

"All right, put new caulk around the upstairs bathtub, too. If you think it really needs it. It is looking dingy," her mother said.

"It's more than dingy, Cynthia. You're liable to get a leak there soon," Grant explained. "There will be water running down the walls, a leak in the kitchen ceiling, and all kinds of problems."

Her mother's expression was skeptical. "In for a penny, in for a pound, I guess. But that's the last of it. Anything else will have to wait for the new owner," she murmured. "He'll be taking over soon."

She meant Kevin, of course. Jean glanced at her mother. It never failed to surprise her how calmly her mother spoke about her own imminent passing. Though Jean still couldn't tell if that calm, offhand attitude was just a smoke screen to hide her fear. She had to be a little afraid. Wasn't everyone?

The phone rang, and her mother picked it up off the table. "Hello, Vera," she said. "How are you today?"

Jean wondered if listening to the old women chatter would make Grant impatient. Once her mother and Vera Plante started talking, the call could go on for an hour. He sat looking down at the repair list, making small notes in the margin.

"A party Friday night? What time would that be? Well . . . I suppose I can join you. If Jean drives me. Let me ask her."

Her mother covered the phone with her hand. "Vera is having a little get-together for the Christmas Fair committee on Friday night. Can you drive me there?"

"Of course I can." Jean was happy that her mother wanted to go.

Cynthia put the phone next to her ear again. "Jean will bring me over. What time should I come?" She paused, listening. "Crochet hooks? I think I have some extras. I have to look in my knitting bag. I'll call you back later and let you know. Someone is waiting for me," she said, glancing at Grant. "I have to go. Good-bye, Vera."

"Now, where were we? Oh, right. You were putting in new caulk around the upstairs tub. And that's absolutely it."

"That's it," Grant agreed.

"So you'll be done with everything on Friday?" her mother asked.

"That's right. Too bad you're going to a party. I thought we could celebrate." Jean knew he was teasing and so did her mother, Jean was sure. But Cynthia seemed flustered and even blushed a little.

"What a silly idea. What is there to celebrate? You've just done a few simple repairs. One would think you renovated the Taj Mahal." Her words were blunt but her tone was humorous. He had the rare knack of bringing out a pleasant side in her mother, Jean thought, one she didn't show to most people.

Grant stood up and put on his jacket, then picked up his knapsack. "The Taj Mahal could use a little fresh paint here and there. Maybe that will be the next project."

Cynthia gazed up at him. "I wouldn't be surprised. Send us a postcard." She looked over at Jean as if to say, "See what I mean? Here one day, heading for the wild blue yonder the next."

Grant was at the back door, about to go. He suddenly turned and looked at Jean. "Looks like your Subaru is blocking the truck. Mind moving it for me?"

"Oh, sorry." Jean grabbed her coat and car keys. He opened the door and politely let her pass through first. Once they were outside, she said, "I meant to leave it on the street. I just forgot."

"That's all right. I would have moved it for you. I just wanted to talk to you alone for a minute before I left."

He was walking beside her down the path to the driveway. When he turned to smile at her, his face was very close. The sun had not quite set; the horizon in the west glowed with layers of gray-blue, lavender, and pink clouds. The eastern skies were already inky blue, with the first stars starting to appear.

They reached her car, and he turned to her. "Would you like to have dinner with me Friday night? It sounds as if your mother will be occupied. I thought we could go out someplace nice."

"To celebrate the repairs?" She was thrilled by the invitation but couldn't resist teasing him.

"That's not exactly what I had in mind. Besides, it's not like I renovated the Taj Mahal."

She laughed. "I'd love to have dinner with you. I'll drop my mother off at Vera's and we can leave from there."

"Good idea. I look forward to it, Jean." He smiled down into her eyes.

"Me, too." Did she sound too eager? Too interested? *Maybe I do,* she thought. *But he already knows that.*

CHAPTER TWELVE

⌖

ᴇʏ, ᴘᴀʟ. Yᴏᴜ'ʀᴇ ʜᴏᴍᴇ ᴇᴀʀʟʏ. Dɪᴅ ʏᴏᴜ ᴘɪᴄᴋ ᴜᴘ ᴛʜᴇ flooring for the Turners?" Sam turned at the sound of Darrell's heavy steps entering his office. Sam had been watching TV but turned it off as he greeted his son.

"Picked it up, had Mrs. Turner look it over, and stored it in a safe place so it can age a few days. Just like you said. I even had a little time to spare and stopped at Village Hall." Darrell's face lit with a smile. "I showed Inspector Hepburn my drawings and plans. He agreed to work on the project with me. He said the town has needed something like this for years and it's very worthwhile. He said he'll talk to people on the town council about it, and he's even going to find an architect who will sign off on everything."

Sam was surprised to hear that. Jim Hepburn was a cautious, conservative guy. Was he actually going to jump on board with this pie-in-the-sky plan? Cooked up by a college kid, no less? Even if the college kid in question was his son, that still didn't make it feasible.

"That's surprising," Sam admitted.

"Why do you say that?" Darrell flopped into a big leather armchair.

"I just think it is, that's all. I know Jim. He's not the kind of guy who goes out on a limb. In fact, he'd have to inspect and certify the limb ten times before he'd even think of it."

Darrell didn't even crack a smile. "He's taking me seriously, Dad. That's what counts here."

"I take you seriously," Sam replied. "But I don't think you have any idea how complicated this project will be. Have you even figured out a budget?"

"I did. Sort of," Darrell added more honestly. "I need to do more research for that. I thought maybe you could help me."

"Me? That's over my head, pal. Home extensions, new kitchens, dormers—that's my territory. I have no idea how to estimate the cost of an apartment complex. I do know it will cost millions in supplies and labor. Where is all this money going to come from?"

He could see Darrell was getting uncomfortable, but Sam wasn't ready to let up yet. He had gone easy on his son the first time around, but Darrell had to face the hard facts. This idea was fine for a school project; brilliant, in fact. But no way was his son going to actually build it.

"I don't have all the answers yet. Obviously. I just started working on it. But I'm making good progress every day. I figure if I take off spring semester and work on it all summer, too, I can make this happen. I can find the financing somewhere and find the right people, like Inspector Hepburn, who will believe in this project and help me get it off the ground."

Sam hardly heard Darrell's entire, impassioned speech. His mind got stuck on the phrase "take off spring semester."

"You can't take off your last semester of school. You have to graduate. Even if you could get the funds, the permits, the insurance, and a million pieces of the puzzle to fit together, you need your BS and you need to start grad school."

"I'll finish my degree, Dad. BU will still be there. What do a few more courses matter when this project will give me huge, practical experience? Isn't that what an employer wants to see on a résumé?"

"An employer wants to hire a college graduate, Darrell. With a real diploma. You know that. I will not allow you to take off the spring semester. You have to go back to school. That's final." Sam knew he was shouting now, but his son was so stubborn. Sometimes that was the only way to get through to him.

Jessica rushed into the room, wearing an apron. Which meant she was in the middle of cooking. "What's going on in here? What are you two arguing about?"

Darrell came to his feet. "I'm not arguing. Dad is. Ask him." He stalked out of the room, practically knocking his mother over as he headed for his room.

"What is it, Sam? Did Darrell mess up at one of the jobs again?"

Sam shook his head. "Nothing like that. You know that idea Darrell has for renovating the old cannery into an apartment complex?"

"He showed it to me the other night. His school project. I think it's great," Jessica said.

"I do, too. Did he tell you that he thinks he can actually build it? An apartment complex. Just like that." Sam snapped his fingers. "He's been researching grants to get the funding and talking to a lot of people at Village Hall."

Jessica sat down on the edge of the chair. She looked surprised, but

Sam could tell she did not disapprove of the idea. "That's very ambitious."

"Yes, it is. I'm proud of the way he thinks, wanting to use his education and talents to help people. At least, I was at first. But now he says he doesn't want to go back to school for spring semester. He said he doesn't care if he graduates."

Jessica looked distressed. "I guess this job as your foreman has given him a taste of being out in the world. I think he's eager to follow in your footsteps, Sam. You know that his whole life he's only wanted to be like you."

"I know." Sam's tone was wistful. "But let him be like me after he has a few diplomas hanging on a wall. Let him be *more* successful than I am. The truth is, Darrell will never be able to make this big project come about. Even a developer with a track record would find it hard to pull it all together."

"And you were trying to give him a taste of reality?"

"He just blindsided me," Sam admitted. "That's what happened. I totally lost it when he said he was going to take off and not graduate."

Jessica met his glance with a sympathetic look. "It took you by surprise. It pushed your buttons."

"You've heard me say this a hundred times, but it's true: I should have finished college. I see that now. I always told myself I'd go back and finish someday. But life starts happening and I just never did."

"I know you regret that, Sam. Maybe you will go back to school someday. You never know. Look at Lucy Bates. She became a nurse in her forties. People do it all the time."

Sam smiled. "After Tyler and Lily are finished, you mean? Lily wants to go be a veterinarian. A *vegetarian* veterinarian," he corrected. "No . . . I think it's too late for me. But I can't let Darrell make the same mistake. It's fine if he wants to build things that are bigger and more significant than anything I ever did. That's what I want him to do. I want him to have all the advantages I never did. But he has to finish school."

"I agree. I'll back you up on that, too," Jessica promised.

"Thanks, honey. Let's hope Darrell figures this out on his own. I don't want to argue about it again. I think he'll have to face the facts soon—that this very big plan won't work out."

"I hate to see him disappointed." Jessica rose and squeezed his hand, then left the room.

Sam was left alone with his thoughts and conflicting feelings. He felt bad now for losing his temper. He would apologize to Darrell for shouting. It was not the best way to communicate. But that didn't mean he would change his mind. Darrell had to return to school and graduate. There were no two ways about it.

"ARE YOU GOING TO VERA'S PARTY, TOO?" BARBARA ASKED. "YOUR mother is excited about it."

"Is she ever." Jean shook her head and smiled. "I'm dropping her off then having dinner with Grant Keating."

"Finally. A real date. That's progress." Barbara looked pleased. "Can I see your dress?"

Jean held it up for her, a navy blue wrap style made from a silky material. Barbara looked impressed. "Very nice. That color does wonders for your eyes."

Jean laughed and smoothed a dress sleeve on the ironing board. With her fair complexion and blue eyes, shades of blue were flattering on her. But wonders? "Thanks but that sounds . . . extreme."

"You know what I mean. It's nice to dress up from time to time."

"Frankly, I'd forgotten how much work it is," Jean said with a laugh.

"Hair, nails, makeup. I've been wearing jeans and sweatshirts every day since I came to live here. And just shooting for basic hygiene."

"He must really like you if you've never made an effort and he's asked you out anyway. In fact, I'd say he's crazy about you," Barbara teased.

Jean looked up at her. "We have fun together. I enjoy Grant's company. But I'm not sure dating him is a good idea," she confessed. "I get the feeling he's only in town for a short time and will take up and leave whenever the mood strikes."

"From what you've told me, you're not planning to stay in town very long either," Barbara reminded her. It was true, too. Jean doubted she would stay in Cape Light after her mother passed on. "I say just go for it. He's very attractive—in a scruffy, unkempt way—and who knows? People can change their plans."

Jean didn't answer. She knew that Grant had feelings for her, but she doubted those feelings ran deep enough for him to change his ways or his plans.

"I'm thinking of this as a fun night out with a friend. Nothing more, nothing less."

Barbara nodded as she pulled on her coat. "Good attitude. Though personally, I have the feeling the evening will fall into the *more* category. I expect a full report on Sunday."

Jean had to laugh at Barbara's request. "I'll report in, no worries."

After the nurse left, Jean went into her mother's room to help her get dressed. She found Cynthia in her bathrobe, sitting at her dressing table. Barbara had helped her shower, and earlier in the day Jean had put her mother's thin white hair up in pin curls. Jean had offered to style her mother's hair with a blow dryer, but Cynthia had insisted on an old-fashioned set with bobby pins. Now her mother had removed the hairpins and was combing out the wavy white tufts.

Jean stood behind her and met her gaze in the mirror. "Your hair looks very nice, Mom. You were right. The pin curls worked out well."

"I know my own hair by now. What's left of it." She handed Jean a can of hair spray that looked decades old. "Give me a little spray, please. Not too much. I'll close my eyes."

"All right. Here goes." Jean squeezed lightly and waved the can around, careful not to press too hard on the nozzle. "How's that?"

Her mother touched her hair, pushing it into shape. "It will do for Vera's house. It's partly a party and partly a way to get us to finish up the last of the craft items. We're going to crochet the rest of the pot holders and place mats. I hope it's not too tedious. I want to see the fair tomorrow. I don't want to be tired out."

Her mother had mentioned going to the fair a few times. Jean also hoped she was not too tired. It was one thing to attend the Sunday service, but the Christmas Fair could be chaos. If they went at all, it would be early, before the rush, and they would only spend a short time there.

"If you feel tired, you don't have to crochet. You can leave early. Just call me. Now, what would you like to wear?"

"The red dress with the black velvet collar. I always wear that during the holidays."

Jean remembered the dress well and found it in a dry-cleaning bag at the back of the closet. Her mother wore a full slip under her robe, and as Jean helped her into the dress, she couldn't help noticing how her mother's body was deteriorating, the yellow cast of her loose skin and her swollen joints.

Her mother tried to slip her wedding ring on, but it wouldn't go over her swollen knuckles. "What's the use? Everyone there knows I was married." She sighed and tossed the ring back into the crystal dish on her dresser.

"How about earrings? These pearls would go well."

Jean fit the earrings on and her mother looked satisfied. Jean helped her with a bit of makeup next, some foundation and lipstick. Cynthia had never worn much makeup, even when she was young. She had been so pretty, she never needed it.

It was a struggle to slip on the short stockings that just reached above her knee, but her mother insisted. "A lady doesn't go out without stockings, Jean."

Jean put her mother's boots on last and helped her into the living room. "We'll leave at about a quarter to seven. We have plenty of time."

Jean's freshly pressed dress was hanging near the stairs, and she picked up the hanger.

"Are you going somewhere, too?" her mother asked.

"I'm having dinner with Grant," Jean replied. "While you're at the party."

"Oh . . . I didn't know that. When did he ask you out?"

"Wednesday night, after you got the invitation from Vera."

"I see." Jean's mother sat back on the sofa, looking as if she had figured out some great mystery. "Well, you know what I think of him."

"Yes, I do." Jean hoped to be spared another lecture about Grant's frailties and faults.

"He's intelligent and can carry on a decent conversation. But you shouldn't get your hopes up. I doubt this will lead to anything."

"We're just having dinner, Mom. I don't expect an engagement ring."

"Good. Then you won't be disappointed."

Jean turned and walked up the stairs, saying only, "I'll be down soon."

Jean came downstairs a short time later. Her mother looked her over, from her smooth, blown-out hairstyle and makeup to her high-heeled boots, but didn't say a word.

Jean drove over to Vera's and parked in the driveway, wondering what would be the best way to get her mother into the house. Grant came out and offered to help. He had obviously been watching for them. Together, they managed to get her mother inside. "You look lovely tonight, Cynthia," Grant said as he helped her with her jacket.

Her mother shrugged, though Jean could tell she was pleased by the compliment. "I've had this dress for years."

"I can see why. Red suits you."

Her mother glanced up at him. She didn't have any more tart comebacks and even smiled. Jean could tell she had noticed Grant's transformed appearance, too. Jean was hoping her mother wouldn't say anything, one way or the other. She feared that whatever her mother came out with would be rude.

Jean thought he looked very handsome. Not that she didn't think he was handsome ordinarily. But he had made some effort, with a smooth shave and maybe even a haircut. She had never seen him wear anything but jeans and his khaki utility jacket. Tonight he was dressed in a brown tweed sports coat, a tailored shirt, and brown dress pants.

A few of the guests had arrived, and they greeted her mother cheerfully. They were already enjoying drinks and appetizers, and some had started to crochet.

"You sit right here, Cynthia. I'm so glad you could come. I saved this seat just for you." Vera helped her mother to a large armchair in the middle of the living room.

Once she got Jean's mother settled, she stood up and smiled at Jean and Grant. "Don't worry about a thing. You two have a nice time."

"Thanks, Vera. Enjoy the party," Jean said.

"I'm enjoying it already," Vera replied.

A SHORT TIME LATER, THEY ARRIVED AT THE SPOON HARBOR INN and were seated at a table with a view of the small harbor. The dining room had a classic, old-fashioned look, with a low beamed ceiling, brass fixtures, and tables covered with white linen and topped with small candles.

"Vera recommended this place. I hope it's all right with you?" Grant said after ordering two glasses of white wine for them.

"My family used to celebrate special occasions here," she told him, "but I haven't been back in a long time. The food was always tasty. I do love the atmosphere."

"I'm glad you're pleased. Let's see if it's still as good as you remember." They studied the menus as a waiter brought their drinks to the table. "Once upon a time," he went on, "I used to eat out a lot. At the trendiest places I could find." He closed the menu and looked over at her. "It feels like all that happened in a past life. The Clam Box is about my speed these days."

His comment made her curious. "What past life was that? Or is that question too personal?"

He sat back and took a sip of wine. "I used to own an advertising agency. A very successful one, too, in Boston. I was living the good life, lunch and dinners with clients at five-star restaurants. Flying all over to conferences and presentations. You've been in that business. You know how it can be."

"I was just a worker ant in the art department, but the executives treated themselves very well."

Grant smiled. "That was me. I treated myself well . . . too well at times. Maybe you'd say I was spoiled. I felt I'd worked hard and deserved my rewards. My family was never poor, but my parents struggled financially. I felt that being a success meant having more than they ever did and being able to take care of them, too. Which I did. But I also placed a great deal of importance on material possessions, the signs of my success—custom-made shirts and shoes, fancy cars, luxury vacations. You get the idea."

"I do. But you don't seem at all that way now. Why did you change?"

The waiter returned to the table, and they ordered salads and main courses. Grant waited until the waiter was gone before answering her question. "The other day, I mentioned that I was married back then. We were trying to start a family, and my wife had some routine tests. The doctors found a rare blood disease—a type of cancer that is fatal ninety-nine percent of the time. She died soon after the discovery, and I was crushed. Everything I'd worked for, everything I'd achieved and acquired, suddenly seemed without meaning or worth.

"I was very angry at first. Shocked and angry. I could barely put one foot in front of the other and carry on my life. I finally pulled myself together and sold the company. Then I set off with just my cameras and the bare essentials in a backpack. I traveled around the world, all the places my wife and I had planned to go someday. Maybe taking pictures saved me. Photography was my first love. In college, I studied with some great teachers and had hoped to be a professional photographer. But I got distracted by the advertising world and the money-making game once I left school. I always told myself I would go back to shooting photos someday. When I'd made enough money and could retire early. After my wife died, that was the only thing I wanted to do. The only motivation for getting up in the morning. And by living simply and immersing myself in different cultures and foreign places, taking photos every minute of the day, I managed to recover."

"That sounds like an amazing journey and a lot of photographs," Jean said.

He laughed. "It was. I haven't printed half of them. But I do look back at the files from time to time."

"That was very brave," Jean added. "Few people would have the courage to do what you did. To change their life so radically."

He looked pleased and a little embarrassed by her compliment. "I'm not sure courage was part of the equation. I was trying to *save* my life. And I did have a good cushion of savings from the sale of the business and our house in Boston. It's been invested well. Keeping my needs simple, I don't need to worry about an income from a nine-to-five job. I know few people can say that, and it's a real blessing."

"It's quite a story," Jean said. "You told me the other day that your whole life changed when you lost your wife, but I had no idea."

"I'm sure everyone in that situation feels immense loss. But I guess I had a radical reaction. Her death made me question everything. I've come to think of this new chapter in my life as my wife's final gift. I'm far happier now than I was on the fast track," he said. "Life goes on for the living, Jean. You can't put off the things you want to do and love to do. Tomorrow isn't guaranteed for anyone. That's another lesson I learned."

"Good advice," Jean agreed as the waiter brought their salads.

"So, I told you my story," Grant said. "Let's hear yours. Have you ever been married?"

Jean was surprised by the question, though she knew she shouldn't have been. "I was married in my twenties. It didn't work out, which was for the best," she replied. "I've had some serious relationships since, but none that led to marriage."

"Really? I'm surprised. I'm guessing that must have been your choice."

Jean wasn't sure what he meant. Was he saying that many men must have wanted to marry her, but she was too particular? Or that she had avoided marriage in some way?

"You left Portland a few weeks ago and came back to Cape Light, where you grew up. You seem to be at turning point in your life, too," he pointed out. "What do you love to do? What gives you the most happiness, Jean?"

Jean had never seen her recent choices in that light. But once he framed it that way, she had to admit there was some truth to it.

"I love to do my own artwork. Especially the illustrations for the children's book I've been working on. I've made a lot of progress since I moved here."

He looked delighted by her reply. "Can I see them sometime? An authorized viewing this time," he added, reminding her of how he had picked up the sketches in the shop without asking the day they met.

"I guess so," she replied. "No one has seen the illustrations yet. They're not done."

"Whenever you're ready," he said kindly. "I'm sure the project is wonderful."

Jean thought he was being very sweet. He had only seen a page or two. How could he tell if it was wonderful or not?

The waiter returned with their main courses. Jean had ordered flounder and Grant was served swordfish. She thought everything looked and tasted delicious but wondered what Grant—with his sophisticated past and palate—would think.

She watched him take a bite of his fish. "This is good. Not fancy, but amazingly fresh. Just as it should be. How is yours?"

"Just right," she said honestly. "Save room for dessert. I remember that course to be the high point."

He smiled at her. "Thanks for the tip." They ate for a while in silence. "Has there been any progress persuading your brother to visit for Christmas?"

"None at all. I did reply to his e-mail. All I could say was that our mother wasn't doing well and I still thought he should reconsider. I'm certain this Christmas will be my mother's last," Jean admitted. "But I couldn't come right out and say it so starkly in my note. Maybe I should have."

He reached across the table and took her hand. "Jean, I'm sure he realizes that by now. Or he's just in denial. You can't blame yourself for his decision."

"I know. But I still wish he would change his mind," she said. "My mother can be difficult, but she's been amazingly stoic, facing her illness with acceptance and courage. She has a lot of faith," Jean added. "I think it's meant a lot to her to go to church the last few weeks, and I know she wants to be there for Christmas this year. I'm glad I can at least give her that."

"From what I've seen, you've given your mother a lot more than that since you've been here. You've made it possible for her to join the world again, to socialize and return to her painting."

Jean felt pleased by his words but couldn't give herself that much credit. "We still bicker at times. I always feel bad afterward. I'm sure it's not good for her health. She's still quite sick, but getting out of the house lifts her spirits. She didn't attend church much when I was young," Jean recalled. "My father would take me and my brother. I think now that she's older and reaching the end, church is more important to her."

"I've been to cathedrals, temples, and mosques all around the world. Searching for some answers, I guess. I haven't tried Reverend Ben's sermons yet, but maybe I will soon. I think Christmas draws everyone to church, even wandering souls, like me."

"All who wander are not lost," Jean countered.

Grant smiled. "I hope so."

The waiter had cleared their dinner dishes and took their order for dessert. Grant ordered an apple cobbler with ice cream and Jean asked for the chocolate cake.

"I've been wondering," he said, once the waiter had left. "What will you do when your mother is gone? Will you leave or stay in Cape Light?"

"I'll probably leave. I expect Kevin will want to sell the property right away. He has no interest in coming back here. I'm sure he'll give me time to find someplace to live. But I see no need to prolong the situation." She looked up at Grant, trying to gauge his reaction.

They were talking about a time in the future when they wouldn't see each other anymore. She didn't like thinking about it and wondered how he felt. Did it matter to him at all?

"I'll probably look for a job in Boston, something in graphic art. Back to the real world again," she said, trying to inject a lighter note.

"I see. Nothing to keep you here?"

"Not really," Jean replied, curious about his question. He already knew the answer, she thought. Though, if he were to stay in town, she would figure out a way to stay. And Boston wasn't that far. They could still see each other. If he wanted to.

The waiter returned with dessert and set the dishes before them. Grant had coffee but Jean declined. She took a bite of her chocolate cake, the restaurant's specialty. It was still decadently rich and totally delicious.

"That looks good," he said, watching her.

"Oh, it is," she replied. "Would you like a bite?"

He reached over with his fork and took a small bite from her plate. "Wow, pure chocolate."

"That's why I like it. I can't live without chocolate. Even if I wanted to simplify and give up material pleasures."

He laughed. "No worries, chocolate is allowed. I'll write you a note."

His reply made her smile. Then she realized that she sounded as if she were projecting some future with him. She hadn't really meant it that way, had she?

She quickly tried to change the subject. "How about you, Grant? You said you've almost finished your photo essay. Will you stay and work on a new subject?"

"I don't think so. I'm not sure where the new year will take me. Up north somewhere, maybe? I've heard Prince Edward Island and Nova Scotia are beautiful."

"Then that's one place I've been but you haven't," she said, making him laugh again.

"It's settled. You should be my guide."

Jean was sure he was just teasing. *If only,* she thought. She would run off with him in a heartbeat, that was for sure.

"We were there on vacation when I was very young. All I remember is a cottage by a beach and a lot of wild strawberries. Maybe some poison ivy?"

"Sounds perfect to me. Except for the poison ivy, of course." His expression made her laugh. "Poison ivy is *not* required."

The hours had passed quickly. When Jean finally noticed the time, she realized the party at Vera's was probably winding down. Grant took care of the bill and they headed back to the village.

GRANT PARKED IN FRONT OF VERA'S HOUSE. ALL THE LIGHTS WERE still on, but Jean noticed fewer cars parked along the street. She guessed that her mother must be eager by now to go home, but she couldn't help lingering a few moments more, alone with Grant.

He seemed to feel the same way and turned to her with a wistful look.

"Thank you for having dinner with me, Jean. That was the nicest evening I've had in a long time."

Jean felt the words catch in her throat. "Me, too," was all she could manage.

His gaze sought hers and he moved closer. Then he put his arms around her and kissed her. She felt his hands in her hair and clung to his strong shoulders. "You're so lovely, Jean," he whispered. "And the evening passed much too quickly. It's hard to let you go."

Jean sighed and leaned back. "I know," she said quietly. "But I'd better get inside. It's getting late."

Jean left the truck and Grant followed her up the path to the porch. Vera lived in a stately Victorian that was furnished with antiques throughout and maintained in perfect condition. After Vera had lost her husband, it was hard for her to remain in such a large house. She managed by renting furnished rooms short-term to people who came through town. Jean knew the residence was technically a boarding house, but she doubted there was ever one as elegant.

Jean rang the bell and Vera came to the door. "Oh, Jean. Didn't your mother call you? She felt tired and Emily Warwick drove her home."

Jean was surprised and then felt embarrassed. "She didn't call. Unless I missed it." She pulled out her phone and checked. No call from her mother showed up on the screen. No call at all.

"I'm sure she's all right. Don't worry, dear," Vera said quickly. "I think she wanted to turn in early, so she would get enough rest to come to the fair tomorrow."

"Thanks, Vera. I'll say good night then."

"Good night, Jean." Vera glanced at Grant. "I'll leave the door unlatched for you, Grant," she added, and then left them alone.

Grant looked down at her. "I'm sorry I kept you out so long . . . again."

"If that's the only thing you ever have to apologize to me for, you're definitely ahead of the game," Jean said. "I should have guessed the party would wear her out quickly. I'm sure she's fine. But I'd better go."

"I'll walk you down to your car."

"No need. I'm fine." Jean touched his arm. "Thanks again. I had a wonderful time."

"I did, too. And I don't need to keep fixing things in that cottage in order to see you, do I?"

Jean had already begun walking down the path to the street. She turned and laughed at him. "Nope. Though I did consider causing some minor damage so you'd have to come back."

She heard him laugh as she climbed into her car and headed home. She felt as if she had been on another planet all night—a wonderful planet where she felt attractive and interesting, even desired—and was suddenly coming back to Earth. She wondered if her mother had somehow gotten herself into bed, but doubted it. She hoped her mother would be too tired to talk—and too tired to carry on about needing a lift from Emily Warwick.

The house was dark when Jean unlocked the front door. She found her mother asleep in the living room, in her recliner. Jean gently touched her shoulder. "I'm home, Mom. Let me help you to bed."

"Jean. Where have you been? What time is it?"

"Not that late," Jean said. "I went to Vera's first. I didn't know that Emily gave you a ride home."

"Well, she had to. I couldn't get in touch with you."

"Did you try to call? I didn't hear the phone ring. Or find a message from you."

Jean could see her mother was in a very sour mood and arguing with her would do no good. But she couldn't help asserting the simple facts. "You look too tired for the walker. I'll bring the wheelchair."

"Never mind. Help me up. I don't want the chair," her mother insisted. Jean brought the walker, and with some struggle, got her mother standing and pointed in the right direction.

She followed close behind as her mother made her way slowly to the bedroom. "How was the party? Did you have fun?"

"It was fine. A little too much chitchat for me. Vera just wanted to finish the pot holders. That's why she had us over."

Jean suspected the Vera had made a very nice party for the group and that her mother had enjoyed herself more than she was letting on. "It must have been fun to get together," Jean said.

"Great fun. I was jumping with joy," her mother replied sarcastically. "I'm sure you had a much better time. You totally forgot me. I felt abandoned. It was so humiliating to have Emily Warwick take me home."

"I'm sorry, Mom. You should have called." Jean had managed to get her mother's dress, stockings, and boots off, and looked through her drawer for a nightgown.

"I don't know why you went out with him in the first place. Sheer boredom, maybe. Or perhaps he flatters you. He's no better than a day laborer, living in a boarding house. And most of the time, his appearance is appalling."

Jean took a breath to get hold of her temper. "He's far from a day laborer, Mom. You know that. Do you expect him to wear a tuxedo to clean the mold off the bathroom ceiling?"

"Don't be snide. You know what I mean."

"No, I really don't. He's a very accomplished photographer, and he used to own an advertising agency. He's traveled around the world and has values I admire. You should understand that, being an artist yourself."

Her mother raised her arms and allowed Jean to pull on the nightgown. She patted her hair afterward and sighed. "An advertising agency. Really. I guess you believe him, too." Before Jean could reply, she added, "Do what you wish. You're too old to listen to anything I say. Even though I say these things for you own good. Your father expected great accomplishments from you, but frankly, I never did."

Jean felt stunned by her mother's rebuke. She knew Cynthia hated to be proven wrong and would argue fiercely to save face. But still, the words stung in a way that Jean had thought she had long outgrown.

Jean left the room feeling cowed and deflated. She stood in the dark living room and wished that her father was alive. She was his favorite and could still remember a golden time when he was alive and she was an outgoing child, spirited and happy, feeling so sure of herself because she was sure she was loved. After her father died, she retreated into her inner world. It was a great loss. One she knew she had never really recovered from.

Of all the things her mother said, what hurt most was to think that her father would have been disappointed in her.

Maybe her mother was right. She had never accomplished anything of note, not even marrying and raising children. But another voice insisted on being heard: *Grant Keating likes you. He thinks you're special. He wants to see your illustrations and is sure that the work is wonderful. He's accomplished a lot and met a lot of people in the world. More than your mother ever has.*

Remembering all that and Grant's tender good-night kiss boosted Jean's spirits again as she headed to bed.

CHAPTER THIRTEEN

*J*EAN WOKE TO THE SIGHT OF A CLEAR BLUE SKY. SHE FELT relieved. There had been talk of snow flurries, and she worried that bad weather would make her mother's trip to church this morning for the fair an even greater challenge. Her mother had been insistent about taking part, even for a short time, and Jean doubted she could talk her out of it. At least the weather was cooperating, and it would bring even more crowds to the fair today.

She went downstairs and started the coffee, then went into her mother's room. She was surprised to find her mother still fast asleep, breathing deeply. Her color wasn't good. She had probably needed oxygen during the night but hadn't put on the mask, even though Jean had left it well within reach.

Jean touched her shoulder. "Mom? Do you want to get up? It's past nine. You wanted to get to church early," she reminded her.

Her mother shook her head but didn't open her eyes or even try to sit up. "I'm very tired, Jean. I don't feel well. Leave me be."

Jean wondered what was really going on. Her mother seemed more irritable than tired. Maybe that was all it was. "All right. You can sleep as late as you like. But you need to take some pills. I'll bring them in for you in a few minutes."

Jean left the room, unable to ignore a spike of worry. She had rarely seen her mother like this. The party must have tired her out more than Jean had realized.

She made her mother a tray with tea and toast, along with her medication. Cynthia sat up briefly, hardly ate a bite, but did take her pills. Then she slipped down under the covers, looking exhausted by the effort.

Jean sat with her a moment until she fell asleep again. Her breath was raspy, even with the aid of oxygen. Her color was definitely not good.

Back in the kitchen she called Dr. Nevins's office and left a message with the answering service. She called Barbara Crosby next. Barbara was not due to visit until Sunday, but when Jean described her mother's condition, the nurse said she would come by soon.

"She might just be tired from the party. Don't worry, Jean. Let's see what Dr. Nevins says. I'll be there as soon as I can."

Jean thanked her and hung up. She wished Barbara could come right away, but the nurse had other patients to see, and it was good of her to come at all today.

Jean didn't know what to do with herself while she waited. She had already decided to take a break from cleaning. After breakfast, she took out her artwork and set up on the kitchen table. Then she set her phone alarm to make sure she looked in on her mother every ten minutes. It was hard to concentrate. She looked over her work, but couldn't focus enough to make any progress.

She didn't even need the alarm. Each time she checked, there was no change in her mother's condition. Her mother slept deeply, an unnaturally deep sleep for the time of day, Jean thought. Cynthia seemed unaware of Jean being in the room, even when Jean adjusted the covers or the oxygen tube in her nose.

Jean heard the phone ring and ran back to the kitchen. It was her mother's specialist, Dr. Nevins. It had taken less than an hour for him to get the message and call back, but it definitely felt longer.

Jean quickly described her mother's symptoms. "She went out last night. A get-together at a friend's house for a few hours. She must have gotten home around ten or ten thirty at the latest," Jean explained. "But maybe the outing was too tiring for her?"

"That's possible, Jean. But, as I've explained, your mother's heart is getting weaker and her organs are starting to fail, especially her liver and lungs. She could have stayed at home last night and still woken up this way today. There's no way for us to know."

"I understand," Jean replied. The facts of the matter, stated so plainly, made her feel sad. "Is there anything I can do for her? Any medication you can prescribe to help her?"

"I can't prescribe anything over the phone without seeing her. My first concern is pneumonia. I don't normally make house calls, but I'll come see her if I can. The problem is I'm out in Worcester, giving a talk. I won't be back in Cape Light until this evening." Jean knew that Worcester was a good hour and a half way. "I don't think you should wait that long," Dr. Nevins went on. "I think you should call an ambulance now, and she should be admitted to the hospital."

The last thing Jean wanted was to fail to give her mother proper care. But she also knew Cynthia did not want to be hospitalized.

"Do you really think that's necessary? Barbara Crosby, her visiting nurse, is coming soon. Maybe she could examine my mother and call you, and we could decide from there?"

Dr. Nevins didn't answer for a moment. "All right. I know Barbara and trust her opinion. Keep your eye on your mother and call me if there's any sudden change. I know it's hard, but make your mother take liquids at least. She mustn't get dehydrated. And have Barbara call me as soon as she takes a look at your mother."

The doctor gave Jean his private cell phone number so that she didn't have to call the service again, and they said good-bye.

Jean still felt nervous but somewhat reassured by the plan. Too distracted now to even think of painting, she gathered up the illustrations and slipped them back into the black portfolio.

She heard a knock on the back door and hoped that it was Barbara, though she had never come in that way before. She turned and saw Grant peeking through the window.

"Morning," he said when she opened the door. "I came to pick up a ladder I left in the shop and saw you in here. I thought I'd say hello."

Jean thought he might call, but a visit was even better. "Come in. Would you like some coffee? It's still warm."

"No thanks. I can see you're working." He glanced at the paints that were still out and the portfolio on the table. "Am I not allowed to look?" He pulled his knit cap down over his eyes, making her laugh.

"I just put it all away."

"You said I could see it when it was finished, remember?" he reminded her. "Getting any closer?"

Jean felt a flock of butterflies in her stomach but forced a smile. "I have a bit more to finish, but you can see what's done so far." She forced herself to pick up the portfolio and hand it to him. "Just be careful with it. It's my only copy."

He looked shocked and held out the folder as if it were very fragile. "Are you sure? I was only teasing you, Jean. I can wait if you're not ready."

"You'd better take it, before I change my mind."

He laughed. "I'm honored. I'll take good care of it. I can't wait to see what's inside."

Jean felt flattered by his excitement but also nervous, worried that he might think the illustrations were an amateur mess.

"I'm surprised to find you home," he said. "I thought you were taking your mother to church today, for the fair."

"She's not feeling well. She's still in bed. I just spoke to her doctor. He's worried that she has pneumonia and wanted me to call an ambulance. But Barbara Crosby is coming to see her soon. We'll decide then what to do. She might just be tired out from Vera's party."

Grant looked concerned. "I'm sorry to hear that. I hope she will rally soon. Let me know if I can help you. At least it didn't snow today," he said, glancing outside. "I'm meeting a friend in Newburyport. We're going to shoot some photos of the harbor."

"That's a beautiful place. The village looks wonderful this time of year." Jean wondered if he had planned to ask her to tag along. Maybe he would have if her mother hadn't been sick. She loved Newburyport and would have liked to spend the day there with him.

"I'll call you later to see how your mother is doing," he said.

He said good-bye and left, the packet of illustrations tucked under his arm. Jean felt a tinge of melancholy as she saw him drive away but reminded herself that he had come by to see her. Even if he had not asked her for another date, that was a good sign.

Jean was putting away the last of her paints and drawing supplies when Barbara arrived. They went straight back to her mother's room.

Cynthia was still listless and groggy. Barbara quickly took her vital signs. Then persuaded her mother to drink some water before she laid back on the pillows and closed her eyes again.

"She hasn't had a stroke, and I don't hear signs of pneumonia,"

Barbara said, easing some of Jean's fears. "But her heart is definitely working very hard, Jean. I'll call Dr. Nevins and see what he wants to do."

"I'm awake you know. I can hear everything you say," her mother mumbled. "There's no need to talk about me as if I wasn't in the room."

"Sorry, Cynthia. I'm going to call Dr. Nevins. He wants to know how you're doing."

"I could be better," her mother replied. "And I could be worse. Tell him that for me."

Barbara dialed Dr. Nevins on her cell phone, described Cynthia's symptoms, and relayed her vital signs. "I see. Yes. I'll tell her that—"

"I can speak to my own doctor, for goodness' sake," Jean's mother said in her loudest voice yet. "Give me the phone, please."

"Hold on, she'd like to speak with you, Doctor." Barbara handed down the phone, and Jean watched her mother struggle to sit up.

"This is Cynthia Whitman. Your patient. Do you have something to tell me, Doctor?"

Jean and Barbara glanced at each other, sharing a secret smile. Jean's mother listened for a few moments, then said, "Absolutely not. I have no need of a hospital. I'm really past that point. If this isn't the end, I'll get through it. I've had setbacks like this in the past. If it is indeed the final act, I want the curtain to go down while I'm in my own bed. The only way I'm leaving this house, Doctor, will be feet first."

"She still knows her mind. That's a good sign," Barbara whispered to Jean.

"You come by if you like. I'll be here. I'm not going anywhere today," her mother said to the doctor. "I'm going to put my daughter on. You can make the arrangements with her."

"I've told Barbara to take a blood test. We need to rule out pneumonia or some other infection," Dr. Nevins explained when Jean took the phone. "Keep working on the fluids. I'll be by around five o'clock. I'd prefer that Cynthia be admitted to the hospital, but we'll respect her wishes."

"Good," Jean said. "I think that's what we have to do." Barbara took the blood specimen then spent some time making Jean's mother more comfortable. Jean went into the living room and dialed her brother.

Kevin picked up on the first ring. "Hi, Jean. What's up?"

She could tell from his cautious tone that he was wondering if she had called to bug him again about coming home for Christmas.

"Mom isn't well, Kevin. She's very weak and could barely rouse herself to talk to the doctor. Dr. Nevins wants to put her in the hospital, but Mom refused."

"Is she that bad?" He sounded concerned and alarmed. "Maybe she should go, Jean. No matter what she says."

"I was thinking the same way. Until I heard her talk to the doctor. She's perfectly lucid and able to make the decision for herself. That's the hard part," she added. "Her nurse came by, Barbara Crosby. She examined her and doesn't think it was a stroke or even pneumonia, thank goodness. The doctor is nice enough to come by later. I can call you back and let you know what he says."

"Sure, call me back. Can I speak to Mom?"

"Of course. Barbara is with her now. I'll bring the phone back. Hold on."

Jean returned to her mother's room. Barbara had bathed her mother and combed her hair, and taken her to the bathroom. Cynthia looked a bit better, sitting back against a pile of pillows.

"It's Kevin, Mom. He wants to talk to you."

Her mother stretched out her hand and took the phone. "Kevin?

What did Jean tell you? I don't want you to worry. I'm not half as bad as they make me out to be."

Her mother listened for a moment, then said, "Oh, you don't have to do that. I'll be fine in a day or two." She paused. "Of course I'd like to see you. I'd love to see you. But you don't have to go to all that trouble. Don't you need to be in the office?"

She listened again, then nodded and smiled. "All right, dear. If you insist. But don't be mad if you find me dancing a jig, and you've come all that way for nothing." Jean couldn't hear Kevin's reply, but her mother laughed. "I hope so, too, dear. You have a safe trip. See you soon."

She handed the phone back to Jean. "Kevin is coming. He wants to speak to you again."

Jean took the phone, feeling surprised and relieved by the news. If her mother was facing her final days, Jean was glad she would not be alone. And her brother needed to be here. She was relieved he had realized that.

"I'll let you know when I've made my reservations, Jean. I'll be there as soon as I can," he said. "Let me know what the doctor says."

"I will, Kevin. I'll speak to you later. Thank you for . . . for coming home. I know it means the world to Mom. No matter what she says."

He was silent for a moment. She sensed that he felt uncomfortable. "Thank you for taking care of her, Jean. I'll talk to you later."

Barbara left but told Jean to call if she needed anything at all. "Even if you just want to chat. And do let me know what Dr. Nevins says when he comes by later. I'll be by tomorrow afternoon, but call if you need me sooner."

Jean thanked her, grateful for her concern and her friendship. She felt too distracted the rest of the day to do much. She sat in her mother's room with a book but couldn't concentrate.

She considered calling Grant. He said he would call for an update on her mother's condition. She assumed he meant later that night. He was probably busy now in Newburyport, taking photos. She didn't want to bother him. She didn't want him to think she was too clingy after just one date. She decided to wait for him to call her.

She finally gave up on the book, went into the kitchen, and took out some ingredients for baking. Baking or cooking never failed to soothe her nerves, and she had the perfect excuse today to make cookies. Next Sunday was Christmas Eve, and even though it was only herself and her mother and now Kevin in the house, it wouldn't feel like Christmas without some sweet treats.

Dr. Nevins arrived a few minutes after five, just as he had promised. Jean showed him back to her mother's room. Cynthia was asleep again, sitting up against the pillows, her head flopped to one side like a broken doll.

She woke up and blinked when she heard Jean and the doctor come into the room. "Dr. Nevins. I forgot you were coming to see me. Don't you know that doctors never make house calls anymore?"

Dr. Nevins smiled. He was a dapper-looking man with silver hair and an expensive navy blue suit. "Only for my favorite patients, Cynthia. Don't let it get around." He sat on the edge of her bed and took out a stethoscope from his bag. "Let's listen to your heart, please," he said, his expression turning suddenly serious and focused.

He listened a long time then listened to her lungs. Then he gave her a complete examination. At last he said, "We need to wait for the blood test to come back to be certain, but I don't believe that you have pneumonia."

"That's good news," Jean said.

"There is a great deal of fluid in your lungs, Cynthia. If it was anyone else, I'd be calling an ambulance right now."

"We've already discussed that. My mind is made up."

"Yes, I know. That's why I'm not pressing it. I'll let you have your way, this time. We'll wait and see how it goes."

"My son, Kevin, is coming from California," she said. "You'll have to talk to him from now on. He'll stick up for me."

Jean felt a jolt. As if she had not been sticking up for her mother?

"I look forward to meeting him." The doctor rose and took his bag. He said good-bye to Cynthia and promised he would see her soon.

Jean walked the doctor to the door and gave him his coat. "Keep an eye on her," the doctor said, his tone concerned. "She might surprise us and come through this. We should know more by tomorrow. You can call me any time."

"I will, Doctor. Thanks again for stopping by."

"Cynthia has been my patient for a long time. And you've been a very good advocate for her, Jean. She's lucky to have you in her corner," he said quietly.

Jean thanked him and said good night. As she closed the door, she wondered if her mother intended for Kevin to be the one to deal with the doctors now. He was officially her mother's medical proxy, but she doubted Kevin wanted it that way. For one thing, he had barely been in the medical loop the last few years. Jean had at least come home from time to time to drive her mother to tests and appointments with her specialists.

Her mother might get over this crisis and be back to her old self in a few days. But the end was clearly closer. Jean had many regrets about their relationship—too many to be papered over by coming to live here and taking care of her mother these last weeks. It just didn't work like that, Jean realized.

* * *

REVEREND BEN NOTICED THAT CYNTHIA AND JEAN WHITMAN WERE not at the service Sunday morning, but he didn't think much of it. Many seniors didn't feel well from time to time and found it hard to come to church every week. He found out during Joys & Concerns that Cynthia was feeling poorly. Vera Plante announced it and asked for prayers. He usually visited sick members of the congregation and shut-ins on Mondays, but he was concerned about Cynthia. Her condition seemed so fragile the last time he had visited. He called the Whitman house right after the service and spoke to Jean.

"I'd like to come see her this afternoon, if that would be all right. Do you think she's up to having a visitor, Jean?"

"I think she'd like to see you, Reverend. She isn't very talkative, but she did mention that she missed going to church this morning."

He left from church and arrived at Cynthia's house a few minutes after twelve. Jean led him back to Cynthia's room. Even though the house looked exactly the same, the sense of illness hung in the air. A certain stillness and tension. A sense of waiting. It was hard to express exactly, but he knew the feeling well by now. He'd encountered it many times, in many houses.

Cynthia's room was dimly lit, but he found her sitting up in bed. She was asleep with the Sunday newspaper spread out on the quilt. "She wanted to read but must have dozed off," Jean said. She touched her mother's shoulder and gently woke her.

Cynthia's small blue eyes blinked and focused on him. "Reverend Ben. I thought for a moment I'd imagined you standing there."

"It's me, Cynthia. I've come to see you. How do you feel today?"

"Oh, I've felt better . . . and I've felt worse. I think I've improved a little from yesterday," she added, glancing at Jean.

"She has a little more energy today. Her nurse is coming later. We'll see what she thinks."

"For goodness' sake, I know if I feel better, Jean. I don't need that Barbara Crosby to tell me."

Reverend Ben smiled. Her voice was raspy but her spitfire spirit was still intact. That was a good sign.

"Why don't you bring us some tea, Jean?" Cynthia said. "I could use a cup and I'm sure Reverend Ben would like some."

"I don't want to wear you out. I won't stay long."

"At least have some tea. When the minister comes, you have to offer him something," Cynthia said, making Ben laugh.

"The kettle is on. I'll bring it in a moment." Jean left the room, and Ben took a seat next to Cynthia's bed.

"I'm sorry you couldn't make it to the fair," he said. "It was a great success. Everyone was talking about your ornaments. They sold out very quickly. Jessica Morgan ran that booth, and she even took down phone numbers of people who want to order more from you."

Reverend Ben could see Cynthia sit up a little higher, her expression lighting with pride. "I won't be making any more of those. But it's nice to know."

Jean returned with the tea, gave them each a cup, and left a dish of cookies on the nightstand. The cookies looked homemade, with Christmas decorations. He took a peanut butter cookie and Cynthia selected a butter cookie, in a star shape, then dipped it in her tea. He thought that was a good sign, too.

"I'm not hungry for regular food. Jean has to nag me. But I still want my sweets," she said.

"These cookies are good enough to encourage anyone," he replied, taking a bite of his.

"I gave everyone a scare. Even Kevin. He's coming back from California," she told Ben. "But it's not quite the end. I think I'll get through this episode, but it doesn't bode well," she admitted. "If not this time, it will be soon. I know what you're going to say," she added, setting her tea aside. "No one knows the day or the hour, except God above. But the road signs are telling me it's closer."

Ben couldn't argue with that. "You seem . . . resigned, Cynthia. Is that really so?"

"Yes . . . and no. I have regrets, Reverend. More than I expected," she said in a quieter tone. "But it's too late to do anything about them. That's the very definition of a regret, wouldn't you say? Things that you want to do over. That you know you could have done differently or better. But you can't go back in time. That's the problem now."

"I understand. If it's any comfort, there is no life ever lived free of regrets, Cynthia. No life," he repeated.

She shrugged, her thin shoulders sharp and gaunt under her nightgown. "Maybe so. But knowing that doesn't make it any easier."

"We can't change the past. That is so. No one is perfect. God didn't make us that way."

"Why didn't He? Wouldn't that have been easier?"

"I'm not sure. Maybe because He wants us to experience free will and forgiveness. Forgiving those who have wronged us and asking for forgiveness for our own missteps and misdeeds. Just the way He forgives us, if we ask Him to and are sincerely repentant." He gazed down at her. She seemed to be considering his words carefully, not just engaging in some polemic sparring match.

"It's all in the Lord's Prayer," he reminded her.

"Perhaps," Cynthia replied finally.

"Is there anything specific that you'd like to talk about with me, Cynthia? I only ask to offer comfort and, perhaps, advice. I'm not here to judge, believe me."

He had a feeling that Cynthia's regrets had to do with her children, especially Jean. But he doubted she was ready to put those difficult realizations into words.

She met his gaze for a long moment, her blue eyes glassy. He thought she might cry. But finally, she looked down again at her bed and shook her head. "There's nothing more I have to say. I will think about what you just said, Reverend."

He leaned over and patted her hand. "I don't want to wear you out. I'd better go."

"Yes, you probably should. Thanks again for stopping by."

"Anytime. Please call me or have Jean get in touch if you'd like to talk again. Or if you just want me to sit with you."

"I will, Reverend." She leaned back on her pillows and closed her eyes.

Ben rose and picked up the teacups. He took them out to the kitchen where he found Jean reading the newspaper. "Your mother is resting again. We had a good talk. She thinks that she'll get through this setback. Sometimes, in these situations, if a patient believes that they'll get through it, it makes all the difference."

"She's definitely improved today. My brother is coming tomorrow. That news has given her a huge boost."

"I'm glad to hear you'll have some help caring for her. Whatever happens now, I hope you'll take comfort knowing you've done all you could to ease your mother's final days. Which I'm sure has not always been easy."

"No . . . it's not," Jean admitted.

"Please call if there's anything I can do to help. I can come any-time, day or night," he reminded her. She thanked him again and he said good-bye, then headed out to his car.

He had a feeling that Cynthia would want to talk more before very long. He sensed that she carried some burden and would not be at peace until she allowed herself to let it go.

CHAPTER FOURTEEN

⌒⫧⌒

*G*ET THE DOOR, JEAN. FOR GOODNESS' SAKE. YOUR BROTHER is standing out there in the cold."

Jean had already jumped off the couch at the first note of the doorbell. She knew her mother was excited about Kevin's arrival. Cynthia had been watching the clock all day, even though they knew that his flight would not get into Boston until five, and he most likely would not reach the house before seven or even eight.

Jean went to the door, feeling excited and a bit anxious. When her brother's warm, familiar gaze met hers, her heart filled with happiness. "Kevin, you made it!" She pulled open the door and grabbed one of his suitcases.

He took the other bag inside and leaned down to give her a hug. "Hello, Jean. So good to see you." He stepped back and stared down at her. "You look terrific. I think coming home agrees with you."

"You look well, too. Let me take your coat." He looked very fit, though a bit older. She noticed touches of gray in his dark hair. She guessed that she must look older to him, too, but he was too nice to say that.

"Why are you two standing out there yakking? Don't I deserve a greeting, too?"

Kevin looked at Jean and they shared a sibling look. "She sounds in fine form," he whispered.

"She's perked up considerably, knowing you were on the way," Jean whispered back. "But she's still in bad shape."

She followed her brother into the living room. Her mother was beaming. She couldn't get up from her chair but held open her arms. "Come here, son. Let me give you a kiss. Aren't you a sight for sore eyes."

Kevin leaned down and kissed their mother hello, then sat in a chair close to hers and held her hand. "How are you doing, Mom? I heard you've had a rough time the last few days."

"I hit a bad patch," Cynthia admitted. "But I made it through. It was good of you to come. But it probably wasn't necessary. I told you that on the phone."

"I'm here now. I'm relieved to see you're feeling better."

"How long can you stay?" Cynthia asked eagerly.

"I thought I'd stay through the holidays." He glanced at Jean. "I'd already scheduled some vacation time, so it isn't a big deal to be out of the office."

"That's wonderful." Cynthia seemed as happy as a child. "Isn't that good news, Jean? We'll have a nice Christmas together. The way we used to."

"That's what I was hoping, Mom," Kevin said.

Jean met Kevin's gaze. She was never one to say "I told you so," but she felt that he was thinking now she had been right to call and even e-mail him. It had taken an emergency to get him home, but at least he was here, Jean thought. No need for recriminations.

"Are you hungry, Kevin? I can heat something up for you," Jean offered.

"I'm fine, thanks. I ate on the plane." He turned to their mother. "You look tired, Mom. Can I help you back to bed?"

"That would be nice, dear." Their mother patted Kevin's arm, as if testing that he was actually there. "I need my wheelchair. I'm not up to using the walker right now. Though I normally do," she quickly added.

"At least you've been sitting up and out of bed today," Jean said, rolling over the wheelchair. "One step at a time."

"Yes, one step at time, Mom. I'm here to help now," Kevin said, then scooped up their mother as if she weighed nothing at all, and set her down in her chair. "Jean and I can take care of you together."

"So much attention. It's really not necessary. I'm quite overcome," their mother replied. But Jean could tell she was elated, floating on a happy cloud.

Kevin came into the kitchen a few minutes later. Jean had made a pot of tea and set out some of the Christmas cookies. Her brother had always been a big fan of her baking.

He sat down at the table, and she brought the teapot over and sat across from him. "She fell asleep as soon as her head hit the pillow," he said. "I can see that she's lost a lot of ground since the last time I was here. But her spirits seem good."

Jean wondered when Kevin had seen their mother last. Was it a year ago, or maybe two? She didn't want to ask him and get off on the wrong foot. "Her mood goes up and down. But she's gotten a big boost seeing you."

"What does the doctor say now? Anything new?" His expression was serious and concerned, which reminded her of their father, Jean realized. Kevin had always been handsome, tall and lean with dark hair and eyes. Now he was in his early forties and his looks had matured; he resembled their father even more.

"Nothing that I haven't told you. She's been taking some heavy medication that has cleared up the fluid retention. But it causes other problems. It's worked this time, but just barely. Her heart is wearing out, Kevin. There's nothing more that they can do about that."

"I understand." He looked very sad, his eyes glazing over with tears. He rubbed them back with his hand. "I'm sorry you had to deal with this on your own, Jean. I should have come sooner. That was wrong of me."

She was surprised by his apology. "You're here now. That's what counts."

"It's good of you to say that. But I haven't been fair to you. Neither has Mom. She never has been. I can't understand why. And now you've been so good to her. That takes a lot of character, Jean. I admire you for that."

"No thanks necessary. I felt it was just what I should do. I'm glad you're here now. We have plenty of time to talk, Kevin. It's been a big night."

Jean felt tired and emotional. She wasn't ready to talk about their family drama, though she appreciated that her brother recognized these issues.

"What do you think of the house? We've been working on it. I've cleaned out a lot of the rooms. Though there's plenty more to do."

"It looks great. I noticed right away."

"Mom hired a handyman to do the repairs. He's a photographer, actually. He's been a big help and is good with Mother. He has a knack for handling her," Jean added with a smile.

"He sounds like a man of many talents," Kevin said.

"He is. Maybe you'll meet him while you're visiting," Jean replied. Grant had sent a text early Sunday morning to ask about her mother, even though he had said he would call. Jean replied but hadn't heard from him since. It had only been three days since their night out and she assumed he was busy. But it still stung a bit that he had not been in touch with her more, especially since he knew about her mother's setback.

"Where will I sleep tonight, in my old room?" Kevin asked.

"Yes, I aired it out and changed the bedding, of course. But I didn't clean out any of your things. It's still the Museum of Kevin," she said with a grin. Her mother had not touched one Little League trophy or rock star poster.

"Don't worry, I'll take care of it. I'll have plenty of time to help you in the house while I'm here, too. No need for the handyman anymore."

"Good to know," Jean said, though it made her a little sad to think that even that excuse to be in touch with Grant was gone now.

"I CAN GET THE HANG OF THIS, JESS." SAM TOTTERED OUT OF THE doctor's office and onto the sidewalk. "You just go ahead and open the car door."

"Are you sure? Darrell, stay close to your father. He might fall." Jessica sounded nervous. It wasn't helping Sam's concentration.

Three weeks had passed since the accident, and the doctor had just taken off the long cast on his left leg and given Sam a shorter one, just to his knee, and a soft cast on his broken foot. His right shoulder was still too fragile to handle a crutch, so Sam was given one crutch for his left shoulder and a cane. The arrangement was awkward, but Sam was happy for any change that got him free of the wheelchair.

"Easy does it, Dad. You need to build your strength up again," Darrell said.

Sam knew that was true, but he didn't like being reminded. He had tried to use hand weights and do the leg exercises he was able to manage. But it hadn't been enough to keep him fit.

"The doctor said you can start physical therapy tomorrow," Jessica said. They had reached her SUV, and she opened the passenger side door. "You can make an appointment as soon as we get home."

Sam stopped on the sidewalk. "I'd rather ride in the truck right now. Darrell can swing by the jobs and I can say hello to the guys. Let them see that I'm still alive."

His wife didn't look convinced. "Are you sure? You've had a big morning. The jobs will all be there tomorrow."

Before he could reply, his son spoke up for him. "Come on, Mom. He's dying to get out there. You know he'll drive you crazy today, crashing around the house."

"Good point," Jessica said. "Can you get in the truck, Sam? The seat is high."

Sam smiled, relieved he'd won. "Darrell can give me boost. I'll get in there one way or the other."

"All right. But bring him home if he gets tired, Darrell," she said. "And try to stop by your grandmother's today. She has a few repairs she needs you to take care of. Nobody wants Ezra climbing any ladders."

"Okay, Mom. I'll stop there later, on my way home."

"You can drop me off first," Sam said quietly, sharing a secret smile with his son. It was no secret that he was not his mother-in-law's favorite.

With some effort on Darrell's part, Sam managed to get into the truck. He felt giddy with happiness as they drove away from the doctor's office and headed to the village.

They stopped at the Marino house first, the site of his accident. Darrell parked in front and turned to him. "Hard to come back here?"

"Nah . . . it's just a house," Sam said, though the sight of it did bring back sharp memories of his fall. "I won't get in and out of the truck. That's too much bother. Go inside and tell the guys I'm here. I'd like to talk to Bart if he's around."

"Sure thing." Darrell hopped out and headed into the house. The project had come a long way. Sam could see that just from the outside. Darrell had done a good job keeping the projects on track. If he minded his father coming back on the scene and checking up on him, he didn't let it show. Not so far anyway, Sam thought.

Sam's crew poured out the front door all at once, all eager to see him. He spoke to them from the cab of the truck and had a one-on-one with Bart Begossian. Bart had only good things to say about Darrell, which made Sam feel proud.

It was the same story at the other jobs. The clients were happy to see him, but clearly felt secure with Darrell managing their renovations.

"I don't know, Darrell," Sam said as his son drove away from the Turners' house. "You've got such great reviews, I'm not sure I'm even needed anymore."

Darrell laughed. "You know that's not true."

"True or not, they're going to be stuck with me again once you go to back to school."

The words had just slipped out. He glanced at his son, who had no reaction. They had not talked about the question since their argument, though Sam had apologized for raising his voice.

"I guess so," Darrell said, finally.

Sam felt relieved. Maybe Darrell had accepted the situation. But a few moments later, Sam realized that was not the case. Darrell pulled up in front of the cannery and parked the truck on the road's shoulder.

"Why are we here, Darrell? I've seen the cannery."

"I know. But I thought this was a good place to share some news. I've been waiting for the right moment to tell you. The town council reviewed my proposal, and it looks like they will be willing to donate the building and be paid back later, once the project is up and running."

Sam knew his son expected to be congratulated and expected him to be happy about this surprising turn of events. But Sam felt terrified. This was exactly what he didn't want to happen.

"Donate the building? Are you sure?"

"I'm sure, Dad. I'm positive. They put it all in writing."

"And what proposal was this? Those renderings you showed me on the computer?"

"Those sketches were part of it. I put it all in writing, too. I e-mailed it to you, but I guess you've been too busy these days." Sam could tell Darrell was hurt that he hadn't read the proposal, but his son's sarcastic tone got under his skin. He remembered now. He opened the e-mail and the attachment but hadn't read it through.

This was getting too real, too fast. Still, he didn't want to lose his temper again.

"I looked at the proposal. Most of it," Sam finally replied. "You did a great job. I can see why the town council was persuaded." The plan was wonderful, with open spaces and common areas and beautifully designed living space. No one could say it was not. "But now it's time to hand the ball over to someone else, like Charlie or even Jim Hepburn," he continued. "You should feel proud that you took it this far. But look at it logically—you don't have the qualifications or experience or time right now to see this through. You have to go back to school and finish your degree. Not to mention, your main focus right now should be on my business. That's what puts food on our table and a roof over our heads, and pays your school tuition."

His son sat facing forward, staring out at the cannery. The day had started off sunny, but now a low, nickel-colored sky hovered. Well-matched to the mood in the truck, Sam thought.

"I have time to work on this project and take care of the business, too," Darrell said finally. "You just told me that everyone is very pleased and all your projects are right on track."

"I know what I said. That's all true. But you still need to find someone else to take on this warehouse renovation. You'll be back at school in a few weeks. You certainly can't manage it from there. Not with the full course load you need to graduate."

"I already told you. I don't want to go back to school. This is too important to me, and you'll still need my help in mid-January."

Sam felt his temper boil up but was determined this time not to blow. "Look at me. I'm on the mend. If I need some help, I'll figure it out once you're at school. Business is always slow after the holidays. It'll give me time to catch up. By March, I'll be up to speed again."

"That's when I'll be able to work on the warehouse full-time, and construction can begin," Darrell countered.

"That's when you'll be finishing your senior year, and in May, we'll watch you march in graduation," Sam shot back.

"You don't understand, Dad. If I abandon the project now, it will just fizzle out. Or worse, some private investor will jump in and turn the place into high-priced condos. Do you want to see that happen?"

"Of course I don't. But I want to see you finishing college. That's the most important thing to me now. If you leave a semester short of graduation, you may never go back. I know how it is. I left school, thinking I could go back anytime and finish my BA. But time passes quickly. You look back one day and see that you've lost the thread."

"That won't happen to me." Darrell's tone was so typical of a know-it-all young adult, Sam almost had to laugh. "Besides, a lot of famous people didn't finish college. Bill Gates and Steve Jobs. Even Frank Lloyd Wright quit school after one year. I wonder what his father had to say about that."

"Frank Lloyd Wright didn't finish college?" Sam couldn't hide his surprise. But he quickly recovered. "Okay, some geniuses squeak by without college. Good for them. Most people have to finish to get anywhere, to get hired for good jobs, and to be taken seriously. You know that's true. It's not worth arguing about."

"I agree," Darrell said, giving Sam some hope. "I don't want to argue with you either. I'll finish school. But not on your schedule, Dad. I can't go back for spring semester and give up this project. I'm old enough now to decide this stuff for myself."

Sam took a deep breath and stared out the passenger-side window a moment. That cannery . . . if he had a stick of dynamite, he'd blow it up. *Maybe even that wouldn't solve things,* he thought glumly.

He turned back to his son, who sat waiting for his response.

"I'm sorry to put it this way, Darrell, but if you don't go back to school, we will not support you. If you're old enough to make this decision, you're old enough to earn your own way. And that includes your car and your cell phone and everything else we supply that you seem to take for granted."

Darrell turned to face him, his dark eyes angry. "I thought you would be proud of me, having such a great idea and following through on it. Isn't that what you taught me? Isn't helping ten families, or maybe even more than that, more important than sitting in boring classes for the next four months?"

"There will be another abandoned warehouse somewhere, I promise you."

"Really? Thanks a bunch for the advice, Dad. That's pretty condescending."

Sam didn't reply. He hadn't meant it that way, but could see that was the way it sounded. "I'm sorry, Darrell. You know what I meant."

"Yeah. I think I do." He son started up the truck and backed out of the parking space, the sandy dirt spinning from under the rear wheels. "If you don't want to support me, let's start right now."

"Hey, slow down. Where are we going in such a rush?"

"I'm dropping you off at home. Then I'm getting some stuff and moving out."

"No, you're not. Calm down. I never said you had to move out of the house."

"Didn't you? It's just as well. Don't worry, I'll keep working for you. That's all you're really worried about."

"Darrell . . . don't say that. I'm worried about you. About your future. I'm sorry you can't see that."

Darrell didn't reply, just stared straight ahead at the road. They were soon home, and even though Darrell stood by Sam's door with a stoic expression, Sam didn't want his help getting out of the truck cab. It hurt a little to land, but he stifled a groan and waddled into the house on his own.

Darrell stomped up to his room, emerged a few minutes later with a duffel bag, got back in the truck, and drove off again. Sam felt his heart drop like a stone. Was the boy coming back tonight? Was he coming back . . . ever? How would he explain this to Jessica?

Jessica came out of the kitchen to greet him. "I bet it felt good to get out and visit the jobs. But you must be tired by now."

Sam stared up at the stairs and then back at his wife. "It started off fine. But Darrell and I had a fight. He still refuses go back to school, Jess. And now the town council is saying it will donate the cannery for the housing project, and he's all fired up about quitting school and building this thing."

"Oh my goodness . . . of course he'd be encouraged by that decision."

"I understand," Sam said, shrugging out of his jacket. "But he can hand it off to someone with the proper experience and qualifications. He has to graduate. I told him if he didn't go back, we wouldn't support him."

Jessica looked shocked. "You didn't actually say that, did you?"

"Well, I was hoping it would change his mind." Sam's voice dropped as he said, "He's taken off. Says he's moving out."

Jessica looked as if she might cry. "It's almost Christmas, Sam. Was that really necessary? What if he disappears and doesn't tell us where he's staying?"

"He said he would still go to work. Don't worry, we'll be in touch with him. Maybe he just needs some time to cool off. He might even be home tonight, Jess."

"I hope so," she said, shaking her head as she headed back to the kitchen.

Sam hoped so, too. Darrell could be so stubborn. Sam never thought it would come to this. He felt guilty, thinking he went too far with his ultimatum, and now Jessica was upset, too.

DARRELL THOUGHT HE COULD COUCH SURF AT HIS FRIEND TOM'S house. But Tom didn't reply to his text messages, and Darrell didn't want to just show up. That wasn't cool. He decided to try again later. He found himself in the village, near his grandmother Lillian's house, and remembered he had promised his mother he would visit and do some repairs. It seemed as good a place as any to kill time until Tom got back to him.

"Darrell, my boy. How good to see you!" Grandpa Ezra swung open the door as if he were welcoming royalty. "To what do we owe the honor of your visit?"

"To the dead lightbulbs in that chandelier, I suspect." His grandmother Lillian came into the big center hall from the living room. "We've been living in the dark for weeks. Someone could have broken a hip."

Ezra closed the door and ushered him in. "I was more than willing to replace those lights, but some people will not let me near a ladder these days."

Darrell knew very well who he meant. "I can fix the light fixture in a flash, Grandpa. No problem. And I'll take care of whatever else you need."

"You know where the ladder is," his grandmother said. "Ezra, where did you put those special bulbs Jessica bought for us? In the pantry?"

"I believe so, dear. I'll come help you look." Grandpa Ezra trotted off, following his wife. Darrell found the ladder he needed in the basement and carried it up the stairs.

They were both waiting for him in the foyer. Ezra held the lightbulb package, and his grandmother stationed herself next to the ladder to hand them over. *How many grandparents does it take to change a lightbulb?* Darrell mused. He knew there was a joke in there somewhere; he just couldn't pull it together.

"I'll hand them up to you when you're ready," his grandmother said. "And you can hand me down those duds."

"Do they need to be recycled?" Ezra scratched his head. "Everything needs to be recycled these days. And all in separate containers, no less. It's become a full-time job."

"Very true, Grandpa," Darrell said. He climbed to the top of the ladder and could hear the old people sigh, feeling nervous though there was nothing to fear.

"You're so high. Be careful. Watch your step," his grandmother commanded.

He looked down at her, recalling the first time he had ever been in this house. Sam and Jessica had brought him to a family dinner before they adopted him. At the time, his grandmother disapproved of the adoption and wasn't very nice. He didn't help win her favor by misbehaving all during the meal, nearly pulling down the tablecloth while crawling under the table, then using a small area rug as a sled.

He recalled flying down the long staircase. When he landed, he smashed his grandmother's antique Oriental bean jar.

Darrell looked down from his perch and tried to find the replacement.

"Are you all right up there?" Lillian called to him. "You aren't dizzy, are you?"

"These young people don't eat right. They skip meals and get low blood sugar," his grandfather murmured.

"I'm fine. I was just . . . looking over this fixture. It's remarkable, Grandma. A real antique," he shouted down, though that had not been what he'd been thinking about at all. But he knew the compliment would please his grandmother.

"It's from Lilac Hall. It's been in the family for years. You can have it when I'm gone if you like it that much," she added.

"Thanks, Grandma. But I hope you're not going anyplace soon. I don't need it that badly."

His grandfather laughed. "Good one, Lillian. The boy's got a sharp wit."

"Yes, he does," Darrell heard her murmur.

High praise from Grandma Lillian. She would never be the cuddliest grandmother in the world. He had known that for a long time. She would never bake a cookie or even carry pictures of her grandchildren in her wallet. But Darrell knew she sometimes had a surprisingly generous side. He also knew he had earned her respect through his intelligence and achievements.

Ezra had always been a fan and was a wonderful grandfather to all the children in the family, even though he was actually a step-grandfather. He'd never had children of his own and truly loved his wife's family.

After the antique chandelier was firing on all cylinders, there were several other small tasks to take care of—a drafty door, a sticky window, and a clogged drain. His friend Tom had never answered the texts, and Darrell was giving up on him, though he didn't know who else to call. Most of his local friends were still away at college, finishing up their semesters.

"Would you like to have dinner with us?" Ezra asked. "We're having Chinese food. Your grandmother permits me the indulgence once a month."

"Chinese food?" Darrell was surprised at the menu. "Sure, I'd love to stay."

Ezra looked so pleased, Darrell thought he might clap his hands. "Lillian, set the table for three. Darrell is staying for the Chinese food."

A short time later, he was sitting with his grandparents in their dining room, just the three of them at the long table. His grandparents often employed housekeepers who would cook and serve dinner, but Darrell saw no such person in sight. His grandmother was notorious for losing help. Everyone quit on her.

She was also fiercely independent and had to have things a certain way. She had set the table herself, with silver flatware, linen napkins, and good china. She had emptied the plastic takeout containers into china bowls and arranged egg rolls on a silver platter. He wasn't surprised. That was just who she was, he'd come to realize.

"Moo shu pork, my favorite," he said, placing a pancake and a few spoonfuls on his plate.

"Mine, too," Ezra agreed.

"If you need any other repairs, I can take of them after dinner," Darrell told them.

"I don't think there's anything more, Darrell. Though you certainly took your sweet time getting here." His grandmother was eating wonton soup—very slowly, he noticed, examining each spoonful before she put it in her mouth.

"Don't you know Darrell is very busy these days?" his grandfather countered. "He's running his father's business. A great deal of responsibility."

"He's an adult, about to graduate college. He should be able to handle it," Grandma Lillian replied.

"Tell that to my father," Darrell cut in.

Ezra peered at him over the metal rim of his glasses. "Your father must think you're very responsible if he has you managing his business."

"It's not that, exactly. And by the way, he calls or sends a text message every ten seconds. Would you say that shows a mammoth amount of trust?"

"He's probably bored, stuck in the house all day. He's normally such an active man. I wouldn't take it personally," Ezra advised. "What is it, exactly? Did you two have an argument?"

His grandmother was looking at him now, too. Darrell felt put on the spot. He didn't want to talk about his father behind his back, but he knew that his mother was bound to tell his grandmother and Aunt Emily sooner or later. And his father would definitely tell Aunt Molly. There were few secrets in his family.

Darrell explained how he had noticed the cannery and had the idea to renovate it and turn it into attractive, affordable housing. And how the town council was even willing to donate the property, but his father still wouldn't let him take off a semester to see the project through and actually build it.

"He said if I don't go back to school, he won't support me."

"My goodness." Ezra stared at him, his fork in midair. "That's serious. Don't you think that's serious, Lillian?"

His grandmother didn't seem as alarmed. "Your father has a temper. Everyone knows that," she said curtly. "Did you know that cannery was once owned by the Warwicks? It was part of your grandfather Oliver's inheritance."

"I did learn that. I've been doing a lot of research about the property. And about grants I can apply for to finance the building."

"Have you really?" His grandmother looked impressed. "That's a very ambitious project. Though I'm not sure I like the idea of affordable housing. What exactly does that mean? If one can't afford a neighborhood, why should one be able to live there?"

"Lillian, please, none of that talk. Darrell has the right idea. I'd love to see the plans, if you have the time to show them to me."

Darrell was pleased by his grandfather's interest. "Everything is on my laptop. It's out in the truck. I'll bring it in after dinner."

"Really? That would be splendid. I'd love to sit down and look it over. Much more fun than watching the news on TV."

"I'd like to see it, too." His grandmother put a few spoonfuls of

KATHERINE SPENCER

white rice on her plate. Darrell spotted one shrimp with most of the sauce scraped off. "How did you leave it with your father? Did he say he wouldn't support you as of today? Or only if you don't go back to school?"

"If I don't go back . . . But I said it could start right now if that's what he really wanted. I'm going to spend the night at a friend's house. If he ever answers my text."

"At a friend's house? When we have more empty rooms upstairs than the Charles Hotel?" His grandfather shook his head. "No, sir. You stay right here. We'd love to have you."

Darrell hadn't even thought of it. He looked over at his grandmother. After all, it was her house.

"You may stay if you'd like, for as long as you'd like," she said. "If you're lying low, it's much better to hide out with relatives. No need to give strangers a chance to gossip about our family."

"Good point, Grandma," Darrell agreed, hiding a smile. Leave it to his grandmother to consider the gossip angle. He also knew she might be enjoying undermining his father.

He was sure that if he stayed with his grandparents, it would soon get back to his family. But he wasn't out to worry them. He just wanted to get some distance from his father and this endless argument. Sam was trying to teach him a lesson, but if he thought Darrell would give up this easily, his father was the one would who would be learning the lesson.

"I HAD A BIG FIGHT WITH DARRELL YESTERDAY," SAM TOLD HIS SISter, Molly. "He got so mad at me he didn't come home last night."

They were sitting in her bakery on Wednesday morning.

Sam had been eager to get out of the house, and Jessica needed to

260

take care of some Christmas errands in town, mostly shopping she couldn't do when Tyler and Lily were around.

Sam had felt like a dog who loved to ride in the car, hopping on his crutch and cane as soon as he heard Jessica jangle the car keys. He would have preferred to be out with Darrell, visiting the jobs, but that card was off the table. For today, at least.

Sunday was Christmas Eve. Sam hadn't given Christmas much thought, he'd been so wrapped up in his injuries, and now this problem with his son. But in the village, there was no escaping the Christmas spirit. Every inch of his sister's bakery was decorated with pine garlands, wreaths, red bows, and big ornaments that hung from the ceiling. Sam ducked down and sat at a table near the window, content to visit with Molly and watch the world go by while Jessica swept Main Street.

"What was it this time? Did he smack up the truck?" Molly had already served him a coffee and a banana nut muffin. She set down a frothy cappuccino at her place and took a seat across the table.

"I would have welcomed a dented fender compared to this debate. He's so fired up about a plan he's put together to renovate that old cannery off the Beach Road that he doesn't want to go back to school."

"The cannery, right." Molly nodded. "He told me about that place. I think it was the first day he spotted it. He was definitely excited about it. As if he struck oil in your backyard."

"The town council looked over his plan and decided they would donate the building. He would pay them back over time. And that was all the boost he needed to put him over the top."

"That is a big problem solved," Molly said in her most reasonable tone. "You can't blame him. He must have inherited the Morgan gift for gab. Actually, he learned it from watching you."

Ordinarily, Sam wouldn't have let his sister's teasing dig get by without a comeback, but this was no time for one of their very childish—but fun—insult contests.

"So, where did he sleep? On a park bench?"

"He stayed over with Lillian and Ezra."

Molly made a sour face. "Ouch. I would have taken the bench."

"Me, too," Sam agreed

"I'm sorry, Sam. This is a big one. If one of my kids refused to go back to school so close to graduating, it would make me crazy, too. But I'm also very proud of the boy. He's not just book smart; he's a real doer. And he's so young. Imagine what he'll do once he's older."

"Not just older. Once he has his degrees," Sam corrected her.

"A piece of paper doesn't make you an adult, Sam. You and I know that. I know you have the best intentions and still want to protect him. But he's not that scared little boy you rescued anymore. He's an adult and you need to start treating him that way. If he takes a leave from school, he'll be the one to pay the consequences."

Sam knew there was some truth to her words. Of all his children, he worried about Darrell the most. Darrell was smart, capable, responsible—all those things. But it was just a habit Sam had, ingrained from the time when Darrell was very young. Sam still felt a fierce love and protectiveness toward him, toward all his children. But for some reason, especially for Darrell.

"I do tend to worry and hover about him," he admitted. "I want him to benefit from my experience and bad decisions. You want that, too, Molly."

"We all do," she replied. "But there are limits. At a certain point you have to let go and let them make their own mistakes."

Molly had four girls, two from her first marriage, a stepdaughter from her second marriage, and her youngest, the child of her second husband, Dr. Matt Harding. Two of her girls were older than Darrell, and further on in life. Molly had been through some dramas with them, and he knew he should respect her advice.

"I know what you're saying, Moll, and mostly, I agree. But this is one mistake I don't want Darrell to make."

"Obviously. But how can you stop him?"

"I really can't," he admitted. "I can see that now. But there's one more big hurdle for the apartment project. The county has to approve the area for multiple-unit occupancy. If the review doesn't go Darrell's way, all this arguing will be for nothing."

"And so will all of Darrell's hard work, sounds like to me," Molly pointed out.

"I'd feel bad about that, honestly. But I still hope the project won't get that approval. That would solve everything."

"For you and Jess, you mean. Darrell will be crushed. He might even dig in his heels and fight it. I wouldn't bet against that happening."

Sam didn't want to think of that possibility. He knew how persistent his son could be. "I hope not. I hope he finally sees reason," Sam said. "In time, Darrell will realize it's all happened for the best."

"Okay, that's a good attitude. And if it the approval goes Darrell's way, I hope you have the same outlook."

Sam didn't know what to say to that.

CHAPTER FIFTEEN

B Y FRIDAY, CYNTHIA WAS GREATLY IMPROVED, SPENDING most of the day out of her bedroom, sitting in the kitchen or living room. She even talked about going into her studio to paint, though she wasn't quite ready for that effort.

She was definitely well enough to supervise Jean and Kevin's efforts at decorating the house, which began after lunch.

"I always put fresh greens along the mantel. With the brass candle holders and *wine*-red tapers. A shade close to maroon or burgundy. Not bright red, please. That looks garish."

"I'll look for wine-red candles at the store," Jean promised. "I'll put the candle holders there for now." She had found a few boxes of decorations in the attic, and her brother helped carry them down. Her mother seemed surprised at the project, then pleased. "We don't need to put everything out. But a few good things would be nice," she said as Jean rummaged through the first box. "I can decorate the wreath. There's a bag with the ribbons and pinecones. I like to put sprigs of fresh holly in the branches. There are some angel ornaments I hang on it, too." Her mother rolled her wheelchair over to the box, as excited as a child to pick through it. "You must put this one out. The music box with the ice skaters."

She held up a stained, dented box. Jean knew what was inside. The mirror of the ice skating lake was cracked and one of the skaters was missing a foot. But she set it up on the coffee table nonetheless.

Her brother had been stringing lights outside, around the front door and on the bushes in front of the porch. "I cut some fresh greens. That should come in handy," he said as he came inside.

He showed the bunch of branches to their mother, who looked as if she had been presented with a dozen long-stemmed roses. "Lovely idea. Put that in the white Lenox vase. Get some baby's breath at the florist, Jean, and some white flowers to mix in . . . Not carnations. You know how I hate carnations."

"Yes, Mom. I remember." Jean had taken out several more boxes and flipped open the lids to examine the contents. Most were ornaments, not useful this year since there was no tree.

"I should string some lights in here," Kevin said. "Small lights around the bay window?"

"That would be great," Jean said. "I can hang some of the ornaments on ribbons in front of the window, too. Don't you have a table-top tree somewhere, Mom?" Jean turned to a carton that wasn't opened yet. "I think it's all decorated and you just plug it in . . ."

"That old thing. I don't want to put that out this year. I'm sure we can do better." Cynthia turned her wheelchair around to face them. "I want a real tree. A big one. Kevin can move the side table and put it in that corner." She pointed to the corner of the living room, to the left of the fireplace. The spot where the Christmas tree always stood when Jean was growing up.

She recalled many nights around Christmastime, lying on the floor in front of the fire, with no other lights on in the room but the burning embers and the colored lights on the tree. Seen through the prism of her drowsy, blurred vision, the sight was magical; the ornaments of elves, reindeer, and angels looked as if they might very well be alive and watching her, too.

Kevin stood near their mother's wheelchair, a bunch of lights in his hands. "Great idea, Mom. A tree makes it really feel like Christmas."

Jean thought so, too. "Kevin and I will go to Sawyer's and pick one out."

"You can't go without me." Her mother's expression was indignant. Jean glanced at her brother. *Some help here, please?* she tried to telegraph. "I don't think that's a good idea, Mom," she said as tactfully as she could. "I know you're feeling better, but it's so cold outside."

"You'll be too tired to help decorate later," Kevin agreed.

"If I'm tired, I'll rest for a while. We can put the ornaments on tonight. Or tomorrow. You need to let the branches fall a bit if it's a fresh tree." Cynthia looked over at Jean. "I'll stay in the car and watch from there. You can even cover me with blankets."

Jean sighed. She could tell from her brother's expression he was ready to give in, too. "All right. But you have to dress warmly. Pants, a sweater, and boots. Two sweaters," she added, half joking and half serious.

"Whatever," her mother replied, in a rare moment of agreement. "Let's get going. There's not much time before Christmas. I hope there are some good trees left."

She turned her wheelchair and began to roll toward her room with more energy and strength than Jean had seen her display for days.

*   *   *

"IT'S STILL THE SAME," KEVIN SAID, AS JEAN PULLED UP TO SAWYER'S Tree Farm. She had to agree. From the white split-rail fence that surrounded the rows of trees to the hand-painted sign in front and the Christmas Cottage, where she recalled tree trimmings of all sorts were for sale, along with hot chocolate and rides on a horse-drawn cart or sleigh. The tree farm had not changed one bit from the image in her memory.

"Jack Sawyer still runs it with his wife," Cynthia clarified. "He has a nursery and landscaping business in the summer." She was cozily seated in the back seat, with her feet up and a pillow to support her back. Jean had covered her with a quilt and an afghan, making her complain that she felt like a mummy.

"I want a big Douglas fir," Cynthia proclaimed. "Not one of those spindly pines. Bring the good ones here and show me."

Jean nearly rolled her eyes at the instructions but left the car without comment. As she walked toward the rows of trees with her brother, they both started laughing.

"She's impossible, isn't she?" he said.

"She's very strong-willed. Difficult for us, at times. But it has gotten her this far."

Jean saw a sign for the Douglas fir section, and they walked into rows of trees that were already on stands. She also saw more trees stacked against the fence, tied up with plastic netting.

In the first row she found a nicely shaped tree. Not too tall, with a classic Christmas tree shape. She walked around to the other side, checking for any empty spots in the branches.

And came face-to-face with Laurel Milner. "Hi, Laurel. Out tree shopping?"

"I am. With my kids, though I may have lost them," she joked. "We usually get our tree earlier, but we just moved into our new place. We'll have a lot of unpacked boxes and a Christmas tree in the middle, I guess. Kids need a tree on Christmas morning."

"How else is Santa going to come?" Jean agreed. She glanced around, wondering where her brother had disappeared to. The situation was awkward. Should she tell Laurel she was here with him?

"Jean, I think I found a good one. What do you think?" Kevin walked toward them, gripping a large tree with both hands. The branches blocked his vision, and it wasn't until he set it down that he realized Jean was not alone.

"Look who I found Christmas tree shopping," Jean said. "It's Laurel."

From the look on her brother's face, Jean knew he had already realized that. He stared at Laurel as if she'd just dropped down from another planet. She was staring at him the same way.

"Kevin . . . Jean didn't mention you were visiting."

"I came in on Monday night. Our mother's been ill, but she's made a good recovery."

"I heard that in church," Laurel replied. "I'm glad she's feeling better. I'm sure she's thrilled that you're home for the holidays."

"It's good to be back." When he smiled at Laurel, Jean could see his shock had melted into sheer happiness at seeing her again. "How about you? Are you here visiting your parents for Christmas?"

Jean drifted down another row of trees. They didn't even notice. She found a nicely shaped tree a few rows back and brought it over to the car to show her mother.

Her mother examined it through the window. "Not bad. Let me see the other side."

As Jean slowly turned the tree for her inspection, Kevin walked over to the car, carrying two more. He looked very happy, and Jean knew why.

A few minutes later, they had selected a tree, and one of the tree-farm helpers tied it to the top of the car. Jean added some pine garlands and a big wreath for her mother to decorate.

"That was fun," Jean said as she started her Subaru.

"It was," Kevin agreed. He was looking out the window. To catch a last glance of Laurel? They would have to talk about that later, out of their mother's earshot.

But Jean couldn't help saying one thing. She turned on the radio, so her mother couldn't hear. "She's still just as pretty, isn't she?" Jean asked quietly.

Kevin smiled and nodded. "Yes, she is. Even more so."

When they arrived home, their mother was predictably tired from the outing and went into her room for a nap. "Tell Kevin to put the tree in the stand. We'll trim it tonight. Order some pizza. It's too confusing for you to cook."

Jean had forgotten that. Her parents always ordered pizza on tree-trimming night. "Good idea." She helped her mother into bed and pulled up the quilt.

While her mother rested, Jean did more decorating. She took out the snow globes and draped pine garlands along the fireplace mantel, then hung out their stockings. Her father's Christmas stocking was also in the box and she picked it up a moment, looking over the embroidery on top that said "Dad." She wrapped it in tissue paper and put it away again.

Christmas was exactly three days away, and she still hadn't bought any gifts for her mother or brother. It was too late to go to town today, but she would go out tomorrow, first thing, she decided. She had considered getting Grant a gift, too. But that was last week, right after their date and before he had gone missing in action on her.

Since stopping by Saturday, he had sent one text message, to ask about her mother. Then a photo of Race Point Beach in Provincetown, e-mailed to her on Tuesday. She couldn't quite figure that out. The last she had heard, he was going on a daytrip to nearby Newburyport, not all the way out to the very tip of Cape Cod.

It had hurt her to feel so encouraged by their evening out and then be cut off so quickly. Grant had clearly done his best to put distance between them the last few days, physically and emotionally. As if the closeness they had shared Friday night had scared him. That was her theory, anyway.

She had seen men react that way before. But she thought he was different. Jean hated to admit it, but her mother had been right. Grant was intelligent and charming, and could be so thoughtful and caring at times. But he was not someone she could rely on. He was not interested in finding out if the connection they shared—which Jean thought was so wonderful and easy and rare—could last and grow into something more. It had been obvious. And she hadn't wanted to see it.

Jean had told herself the future didn't matter. She, too, was just passing through this place. But she had been wrong. She could see now that it did matter. She couldn't let herself get any more attached to him. It would only become more painful.

A short time later, her mother and brother emerged from their rooms. The pizzas were ordered and they began to decorate the tree.

"Good choice, Mom," Kevin said, hanging his favorite ornaments, a set of three matching penguins. "This tree has the perfect shape."

"I still have a good eye," Cynthia said. "You need to hang those penguins a little higher, dear. No one will see them down there."

Kevin had wheeled Cynthia close enough to the tree for her to hang a few ornaments on her own, but she was mainly directing Jean and Kevin on where she thought everything should go.

The doorbell rang. "Must be the pizza. I'll get it," Jean said.

She grabbed her wallet and pulled opened the door. But she did not find the pizza delivery boy there. It was Grant.

"Hello, Jean. I saw that you were home. I hope I'm not interrupting anything?"

Jean was surprised to see him . . . and then felt annoyed. She finally opened the door wider and stepped aside so he could come in. "We're decorating our Christmas tree. My brother is here. He came in from California on Monday."

"That's great. I bet you're happy to see him."

Grant walked in and took off his hat. It was the felt hat he had worn the first time she had met him, the one that made him look like Indiana Jones. She had thought so at the time, anyway.

"I am. My mother is over the moon," she added, in a quieter voice. Still confiding in him? *Quit it, Jean. It's a bad habit.*

"Would you like to meet him?" *Just being polite—or too nice to him?* She wasn't sure.

"All right, just for a minute." He left his hat on the hall bench, but kept his jacket on and followed her into the living room.

Her mother was hanging a candy cane ornament from the tip of a branch and turned to look at them. "Hello, Grant. What brings you here?"

"I just stopped by to say hello. I heard you've been ill, Cynthia. It's good to see you up and around."

"Up to my old tricks. I suspect you are, too," she added, glancing at Jean.

Jean ignored her comment and the look. "This is my brother,

Kevin," she said, introducing the two men. "Kevin, this is Grant Keating. He did all the work on the house."

Kevin stepped forward and stretched out his hand. "Nice work you did for us. I'm a little handy, but those jobs would have taken me months."

"Glad I could help." Grant smiled briefly, but Jean could see he felt uncomfortable. *Which he deserves,* she thought. Then she felt guilty about being mean-spirited.

"That's a very pretty tree. It's got perfect symmetry, and it's just the right height," Grant observed, glancing to the top.

"We're pleased with it," her mother replied. She was fastening a wire hook to a Christmas ball and didn't look up at him. Jean could tell she was annoyed by his unexpected visit and wanted him to go.

The doorbell rang again. "I'll go," Kevin said. "It must be the pizza this time."

"You haven't had dinner yet. I'd better go," Grant said.

"It's just pizza. Would you like to stay?" Jean knew she shouldn't have asked, but her resolve to act cold and distant was fading quickly. If she'd ever had any at all.

"Thank you, but I've barged in on your family time long enough." Grant said good night to Jean's mother, and Jean walked him out to the foyer, passing Kevin who was carrying in the pizza.

"Good to meet you, Grant. See you soon," Kevin said.

"Hope so," Grant replied.

Jean stood alone with him near the front door. "Good night, Grant. Thanks for stopping by."

"Good night, Jean." He looked down at his hat a moment but didn't put it on. "Listen—before I go, I just want to tell you that I looked over your illustrations. I think they're great."

"You do?" Part of her was elated at the news, another part cautious.

Was he just saying that to get on her good side again? "Not too amateurish? I doubt they're good enough to publish. I was just practicing."

"They're not amateurish at all. You have your own style. It's very distinctive. I think you should submit the work to a publisher."

"Oh, I couldn't do that. It's not even finished."

"There's enough of it finished to make a good submission," he said. "You could get a contract on what you've done so far."

Jean didn't know how it worked exactly. "Thanks for the advice. I'll think about it."

"Please do." His praise for her work was encouraging. She had to grant him that.

He seemed about to leave again, finally. Then he paused. "Listen, Jean . . . I'm sorry I've been out of touch. My friend came in from out west, and after Newburyport he really wanted to see the Cape. He'd heard so much about the light and the beaches and all that. We went out there for a few days, unexpectedly."

"So I gathered from the picture you sent of Provincetown. It's a nice time of year for the Cape. Nicer than summer in some ways." She was trying her best to sound as if his apology didn't matter to her one way or the other.

"We took some interesting photographs. I'll show you sometime. But I should have been in touch more. Especially since your mother was sick. I'm sorry I wasn't around to help."

She shrugged, avoiding his gaze. "It's okay. My brother is here now. He's been a big help."

Grant nodded then put his hat on. She hadn't meant to rebuff him with the comment, but maybe it had come out that way.

"I'm glad he finally decided to come. I know you were worried about that," he said simply. "Good night, Jean. I'll see you soon."

She said good night and closed the door behind him. Then she stood there a moment, wondering why he had really come.

He obviously felt bad for being out of touch. But did his apology really change anything? Did it make him more reliable? Did it prove that he wouldn't hurt her like that again? Jean didn't think so.

"I'D LIKE TO MAKE A NICE DINNER FOR US TOMORROW, CHRISTMAS Eve," Jean told her mother and brother. They had just finished breakfast but were still at the table. Jean was starting a list for the supermarket. "What would you like, Mom? You always made roast duck. Is that your favorite?"

"Duck was your father's favorite. I always find it too gamey tasting. I like beef. A rib roast would be nice. With mashed potatoes on the side?" she asked hopefully.

"We can't forget the mashed potatoes," Jean said, adding the spuds to her list. She would have preferred a more interesting side dish. Or fixing the potatoes some other, more adventurous way. But obviously, Christmas to her mother meant mashed, with plenty of cream and butter.

"Sounds good to me." Kevin had been reading the newspaper but folded it and put it aside. "I can help, Jean. You just give me jobs. Tell me what to do."

Her brother had gone out of his way the last few days to share the housework and care for their mother. Jean not only appreciated his help but suddenly realized how much she had been shouldering on her own.

"I will give you jobs," she promised. "Don't worry."

"We'll have to eat late," her mother said. "The church service starts at half past five. It won't be over until seven, with all the singing."

Jean looked up from her pad. "I don't think you're well enough to go to church, Mom. Not this weekend."

"Of course I am. I went out to buy a Christmas tree yesterday, didn't I?"

Jean glanced at her brother. *Some more help here?* she silently implored.

"That was different, Mom," he said. "You were in the back seat the whole time, wrapped in a million blankets. And we were out of the house less than an hour."

"We don't want you to have another setback," Jean explained.

"For goodness' sake, I don't need your permission." Her mother's sharp blue eyes moved from her son to her daughter. "I thought it would be nice if the three of us went together. If you don't want to go, that's your business. I will not miss the Christmas Eve service tomorrow night. Unless I die in my sleep tonight, which is certainly possible."

Jean had no answer for that. She looked at Kevin. Clearly, he didn't have one either.

"If you won't take me, I'll call Vera. She'll be happy to pick me up. Or Reverend Ben can find someone willing to drive me."

Jean heard someone at the door. "I think that's Barbara. Let's see what she thinks," Jean said as she left to let the nurse in.

"I don't need that Nurse Crosby's permission either," Jean heard her mother say. Jean didn't think the question would rest on Barbara's say-so, but the interruption was convenient.

While Barbara was tending to their mother, Jean and Kevin talked it over. "I know she's very frail, but I think we have to risk it," Jean said. "The doctor says every day now is a gift. If going to church tomorrow night will make her happy, that's what we have to do."

"I agree. I didn't realize how . . . how serious the situation is until

I saw things firsthand." *How close their mother was to the end,* Jean knew Kevin meant to say. "Whatever she wants now—no matter how unreasonable it seems—we need to make it happen."

Jean was glad to hear her brother agree, though her mother's wishes really weren't much at all. A rib roast and mashed potatoes for dinner? Attending the church service? Maybe just being in her own home and having her children close at hand—especially Kevin—was enough to make her happy. Jean certainly hoped so.

"Sam, you're going to hurt your neck if you sit like that all night. Then you'll be at the orthopedist for something new."

Sam turned to Jessica, who sat beside him in the pew. Tyler sat next to Sam and Lily sat next to Jessica. He glanced at his family, feeling a hole in his heart. Resigned, he turned to face forward, toward the altar, which was filled with white candles and decked with pine boughs.

The Christmas Eve service had not started yet but Carolyn Lewis, Reverend Ben's wife, was playing the organ. A crèche was front and center, the animals and figures assembled. The only figure missing was the swaddled infant.

Sam had really wanted to wait outside and have a private word with Darrell. If he arrived at all. But Jessica had told him that would be too much. Sam hadn't seen him or spoken to him directly since their argument. Darrell had continued working for Sam, but would only communicate via text messages.

"He knows where the party is tonight," Jessica had reminded him as they got ready to leave for church. "We can't force him."

"I know," Sam replied. "I just want to tell him I'm happy to put aside this feud on Christmas. To put it aside forever, if he'll let me. I want him to come home."

"I do, too. But he's living with my mother, Sam. He's not exactly out on the street."

Sam had to smile at the observation. Luxury and refinement were Lillian Warwick's middle names. "I bet he misses the sports channels at our house. I doubt your mother has the Boston Fan package."

It was easy to joke about the situation at home. But in church on Christmas Eve, Sam felt differently. He wanted his family to be there together. Like they always were. But this year, at least, it seemed not to be.

Jessica nudged his arm with her elbow. "They just came in. Tucker found them seats on the right side. My mother must be mad as a bee. You know how she hates to sit in the back."

Sam turned again, craning his neck to see. "Is Darrell with them? Oh . . . I see him. When did he pick up that suit and tie?"

She shrugged. "I don't know. He must have come by for clothes at some point when we were out. Unless my mother bought it for him."

That was possible. His mother-in-law would insist that Darrell wear a suit to escort her and Ezra to church.

Jessica nudged him again. "Don't stare," she whispered. "I think it's a good sign. Maybe they'll all go to Molly's."

"Maybe. Let's both say a prayer," he whispered back.

JEAN'S MOTHER WAS IN FINE SPIRITS AS KEVIN ROLLED HER UP THE side aisle of the sanctuary. She waved and sent Merry Christmas wishes to nearly everyone they passed, like a celebrity.

She looked her very best, Jean thought. Anyone who didn't know her wouldn't guess how sick she was. Jean had helped her do her hair and dress in a dark green velvet suit. It had taken some time to dig out her good jewelry, which was stashed in various hiding places around the house. But Jean finally found it all, like winning a treasure hunt: a gold charm bracelet, a jade cocktail ring, and a large circle pin. And finally, gold earrings studded with tiny diamonds and bits of emerald.

"These were my mother's and her mother's before that," Cynthia said, "the only jewelry passed down through my family."

Jean had heard that before. But this time, she thought her mother might say, "I'm leaving them for you, as a keepsake."

But she did not.

The organ was playing as they came in. The church was already very crowded, even though Jean thought they had left enough time. She felt overwhelmed, looking around for a space to fit the wheelchair with seats for herself and Kevin. They could split up, she thought, though that would ruin things a bit.

"Jean, Kevin . . . over here." Grant walked toward them and directed her brother to the perfect spot with space for the wheelchair and enough empty seats so that they could sit together. While Kevin parked the chair and helped their mother get comfortable, Jean squeezed into the pew and took a seat. Grant came in from the other side and sat beside her. He looked very handsome in a navy blue suit and red tie. She could suddenly see him as an advertising executive, though it had been hard to picture that before.

"Thanks for helping us," Jean said.

"Happy to help. I wondered if you were coming, with your mother not feeling well."

"She isn't well. But she insisted. We just want her to be happy now."

"She definitely looks happy. She's positively glowing." Before Jean knew what was happening, he slipped out a camera and took several quick, candid photos of Jean's mother, smiling and talking to the people who sat nearby. Then just as quickly, he stashed the camera in his pocket.

"You like to take candid shots, don't you?" Jean said.

"People are the most genuine when they don't think anyone is watching. Certainly when they don't know they're being photographed."

Jean thought that was true. She wondered what had happened to the photos he had taken of her out on the jetty the day they had been on the beach. Maybe the photos had not come out well. Maybe she looked so awkward he didn't want to show them to her. Either way, she didn't want to ask him.

The organ struck an arresting chord, and the congregation grew silent. The choir was gathered in at the back of the sanctuary, dressed in their long red robes and white collars. They marched down the center aisle singing "Joy to the World," one of Jean's favorite carols. Reverend Ben followed the choir at a solemn pace, wearing a long white cassock and, around his neck, the Christmas scapular.

The many voices and booming organ chords filled the church. Jean felt goose bumps. She glanced at Grant and he smiled, enjoying the moment with her.

Kevin turned to her and squeezed her hand. She could see that their mother was holding on to his other hand, watching the procession with utmost concentration. Kevin met Jean's gaze. The unspoken message in his eyes filled her heart.

As the service continued, there were many hymns to sing and not nearly enough hymnals. Kevin shared one with their mother, and Jean shared with Grant. He held it open for her and pointed when she lost her place. Singing was not her finest talent, but he had a deep, smooth voice and appeared to be reading the music. She enjoyed listening to him sing, though she tried to act as if she wasn't taking notice.

When the service was over, the aisles filled quickly and it was slow going with the wheelchair. Then the chair got stuck and Kevin couldn't get it moving.

Grant moved forward to help him. He kneeled down and made a quick adjustment. "It was the brake. It should work now." Grant stood up and brushed off his hands.

Jean's mother looked up at him. "Thank you, Grant. Merry Christmas."

"Merry Christmas, Cynthia. You look lovely tonight. And very happy."

"Christmas is a time to put aside cares and savor the moment. Don't you think?

He looked amused at her philosophical turn. "I agree. And to put aside grudges, too."

Jean wondered if that last bit was about the way she had cooled toward him, but a smile hovered at the edges of Cynthia's mouth, as if perhaps she understood a message he meant for her. But all she said in answer was, "What are you doing tonight? Would you like to have dinner at our house? Jean cooked all day. We have enough for an army."

Jean felt color rise in her cheeks. Why did her mother invite Grant to dinner? She had rarely said a good thing about him.

"I'm sure Grant has plans," Jean cut in.

"I'd love to join you," he said. Jean's heart skipped a beat. "But Vera invited me to have dinner with her family. I don't want to disappoint her."

"Of course not. Have a nice time, then. Vera's a very good cook," Cynthia assured him.

Jean felt simultaneously disappointed and relieved at his reply. She wondered if he could tell. He offered to help get her mother into the car, but Jean told him they would be fine.

Grant left them—Jean saw him greeting George Krueger, who owned the hardware store—leaving her to wheel her mother the rest of the way down the aisle. Where had her brother gone? He seemed to have disappeared.

"Why did you invite Grant to dinner, Mom? I thought you didn't like him."

"I don't approve of him. There's a difference," Cynthia said. "Maybe I've been unfair. I don't know. I'm glad he has somewhere to go. It's Christmas. I don't think anyone should be alone."

They had finally reached the narthex, which was crowded with congregation members waiting to greet Reverend Ben. "Let's get home," her mother said. "Where's Kevin? Do you see him?"

Jean was wondering the same thing. Then she spotted her brother talking to Laurel and her family. Laurel looked beautiful in a long blue velvet dress. Her son and daughter, dressed up for the holiday, looked adorable, too. Both stared up at Kevin with wide, curious looks.

Kevin and Laurel looked happy and somehow connected, Jean thought. Maybe the spark was still there. Jean wondered if she should distract her mother so she didn't notice them. Kevin didn't need her interfering again.

Vera appeared and bent down to give Jean's mother a hug. "Merry Christmas, Cynthia. I'm so happy to see you here tonight."

"Glad to be here, Vera. Glad to be anywhere right now," her mother said with a laugh. "Enjoy your family. Merry Christmas to you, too."

Vera was soon pulled away by another well-wisher. Kevin had crossed the crowd and took the handles of their mother's chair, and they made their way out of the church and into the cold, bright night.

"How are you doing, Mom?" Jean asked once they were all in the car. "Are you tired?"

"Not one bit," her mother said, though Jean thought her breathing sounded labored. "It was the best Christmas Eve service I can remember."

Jean felt good, hearing that. She smiled and leaned closer to her brother. "I'm so glad we got her here," she whispered.

"I am, too," he whispered back.

CHAPTER SIXTEEN

〰

*I*T HAD BEEN IMPOSSIBLE TO CATCH UP TO DARRELL AND
his grandparents after the service. Even if Sam had been
fit—which he definitely was not, ambling along on the crutch and
cane. Lillian, with her typical impatience, had hustled them out of the
church quickly.

He had been watching the door at Molly's house for almost an
hour and had almost given up hope his son would come to the party,
when he heard Lillian's distinctive voice in the front hall. Molly's husband, Matt, had answered the door and let them in. Sam took a few
steps toward the hallway and spotted Darrell walking in behind Ezra.

"Sorry we're late," Ezra said. "Lillian had to go back to the house
for something. As usual." He shook his head in dismay.

"I forgot to put on my rings. I felt half dressed," Sam heard his
mother-in-law reply.

Sam stood back and waited. He wasn't sure what to do or say

when Darrell came in. But Lily and Tyler had no qualms. They ran forward and greeted their grandparents. Then Lily flung her arms around her big brother's long legs, as if he'd been gone from the house for years instead of just a few days. "Darrell! We miss you!"

Tyler stood near Darrell, too. He was too old for lavish shows of affection, but Sam knew he had missed Darrell very much the last few days and didn't understand what was going on.

Darrell returned his sister's hug then mussed up Tyler's carefully combed hair. "Hey, punk. What's up? Smells good in here."

"The food is awesome," Tyler reported. "You got to try these little meatballs Aunt Molly made." He tugged Darrell's hand toward the buffet.

Sam watched and waited. He and Darrell were soon face-to-face. Darrell met his gaze but Sam couldn't read his expression. Was he still angry? Embarrassed? Confused?

Sam took a breath. "Hello, Darrell. I'm glad you came tonight. It means a lot to . . . your mother."

"Hello, Dad." Darrell nodded then crossed his arms over his chest.

Sam wasn't sure what to say next. "Nice suit. I don't remember that one."

"Grandma bought it for me. She said it will come in handy for interviews and meetings."

"Oh, it will. Very professional looking." Did he mean job interviews, after he graduated? Or meetings for his cannery project? It looked like Lillian was taking Darrell's side in this argument. Sam thought she would, just to spite him.

"I should say hello to Mom. Where is she—back in the kitchen?"

"Probably. Try to get her out of there, will you? It's Christmas."

Even though his sister hired help to serve and clear up at her massive Christmas Eve celebrations, somehow the women in the family always ended up huddling together in the kitchen. At least until the main course was served.

"I'll try," Darrell said.

As he turned to walk away, Sam touched his sleeve. "Hey, I just want to ask you something. Can we please agree to disagree about this going back to school thing? I don't want to spoil Christmas for everyone. I don't think you do either."

"Okay. Sure. I don't want to cause any family drama either. It's cool with me. But I haven't changed my mind at all."

I haven't either, Sam wanted to say. But he knew it would be completely dumb to press his point now.

"I understand." He patted his son's arm in an affectionate gesture. "Merry Christmas, Darrell."

"Merry Christmas, Dad." Darrell finally smiled and Sam felt worlds better.

"You'd better find your mother. I don't think she even knows you're here." He watched his son make his way across the big rooms and then duck into the kitchen. Tall and lean, Darrell looked like a grown man in that suit tonight. Sam felt proud and sad at the same time. He swallowed back a baseball-sized lump in his throat.

Pull yourself together. Don't get all weepy, Sam coached himself. There was still a long way to go to make amends with his son, but at least they would have Christmas.

WHEN THEY GOT HOME FROM CHURCH, JEAN'S BROTHER KEPT THEIR mother company in the living room while Jean put the finishing touches on dinner. Kevin had been a big help getting the meal together—chopping and dicing, setting the table, and washing pots. Everything in the kitchen was organized and ready to go.

As Jean suspected, her mother needed oxygen and put on the apparatus without complaint. She sat in her favorite chair, sipping a glass of sherry and watching the fire Kevin had built in the hearth. He had set Cynthia's old stereo system to a classical music station that was playing Christmas pieces by composers of the Baroque era.

"I love the harpsichord," Cynthia said. "I love the harmonies in this music. They say it stimulates your brain."

"Is that how you've stayed so sharp all these years, Mom? Listening to Bach and Mozart?" Jean heard Kevin ask.

Her mother laughed. "I think it was my temper," she replied. "Though even that's getting dull. Like an old knife that won't cut anymore. It's just as well, I suppose."

Her tone was one of good humor, without bitterness or regret. Jean was glad of that.

Her mother seemed pleased by the array of holiday foods on the dinner table. Especially the mashed potatoes, which were actually her entrée, Jean noticed, with a small portion of rib roast on the side. Overall, despite her excitement about the meal, her mother actually ate very little, even though Jean had been careful to cook everything salt free.

"Delicious, Jean," her brother said between mouthfuls. He didn't seem to notice the absence of the salt, Jean noticed. "I had no idea you're such a great cook."

"I haven't had a bad meal since she arrived," Cynthia said before Jean could reply. "Doesn't take after me that way, that's for sure."

Kevin glanced at Jean and grinned. "No offense, Mom, but I'd say that's a good thing."

Kevin cleared the table and Jean served dessert in the living room. Along with the cookies, she had made macaroons and a trifle, her mother's favorite, and the only complicated recipe her mother had ever been able to prepare.

"Look at that," her mother said. "Where did you find the bowl? I thought I'd lost it."

"In a box in the pantry, under some tablecloths. I wanted to surprise you."

"I am surprised. And I can't wait to taste it. It looks much nicer than mine ever did."

Jean served Cynthia first, with a crystal dessert dish. Even though it was just the three of them, Jean thought it was important to use all the best things her mother owned—the china and crystal, the silver flatware and lace tablecloth. In the face of her mother's condition, these material possessions seemed meaningless. But if they made the evening a little more festive and enjoyable for her, they had served their purpose.

Kevin added another log to the fire. "Did you really want to sing carols, Mom? Jean found the old books."

He showed their mother the worn booklets of Christmas music that had been packed away with the decorations. The booklets would come out every year, and their father, who played the piano, would lead them through every page, frustrating Jean and Kevin to no end, since all they wanted to do by then was open their presents.

After their father died, Cynthia sold the piano and threw away all his music. Except for the carols.

During dinner Cynthia had mentioned carrying on the tradition. She picked up a booklet from the table and leafed through it, her expression wistful.

She looked up at Jean and Kevin. "I'm a bit tired for singing tonight. Let's do it tomorrow."

"Good idea. We have all of Christmas Day to celebrate, too."

Jean thought her mother did look tired all of a sudden. She wondered if she would want to go to the Christmas Day service but decided not to ask. She would wait to see how everyone felt in the morning.

She and Kevin put their mother to bed. Jean stood in the doorway a moment with her brother. A small light on the dresser was always left on now; it cast the room in deep shadows. Jean could see that their mother was already asleep.

"Look, she's smiling," Kevin whispered. "She had a good day."

"Yes, I think she did," Jean agreed. "We were able to give her that."

As they cleaned up the living room, Kevin took a phone call. Jean could tell it was Laurel. The conversation was brief, but Kevin looked pleased when he slipped the phone in his pocket.

"Laurel is having trouble putting together a bicycle for her son, Tim. Santa is supposed to bring it tomorrow morning. Would you mind if I went over there later to help her? I mean, after you've gone to bed." She could tell he felt torn but really wanted to go.

"Don't be silly. Go now. I was just going to read awhile and turn in."

"Are you sure? I feel bad leaving you here all alone," he admitted.

"I'm positive. And happy to hear that"—she didn't know quite how to put it—"that you and Laurel are . . . renewing your acquaintance?"

It sounded so formal put that way. But Kevin understood her meaning. "We are. We have a lot of catching up and talking to do. But I have a good feeling about this."

"I'm glad," Jean said. "I saw Laurel at church a few weeks ago, but I never told you. I'm sorry. I thought talking about her might bring back bad memories."

He had already grabbed his jacket and car keys. "That's all right. I'm not sure how I would have reacted. I probably would have stayed in California and brooded. It was better this way, to be surprised meeting up with her again."

After Kevin left, Jean sat alone in the living room, watching the fire and gazing at the Christmas tree. She was tired and ready for bed, even though it wasn't very late.

She thought about Grant. If he had come to their house for dinner tonight, they would be sitting here together. The thought made her feel lonely. But she reminded herself how she had started to trust him, and he had disappointed her. She would be a fool to let him win her over again and hurt her even more the next time.

JEAN WOKE TO THE SCENT OF FRESH COFFEE. SHE FOLLOWED IT DOWN to the kitchen to find that her brother had already been to the bakery and put together an enticing breakfast.

"Merry Christmas, Kev." She reached up on tiptoe and kissed his cheek. "How nice of you to make us breakfast. This looks great . . . and super fattening," she added, pouring herself a mug of coffee. "Mom will like it. She has a real sweet tooth lately."

"I noticed," he said. "I checked on her before but she was still sleeping. I thought she'd be eager to open presents."

"I'll go in. She should be awake by now."

Her mother's bedroom was dark and her mother was still fast asleep. Jean raised the window shades halfway, then sat on the edge of the bed and gently touched her mother's shoulder.

"Mom? It's time to get up. It's Christmas. Don't you want to see your presents?"

Cynthia's eyelids fluttered and she turned her head. "I know, Jean . . . but I'm very tired. You and Kevin have Christmas without me."

Jean felt alarmed by her mumbled words and labored breath. It sounded as if she were underwater. The same as the last time. Possibly worse. The oxygen tubing had fallen out during the night, and Jean quickly fit it back into her mother's nose. Jean moved the covers and checked her mother's legs and ankles. They were swollen to nearly twice their normal size. She was holding way too much fluid. Had her mother overindulged last night at dinner? Jean didn't think so and she had cooked without salt, her mother's dreaded enemy. Jean wished a few bites of trifle and sips of sherry were to blame for this setback. Her mother could recover from that. But in her heart she knew this time it was more. Much more.

Jean quickly grabbed a glass of water and held her mother's head up so she could swallow her pills. Then she ran out to find her brother.

"She's not well, Kevin. She's holding a lot of fluid and can barely speak or breathe. I gave her some medication but we have to call Dr. Nevins."

"I'll call. You go back and stay with her. Maybe I should call an ambulance," he said.

"I'm sure she doesn't want that. We had a big debate about it last time." She looked up at her brother and met his gaze. "She wants to die here. Those are her wishes. No extreme measures. You're her medical proxy, I thought you knew."

"She's told me that. It's just that . . . well, I can't accept that this might be the end. If we get her into a hospital, maybe there's something they can do?"

"I'm sorry, but the doctor has been very clear. There's nothing more, Kevin. That's the way it is with her condition. And she would hate being in a hospital. Why don't you talk to her? I'll call Dr. Nevins."

He nodded. His eyes were glassy, and he wiped them with the back of his hand. Jean had been living here the past few weeks and was somewhat better prepared, but she knew it was a shock to her brother. Especially since their mother had made such a huge rebound since he had come home. He had not seen the worst or understood the extent of her condition, which was in the end stage.

But he would see now.

DARRELL HAD SLEPT AT HIS GRANDMOTHER'S HOUSE AGAIN ON Christmas Eve night, but Sam was pleased to find him sitting at the kitchen table early Christmas morning.

"Look what Santa brought us," Jessica said. She was at the stove, making breakfast.

Sam took a mug of coffee and smiled. He didn't know what to say. "I guess you didn't want to miss out on opening your presents."

"Mainly, Mom's French toast. But yeah, I'm in it for the presents," Darrell replied, matching Sam's light tone.

"Lily and Tyler are already out there, shaking boxes." Jessica brought a platter to the table, and Sam took a seat across from Darrell. "Someone call them in before this gets cold. We'll open everything later."

"I'll go," Darrell said.

Sam waited until he left the room then looked at his wife. "Did you know he was coming this morning?"

"No, but I hoped he would. I put little gifts in his stocking," she said, matching his quiet tone.

"Do you think this means he's moving back?"

"I can't tell. Let's just play it by ear, Sam. Don't pressure him. That will only make him stay away longer . . ." She set some syrup and butter on the table and took a seat. "I'm just happy he's here and we can have Christmas morning together."

Sam nodded. It would be hard for him to hold his tongue and not pummel Darrell with questions. But he knew Jessica was right. Darrell had agreed last night to put aside their differences and not spoil everyone's Christmas. He was holding up his end, and Sam was determined to hold up his own.

"IT'S AS IF SHE WAS WAITING TO HAVE CHRISTMAS AND NOW FEELS she can let go," Jean told Barbara. "Waiting for Kevin to be here, too."

"That's not uncommon. It happens that way with many patients," Barbara said. "They hold out for what's important."

Dr. Nevins had come on Christmas Day to see her mother and each day since. Barbara had been there daily, too. But it was just as Jean had explained to Kevin. Their mother's heart was failing, and all they could do now was make her comfortable.

Cynthia needed oxygen all the time. Her skin, nails, and the whites of her eyes all had a distinct cast of yellow as her liver failed and jaundice set in. She slept a lot but was still making sense when she was able to speak to them. Jean was glad of that.

The decline had begun on Monday, Christmas Day. Almost two days had passed since then, and that morning Dr. Nevins admitted he was surprised she had lasted so long. "It's a matter of days now. Maybe hours," he had told them.

Jean and Kevin took turns sitting with her. They didn't want her to pass alone.

After Barbara left, it was Jean's turn to keep her mother company while her brother rested upstairs. The ordeal was draining for both of them. Cynthia was sleeping, and Jean tried to read a book by a thin shaft of light that slipped under the window shade. She had been up most of the night and soon felt herself falling asleep in the chair.

She wasn't sure how much time had passed when she woke. The

room was dark. She felt someone lift her off the chair and carry her into the living room, then set her on the sofa and cover her with a blanket. "Kevin?" she murmured.

"It's me," Grant said. When she opened her eyes and tried to speak, he touched a finger to her lips. "Get some rest. I'll watch your mother for a while."

Jean was surprised but exhausted. She closed her eyes and quickly fell asleep again. Grant's appearance felt like a dream. A very sweet dream.

Sometime later, Grant sat at the kitchen table with Jean while Kevin made a simple dinner of scrambled eggs and toast.

Grant and her brother chatted like old friends. Their crisis and Grant's willingness to share in their trouble had brought them all together. Jean felt touched by his unexpected help. He was trying to be there for her at this difficult time, and that meant a lot.

She glanced across the table and met his gaze. He smiled softly and took her hand. She had been kidding herself to think she could get over him so easily. He seemed to be doing what he could to show her that he was sorry for letting her down and that he very much wanted to be part of her life.

She decided to let it be. Her mother was the most important focus for her now. As for Grant, she would just have to see where their relationship led and deal with the consequences later. Right now she expected that to be a bittersweet parting, but there seemed no way to avoid it.

EVEN THOUGH SAM WISHED THINGS WERE DIFFERENT, DARRELL DID not move back home on Christmas. He returned to Lillian's house in the late afternoon on Christmas Day and went back to work the day after on Sam's jobsites. They were also back to the text-only mode of communication, which Sam knew suited millennials just fine, but which he found extremely frustrating.

On Thursday morning, Sam was surprised to receive a call from Charlie Bates. He wondered what the mayor could be calling him about. After a little small talk about Sam's accident and recovery, Charlie finally got to the point. "I've been trying to reach Darrell. Maybe his phone is shut off." *Or just the ringer,* Sam thought, *so he won't have to listen to me call all day.*

"I heard from the county this morning," Charlie went on. "We didn't get the approval for the multi-unit dwelling at the cannery site."

"That's too bad." Sam was surprised and unsure of how he felt about the news. "Is there some route for an appeal?" As much as he didn't want Darrell to fight the decision, he knew his son would try.

"I'm afraid not. They do a study and have a vote, and it's pretty final. I'm sorry. I was getting excited about the idea myself," Charlie admitted. "Your son drew up a good plan. You should be very proud."

"I am," Sam said.

"If he wants to see the letter, he can drop by my office and I'll give him a copy."

"I'll tell him that. Thanks, Charlie."

They said good-bye and Sam sat back, feeling stunned. It seemed as if a huge weight had magically lifted off his shoulders. Then it hit him how disappointed Darrell would be, and Sam knew he could take no pleasure in this outcome.

When Jessica heard the news a short time later, she had the same reaction. She had been in the barn, tending to the animals, and now sat at the kitchen table with her jacket still on.

"Poor Darrell." She looked like she might cry. "We have to tell him."

"I know. But where, when, and how is the question. Should we stake out your mother's house and wait for him?"

She glanced at her watch. "It's almost noon. He'll want to have lunch soon. Maybe he'll meet us at Molly's?"

"Good idea. But you'd better ask him. He might not come if I do." Though it hurt Sam to say that, it was true.

Jessica took out her phone. She sent Darrell a quick text and he answered right away. "He'll meet us there in half an hour."

"All right. Let's go." Sam felt a knot of dread tightening in his stomach. It was going to be hard to face his son with this news.

They were soon sitting at a table in Molly's bakery. Molly was working at her other shop, in Newburyport. Sam felt relieved that he didn't have to explain this family meeting to his sister. She would find out soon enough.

Darrell came in and Jessica waved. He sat down, his glance sweeping over their expressions.

"What's up, guys?"

"Charlie Bates called me this morning," Sam began. "He said he's been trying to reach you. He heard back from the county."

"He did? Already?" Darrell grew instantly alert, and Sam took a steadying breath.

"I'm sorry, son. They didn't approve the cannery site for a multi-family dwelling," Sam said.

Darrell's hopeful expression crashed. The news clearly shocked him. "Are you sure? Why not? What did they say?"

"Charlie didn't go into the details," Jessica said. "They sent a letter to his office. He told Dad you can get a copy."

"Good. Because the sooner I find out why they didn't approve the plan, the sooner I can apply again."

Sam shook his head. "I asked Charlie about that. He said he didn't think you could. These decisions are final."

Darrell stared him. "That can't be, Dad. I don't believe that."

Had Darrell really meant *I don't believe you*? Sam thought that was entirely possible.

Sam struggled to keep his voice even and calm. "You can ask him yourself. I'm only telling you what he told me."

Jessica leaned forward and touched Darrell's arm. "We know this is a shock for you, honey. I know we don't agree about you taking off time from school, but we're both sorry to see you disappointed. We really wish it hadn't turned out this way."

Darrell had been staring down at the table. Now he looked up at them. "Right. Thanks," he said in a flat tone. "But it sure solves your problem, Dad. You have to admit that."

"Darrell, please. How can I be happy to see you so miserable? Do you really think that?" Sam knew his son was upset, but his taunting words hurt.

"I don't know what to think. I'm going to talk to Charlie." He stood up quickly, nearly knocking over the chair.

Sam looked up at him and nodded. "Good idea. Maybe he knows more than he told me."

Darrell didn't reply. He turned and left the bakery.

Sam glanced at Jessica. "He took it hard. Worse than I expected."

"I know. We need to give him some space now, and some time. He's got to work this out on his own."

Sam agreed, though the advice was easier said than taken. Especially since Darrell seemed to think his father was happy to see the plan fail. Sam didn't feel good about that at all.

DR. NEVINS HAD ASSURED JEAN AND KEVIN THAT THEIR MOTHER felt no pain. She was weak, drifting in and out of consciousness. Jean liked to sit by her bed and hold her hand, which was now stiff and clawlike. That seemed to comfort her. It also comforted Jean.

Jean had drifted off just that way Thursday afternoon, sitting in a chair beside the bed. She woke suddenly.

"Jean? Jean?" Cynthia called in a surprisingly clear voice.

Jean sat up, instantly alert. "What is it, Mom? Are you in pain? Do you need something?"

"Closer." Her mother tried to lift her hand but couldn't manage it. "Need to tell you something."

Jean leaned over the bed. "What is it, Mom? What are you trying to say?"

"The gold and diamond earrings. That my mother gave me. I want you to have them." Her mother took a labored breath. "You know the ones?"

Her mother seemed upset. Jean hoped to calm her. "Yes, I know the pair. You wore them on Christmas Eve. They're beautiful. Thank you, Mom," Jean said quietly. Even though it seemed logical that her mother would bequeath her that jewelry, Jean had not felt certain that the heirlooms would be handed down to her. "I'll always think of you when I wear them."

"It's all I can give you now. Maybe you don't want to remember me. I wasn't a good mother."

"What are you talking about?" Jean wondered if her mother was getting confused. The doctor said it could happen with her heart working so hard and all the systems in her body in crisis now.

"Don't talk. Just listen to me. I was not a good mother. To you," she insisted. "I took care of your physical needs, made sure you had clean clothes and did your schoolwork. I taught you some manners. But I never gave you what a child really needs. A mother's love. Unconditional love. I was stingy with you that way. Not with Kevin. Only with you."

"Mom." Jean didn't know how to respond to her mother's confession. It was painful to hear, though she knew it was true. She covered her face with her hands a moment. Then she touched her mother's arm. "You don't have to talk now. Save your energy."

Her mother tried to laugh and managed only a gurgling sound. "For what? I have nothing to save it for now. Let me speak the truth. Finally. I always favored Kevin and treated you badly. Kept you down and discouraged you. That's a sin I'll pay for, I'm sure. I could blame your father, but it came from me. Only me. From bitterness in my heart that I could never wash away."

Jean stared down at her. "I don't understand. What bitterness? Because of your painting? Because you wanted to achieve more?"

"Not the painting. I just acted as if that was the problem. Your father was unfaithful. He had a child with another woman. That woman died when the child was still an infant, and he brought the baby to our house—not here. It was before we moved to Cape Light, when we still lived in Northampton." She closed her eyes a moment as if gathering her remaining strength, then continued. "He brought the baby home and asked me to raise it as our own. Somehow I agreed. The child was innocent, Jean. She didn't deserve to be tossed in an orphanage when she had a living father who wanted to care for her."

Jean drew in a sharp breath, suddenly knowing, but not believing, where this story would lead.

"I could never forgive your father for his betrayal," her mother continued. "I tried to raise the baby as my own. To love her, the same as my son. But just the sight of her was a sharp and bitter reminder, one that cut me to the heart every day."

Jean sat in stunned silence. She was that child, born out of wed-lock to her father's mistress. Her mother was not her natural mother. So many questions and frustrations in her life were suddenly explained. But the story also made her amazingly confused.

"Is this really true? How did you and Dad keep that secret, all these years? Does Kevin know?"

"Only your father and I knew. It's amazing that we kept it to ourselves. I always thought you would find out. Or at least suspect. I know now I just wished that was so. It would have been easier for me. I would have been relieved of the burden of that lie and the hard job of telling you the truth."

"I never suspected. Not once. Though I knew that you and Dad argued."

"We argued a lot. My fault mostly. He tried to make amends, but I wouldn't let him. I wanted him to pay for what he'd done. A debt that was never satisfied. You were caught in the middle, an innocent victim of our battle. I don't expect you to understand. Or forgive me." Her mother paused and took a deep, raspy breath. Jean didn't want her to talk anymore but knew she couldn't stop this confession.

"But maybe, someday, you can find it in your heart. At least now you know the truth, Jean. I am deeply sorry. I was so weak and selfish. Only thinking of myself, my own feelings. That's my only explanation. You're a good woman—even remarkable in your way. You've been kinder, more caring, and more respectful than any daughter I could have ever wished for. Much more than I deserve. Your father would have been proud of you. Very proud."

Jean stared down her mother, weak and frail, so close to death. She wasn't sure what the right response might be. All she had was the truth. "You're the only mother I've ever known. Whoever gave birth to me . . . that's something different. You're my mother, and no matter how you treated me, I love you. I'll miss you when you're gone. I'll miss you very much."

Her mother's eyes widened and tears slipped down her cheeks. She grasped Jean's hand with surprising strength. "Will you, really? In my sorry, twisted way, I love you, too. It was so hard for me to show you. I won't be around to prove it to you now." Still gripping Jean's hand, she closed her eyes, and Jean knew there would be no more talking for a while.

A few minutes later, Kevin came into the room and found Jean crying. He rested his hand on her shoulder. "How is she doing? Has she woken up at all or been sleeping all this time?"

"She woke up. She was talking to me." Jean wanted to tell her brother the secret Cynthia had confessed, but she wasn't ready yet. "She's losing ground, Kev. I think we should call Reverend Ben while she's still coherent. A visit from him could bring her some peace."

Reverend Ben had visited a few times since her mother's decline had started. But there had been no time for them to talk privately. Jean knew that was important now. Her mother would surely pass more peacefully if she confessed the secrets of her heart and he assured her of God's unconditional love and forgiveness.

CHAPTER SEVENTEEN

ARRELL CAME HOME ON THURSDAY NIGHT AFTER WORK- ing and ate dinner with the family. Everyone was happy that he was back, though Sam and Jessica made no comment. Tyler and Lily chatted nonstop, updating him about the animals. He gave them attention and even smiled at their silly stories, but was very quiet and, understandably, downhearted.

Sam took Jessica's advice and did his best to give Darrell some space. No one spoke about the cannery project.

Darrell got up from the table as soon as he finished eating. "I've got some work to do. I'll see you later," he said. "I'm going to send the cannery proposal and plans to my professor. I'll have to mail the model later."

Sam glanced at Jessica. This was thin ice and he was afraid to fall through. "You're still using it as a school project?"

"I did all that work. I might as well send it in."

"So you won't try to appeal the decision?" Jessica asked.

"I spoke to Charlie and Inspector Hepburn and also called some people in the county offices I know now. There really isn't any way to reverse it. That's what they all told me. So, I guess . . . it's over."

Sam didn't say anything more. *This is part of life,* he told himself, *a valuable lesson. Life isn't always fair, and he's not going to win every fight. It's good for him to learn that now.*

He wanted to assure Darrell that he would build wonderful projects like this one someday. But he could see that his son was not ready to be consoled. He was not ready to see the big picture and look to the future. The wound was too fresh.

Jean's mother fell into a coma on Friday night. Kevin had been sitting with her and called Jean to come into the room. "I tried to wake her, to give her some water. She's breathing, but she's totally unresponsive."

"The doctor said it would happen this way. I guess we should call him."

"I'll do it," Kevin said. "How long do you think she'll last now?"

"I don't know. Not much longer."

Kevin put his arm around Jean's shoulder. "I'm glad Reverend Ben came today while she was awake and aware. I think they had a good talk. She seemed very peaceful afterward. I know it's hard, Jean. But this is what she wanted. To pass peacefully, in her own home."

Jean nodded. She pulled a tissue out and wiped her eyes. "I think she's at peace now."

A short time later, Kevin was in the kitchen, on the phone with Dr. Nevins, and Jean walked in. She didn't want to leave her mother alone but needed a cup of coffee to stay awake.

Kevin hung up the phone. "He said he'll come by to see her, but it's what we all expected."

"Did you have a chance to talk with her much?" Jean asked. Kevin had been away so long, Jean hoped he and their mother had talked about meaningful things. She didn't want him to have any regrets.

"We had a few talks. I told her about Laurel. That we met up again and I was hopeful things would work out this time. We talked a lot about that. She didn't apologize exactly for interfering, but she recognized that what she'd done wasn't right. We talked about other things, too." He met Jean's gaze. "How about you? Did you talk to her about anything important?"

Jean nodded, a lump in her throat. "She told me a secret, Kevin. A story that is . . . mind-boggling."

Jean told her brother the truth that their mother had revealed, about her birth.

"Jean." Kevin's voice faltered, as if he couldn't find the words to respond. "I'm so sorry . . . I can't believe she kept that from you—from both of us—all these years."

"I couldn't believe it either. Somehow, she and Dad did."

He moved forward and hugged her. "That explains a lot. Why she and Dad fought so much. One of the reasons, anyway. And why she's always been so unfair to you. Always finding fault. It goes without saying this news doesn't change my feelings for you one bit. You'll always be my little sister. The only one I've got."

Jean appreciated him saying that. She hugged him back. "You'll always be my brother. The only one I've got. I do wonder why Mom and Dad stayed together all those years, after that drama. Especially since they never really made amends. Most couples would have split."

"I wonder, too. But they were both committed to our family and giving us a good upbringing. We have to give Mom credit for that."

"We do," Jean agreed. "She only told me yesterday. It really hasn't sunk in yet."

"It's too bad you'll never have the chance to talk about this more with her. I'm sure you have a million questions."

"I know but . . . but I think all the important the ones were answered." She remembered again how her mother had tried to explain that she did love Jean, in her way.

EVERY YEAR DURING CHRISTMAS WEEK JESSICA ORGANIZED A SKATing party if the pond on their property permitted. This year the pond was frozen solid, and her children invited all their friends to come on Saturday afternoon. They were also excited to show their classmates all the animals at the Grateful Paws Rescue Center. Jessica was prepared for a big turnout.

She had ordered pizza to serve at the house, and also made gallons of hot chocolate and piles of soft-baked pretzels to serve the skaters outside.

Darrell was too old for the gathering and had gone to the gym, his favorite outlet for his disappointment. He spent every spare minute there now. He was still brooding and distant. Jessica reminded herself it had only been two days. Still, she hoped his spirits would lift soon.

Her sister, Emily, came early to help, along with her daughter Jane, who was in middle school. Jessica was counting on Jane to wrangle the younger skaters. She was not great on skates herself anymore and hoped the kids wouldn't get too wild.

Despite her worries, the children were well-behaved, for the most part. There were a few rambunctious boys, but Jane easily got them in hand. While Jessica and Emily watched from the sidelines, their conversation came around to Darrell and the cannery.

"Truthfully, we're relieved that the project hit this roadblock—we want him to go back to school. But we also feel so bad for him. School or not, I wish there was some way the decision could be reversed and the project could continue. Darrell says he looked into appealing, but it's impossible."

"Not necessarily," her sister said.

Jessica was surprised. She had just meant to catch her sister up on the situation, not ask for advice or intervention. But Emily Warwick had been in town and county politics a very long time. If anyone would know how to get around this decision, she would.

"Do you know how to appeal it?"

"I'm not sure . . . but I know a few people who probably do. I'll make some calls, see what I can find out. This is exactly the kind of project I wanted to see in the village while I was mayor. I hate to see it rejected like this. And I hate to see all of Darrell's hard work wasted."

"That's just the way we feel. Thank you, Emily. Thank you so much." Then she thought of Sam. He might be upset to hear that Emily was trying to breathe life back into this plan. "Let's see what Sam thinks," she added in a cautious tone.

"Oh, absolutely. Sam should be on board before I start digging around."

Jessica smiled and poured another cup of hot chocolate for a chilled but happy skater. If anyone could figure this out, Emily could. Jessica hoped Sam would let her sister take a crack at it.

JEAN HELD HER MOTHER'S HAND AS SHE PASSED AWAY PEACEFULLY ON New Year's Day. It somehow made sense to Jean that she would leave them on the first day of the New Year. It was just before sunset, and the room filled with long slants of golden light for a just a few moments as Cynthia's last breath left her body.

Reverend Ben had come right after the service to wait with them. He touched her mother's forehead and said a quiet prayer. "May you be blessed with God's peace and comfort."

Jean leaned over and kissed her cheek. "Good-bye, Mom. I love you."

Kevin did the same. "Mom . . ." he said. He couldn't say more.

Grant was also waiting, standing off to the side in the bedroom. Ever since his surprise visit on Wednesday, he had stopped by daily, bringing them groceries or dinners that Vera sent. He had sat with their mother when Jean and Kevin were both too weary and even helped clean up around the house.

Jean often recalled that Grant knew what it was like to tend to a loved one who was sick and to lose that person. His presence had been quiet and unobtrusive, a comfort to her and even to Kevin.

The funeral was held on Wednesday morning, a small gathering as one would expect for a person so old. Still, many church members were there. Vera, of course, and most all the women who had worked with Cynthia on the Christmas Fair committee. Jean saw Laurel Milner sitting in the back of the church, too. She had come for Kevin, Jean guessed, but it was still good of her, considering how harshly their mother had treated Laurel when she was young.

Reverend Ben's eulogy was not long, but captured Cynthia's character, Jean thought. He spoke of her mother's wonderful talent, her quick wit and intellect, and her indefatigable—and sometimes exasperating—spirit.

He noted that she was not without flaws, quickly adding that no one is. "The challenge in life is to face our missteps and weaknesses, and simply try to do better. To ask for forgiveness from those we wrong and from God above. I believe that Cynthia did try, even in her final days, and that she rests in peace now, embraced by our loving Father."

Jean bowed her head. She felt sure that her mother had told Reverend Ben her secret and was truly repentant. Jean found she didn't mind if the minister knew the truth. She had considered telling Reverend Ben herself, knowing he would give her good counsel about how to understand this news and how to truly forgive her mother.

Jean and Kevin invited everyone back to their mother's house for a small reception. Some women in the church brought food and cakes and set up a coffee urn. Jean had taken out photos of her mother. Cynthia looked young and beautiful, with her striking red hair and blue eyes.

Jean was looking through a family album when Kevin came to sit on the arm of her chair, peering over her shoulder.

"Look at us," Jean said. "We look so silly. Do you remember that little wading pool we had in the backyard?"

"I do. I loved splashing around in it. And look at Mom in that sundress. She was so pretty. She was really very small. But you never noticed, with her personality."

"Like a small stick of dynamite, Dad used to say."

Kevin laughed. "That's very true. You're more like Dad," he said. "Not your looks. I take after him that way. But his kindness and loving nature. I've never seen it more than the past week, and I've been so in awe and thankful."

Jean turned and looked up at him. His compliment left her speechless. He put his arm around her shoulder a moment. "We'll talk more, when everyone is gone." He stood up and walked over to Vera, who was about to leave and wanted to say good-bye.

The house was soon quiet again. Only Grant stayed behind to help clean up, though the women from church had left things in good order. Kevin looked dead on his feet, and Grant told him to take a nap. "You better lie down before you fall down. I'll help Jean. Don't worry." Kevin managed a small smile and thanked him, then went up to his room.

Grant touched her shoulder. "You should rest, too. I don't mind finishing here."

"It's all right. I'm tired but wound up at the same time. I don't think I could sleep right now."

They worked together in the kitchen, putting away food. "It's hard to believe she's not here," Jean said. "I feel as if she's in her bedroom asleep, and then I remember. As much as I knew it was coming, it's still a shock."

"I understand. It will take a long time to get used to the idea." Jean knew that was true. It had taken a very long time to accept her father's death. She turned to him.

"Right before she died, when she was still able to speak, she told me a secret."

"What kind of secret?"

"About my family. Mostly about me." She wasn't sure why, but she wanted Grant to hear the story. It was difficult, but she told him everything.

Jean saw shock in his eyes and then distress as he listened. "That must have been difficult to hear," he said at last. "Especially when she was so weak, and it was hard to express your anger."

"I didn't feel angry, exactly. I was stunned. And things I've always wondered about started to fall into place."

"I always liked your mother. You know I did," he said. "But what she did to you was so unfair. You were just a child."

"She understood that, finally. She told me she was sorry. Truly sorry. I believe she was."

"That's some comfort, I guess. But I hope this will make you see that the way she treated you, the things she said and did, had nothing to do with who you are really—your talents and potential. It was all inside of her, a poison she had no outlet for. You were an easy, innocent target for her unhappiness."

"I do see that. At least, I'm starting to. This confession has shaken everything up, like a snow globe turned upside down. It changes the way I understand my past—and my future. But it's hard to change your idea of yourself overnight."

He glanced at her with a sympathetic look but didn't reply. They worked for a few minutes more without speaking. He handed her bowls of food covered with foil, and she stored them in the refrigerator. "What will you do now? Have you have made any plans?" he asked.

"Not yet."

"How about Boston? You mentioned moving there."

"I probably will. I haven't thought that far ahead yet."

"Of course. I didn't mean to pressure you."

There was a little more to wrap up on the counter, baked goods, mostly. Jean planned to bring all the leftovers to church for their food outreach. The fancy cake and breads would be appreciated.

"I have some news," he said. "My photo essay of Cape Light was accepted by a gallery in Boston. They're planning a show there soon."

"That's wonderful." She smiled at him briefly and returned to her task. She wondered when this show would be and how much he would need to be in the area at the time. How much she might get to see him. "So you're not taking off for Nova Scotia right away?"

"I haven't made any plans for that trip yet. Nova Scotia will be there when I'm ready."

She had to laugh. Typical Grant attitude. She could learn from that.

There were more questions she wanted to ask. Would he move to Boston to work on the show or stay in Cape Light awhile longer? She might move to Boston soon, too, and could see him there. Even if she stayed here awhile, the city wasn't that far. Though she expected that at some point he would disappear from her life entirely, heading off to Nova Scotia or some other distant place. And there was nothing she could do about that.

It was only early evening, but the day had been long and draining. Jean decided all those questions could wait. Perhaps the answers would become apparent without her asking.

Grant left a short time later, taking out all the trash and loading a stack of folding chairs borrowed from the church into his truck. They said good-bye at the back door. "The best thing for you right now is some sleep. Lots of it. Promise me you won't do anything more in the house tonight?"

Jean nodded, touched by his concern. "I won't. I promise."

"Good. Sleep well, Jean. Take some comfort knowing you and Kevin did the best for her. She's at peace now."

He leaned over and kissed her forehead, then touched her cheek with his hand. Before Jean could reply, he turned away and was gone.

JEAN DIDN'T WAKE UP UNTIL NEARLY TEN THE NEXT MORNING. SHE could tell it was late by the way the sunlight filled her bedroom. She lay in bed, the reality of her mother's death sinking in. The funeral was over, but there were still many more tasks to take care of in the coming days: clean out her mother's room, give her clothes away, go through her papers and her paintings. She and Kevin had to visit an attorney in town to review the will. That meeting wouldn't be easy, but she already knew the outcome.

Kevin was already up and had made coffee. He smiled as she walked into the kitchen. "You and Grant took care of all the cleanup. I would have done more this morning."

Jean sat at the table with him. "That's all right. There wasn't much left to do. I'm going to take all those leftovers to church today, for the food outreach Sophie Potter runs."

"Good idea. We can drop the food off before we meet with Richard Barnes, Mom's attorney. I spoke to him this morning and made an appointment for this afternoon to go over her will. I've been meaning to speak to you about the will, Jean. But the last few days have been so busy."

She could see that her brother felt uneasy. And she didn't want him to be. She would never blame him for their mother's decisions. "Don't worry, I know what's in the will. Mom told me that she left the house and just about everything else to you. I know it's not your fault. It's just the way it is. The way she was."

"Actually, there have been some changes. I spoke to her about that toward the end. I asked her to split the property and savings between us. For once in her life, she didn't argue. She told me she was making that change anyway and had already spoken to her lawyer."

"Spoken to her lawyer? But when?"

"Barbara Crosby helped her. Remember when that envelope came from the law office last week?"

"Yes, but I thought she was just getting her affairs in order and wanted to go over the details with you."

"Mr. Barnes drew up a new will and filed it. I didn't intend to keep it from you," he added. "It just turned out that way. But you and I will be joint owners on the house and shop and everything else."

Jean sat silent for a moment, surprised by the news. Another huge sea change in her life, the second this week.

"I'm surprised she changed her mind. She'd been so adamant about you inheriting everything. But at least I understand now how it came about," she said, thinking of her mother's need for forgiveness.

"I want you to stay here as long as you like. You can run the shop if you want to and keep all the proceeds. Or not. That's up to you. Or we can sell everything. Whatever you feel most comfortable with. I think you should decide these matters. You haven't been treated fairly since Dad died. It hurt me to watch, but I was so young. I didn't know what to do about it. I know now I could have done more to make up for that. Especially as we got older. I moved away for my own reasons, my own unhappiness. But I could have thought of you more, too."

He reached across the table and took her hand. Jean returned his grasp, struggling to get her mind around this latest change that so affected her plans and her future.

She took a breath, pulling herself back to the present. "I know you had your reasons for moving away. But I bear responsibility, too. We could have been closer, helped each other more. Taking care of Mom together, I think we've grown closer again. I know you'll go back to California but I hope we'll stay close as time goes on?"

"I know we will, Jean. I'll make sure that we do. We're all that's left of the family, you and me."

"We are," Jean agreed. "But maybe we'll have families of our own someday. It's not out of the question. For either one of us."

He smiled, lifted by her optimism. "That's very true. It's not out of the question at all."

As Jean prepared for their trip into the village, she considered staying in Cape Light, wondering if it was the right choice. She'd come back to this house a few weeks ago, out of duty and dodging bad memories, like cobwebs caught in the corners of each room. But now she saw Cape Light in a new way. No longer the scene of her unhappy childhood, but a restoring place where she had grown more comfortable and confident. And had been given an important key to her history and identity. Little by little, she was starting to see herself differently and knew that she was surely starting a new chapter in her life. But maybe this familiar village and comfortable house—the backdrop of her old life—was the perfect place to do that.

CHAPTER EIGHTEEN

⟋⟍⟍⟍⟋

*D*ARRELL AND HIS FATHER HAD DECIDED THAT FRIDAY, January fifth, would be his last day of work for Morgan Construction. He would leave for school on the weekend.

His father still couldn't drive but physical therapy sessions had helped him be more mobile. Bart Begossian had agreed to pick his father up every day and help oversee the jobsites until Sam was up to speed. Now his dad could drive poor Bart crazy, Darrell thought.

Darrell's classes didn't start until the eighteenth, more than a week away. But he needed time to get organized for the spring semester. He was moving into an apartment off campus with some buddies and looked forward to that change. He was taking a full course load but still wanted to have some fun before he graduated.

It was hard not think about the cannery proposal, as much as he had tried to focus on other things—buying books for his new classes and applying for graduate school. All that made him feel as if he was moving backward now.

Since it was his last day, the guys on the work crew took him out for lunch—to their favorite spot in Essex, famous for huge grinders. It hadn't always been easy taking his father's place, but for the most part, managing the crew had been a good experience and one that he knew would help him later on, at other jobs. It was one positive take-away from his time at home. There were others, too, Darrell knew. If he looked for them.

When he got home that evening, he saw his aunt Emily's Jeep in the driveway, but he didn't see her in the kitchen with his mom, where he expected them to be. He didn't see anybody, and called out from the hallway, "I'm home. Anyone around?"

"Back here," his father called from his office. "Aunt Emily wants to talk to you."

Darrell walked back, expecting his aunt to say good-bye and wish him a good semester at school.

When he walked into the office, they all stared at him—his father, his mother, and Aunt Emily. They were smiling and he thought for a moment he looked weird in some way. Was his shirt on backward or his hair sticking up in a funny way?

"What's going on? Why are you all looking at me that way?"

"We have some news for you," Sam said. "Good news. Your aunt has been calling around all week, working her ex-mayor magic. She found out that the decision on the cannery project can be reviewed again—and hopefully, reversed."

Darrell didn't believe it. First, he couldn't believe his father would be happy about such news. And second, he knew the whole thing was impossible. He took a breath, not wanting to disrespect his aunt.

"I don't know who you talked to, Aunt Emily, but I asked around a lot and got a lot of negative answers."

His father grinned. "Your aunt knows the right people to ask. Or the right questions. But she won't reveal her secrets."

Emily smiled and shrugged. "It's true. The decision can be reviewed again, Darrell. The process will take several months, and you'll have to pay for your own study. But I've spoken to a lawyer, and he seems hopeful."

Darryl stood stunned, but his thoughts were already racing, envisioning the finished project.

"If you want to pursue it," his father added.

"Of course I do." Darrell's temporary flare of hope dimmed as reality suddenly set in. "But who's going to pay for lawyers? You know I can't afford that. I can't even apply for grants until all the permits are signed off on."

"I'll pay for everything. The study and the legal help," his father said. "By the time this process is complete, you'll be done with school and hopefully you can come home and get to work on that cannery again."

"You'd do that for me? You'd even hire a lawyer to fight it?" Darrell couldn't quite believe it. "You're not just doing this because you feel bad for me, are you? I hope it's because you think the project is worthwhile."

"Worthwhile?" Sam echoed. "It's brilliant, Darrell, and beautifully designed. You set your sights high, coming right out of the box. I know I seemed cool about it at times—only because I didn't want to encourage you to leave school. But I've been thinking about things, and I think it's time I set my sights higher, too." His father stood up and leaned forward, holding on to his crutch. Then he stretched out his good hand. "Your first construction project is a good investment for me. And one I'd be proud to partner on with you."

Darrell shook his father's hand then felt himself pulled into a bear hug. He didn't know how to thank his dad. Words didn't seem enough. "Thank you, Dad," he finally managed. "For the help, and the vote of confidence."

"No thanks necessary. You've already shown what you can do. As for grad school, I decided I'm not going to drive you crazy about that either. That step is up to you. Maybe you want to take some time off before you start. Or go part-time while you work on the cannery. I know what I'd like you to do, but I can't make the decision for you.

"Whatever you decide, we know you'll make your mark in the world and do great things." His mother hadn't said a word so far, but when he met her glance, she was beaming. He knew she must be pleased that he and his dad had not only patched things up after their argument, but were going to work on the cannery together.

He leaned forward and hugged his mother and then his aunt Emily. "Thanks, guys . . . this is the absolute best day," he said, not knowing whether to laugh or cry.

"I'm just happy to see you smile again, buddy," his dad said.

A few minutes later, Darrell headed up to his room and Sam looked over at Jessica and Emily. "That turned out well," he said with a deep laugh. "Thanks to you, Emily."

"I was happy to do what I could. And lucky, too."

Sam agreed, though he knew it was more than just luck. If someone had told him a few weeks ago that the cannery situation would work out so well, he wouldn't have believed them. But someone did tell him that, he recalled. Reverend Ben, in the hospital, told him to give his cares over to God and He'd take care of all of his needs. If

Sam would let Him. Sam knew in his heart that heaven had stepped in here, because nothing was impossible for God.

CYNTHIA HAD DONATED A SUM OF MONEY AND TWO PAINTINGS TO the church. Their attorney was going to send the donation from the estate account, but Jean called Reverend Ben and arranged to drop off the artwork on Saturday.

She found him in his office, working on his sermon. He jumped up and greeted her, taking a painting from each of her hands. He held one of the watercolors so they could both look at them.

The first showed the village green and the church, nestled in a deep blanket of snow. The icy, gray blue harbor in the background, in sharp contrast to a clear, blue sky.

Reverend Ben stared down at the picture thoughtfully. "She must have stood out in the snow to capture that moment. And perfectly, too. She was very dedicated to her work."

"She was," Jean agreed. She could imagine her mother standing in the cold, her easel stuck in the snow, the watercolor paints and supplies probably freezing over a bit.

Then they looked at the other painting together. The last painting her mother had worked on, the curved stretch of beach and the lighthouse in the distance.

"She wanted you to have that one, especially. She told my brother. I knew she'd gone back to work on it, but I didn't know she'd finished it," Jean admitted. "All that time I thought she was working on ornaments for the fair, she must have been painting."

Reverend Ben looked at it more closely. "It's beautiful. I remember the day she showed it to me unfinished. But it captures that stretch of the beach even more now. I feel as if I'm standing right there."

Her mother had only been able to finish the painting so well with the help of Grant's photographs, Jean thought.

"It does capture that spot," she agreed. "It's one of her very best, I think."

"Do you have a minute to visit? Sit down. Let's talk. How are things going?" he asked. He offered her a chair near his desk and sat in another.

"Going well, all things considered. Kevin and I are still sorting things out. I was surprised to hear that I've inherited half ownership of the house and other assets."

She could tell the news was not a surprise to Reverend Ben. "When your mother and I spoke the last time, she told me she had changed her will. I'm glad she was at least able to do that for you. Will you stay in Cape Light now?"

"I haven't decided yet. But I'm leaning in that direction. I could do freelance work from here, and I've been working on a book project."

His blue eyes lit up behind his wire-rimmed glasses. "That sounds like a good plan. I hope you stay," he added. He paused and seemed to be gathering his thoughts.

Jean had a feeling he was thinking about something else her mother had told him the last time they spoke. Something more important than her will. But he was being discreet and wouldn't bring the subject up unless she did.

"I had a good talk with my mother before she passed away. A very honest and even shocking talk. Shocking to me." She could tell from Reverend Ben's expression, he knew what she was going to say.

"My mother had a secret. She told me that I was not her real daughter. I hope that she told you, too, Reverend. To unburden herself. She seemed so distressed when she told me. I didn't want her to die believing she wouldn't be forgiven."

"She did tell me, Jean. And that's very generous of you. I believe that God is generous with His forgiveness, if we're truly sorry for the wrongs we've done to others. I know that she was remorseful about what she'd done."

"Yes, she was. I have no doubt about that."

"Still, it must have been a great shock. I can hardly imagine hearing such a thing."

"I was stunned when I heard it. I didn't know what to think. She was brave to tell me the truth, even though she was at the end. She didn't have to. I probably would have never known. Since then, I've had so many feelings—anger, confusion, loss. Even relief. I have to admit, I haven't forgiven her yet . . . . I'm not sure if I can." She shook her head, baffled. "Maybe I don't know how."

"That's totally understandable," the reverend assured her. "This revelation is so fresh. It will take a long time to process it. Forgiveness isn't usually a straight, smooth path, Jean. Though we'd like to think of it that way. Did you ever see a labyrinth walk? We have one in the church garden. It's a meditative walking path in the shape of spiral."

"Yes, I'm familiar with that term, though I didn't know there was one here."

"Congregation members built it a few years ago. It's covered with snow right now, but I like to walk on it when I can. What I'm trying to say is that the path to forgiveness is more of a winding, curling journey that sometimes circles in on itself and can even make you feel as though you're moving backward. But if you keep at it, you are progressing, slowly but surely. And finally, if you make a sincere effort, you can reach the mark."

Jean liked his analogy. "I'll have to remember that, especially when I feel like I'm moving backward. But how will I know when I've truly forgiven her?"

"You'll know it in your heart," he said, lightly tapping his chest. "You'll feel like a stone that's sunk to the bottom of a riverbed and settled there. Peacefully. You'll just know," he promised.

His words gave her comfort and hope. "Thank you, Reverend. I'm going to try that labyrinth, once the snow is gone."

"Please do. And don't hesitate to call me, Jean, or stop by anytime to talk more."

"I will," Jean said, not just to be polite. She knew she would return to talk to Reverend Ben again.

After Jean left the church, she headed across the green. She wasn't ready to go home yet and thought she'd walk around the village and stop in some shops.

Her spirits had been lifted by her talk with the minister. The sun was high in a brilliant blue sky, reflecting on the harbor's dark waters and the small whitecaps tossed by the wind. The harbor was empty, with only the hardiest fishing boats moored there this time of year. But the water wasn't frozen, and most of the snow had melted from the green. She walked up the path that bordered the hill and remembered the wild rides down she had taken with Grant on the borrowed sled.

They had exchanged a few text messages the last few days, but she had been too busy with her brother since the funeral to see him.

Then, as if her thoughts had conjured him, she saw a man walking down the hill toward her. She recognized Grant instantly.

He smiled and waved, picking up his pace to meet her halfway.

"I was just visiting with Reverend Ben," she explained. "My mother wanted the church to have two of her paintings. The one of the lighthouse, especially. The one you helped her with."

"She finished it? I didn't know that."

"I didn't either. I think she wanted it to be a surprise."

"I can't wait to see it. I was just on my way to Reverend Ben's office. He agreed to let me take a few photos. I'm starting a new project, Faces of Cape Light . . . That's just a working title."

She smiled. "It gets the point across. There are a lot of interesting faces in this town, that's for sure."

"I can think of one. The portrait that inspired my idea."

"The photos you took of my mother in church, on Christmas Eve?"

He shook his head. A small smile played at the corners of his mouth. "The shots I took of you, out on the jetty."

"Oh . . . those. I wondered about that. You never showed them to me. I thought they didn't come out well."

"They came out beautifully. You look . . . well, beautiful. I meant to give you prints as a Christmas gift. But now I guess they'll be a going-away present. If you're still moving to Boston?"

He seemed concerned about that question, and Jean felt a spark of hope flare up in her heart. "But if I move to Boston, I won't be a Cape Light personality," she pointed out.

"You'll always be, to me. The subtle, unforgettable essence of the place."

Men had called her pretty, even beautiful. But Jean couldn't recall anyone giving her such a compliment. Not in a very long time.

"Things have changed. I don't think I'm moving to Boston." She told him about the will and how she had inherited half of everything. "I'll be a village personality after all. I'm going to look for freelance work, maybe run the shop and work on a new children's book. Can you drop off the portfolio with my illustrations some time?"

"I have them in my truck to give back to you. But I have to confess something first, Jean. I made copies of your paintings and sent them to a friend who's a children's book editor . . . Are you very mad at me? Please say you're not."

Jean hesitated. She felt angry, but she but didn't want to be. She knew his intentions were good. "You shouldn't have done that without asking," she told him.

"I know. But I thought you never would, and the book is too good to sit in a box somewhere. It can bring a lot of pleasure to a lot of children. And adults."

Jean had never thought of it that way. "What's done is done, I guess. How long do you think it will take to hear back?" Maybe his friend would give her some helpful comments on how to improve her work.

"She got in touch with me this morning," he replied, his smile growing wider. "I was going to drop by your house today and give you the news. She loved the book and wants to see the other paintings right away. If you're willing to do a few revisions, she's interested in offering you a contract to publish it."

Jean was speechless. The only way she could answer was to step forward and give him a huge hug.

Grant hugged her back, nearly lifting her off her feet. "I guess you're not mad at me anymore?"

"I guess not," Jean replied, still locked in their embrace. "But ask the next time, will you?"

"I hope there is a next time," he said quietly. "If you're staying here, I am, too."

She felt her heart skip a beat at his words. "For how long?" she whispered.

"As long as you'll let me be close to you. As long as it takes to get you to marry me." He stepped back, still holding her, and stared into her eyes. "I know I let you down, Jean. And I lost your trust. But I've tried hard to show you the last few weeks that won't happen again. I hope you can believe me."

"You mean when you went to Cape Cod and didn't get in touch for a few days?"

"That's right. I was distracted with my friend. But it was something more. It's . . . this thing I do when people get too close, when I'm feeling too much about somebody. A knee-jerk reaction to push them away. The thing is, I realized, with you, that trick wouldn't work. I couldn't get over you. I couldn't act as if I didn't care. I came back knowing I had messed up and willing to do anything to win you back. I want you to know my wandering days are over. I just want to be with you."

"I want to believe you," she admitted. "But what if you get bored one day and decide to take off for someplace new? Like Prince Edward Island or Nova Scotia? Or Timbuktu?" she tossed in.

"Then we'll go together. You might get some good ideas for your books in Timbuktu. But I think we'll always come back to this place. I have a feeling we can be very happy here."

"I think so, too," she agreed.

Grant kissed her and she felt her head spinning, her heart bursting with joy. She was happier than she had ever been, knowing such a wonderful man loved her and wanted to make a life together. She'd been blessed in so many ways since moving back here. And she knew, feeling safe in Grant's arms, the greatest blessings were yet to come, in the bright future that stretched before them.